Monica Murphy is the *New York*
the *One Week Girlfriend* and the
Californian, she lives in the fo
with her husband and three children.

For more information, please visit her at www.monicamurphyauthor.com,
on Twitter @MsMonicaMurphy,
and on Facebook at www.facebook.com/MonicaMurphyauthor.

Just some of the reasons to fall for the emotional love stories of Monica Murphy:

'Murphy is an incredible talent and continues to show that with each book she writes . . . Readers will be hanging on the edge of their seats wondering what Murphy has in store for this couple. A fantastic book that you simply must read!' *Romantic Times*

'*Owning Violet* owned me from the first page to the last. Ryder and Violet's chemistry is off the charts! Read it, own it, love it' Katy Evans, *New York Times* bestselling author

'An emotional and heartbreaking storyline . . . Monica Murphy pulls the reader in and won't let go' *The Reading Café*

'Monica Murphy succeeds in making a steamy romance between two characters with amazing chemistry and she turns a work of fiction into something so much more. It is a real, tangible, and beautiful thing' *The Life of Fiction*

'I chose this book to be *the* book. The perfect book that would make the world stop for a few hours and suck me into another universe completely. The perfect book that would make my heart race and stop all at the same time. This book is that book! This book is *perfect*!' *The Obsessive Reader*

'OH MY, Monica Murphy really does create the best anti-heroes . . . Having both Caden and Ryder in the same book is almost combustible . . . *Stealing Rose* is a full-steam-ahead, action-packed romance interwoven with finding yourself and your place in the world' *Book Angel Booktopia*

'I am completely and hopelessly in love . . . *Stealing Rose* made me remember e g the very first time'

By Monica Murphy

One Week Girlfriend Series
One Week Girlfriend
Second Chance Boyfriend
Three Broken Promises
Drew + Fable Forever (e-novella)
Four Years Later

The Fowler Sisters Series
Owning Violet
Stealing Rose
Taming Lily

Reverie Series
His Reverie
Her Destiny

Never Series
Never Tear Us Apart
Never Let You Go

MONICA MURPHY

Never Tear Us Apart

Published by arrangement with Bantam Books,
an imprint of Random House, a division of Random House LLC,
A Penguin Random House Company

First published in Great Britain in 2016
by HEADLINE ETERNAL
An imprint of HEADLINE PUBLISHING GROUP

1

Cataloguing in Publication Data is available from the British Library

ISBN 978 1 4722 3719 4

Offset in 11.44/15.78 pt Sabon MT Std by Jouve (UK)

Printed and bound in Great Britain by CPI Group (UK) Ltd, Croydon, CR0 4YY

Headline's policy is to use papers that are natural, renewable and recyclable products and made from wood grown in well-managed forests and other controlled sources. The logging and manufacturing processes are expected to conform to the environmental regulations of the country of origin.

HEADLINE PUBLISHING GROUP
An Hachette UK Company
Carmelite House
50 Victoria Embankment
London EC4Y 0DZ

www.headlineeternal.com
www.headline.co.uk
www.hachette.co.uk

He will cover you with his feathers. He will shelter you with his wings. His faithful promises are your armor and protection.

—Psalm 91:4

Author's Note

Dear Readers,

This book tackles difficult subject matter, things I've been fascinated with for a long time. Since I was young I've read many true crime books (Ann Rule is a rock star in that regard and she will be missed), spent endless hours watching *Forensic Files* and at one point believed the Investigation Discovery channel was made just for me.

I'm fascinated with murderers, specifically serial killers. Why do they do it? Is it a sickness? Do they become so arrogant as they continue with their horrible deeds that they become careless? How do you turn so desperate, so deranged that you kill people for sport? Or that you kidnap children to fulfill some crazed inner need?

I don't understand it. I don't think I want to. But I am fascinated. So when I told my editor that I had this idea for an "unconventional romance," and then proceeded to explain my idea, she didn't immediately tell me, "You're sick and twisted and that would be a no."

Instead, she said, "I love it," and though maybe this means we're both sick and twisted, I'm hoping that's not the case. My goal was to create a couple that shares a very special—and unique—bond that no one else understands. In order to do that, I had to make them both suffer at the hands of the same monster.

This book deals with the rape of a child and I want to make that clear upfront. If this sort of thing disturbs you, please don't read it. I'm not trying to glamorize this subject and I tried my best to handle it with sensitivity and care. Thanks to the stories written by Elizabeth Smart, Jaycee Dugard, and Michelle Knight, I received insight into what it's like to be a kidnap victim and survive. These women are so incredibly brave for sharing their stories—they are true heroes in my eyes.

I also want to mention the National Center for Missing & Exploited Children. They work very hard to help in the search of missing children and to keep our children safe from harm. For more information, please visit www.missingkids.org.

I hope you enjoy Katherine and Ethan's story. I hope you understand their struggle and see that though their love may not be conventional, it is true and real and gives them hope in a situation where they believed they were utterly hopeless. Many times as I wrote their story, they broke my heart. These are two people who are so deeply broken when they're alone, that they only make sense when they're together.

To me, those are the best kind of love stories.

Monica

Never
Tear Us
Apart

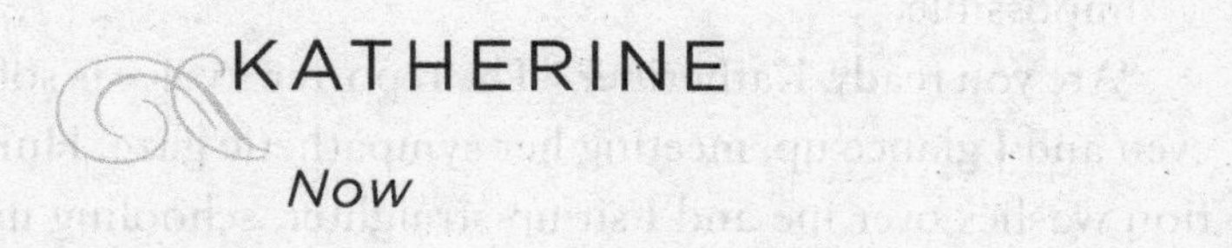

KATHERINE

Now

The lights are bright and hot and I feel little beads of sweat form along my hairline. I don't touch my face, though. I might ruin the makeup that someone just spent the last thirty minutes carefully applying, so I dip my head and wring my hands together instead, noting how clammy my palms are, though my fingers are like ice. A fitting contradiction, considering how I feel.

Nervous. Excited. Terrified. I make no sense. What I'm doing makes no sense, especially to my family.

I'm about to go on camera. Ready to tell my story.

Finally.

The reporter is one I've seen on TV since I can remember. She's famous. Everyone knows her name. She's pretty in that broadcast news way. Perfectly coiffed dark blond hair, bright blue eyes heavily made up. Slashes of peachy pink define her cheeks and her lips are a subtle berry color. She's efficient and knows exactly what she wants. I can tell by the way she commands the room, by how fast the network employees do her bidding. She's strong. Confident. Flawless.

Reminding me that I am most definitely not. All of my flaws mock me, remind me that I'm not perfect. At one point in my life I thought I was pretty close to it, when I was young and ignorant and believed myself untouchable. But perfect is hard to obtain. And once you lose all sight of it, it's impossible to gain back.

Impossible.

"Are you ready, Katherine?" The reporter's voice is soft and even and I glance up, meeting her sympathetic gaze. Humiliation washes over me and I sit up straighter, schooling my expression. I don't need her pity. After feeling hollow inside for so long, unable to dig up even an ounce of bravery, unable to face . . . *any* of this, I finally feel strong enough and I can't forget that.

Only took me eight years and my father's death to make it happen, but I'm doing it.

"I'm ready," I tell her with a firm nod. I hear Mom off to the side, murmuring something to Brenna, and I refuse to look at them, too afraid my strength will evaporate. They came with me, I told them I needed their support, but now I'm wondering if that was a mistake. I don't want to hear Mom's sobs while I'm trying to talk. I don't want to see them watching me spill all of my painful, ugly secrets with horrified expressions and tears in their eyes.

Everyone's shed enough tears over this tragedy that is my life. I should celebrate that I'm alive, not hide in the shadows. I haven't been allowed to talk for so long and I feel almost . . . liberated. Yes, despite the awful things I'm about to reveal, I'm relieved. Free. From the moment I came home, Dad demanded our silence. Particularly mine. He was too embarrassed, too ashamed that he'd failed his daughter.

I heard him say that once, when he and Mom got into a huge fight pretty soon after I came back home. They thought I was sleeping safely in my bedroom but their yelling woke me up, not that I slept much back then. I still have a hard time. But I remember that moment like yesterday, it's burned so deep in my brain. The despair in Dad's voice, that's what drew me out of bed first. That and my name being mentioned again and again, their voices rising.

I slipped out of bed and crept down the hall, my heart racing. I pressed my body against the wall of the hallway and listened, unable to turn away when I realized they weren't just talking about me—they were *fighting* about me.

"You can't keep her under lock and key," Mom had said. *"I know I was always the overprotective one, but I think . . . no, I* know *you're taking it too far."*

"I failed her, Liz. I failed our baby girl and there's nothing I can do to change that."

But he could have changed that, if he'd just accepted me. Hugged me like he hugged my older sister, Brenna, without thought and with plenty of affection. If he'd stopped looking at me with so much shame and humiliation filling his eyes, as if I were some sort of mistake returned home to them, sullied and disgusting. I went from being Daddy's girl to the daughter Daddy didn't want to touch, all in a matter of days.

It hurt me then. It still hurts me now. And he's been dead for over six months.

"We can stop taping at any time if you need a moment to compose yourself while you're telling your story," the reporter reassures me in her smooth, professionally comforting voice, and I smile and nod, thinking in my head that won't be necessary.

I need to tell it, and I don't want to stop, or come back at another time. I need to purge it from my soul once and for all.

More than anything, I need to set the record straight.

There have been endless reports on what happened to me. Countless one-hour documentaries devoted to my case. Two made-for-TV movies and about a bazillion true crime shows.

My face was on the cover of *People* magazine when I was first found eight years ago. Wearing a drab gray sweatshirt and matching pants a female police officer gave me that were two sizes too big, my eyes full of tears as I stared at the camera while they escorted me out of the police station. They were taking me to the hospital so I could be examined.

A shiver moves down my spine at the horrific memory.

I kept that magazine, stashed away in a box. I saved it. My so-called claim to fame. Why I don't know. Not like it documents a pleasant memory.

But it's mine. My life. I can't change it, no matter how much everyone who loves me wants me to.

People magazine wants to talk to me now, especially once they found out about this interview. They want to put my face on the cover again, but I haven't said yes. I don't think I will. Publishers want me to write a book about my experience, but I don't think I'll do it. This one time, I will tell my story from start to finish. The scheduled interview will air for one hour, but I've already been reassured that if I have more to say, the network will give me two.

Must be a slow week, but I don't argue with them. I think I will take the two hours. I have a lot to say. This is my time. My moment.

And then I will never speak of Aaron William Monroe in public again.

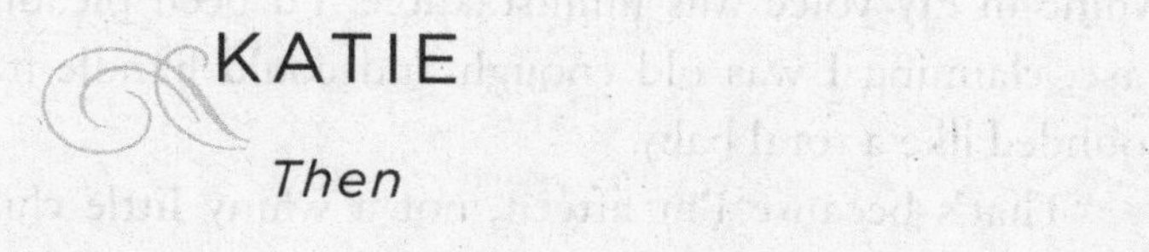

KATIE

Then

The sun broke through the wispy tendrils of fog right about the time we left the hotel. Its intense rays caressed my arms and warmed my hair and face as we headed west down the sidewalk, and I regretted wearing the bright red lifeguard sweatshirt Mom bought me last night at a gift shop. I'd begged her for it, pleading with big eyes and my hands together in mock prayer. She'd reluctantly agreed, griping about the price the entire time.

Despite my love for the outrageously red sweatshirt, it was bulky and would look really stupid if I tried to tie it around my waist.

But I was stuck with it.

The sky was this incredible blue that looked almost unnatural, like out of a painting. The wind was cool, bringing with it the scent of the ocean. Dampness lingered in the air, from both the Pacific and the fog, and I could feel it on my face, taking the edge off the heat of the sun. Pure, unfiltered joy seemed to wash over me and I couldn't remember a time when I'd felt so excited.

Never again would I feel that same innocent excitement.

When we finally arrived, the boardwalk was as crowded as I'd ever seen it and the rides had only just opened. Immediately I launched in, begging Mom and Dad to let us go on our own, and I pulled out all the stops.

"Brenna gets to take off with her friends all the time!" The whine in my voice was unmistakable. I'd been pleading my case, claiming I was old enough and could handle it, but I sounded like a total baby.

"That's because I'm fifteen, not a whiny little child like you," Brenna said condescendingly, glancing over at her best friend, Emily, before they both started to crack up. I hated Brenna sometimes. Didn't really like Emily much, either. They always picked on me. Made me feel dumb.

My best friend, Sarah, glared at the two of them along with me. We seriously didn't need Brenna's commentary to screw up what we wanted so desperately.

To hang out at the amusement park all day by ourselves, not having to tag along with Mom and Dad. Sarah and I were both turning thirteen next month, our birthdays only six days apart, and we were eager for a taste of independence.

"Sarah has her cellphone," I continued, staring at Daddy, pleading with him with my eyes. I could see his gaze waver, the flicker of hesitation, and I needed to latch onto that quickly. "We'll check in every hour, I swear."

"I don't know . . ."

Chancing a quick glance at Mom, I could see that she really wasn't too big on the idea at all. She wasn't the one I needed to convince, though.

Daddy was.

"*Please.* We can meet every two hours if you want. Get together for lunch. It's only ten. We can meet at noon, right over there." I pointed at the nearby food court. "Please, please, *please.*"

"We'll be on our best behavior," Sarah said solemnly, her expression serious. So serious I almost wanted to laugh.

But I held it all in. No way would I blow this, not when we were so close.

"No talking to strangers," Daddy said, pointing at the both of us. I could tell he was this close to agreeing. He was such a softie. "And no leaving this boardwalk, not even to go to the beach."

My heart threatened to burst from excitement. I knew we almost had him.

"Jim, really." Mom's voice was full of disbelief, but I ignored her. Something I'd grown quite good at doing the last few months. We hadn't been getting along. She was always trying to tell me what to do. I was sick of it. Desperate for independence, wanting to forge my own way, not follow after her. What did she know about my life? Things had changed so much since she was a girl, I knew she couldn't have a clue.

"Ah, come on, Liz. She'll be fine," Daddy reassured her before he turned his sunny smile on me. "We gotta let her go sometime, right?"

Mom sighed, and I heard the weariness in her tone. For whatever reason, she'd been stressed out lately. We were on vacation, so why couldn't she just relax? "Call me at ten thirty and let me know where you're at."

Ten thirty? That was less than thirty minutes away. Talk about controlling. "Fine," I conceded, acting all put out, but secretly I wanted to hop up and down. From the way Sarah was shifting from one foot to the other as she stood beside me, I could tell she felt the same.

We were so incredibly in sync with each other, Sarah and I took off running before they could change their minds.

"Don't talk to strangers!" Daddy yelled after us, making us laugh.

"Unless they're cute," Sarah muttered, then she laughed even harder.

I didn't say anything. My best friend had gone boy crazy

right at the end of school and her boyfriend fever hadn't let up. She wanted one. Bad.

Me? I didn't care. None of the boys at school interested me. I'd known pretty much all of them since kindergarten, some even longer because I went to preschool with them. I found most of them irritating. The thought of kissing one of them?

Yuck.

"Please don't wave and flirt with guys all day," I said because I just . . . I didn't want to deal with it. Not today. This was *our* day. Our chance to be by ourselves and ride whatever ride we wanted. Eat whatever we wanted. *Do* whatever we wanted. We had the neon-green wristbands that got us on every ride all day long for as many times as we could stand it, and we were ready.

I didn't want to waste my time flirting with high school boys who'd laugh if they knew we were only twelve. I totally looked twelve, but Sarah didn't.

She looked older.

"Don't be such a downer." Sarah had been smart. No sweatshirt for her, only a T-shirt that she was currently taking off, revealing a bright pink bikini top underneath. She had boobs and I was still pretty flat, but I wasn't jealous. Not really.

"I'm not. I just . . . I don't care about boys today. I wanna have fun." I smiled at her and she smiled in return.

"We're definitely going to have fun. And boys *are* fun. You just haven't figured that out yet." She rolled up her T-shirt and shoved it in the purse she'd brought with her. "Now let's go on the Ferris wheel."

I frowned. How lame. "Seriously?"

"We'll start out small." Her devilish smile grew. "And save

the big one for later." She pointed at the giant white roller coaster looming ahead of us. At that particular moment a train of cars went flying by, the passengers all screaming, most of them with their arms in the air, their hair trailing behind them.

My heart picked up speed just watching them. I couldn't wait.

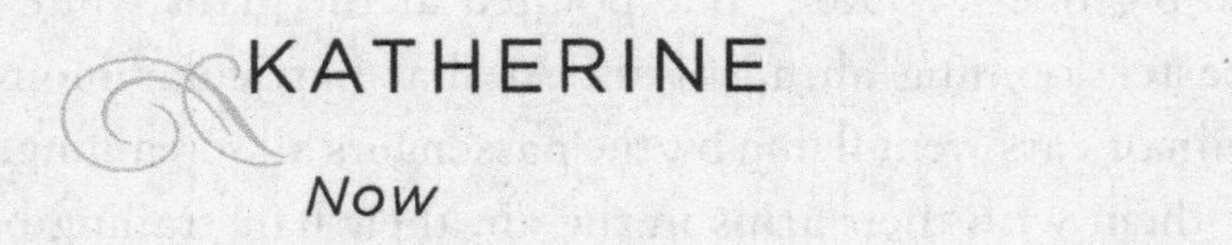

KATHERINE

Now

"And then what happened?"

The reporter's voice knocks me from my thoughts. I'd become lost in them, after not having visited those particular memories in so long. Everyone always focuses on the bad stuff, including myself. What he did to me. How long he kept me. Where he kept me. How he chained me like a dog and blindfolded me and I couldn't see anything and I was so incredibly scared that I peed my pants when he peeled the blindfold away from my eyes that first time. I knew by the determined look on his face what he was going to do to me.

But I didn't *really* know because my sexual education wasn't much beyond a few YA books I'd read with very tame sex scenes and those awful movies they show at school about getting your period and hormones and stuff.

"I had fun that morning," I say, my tongue thick in my mouth because I *did* have fun that morning and there's a hint of bittersweet in those memories. Sarah and I were laughing and being silly, which should make me smile. But it's so painful to remember the good moments of that day. They're completely overshadowed by the bad. "We met my parents for lunch at the food court, just like we promised. I had a corn dog."

The details are still there, a little hazy, but the more I talk, the clearer they become. I remember the seagulls that dive-bombed the tables as we ate. How I dropped the last bite of my corn dog on the ground and the white-and-gray bird swooped in, stealing it before I could even snatch it back.

Not like I would've eaten it, but still.

The reporter smiles, trying to put me at ease I'm sure. "It was a nice day with your family and your best friend."

"Yes." I nod, thinking of Sarah. How we grew apart after everything that happened. How she didn't like to be around me because I made her uncomfortable. She told me that once, both of us crying and not understanding why we couldn't get back to that place we'd been before, when we were best friends. She'd blurted it out, clamping her lips shut the moment the words were said. She looked like she wanted to take them back.

But she couldn't. It was too late. She felt guilty, she said. She hadn't protected me, and I thought that sounded like a crock of crap but I didn't argue with her.

By high school we were strangers. She wouldn't even look at me when we passed by each other in the hallway between classes, and I heard rumors that she said bad things about me. I don't know if any of it was true.

After I left, I never saw her again.

"Do you still talk to Sarah?" the reporter asks, as if she can reach into my brain and know exactly what I'm thinking. I'd heard that she's incredibly intuitive and I should be on guard. She knows just how to get information out of people before they even know they're offering it.

"No." I shake my head, hating how the word comes out like a rasp of breath. The loss of her friendship was the second hardest thing to take, behind my losing my father's affection. Mom and I grew closer. Unbelievably, Brenna became my best friend and closest confidante. She still is.

But that's because I have no friends. I let no one new in. And my old friends abandoned me. Or I abandoned them.

I'm not sure which happened first.

"Maybe she felt too much guilt, after what happened. Do you think she felt responsible for your disappearance?"

"No. I don't know." The words rush out of me and I sound defensive. Young. I swore I would remain cool and composed and the reporter—her name is Lisa—promised she wouldn't ask me uncomfortable questions. She would wait for me to volunteer information.

But I bet she thought the uncomfortable stuff would deal with Aaron William Monroe. Not my long-lost best friend.

Lisa's staring at me right now, trying to pick apart my brain, and I shutter it closed, pressing my lips together so no unwanted words escape. I've created all sorts of defense mechanisms over the years and this is one of them.

"Tell me what happened after lunch," Lisa says.

I take a deep breath and hold it, wondering what I should say first.

This is where it gets harder.

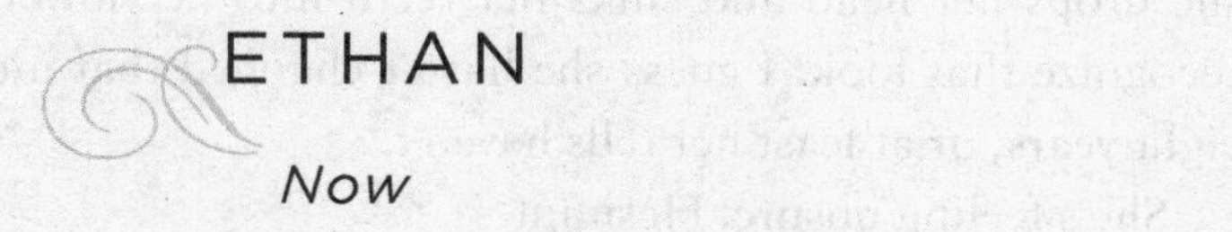

ETHAN

Now

I hear someone else say her name for the first time in years and it stops me cold.

Turning, I glance at the TV where it hangs on the wall of my narrow living room, squinting at the screen. I don't have my glasses on and I scramble for them in my haste, finding them on the counter mere inches from where I stand in the kitchen, and I shove them on my face.

Everything comes into focus and my mouth drops open.

"This week on News in Current with Lisa Swanson, *kidnapping survivor Katherine Watts speaks for the first time in eight years about her harrowing ordeal."*

I stare, completely frozen, as Katherine's image fills my TV screen. Her hair is a little darker, but still that same honey-golden blond. She looks older—which makes sense because come the fuck on, it's been eight years, just like the announcer said, and we've all changed a lot in the past eight years.

A lot.

"I had fun that morning," she says, her soft, sweet voice filling the room, filling my head, making it spin. She sounds the same yet different. Older.

Fun that morning. I'm sure she did. The boardwalk is a fun place to be when you're twelve. I loved it, too. Still do.

But I don't have bad memories that taint the place like she does.

"He was so nice at first," she continues, her voice fading as she drops her head and sinks her teeth into her lower lip. I recognize that look. I guess she hasn't changed that much in eight years, or at least her tells haven't.

She's feeling unsure. Hesitant.

Electricity buzzes through my veins as I watch her, listen to her, savor the sound of her familiar yet different voice. She sounds so composed, so articulate, her words measured, the tone strong. She looks good, too. Pretty with the long blond hair, the big blue eyes, the mouth . . .

I close my eyes for a brief moment and swallow hard. All the memories come at me, one after another, blazing over me like wildfire, and I grip the edge of the counter. The memories are unwanted. I'd banished them from my mind, fought those demons long ago and won. They represent an old part of my life, another part I try my best to forget even happened.

Yet just like that, seeing her, *hearing* her, I'm the old me again, cracked so wide open it makes my heart hurt.

"Seemingly harmless?" Lisa asks in that no-nonsense tone of hers that makes the hair on the back of my neck stand on end. I've had that voice directed at me more than once. When I was a kid and scared out of my mind and I didn't know what to say.

I hate Lisa Swanson.

A new image appears on the screen. Katherine at the time she was found, her tear-filled gaze aimed directly at the camera, distress written all over her young face. She's wearing baggy sweats and her hair is in a sloppy ponytail. A uniformed policeman and woman stand on either side of her, escorting her into the hospital.

Katie. When I see her like that, it all comes rushing back at me, memory upon memory, word after word, promise after promise. My legs feel weak and I grip the edge of the countertop.

You can't be scared, Katie. You have to be brave. You have to come with me.

What if he finds us? What will he do?

He won't do anything to you. I won't let him.

You promise?

I promise.

"Has he ever tried to reach out to you?"

Lisa's back on the screen, her eyes narrowed, head tilted like she's concentrating hard. Like she cares.

Snorting out loud, I shake my head. She cares all right. About her ratings and her money and the next big interview she can snag.

I can't believe Katherine is talking to her.

Katie.

My Katie.

It's been so long since I referenced her like that it sounds foreign. But she was mine. For a tiny bit of time I took care of her, was responsible for her safety. She called me her guardian angel and though I denied it, deep down inside, it felt good, her calling me that. Thinking of me in a good way. A positive way.

Without hesitation I did what was right. I had to. I couldn't let him keep her. He would've . . .

I can't even imagine what he would have done to her.

Not only was I her guardian angel, she called me her hero. She said that to me right before we approached the police station. I can hear her voice, clear as day, ringing in my head.

You saved me from him. You're my hero. Like an angel from heaven.

I didn't believe in God and angels but at that moment, I wanted to. Badly.

"Contact me? No," Katherine says vehemently, shaking her head. "Never."

"Really?" Lisa arches a brow. Yet another image flashes on the screen, a photo of a letter. I recognize that handwriting, and my fingers curl so tight around the counter's edge I feel like it could crumble in my hands.

The next shot is of Katherine, lips parting, eyes going wide. Whatever the fuck Lisa just showed her can't be good.

I know it.

And then his face is there. A photo in black and white, his jaw jutting out stubbornly, mouth drawn into a thin line, eyes blank and dark. His expression is cold, his hair shorn to nothing, and I swear there's a giant tattoo on the side of his neck. Of course.

He is in prison after all. He's had to adapt to the prisoner lifestyle as much as possible or they'd string him up by his dick. Child molester. Rapist. Killer.

My father.

WILL

Then

"Get in here."

I went still at the sound of his voice bellowing from his bedroom, the threatening edge to it. He was drunk. Again. He was always drunk lately and most of the time he ignored me, but not tonight.

Fuck.

I shuffled into his bedroom, my nose wrinkling in disgust at the smell that hit me. I couldn't describe it, not fully. Musty. Stale. Sweat. Booze. Sex.

"Where have you been?" he asked when I stopped in front of his bed. He was laid out on it in his grungy white boxer briefs and nothing else, his skin pale, the hair on his chest stark against the white of his flesh. He hadn't shaved and his hair was wild, sticking up all around his head.

He looked fucking crazy.

"School," I said, looking anywhere but at him. He was hard to look at, this shell of a man who used to be something big, someone important. At least, that was what he told me.

I never saw him like that, but what do I know? I was only fifteen. Ignorant and stupid. Again, things he'd told me.

"Fucking liar," he spat out. "Tell me the truth."

"That's where I was," I insisted. "School. I had football practice." I focused on sports and school so I wouldn't have to come home. So I wouldn't have to deal with him. Most of the time he could give a shit where I was or what I did. I couldn't get why he was acting like this.

Foreboding crept over me, chilling my skin.

He wanted something from me. I didn't know what.

"In the summer? 'Football practice,'" he mimicked, his voice in this high whine that made him sound like he was imitating a girl. Or me with a girly voice. *Asshole.* "Thinking you're a big stud, playing football and basketball and every other fucking sport out there? Trying to get all the girls with that ugly mug of yours?"

I clamped my mouth shut, saying nothing. What the hell did he know? If I said the wrong thing, he'd backhand me. He might've looked like a lazy sloth sprawled across his bed, but the man could move fast when he had to.

I should know. I'd been smacked out of nowhere before.

"I have a new girlfriend," he said, completely changing the subject. "I want you to meet her."

My gaze finally met his and I didn't like what I saw. Amusement burned in his dark-as-the-devil eyes and his lips were curled in a shitty smile. "When?" I asked warily.

"Now," he announced, and at that exact moment, the connecting bathroom door swung open and a woman wearing nothing but a black bra and panties strode out, stopping just in front of me with her hands on her hips.

I stared at her, noted the faint lines around her thin mouth, the hardness in her gaze, just like my dad's. Her hair was an orangey blond and looked fried on the ends. Her skin was pale and ashy in color.

She looked dead.

"Hi." Her voice was rough, like she'd smoked a million cigarettes already in her lifetime, and she probably had. I could smell the faint traces of smoke on her, a smell I recognized since I snuck more than a few cigarettes a day myself.

My one and only vice.

"I'm Sammy." She stuck her hand out, her pink dagger-like nails pointed at me like a weapon. "You must be Willy."

I glared at my dad, hating that fucking nickname so much I wanted to scream. "Will," I corrected her, shaking her hand quickly before I let it go like it was covered in disease. It might've been. "Can I go now?" I asked Dad.

"No." He smiled and patted the spot beside him on the mattress. "Come here, Cookie."

He called all his girlfriends Cookie. I wondered if stupid Sammy realized that. By the little giggle she gave and the eager way she hopped over to the bed, I'd assumed that would be a no.

"You like my new Cookie, Willy?" he asked, squeezing her close and making her giggle even more. "Isn't she sweet?"

No. I hated her. She looked like an old whore off the street. They all did. She was probably addicted to meth or crack or whatever the fuck they liked to do and he was feeding her habit. He liked meth and crack and all that other shit, too. Sometimes. Other times he'd clean up his act and look good. My dad was a great-looking guy when he took a shower, brushed his hair, shaved his face, and dressed like a normal human being.

But right now was not one of those times. He'd slipped and fallen into that dark mental pit of his. I could tell. I knew what he wanted me to do. He'd made me do it before, when I was younger and felt too weak and scared to protest.

No more. I was stronger now. Playing sports, getting my ass clobbered out on the field, out on the court, toughened me up. I could take his ass if I wanted to. We were the same height. I hoped I'd gain a few inches on the asshole. Then what would he do?

I wanted him scared of me like I was once scared of him.

"Sit in the chair over there, Willy." He waved a hand at the worn, pale green chair that sat in the corner of his bedroom. The chair supposedly once belonged to my mother.

The only evidence that remained in our house proving she existed. There aren't any photos of her. He'd torn them all, burned them. Destroyed them, destroying her and my memories of her completely.

"Don't call me that," I said through clenched teeth, hating the nickname. Hating the name in general. It was *his* name. Aaron William. William Aaron was mine. Fucking sucked, being his namesake, even though our names were swapped.

I planned on changing it someday. Giving myself a name that belonged only to me, never to him.

"Willy," Sammy called, tilting her head back like she was howling at the moon. Dad laughed and rolled her over so she was on her back, his hand on her tit, his mouth on hers for a brief moment before he lifted up and stared at me.

"Get in the chair."

"Fuck you," I told him.

"Get. In. The. Chair," he commanded, his voice low and threatening.

"Come on, Willy. He just wants you to watch. He told me you like to watch," Sammy said, giggling when he pinched her nipple to shut her up. But she wouldn't shut up. She started cackling like a witch and he squeezed her hard, rolling over on top of her, his hand on her mouth. She started to scream beneath his hand, the sound muffled, and I took my opportunity.

"Fuck you," I growled again before I turned and fled, running into my room across the narrow hall and slamming the door behind me. I turned the lock and threw myself onto the narrow bed, my heart pounding, the roaring in my ears making it so I heard nothing else.

I stared at my door handle for a long time, waiting for it to start to shake, for him to pound on my door and demand I let him in. He'd done it before. Countless times. When I was smaller he'd grab me by the neck and lead me back into the room, forcing me into the chair.

Forcing me to watch.

Everything inside of me burned and I grabbed my pillow, clutching it tight. I hated him. I hated my mother for leaving me with him. Why didn't she take me? Tears stung the corners of my eyes and I blinked them away, refusing to cry. I'd cried enough. It was finally time to toughen up. I was too old for the crybaby shit.

Three more years. I had three more years of school and then I'd graduate and run. If I couldn't get into college, I'd go straight into the military. The navy. Something like that. Anything to escape. I wasn't scared of anything out there.

I was too damn scared of what could become of me if I stayed in here.

I lay on my bed clutching the pillow to me for a long time, my body tense, my muscles so rigid they ached when I tried to move. Finally I closed my eyes, letting the exhaustion slowly take me over.

He never came to my door.

That was the last time he asked me to watch.

KATHERINE

Now

Are you going to watch?

I stare at the text message from my sister, my fingers hesitating above the keys. How should I answer? If she tries to invite herself over, I'm going to have to turn her down. I don't want her with me tonight. I don't want anyone with me.

Are you?

I send the message and wait for her reply. I'm hiding out, scared of the media's reaction. Tonight, after the show airs, my life has the potential to change completely. It'll be a repeat of what happened before, when we turned everyone away, when we told them we didn't want to talk. That we refused to talk.

In the years since, there have been so many theories about what happened to me. I was a runaway. I asked for it. I wanted to be with him. I wanted to be his sex slave. I was desperate to escape my strict parents. I hated my life. I was a sullen preteen looking for fun. I was a fucking whore who deserved everything that happened to me. I was a dirty cunt who liked to suck dick.

Every single one of those horrible lies had been said about me, spread all over the Web. There are videos on YouTube devoted to my supposed lies. I watched one once and then immediately threw up afterward. I can still remember what the video said.

Temptress. Whore. She enticed him by dressing provocatively. Fucked him because she wanted it. Remained silent after she was rescued because she was guilty. She had secrets to hide. She was a drug addict. A slut. The bitch whore girlfriend of his son and they shared her between them.

Because I survived, for some reason, I've been blamed. I asked for it. For a serial killer to abduct me in broad daylight and keep me captive like his own personal plaything.

My phone dings and I check the message from Brenna.

I really don't want to watch it. I heard enough the day you did the interview.

Wasn't that the truth? I'm about to respond to her when another text comes through.

Mom called and asked if we should all be together tonight. I said I would check with you first.

Um, no. I don't want to be with Mom. She'll cry and try and comfort me and I'm over it. I said my piece. But I do want to watch it. Alone. I want to see how they portray me. Lisa swore up and down that it would be a positive piece. That it wouldn't make me look bad; I was a victim.

I corrected her and said I'm not a victim. I'm a survivor. Big difference.

Huge.

I want to watch it alone. Tell Mom thanks but I need to see it by myself.

I send the text before I can second-guess my decision and wait for her reply.

My parents never moved. Mom is still in the house I grew up in and Brenna isn't too far away, living in an apartment with her boyfriend, Mike. She's a third-grade teacher at the same elementary school we attended. It still blows my mind—my impatient, mean-as-crap older sister teaches a bunch of eight-year-olds every day and loves it.

I moved on purpose. I'm an hour south of where I grew up, in a very small town not far from where the kidnapping happened. I live in the middle point and why this reassures me, I don't know, but I don't like to question my motives too closely.

Considering everything going on, I'm in hiding right now. I've taken all the extra steps to not be found and I like it that way. I prefer it. What with the *News in Current* commercials in constant rotation, highlighting that moment when I'm shown a letter he sent me that I didn't know about—thanks, Mom, for keeping that particular secret from me—and the look of sheer panic on my face right before they go to his mug shot, I'm glad I took those precautions.

That's the moment I hated the most during the interview. Well, that and one other, where I had to vehemently defend the boy who saved me from a monster.

Who saved me from his dad.

My cellphone rings, startling me, and I nearly drop it from my fingers. I glance at the screen and see it's Mom.

Great.

"Darling, are you sure you want to be alone tonight?" She sounds worried. I can hear it, practically feel the emotion vibrating in her voice. "What if you become terribly upset? I don't think this is something you should experience by yourself. We want to be with you." And by *we* she means her and Brenna.

"I appreciate your concern, Mom, but I don't want to come over." I sound stiff. Wooden. Like how I used to talk to Dad.

"How about Brenna and I come over there," she suggests.

"Please, Mom." I sigh and close my eyes, searching for patience. I don't want to get angry. She means well. "I'd rather do this alone. I swear if I feel sad or get scared or whatever, I'll call you."

"Okay." She huffs out a long, tired breath. "Okay. I just—I want to be there for you."

"You always have been."

"Your father . . ." Her voice drifts and she sighs. She misses him. So does Brenna. They're both very fragile and don't talk about him too much because his death is so fresh.

I don't feel the same. I'd already lost him long, long ago.

Saying nothing, I wait for her to continue.

"He may not have reacted the way we wanted him to, but you need to know he loved you the same. Before it happened and after," she says.

She's defending him and I get it, but she's lying. He may have loved me, but not the same. He viewed me as tainted. Not his little girl anymore. A woman in a little girl's body.

I'm almost thirteen . . .

I remember thinking that seemed so old at the time. That I was about to cross that magical bridge from twelve to thirteen, where I'd be transformed into a woman with breasts and curves and her period and maybe even . . . eventually . . . a boyfriend.

That never happened. I starved myself afterward, believing I wasn't worthy of food. Of life. I was down to ninety pounds and didn't have my period until I was sixteen. Never had a boyfriend. Never went to my prom or any school dances. No football games, no parties, no sleepovers, nothing. All of it scared me. Boys scared me. Worse, men petrified me. The male teachers especially. They always looked at me. Examined me. I could feel their gazes crawl over me like tiny ants marching in a line up my legs, over my hips, across my stomach, around my breasts.

The tears spill from my eyes before I can stop them.

"Um, thanks for that, Mom, but I gotta go." I don't let her speak. I end the call and set my phone very carefully beside me on the couch, letting the tears continue to fall.

I'm not okay. I believed I was, but I'm not. I assumed that by telling my story and getting it out of me once and for all, I'd be done. I'd finally feel clean. After spending the last eight years of my life feeling like a dirty, filthy whore—thanks, Internet, for putting those thoughts in my brain—I'd be scrubbed and wholesome and pure again.

But I'm not. I was violated in the worst way.

Mentally.

Emotionally.

So much that the physical violation doesn't even matter any longer.

ETHAN

Now

I sit on my couch, anticipation setting me on edge as I wait for *News in Current* to come on. It starts at nine and runs to eleven. Two solid hours of watching Katie and me feel bad, guilty, all of those things, but I'm also excited. And nervous.

They have to mention me. I'm an integral part of this story—of *her* story. Will they make me look bad? I'm sure of it. I hate Lisa Swanson, and she doesn't like me much, either.

I'd shoved Katie Watts out of my brain so forcefully that I hadn't allowed myself to think about her for years. I couldn't. But now that she's back, she's consumed me. I've spent hours on my laptop looking up information about her, trying to figure out where she is, what she's doing, who she's become.

Unfortunately I couldn't find out much. She's private. No surprise. She didn't change her name beyond shifting to her more formal full name of Katherine. She didn't graduate high school, at least not publicly. Her sister is a teacher. Brenna Watts has a Facebook page with really shitty privacy settings and I scoured it like a stalker, looking for images of Katie, any mention of her, a link to her own profile.

There's no profile for Katie. Not many mentions of her on her sister's page, either. But there's one photo from a year ago of a housewarming party for Brenna and her dopey-looking boyfriend, Mike, celebrating their moving in together. It's a group shot, lots of people crowded in a cramped living room, holding up their glasses in a toast for the camera. Whoever took it must've been standing on a piece of furniture or a footstool or something because it was shot from high above.

I saw her among the sea of people, no cup in her hand but a faint smile on her face. Her hair piled on top of her head in a messy topknot, little tendrils brushing her cheeks, her gaze direct. She looked . . .

Beautiful.

Lost.

Sad.

Lonely.

Broken.

I stared at that photo for a long time. I right-clicked it and saved it on my hard drive like the stalker I am. What would she say if I reached out to her? Would she be happy? Would she hate me? Would she think I was an asshole or would she still believe me her hero? Her guardian angel?

You saved me from him. You're my hero.

Her words ring in my head. Still. Always. They break my heart, pierce my soul like she's never left it.

Which she hasn't.

I glance at the TV and see that the show preceding it has ended, and Lisa Swanson's image fills the screen, her gaze full of false sincerity, her expression one I like to call serious bitch news reporter. I turn up the volume so her voice fills my living room, fills my head, my thoughts, and I want to tell her to shut the fuck up.

But I don't.

Because even though it kills me to admit this, I want to watch.

KATIE

Then

The letters came like clockwork, showing up in my mailbox every other week, usually on Thursday or Friday. I always checked the mail after school; I told him this. We'd emailed each other before but that felt so cold, impersonal. I asked for letters instead and he agreed.

I liked seeing his handwriting, the bold slashes across the paper, the smudges of ink that reminded me he was a lefty and he dragged his hand along the words as he wrote. The wrinkled paper that told me he ripped it out of a notebook. The notes in the margins that were silly and reminded me he was still young.

We were both young, though most of the time we didn't feel like it. We both had to grow up so fast. I believed that's why we were drawn to each other still. Kindred spirits who suffered at the hands of the same man and all that.

I opened the mailbox and grabbed what was inside, slipping my letter from the pile and shoving it in the pocket of my sweater. Entering our house, I dropped the rest of the mail on the kitchen counter and murmured a hello in greeting to my mother's call from the family room.

She didn't push, didn't ask about my day until later, when we were sitting at the dining room table and she tried her best to work past the stilted conversation our family engaged in now. It was almost painful, having to endure the evening meal at the Watts house.

I hated it. So did Brenna.

Shutting my bedroom door with a resounding click, I turned the lock and then dove onto my bed, reaching for the letter in my pocket. I tore into it with trembling fingers, anticipation filling me at the potential of his words. They could be good. They could be bad. Someday these letters might disappear, and I've tried to prepare myself for that. We'd been corresponding for almost a year. He was about the only person I really wanted to talk to. I had no friends at school, not anymore.

Only Will.

I unfolded the letter, chewing on my lower lip as I devoured his words.

Katie,

You keep asking how I'm doing at the group home like you're worried about me or something. I've been trying to avoid that question but I can't hold back any longer. I hate it here. The guys are assholes. They steal my stuff and I got into a fight last week with one of them. I kicked his ass but he gave me a black eye and I got on restriction for causing the fight. Wasn't even my fault in the first place. And I'm still out the fifty bucks he stole from me.

At the rate I'm going, I'll never get ahead, never get anywhere.

Did I tell you I gave up football? Had to let go all my after-school activities so I could find a job. I'm working two, one legit and the other where they pay me under the table. Both suck but at least I'm earning some money. I need to find a new place to hide it all. Maybe I could open up a bank account, I don't know. I think I need an adult to help me with that, which is such bullshit. I can work and earn my own money but can't open a savings account?

Enough of my complaining. How are you? How's school? Did you pass that history test? I bet you did. You studied a lot and you're always worried about your grades. How's your dad treating you? In your last letter you mentioned Brenna has been extra nice to you. Is that still the case?

I wish I could see you. Talk to you. The trial has been delayed again. I know you don't want to talk about him but I'm feeling like the only time I'll ever get to see you is at trial and that just sucks, Katie.

But I know you can't meet me anywhere. I know your parents don't let you out of their sight and that's the way it should be. They need to keep watch over you and make sure you're safe.

If I can't be there, then they have to be the next best thing.

I have to go to work, so I'm sorry I'm cutting this letter short. Just know that I miss you.

Will

I reread the letter, my heart filled with pain at what he was going through. He was so miserable. Working so hard and for what? So someone could steal his money? How fair was that?

But life was totally unfair. I knew that. So did Will. We were the only ones who really got it.

The only ones who really understood each other.

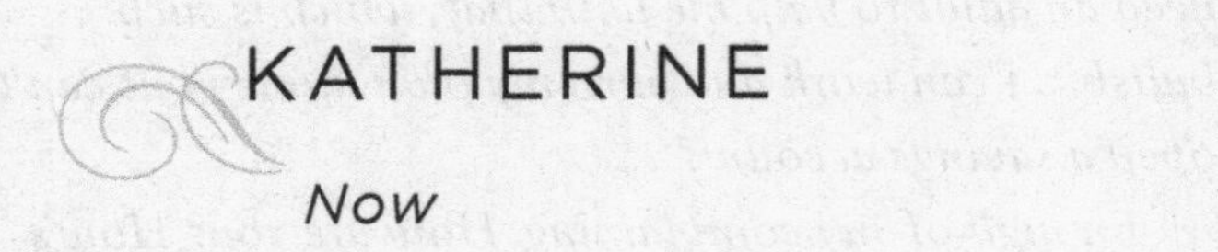

KATHERINE

Now

Watching the interview earlier, seeing the old photos of myself, crime scene photos, trial photos . . . all of the memories came back. One after another, so many of them after having been locked up tight in the darkest, farthest corner of my brain, they assailed me. Overwhelmed me. Ultimately, they brought on a massive headache.

I've heard plenty of stories about how when people have a traumatic experience, their brain protects them by banishing the memory. A girl I went to elementary school with was hit by a car, thrown fifty feet into the air, and she remembers . . .

Nothing. Not a lick of it.

How I wish my brain had protected me from the traumatic days I experienced by blocking out those awful memories, but it never happened for me. I might have done my best to bury those memories on my own, but they're always there. Lurking. Just waiting to come back out and revisit me.

Tonight, I thought of him for the first time in . . . forever. And when I refer to him, I'm not thinking of the big, bad, awful, monstrous *him*.

I'm thinking of the other him. The son. William.

Will.

During the interview, Lisa brought him up first, asking if I'd ever had contact with him after everything that happened. I said no.

I lied.

He reached out to me first, right after everything happened. A handwritten letter in a barely legible scrawl, quick, hard slashes across the lined paper. Words of sorrow and pain, wishes that I was better, hope that I would be okay, and an apology.

A long, heartfelt apology he had no reason to offer. He did right by me. He saved me. He also included a gift with his letter—a bracelet with a guardian angel charm.

I wore that bracelet for a long time, the only thing that kept me feeling safe, kept me going. We wrote each other letters once a week at first, then a couple of times a month. Occasionally emailing, even getting brave enough to exchange texts when I finally got my own cellphone. But ultimately my mother found out about our correspondence and I was forbidden from ever talking to Will again.

She banished him from my life and I allowed it, too afraid to defy her.

I hadn't worn the bracelet Will gave me in years, keeping it safely tucked away in an old jewelry box. But the night of the interview, after it aired, I dug through that box and slipped the bracelet on, my fingers sliding over the charm again and again, wishing for strength. Wishing for courage.

Lisa sent me a skeptical look when I offered up my answer about Will, but I didn't budge. I didn't so much as blink. After a long, quiet moment she informed me she didn't know what happened to him either. Could only assume he'd changed his name, created a new identity, a new life, and moved on.

I hoped that was the case. I didn't like thinking of the alternative. What if he turned to a life of crime like his father? What if he couldn't shake the burden and guilt of being that horrible man's son? What if . . . what if he took his own life and he's no longer alive? I know I'd been tempted over the years. Suicidal thoughts ran rampant in my brain, especially when I was younger and didn't know how to cope.

But I soldiered on. And came out on the other side. Did Will? Was he able to soldier on?

Lisa barely mentioned him during the interview. A few references here and there—and he deserved more than that. He's the *only* reason I'm still alive. She didn't include the clip where we talked about him in the televised interview, either. That made me inexplicably sad.

Will wasn't my enemy. He helped me. I don't care about the many news accounts that implied he was a part of his father's evil plan. He was questioned so much about why he didn't take me to the police sooner. I, too, was questioned over and over again about Will's role in all of this.

Did he molest you?

No.

Did he make you touch him?

No.

Did he have sex with you?

No.

Did he force himself on you? Become violent with you?

No and no.

The police never seemed fully satisfied with my answers.

Didn't they realize he'd been just a kid, like me? I was almost thirteen when it happened. He'd been fifteen. *Close enough to an adult*, one of the cops muttered under his breath during my initial questioning. *We've thrown murderers into prison that were younger.*

It wasn't true, what they were implying. He was my hero.

My angel.

My response to his letter and gift was a card full of gratitude, written in girlish script. I sent him a small gift as well, the only thing I could manage considering I was still a child and I knew without a doubt my parents would be furious if they found out I was corresponding with my kidnapper's son. It didn't matter that he saved me. In their eyes, Will was the enemy.

Halfway through the interview, I gave up watching and was on my laptop using Google. My search results came up empty. I think Lisa was right. He must have changed his name, his identity, and moved far away.

The interview is over but I'm still searching and when I finally sit up straight, my back aches, as do my shoulders. I glance around, see the late-night talk show host smiling and cracking jokes, and I turn off the TV, unable to take the cued laughter coming from the audience.

Fake. Everything feels fake. Unreal. I hold my hand out in front of me and curl my fingers, stretch them back out, my knuckles popping, and I notice that my fingers . . .

They're trembling.

Slamming my laptop shut, I leap from my chair and roam through my tiny house, restless. Mom texted me after the interview was over, asking if I was okay, and I reassured her that I was fine. And I am fine. Watching myself on TV is . . . weird, but hearing myself retell the story was cathartic. I'd been holding those words in for so long, it's rather liberating, knowing my story is out there now.

My shame is there for everyone to see.

It's late and I'm tired. I need to go to bed, so I go through the motions. Wash my face, brush my teeth, brush my hair and pull it into a messy bun on top of my head. I stare at my reflection in the mirror, my plain features, my washed-out blond hair, pale blue eyes. I feel . . . empty.

Bland.

Blank.

I change into a T-shirt and sweatpants and toss my clothes into the laundry basket. My routine is the same every night. I never deviate. I like routine. It makes me feel in control.

Safe.

Slipping in between the covers, I climb into bed, plug my phone in to charge, then turn off the lamp on the bedside table. The house is quiet, eerily so, and usually I like that. I live at the end of the street on a cul-de-sac; the backyard ends where the forest begins. Mom thought I was crazy, wanting to live in a house that butts up against a forest.

She's afraid someone will lurk in the shadows, Brenna had told me, trying to make a joke of it though I know she was serious.

They're all lurking in the shadows, I'd replied. *It doesn't matter where we are, what we do. If they're out there, they'll find a way to get us.*

Brenna told me I was morbid. She's right. I *am* morbid. When you've already faced your death once, what do you have left to fear? I tell myself that I should be living balls out. Not hiding away in my safe little house with my safe little routine and my bland, blank existence.

It's not that easy, though. Not being afraid. Believing that you're brave. I admire those who can move through life without a care in the world. Who do whatever they want whenever they want to.

I can't do that. I won't allow myself. I'm too scared.

For now, I stay here. My house, the quiet, the neighborhood, old Mrs. Anderson who lives next door and can be a bit of a busybody sometimes though I know she means well—it all reassures me.

Just like my routine.

As I lie here in the darkness, letting my thoughts wander, my mind fills with images of a fifteen-year-old, terrified Will. I never took the bracelet off and I rub my thumb over the charm again and again.

Sleep finally comes, but fitfully. I wake up almost every hour, the red numbers on my old alarm clock—the one I've owned since before, when I was just normal Katie—mocking me in the dark. Some things I can never get rid of. The stupid alarm clock is one of them.

My fears are another.

I imagine leaving. Running away like Will did. I envy him his freedom. Of being able to shed his skin and pretend to be something else. Someone else. Even if I did run away and came up with a new name, a new life, I know the remnants from my old one would cling to me. The worry. The fear. The sadness.

They're hard to get rid of.

Even harder to live with.

WILL

Then

I stood outside the storage shed, my entire body trembling as I paused in front of the door. I'd left her in there. I found her last night and walked away. I couldn't begin to explain why. What I did . . . was wrong. She begged me not to go.

Begged me.

And I left her anyway.

My stomach churned and I closed my eyes, breathing deep. I had to go inside. She could still be in there, scared out of her mind and needing me to take care of her.

But what if she's not in there? What if she's gone? What if he . . .

No. I shook my head once, banished the thought. She'd be there. She had to be.

With shaking hands, I turned the combination on the lock and yanked it open, then slowly pulled open the door. The hinges creaked, the sound loud in the otherwise quiet of the mid-afternoon, and I stepped forward, blinking against the darkness from within.

My nose wrinkled, I entered the storage shed, ducking my head since the ceiling was so low. It stunk inside. Bugs buzzed around me and I swatted at them, my eyes slowly readjusting so I could make out various shapes within. Stacks of boxes, a jumble of old furniture.

A dirty old mattress on the ground with a girl curled up on top of it.

I stopped in my tracks, my breaths so harsh my throat felt raw, my head spinning. I'd almost hoped I dreamed the entire thing, but she was real. Chained to the wall, shackles around her ankles. The blindfold was gone, duct tape stretched across her mouth in its place. She was in the fetal position, her head tilted downward, her matted blond hair a mess about her head.

Fuck, I thought I was going to be sick. My head swam, as did my stomach, and I stumbled over something unknown, causing her to sit straight up, her eyes opening and then squinting as she tried to decipher who I was.

A muffled scream came from beneath the duct tape and I crouched in front of her, reaching out to touch her hair, snatching my hand back when she recoiled from me. Her eyes filled with tears, streaking her dirty face as they fell, and she screamed again, the duct tape preventing the sound from carrying.

"I want to help you," I whispered as I fell to my knees on the filthy mattress. She scurried away from me, retreating to the wall, the chains clanking against the wood floor. "Please."

I couldn't believe what I was seeing. There was a prisoner being held mere feet away from my house. A girl—I knew she was younger than me, she didn't even have boobs, so I pegged her around eleven, twelve. No older than thirteen.

And my father was holding her captive. I could hardly wrap my head around the thought.

"I need you to trust me." I took a deep breath, as my brain tried to come up with the right thing to say. How could I earn her trust when I left her here once already? "Let me take the tape off."

She screamed again, the sound louder this time, and she shook her head furiously, her hair going everywhere. Her arm lifted and she pointed an accusatory finger at me and it was like she stabbed me in the heart.

Blame. That's what I felt. She blamed me for leaving her.

I couldn't hold it against her. I *had* left her. But what was I going to do? I'd freaked out. I almost didn't believe what I was seeing.

"Let me make it up to you," I whispered as I scooted closer to her. She eyed me warily, the tears still spilling down her cheeks, the stretch of tape covering her mouth, the entire lower half of her face. "I'll take the tape off. We can talk."

First time I found her, I'd barely spoken to her. I'd panicked, not knowing what to do.

Now, tonight, I planned on doing the right thing.

I approached her like she was a wild animal and I wanted to tame her, moving slowly, an inch at a time. I never let up on talking to her, trying my best to soothe her with a low voice and reassuring words. She never took her gaze off me as she sat trembling against the wall.

Until finally I was right next to her and I reached out, touching the tape with my fingers. She flinched but didn't jerk away, and I took that as a good sign. "This is going to hurt," I murmured. "I'm going to rip it off. Better that way."

Before she could give me any sort of sign that she approved or protested, I tore the tape off her face with one vicious tug. A sob escaped her the moment the tape was gone, the sound startlingly loud in the storage shed, and she toppled toward me, her wrists wrapped in the same chain that circled her ankle. I caught hold of her, her face in mine as she started to babble.

"Take me away from here, please. I need to find my mom and dad. My sister. My friend. Please take me somewhere safe. Please. Please, I'll do anything. They'll pay you. I promise."

She started to cry and I wrapped my arms around her waist, holding her close, patting her back awkwardly. I didn't know what else to do, how else to comfort her, but she never said a word. Just cried on my shoulder, her tears soaking through my shirt, her painful sobs hurting me, too. My chest ached. My throat and eyes burned.

I'd never seen such an outpouring of emotion and fear. Never had someone affected me this way. I felt her sobs, muffled by my shoulder, wrack her thin, trembling body.

What had my father done to her?

I couldn't begin to imagine.

"We'll leave," I whispered as I tentatively rested my hand on her hair. Anything I could do to reassure her. "Later tonight."

She leaned away from me, the horrified expression on her face one I'd never be able to forget. "What do you mean, later?" She shook her head. "I can't wait. I have to get out of here now."

"We don't have a choice," I said firmly.

"He'll come back," she countered. "Ev-every time he comes back, it's worse. I don't know if I can—if I can stand it."

I took a deep breath, pushing all thoughts of what he might have done to her firmly from my brain. "It can't be helped. I have to prepare first."

"Prepare what?" she practically shouted. She pulled out of my embrace, pressing herself against the wall, like she couldn't stand to be near me. The chains clanked against the floor, reminding me that she was a fucking prisoner, and disgust filled my stomach, making me nauseated. It took everything within me not to turn my head and puke my guts out. "Do you have the key?"

I frowned. "Key to what?"

"To these?" She lifted up her bound wrists, then her foot, showing the tiny lock that held the chain onto her ankle. "I need these chains off."

I shook my head, feeling unprepared. How was I going to get that damn chain off of her? "I need to find bolt cutters."

"You need to get me out of here is what you need to do. *Now.*" She stressed the last word, her tears all dried up, determination written all over her face. Her blue eyes shone, still damp with tears, and I was suddenly taken with the realization of how pretty she was. "He's going to kill me, you know."

My mouth went dry. How could she be so composed, so calm, while she said that? "No he won't."

She started to laugh but it sounded crazy. Like maybe she was losing her mind. "He will. I've seen the look in his eyes. He's—he put his hands around my neck, like he wanted to choke me to death." She was crying again, though I don't know if she realized it. "He can't let me go. He has to kill me. I've seen his face. I've seen his everything."

She turned away from me, pressing her face into the wall, like she couldn't stand looking at me any longer, and I kneeled there on the disgusting mattress, feeling helpless. Hopeless. Then anger surged through me, making my blood spark with fiery heat, and I clutched my hands into fists. "I won't let him touch you ever again."

She didn't bother looking at me. "Go away."

Her words shocked me. Didn't she want my help? Or had she already given up? "Tell me your name," I demanded rather than asked. I wanted to tell her mine, to give us a connection.

"No." She glared at me from over her shoulder, her hair flopping over one eye. "Leave me alone. You don't really want to help me. You're too scared you'll get caught."

I could hardly begin to comprehend what she said to me. She couldn't mean it. Was she willing to give up everything, her entire life, so she could . . . what?

Die at the hands of my father?

Screw that. *Fuck* that. I refused to let that happen. I was going to save her. I had to. It was the only choice.

"I'll be back," I told her as I stood and brushed off the front of my jeans. She still wouldn't look at me, her face mashed into the wall, her shoulders gently shaking, as if she was still crying.

Seeing that, hearing her quiet sobs . . . it broke my unbreakable heart.

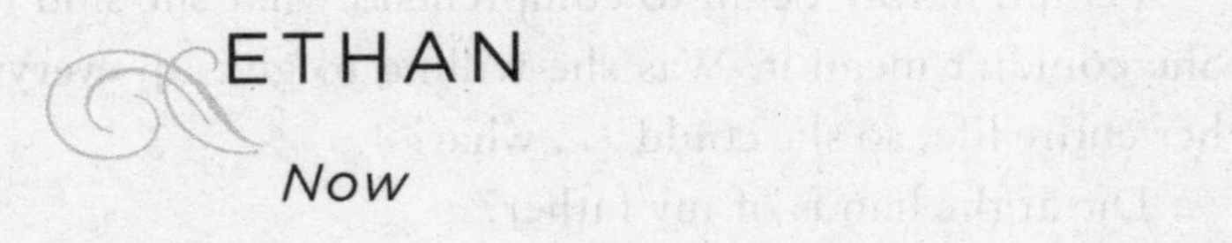

ETHAN

Now

I found her.

My pursuit of one Katherine "Katie" Watts was relentless. After watching her interview with Lisa Swanson, I spent almost a week scouring the Web for any bit of information I could unearth. Every news article I could find about the crime and her discovery, I read; some of it I'd seen before, after it first happened. Every crime documentary created about her, I watched on YouTube, Hulu, Netflix . . . all of them. Again and again. Over and over. Some I'd seen but many were new, coming out after I forced myself to let her go, pushing her and what happened between us out of my brain.

Now I was looking for a clue. A glimmer of truth, a bit of information I might've missed before.

It helped. After some slightly unethical searching on the Web, I discovered where she lived growing up, where she went to elementary school, and who her best friend was, the one that accompanied her the day she was taken. Her name had been withheld on the media but I scoured the court documents until I discovered it on the witness list.

Sarah Ellis was easy to find. Her Instagram, Twitter, and Facebook accounts popped up with ease, even with all the other Sarah Ellises out there. But it didn't look like she was in contact with Katie anymore, so there was no point in pursuing her.

I finally stumbled upon some pertinent information by accident. Legally, too—during a civil search, I found the documents for the purchase of Katie's house.

Meaning . . . I had her address.

I pulled up her house on Google Maps and studied it. Older. Small. Tiny front yard, rosebushes line the white fence. There's a little porch with a swing on it. It looks like a safe neighborhood, quiet, that borderlines a grove of towering pine trees.

She's lived there a year. The deed is in her name only. No guy. I'm assuming she doesn't have a guy.

I'm really fucking hoping she doesn't have one.

The interview is on right now—I'm watching it again because there's something about Katie's voice that soothes me. Gives me hope. Makes me yearn. We'd forged such a connection then, when we were young and felt like no one else understood us. Her parents severed that and I told myself it was for the best. I didn't need her, didn't want to need her, so I forgot about her.

Or so I thought.

Now I'm fucking obsessed. I want to meet the Katie of today and tell her I'm sorry. That I hope she's happy. I want to ask her if the ghost of my father still haunts her.

Because he haunts me. Constantly.

"What are your plans for the future?" Lisa asks Katie. The interview is almost over.

"Right now I just live day by day," Katie responds, her sweet voice filling my head, invading my thoughts. I pause in my search and lift my head, studying her image on my TV.

So beautiful. Her golden-blond hair is long and wavy at the ends and her blue eyes are dark, like a midnight sky. She looks innocent. Like an angel.

She could be my angel. She could save me. If I could just see her, talk to her. Just once.

"You must have some plans, don't you? Things you wish for? A career? Marriage? Children?" Lisa persists.

The flinch is there, so subtle I'm sure the average person wouldn't notice.

I do, though. I saw it. Her eyes flickered the slightest bit and a twinge made her wrinkle her nose. She didn't like those questions.

"I don't know what's in store for me. I'm going to school, living on my own for the first time, and I like it. I do hope that someday I will find someone, but I . . ." Her voice drifts and she's silent for a moment. She bends her head, her hair falling in front of her face, and I watch, mesmerized yet again, even though I've seen this many times. "I'm not sure it's in the cards for me," she finishes softly.

"What isn't in the cards for you? Marriage?" Lisa is like a dog with a bone. She never lets go. Not until she gets what she wants. And she wants to sexualize Katie. In a nice way, in a proper way, with marriage and children and all the things we're expected to do as good little citizens of the world.

"All of it," Katie says with a nod, lifting her head, her gaze meeting Lisa's once more. "I don't know if I'm capable of it. Of trusting anyone."

And that last sentence is what kills me.

He ruined everything. Fucking everything for this girl. She trusts no one. She believes she can love no one. Worse, I wouldn't doubt for a moment she thinks she's unlovable.

I can relate. I *am* unlovable. At least, that's what I always believed, for all these years as I continued on and tried to find a new way to live my life. Not under the shadow of my father, who sits on death row almost gleefully. I wonder what he thinks of Katie's interview.

Because I'm sure he watched every single fucking second of it. Just like me.

Just like me.

KATIE

Then

He wasn't coming back.

I figured he was full of crap. A liar. I didn't know who he was. Or what his name was, either. What did he want? How did he find me? I didn't even know where I was. I caught a glimpse out of the storage shed's dirty window the first night I was brought here, right before the man slipped the blindfold over my eyes and shrouded me in darkness. But all I saw was an empty backyard, with the exception of a lone, faded and chipped horse that looked like it came from a carousel leaning against the fence. Seeing that horse made me feel sad. It didn't belong here.

I didn't belong here, either.

The man hadn't come back since early this morning. He brought me a donut for breakfast and I devoured it, not caring that the glaze was damp and sticky and that it tasted stale. I was starving. I was still starving. My stomach growled and I pressed my forehead against the wall, closed my eyes, and willed the hunger pains to go away.

My mom's face loomed in my mind and I squeezed my eyes closed even tighter, trying to cling to hope, to the future. I saw her face, Daddy's face, my sister's face, Sarah's face, and I hoped they weren't too worried about me. That they were looking for me. Were they? Would they find me? Would anyone find me?

No.

The tears came. Slowly. My eyes burned, my throat ached, and I swallowed the sob, forced it down like it was food and would sustain me for a little while longer. I needed *something* to sustain me. I'd lost all hope. He'd be back soon. He'd touch me, force himself on me, put his mouth on me, and oh my God . . .

I banished the thoughts, the horror, the realness from my brain. Shuttered it closed, like I'd become so good at doing.

When I shifted my legs, the chains were loud as they clanked against the floor and I winced at the twinge between my legs. I hurt everywhere, but especially there. I was bruised and battered, the inside of my thighs black and blue, my chest, my legs and arms . . .

Marks everywhere. He was brutal in his handling of me. Like I was a rag doll, tossing me around, readjusting me, spreading my legs, moving my arms, tilting my head just so. He wanted me to look a certain way, every single time, and I didn't understand it.

I thought about his hands. Blunt fingers. Wide palms. The sound they made, like the crack of a gunshot when he slapped my face. The sting of my skin every time his hands made contact, the crawling just beneath my flesh, like little worms twisting along my muscles and bones, burrowing deeper inside me. I shivered, and fear made my stomach clench. He'd be here soon and I didn't know if I could take another visit from him. I didn't know if *he* could take another visit. After what happened last time . . .

I tried to swallow. My throat was scratchy like sandpaper, the tendons enflamed. I had bruises there around my neck. I wouldn't doubt if they were formed in the imprint of his fingers, five little marks on one side, five purplish smudges on the other. From when he choked me so hard my head hit the mattress with a dull thud again and again and I swore I was going to black out.

I'd *rather* pass out. So I wouldn't have to suffer anymore. I was already so tired of this. Exhausted. It had been only a few days. I'd lost count exactly how many, but I couldn't stand it anymore. I needed to go. I needed to escape before he ended me for good—

The door of the shed suddenly swung open, letting in a sliver of waning sunlight, and then it was gone, the door shutting with a foreboding, soft click. I went stiff, tried to hold my breath so I could hear him sneak in.

The softness was what scared me the most. I'd rather he come blazing in here, his anger palpable, his voice loud. Instead, he crept in like a sneak. Like your worst nightmare come to life. Quiet and calculating, and with an eerie smile on his face.

I kept my back to him, my muscles rigid despite my trembling. Everything inside of me ached and I pressed my dry, cracked lips together, trying to keep in the whimper that wanted to escape.

"Hey."

At the sound of the soft male voice I whirled around. Shock and relief caused tears to spring into my eyes and I sagged against the wall. "You came," I breathed.

He moved toward me, the boy who I'd thought was a liar. I was wrong. He stood in front of me like my hero come to life, his dark eyes intent as he studied me, his mouth drawn into a thin line. My gaze dropped from his face to see he carried something I'd never seen before in his hand. It had long handles and the metal tip reminded me of pliers.

It looked like a weapon. Like he could raise it above his head and smash it down on me in seconds.

"A bolt cutter." He lifted it up and I flinched, which he noticed. His gaze filled with pain, he settled on his knees at the edge of the mattress. "Come here—it'll be okay. I won't hurt you. I want to cut off the chain. First from your ankle, then your wrists. It'll be easier that way."

Relief filled me again and my heart practically sang with hope. I moved away from the wall, thrusting my leg out toward him, desperate to be rid of the chain once and for all. I couldn't miss the way he winced when he saw the bruises on my calf, my knee.

My thigh.

He ignored the bruises, the marks. His dark eyebrows scrunched together as he bent over my leg, his black-as-night hair falling over his forehead. The hair was unnaturally dark and I wondered if he dyed it.

I also wondered why.

"Tell me your name," he huffed out as he reached for my ankle, his touch tentative as he maneuvered my foot just so. The action reminded me of *him*. Of the man who took me, and for a quick moment I seized up, my chest tight, my heart pounding.

"Tell me yours first," I whispered, the words rushing out of me, almost slurring together. My head felt woozy and I knew it was from lack of food. I was so hungry, so thirsty.

He lifted his head, his gaze meeting mine once more. Dark and direct, serious and full of fear, he looked just as scared, just as unsure as I felt. "Will," he whispered.

"I'm Katie," I whispered back, flinching when I felt the cold, thick metal of the tool as it curled around the chain and brushed against my skin.

"Don't move, Katie," he warned me, his gaze dropping from mine once more so he could concentrate on the task at hand. I watched, too. Noted how his hands gripped the handles of the bolt cutter and he inhaled deeply, as if he needed to prepare himself. Give himself strength. "I don't want to hurt you."

My heart tripped over itself. That was the exact moment I knew this boy was my guardian angel, sent to protect me. Only me.

He was mine.

KATHERINE

Now

"So." Dr. Sheila Harris folds her hands in her lap, the docile smile on her face unassuming. Nonthreatening. "How's your week been? Have you been making progress toward your goals?"

I tear my gaze away from hers, keeping it focused on my fingernails. My cuticles are a mess and I pick at them, tear one so hard I start to bleed. She asks me this question every single time I'm here, though the goals part is new, a reference to the conversation we had last week. "Oh, you know. The usual. I did an interview on national television with Lisa Swanson. No biggie."

"I saw the interview." Amusement laces Dr. Harris's tone. She'd known I was doing it. The interview had been a topic of discussion for a while. It was part of my plan. One of my goals in the hope that I'd find peace, find strength.

Not sure if I agree with those goals, but I'm trying.

"What did you think?" I ask.

"I thought you were very brave," she says, her tone now solemn. "You revealed more than I expected."

Lifting my head, I study her covertly. She's watching me, that neutral smile still planted on her face, ever patient, ever kind. "I wanted to be completely honest and open."

"Do you think that was smart?"

I think about it before I answer. "I'm not sure. It's been crazy," I admit. "All sorts of media outlets reaching out to me.

Agents. Publicists. Magazines. Websites. They all want to talk."

"You didn't think that would happen?"

"I knew it would. That part didn't come as a surprise." I'd been fully prepared. Or so I thought.

"What did, then? Come as a surprise?"

"I don't know." I shrug. I'm lying. I just don't want to admit that I thought I would feel better after I told my story. That I'd somehow feel purged clean. Stronger.

The problem? I don't feel any different than I did before the interview aired. Oh, at first I did. I felt relieved, like I purged it all out of me. But now? I'm the same. No different.

Not healed.

"A lot of people are curious," Sheila states.

"That definitely surprised me. The sheer number of people who've watched the interview and want to know more." I stress the word *more* because it's something they've said repeatedly. More of my story, more about my future, more about my past, more, more, more. I feel like I'm being torn in twenty different directions and I don't know which way to go.

"I don't think you should've been surprised. The media gobbles this sort of story up. Look at those poor girls who were held captive all those years in Ohio. And Elizabeth Smart. Jaycee Dugard. The world was enthralled with their stories. They still are. Every one of them has published a book, done multiple interviews. Some speak in public venues. They've turned their tragedies into a message of hope and strength."

"I'm not sure I'm capable of that," I admit.

"It's something we can work on, don't you think? Not that you need to become a public figure, but trying to find that purpose? Digging deep and discovering your inherent strength?

It's in there, you know," she says, her tone assured. Like I should never doubt her.

"You really believe that?" I hate that I sound so full of doubt.

"Do you?"

"I don't know." I heave a big sigh. "I sometimes wonder if it was a mistake, doing that interview."

"How do you feel at this exact moment?"

"I wish I were a hermit," I say without hesitation.

Dr. Harris laughs softly. "You're already a self-proclaimed hermit."

Ouch. I change tactics. "I wish I didn't exist."

The laughter stops. "You don't mean that."

I shrug. Give no verbal reply. It's true. If I didn't exist, I wouldn't have to deal with any of it. I brought this on myself, so I have no one else to blame.

That's not true. I blame Aaron William Monroe for doing this to me. I wouldn't still be suffering if he'd just murdered me and been done with it. Done with me.

The thought alone makes me flinch, as if his rough, icy fingers are wrapped around my neck at this exact moment and are trying to choke the life out of me.

"Are you all right?" Dr. Harris asks, and I say nothing. I'm sure she saw me flinch. She doesn't miss a trick, my therapist.

We remain quiet for a few minutes, the ticking of the clock that sits on a nearby bookcase the only sound. It drives me nuts, that repetitive tick-tock, tick-tock. I think she has it in here on purpose, to drive all of her patients insane so we have no choice but to fill the silence with our problems and troubles.

Finally I can't take it anymore.

"I wonder sometimes what would've happened if he'd—killed me," I admit, swallowing hard.

"You'd be gone. There's nothing to wonder. You'd have no future. You'd have been a dead twelve-year-old with a devastated family and a man would have been free to kill numerous other girls after you," Dr. Harris says point-blank.

She's trying to shock me, convince me my train of thought is pointless without saying it out loud. She can't tell me whether what I think is right or wrong. That goes against her counselor's code or whatever.

"Would it have been better, though?" I ask. "Not for my family. They would have suffered no matter what." I think of my father, then immediately banish him from my mind. I'm still upset over the way he treated me, but there's nothing I can do about that. He's gone. "For me," I add, lifting my head to meet her gaze. "Would it have been better for me?"

Her face is impassive as usual. God, I wish this woman would show an iota of emotion. Just once. Though I guess this is what makes her so good at her job.

"It would be over," I continue. "Done, you know? I mean, look at me. I live a shell of a life. I rarely leave the house. I go to school from home. I don't really have friends. A nonexistent social life with the exception of hanging out with my sister and her boyfriend on occasion, and that's just lame. And of course, no man will ever want to . . ." *Be with me. Touch me. Kiss me.*

My voice drifts and I clamp my lips shut, closing my eyes to ward off all the ugly thoughts. They bombard me at the worst times, always when I'm feeling low, knocking me even lower, taking my breath and my strength, all in one swoop.

"Are you feeling lonely, Katherine?"

I open my eyes and drop my head again, not wanting to see any sort of pity in her gaze, not even a glimmer. She may remain stoic most of the time, but every once in a while her eyes give her away. Just for a second, almost as if I imagined it. "Sometimes," I admit.

"You should try and get out more. Join a club or something," she suggests.

I start to laugh but there's no humor in it. "Right. A club. Which one should I join? Do you think a surviving victims of serial killers group exists?"

She ignores my sarcasm. "There are all sorts of support groups out there, Katherine. I'm sure you could find one that suits you and your needs. I have resources. Plenty of information I can send home with you."

Information she's tried to shove on me before. No thanks. Not interested. "I can't go out in public right now. People might recognize me."

"You're the one who wanted to do the interview," she points out, and that does it.

I'm sort of pissed.

"You're right. I thought it would be therapeutic, considering these visits really aren't." I leap to my feet, my entire body shaking I'm so upset. "I should go."

Dr. Harris looks up at me, one brow lifted. "Do you think that's wise?"

"I don't know." I feel like I'm about to crawl out of my skin. "I don't think it matters. I can't help the way I feel."

"You're conflicted."

"Always."

"Why?"

I slump back into the chair, all the air leaving me, my lungs feeling deflated, my head spinning. "I don't know. I want to live. I'd rather be dead. I want to be strong. It's so much easier to be weak. I want to confront my fears and face them head on. I want to run away and pretend I don't exist."

"But you do exist. You're trying your best to be strong." She leans forward in her chair and I want to shrink into mine. "First thing you tackled was the interview. Telling your story."

"So?" My voice is small and I curl my arms around myself, suddenly cold.

"So you did that. And you survived it. Came out on the other side. You should be proud of yourself." Her voice is firm, as if she's trying to parlay her strength onto me. "Are you?"

"Proud of myself?" I scoff. "No. What do I have to be proud of? All I did was survive."

"You escaped. You identified a serial rapist and murderer, and thanks to you he was caught."

"It wasn't all me. I had help." I think of him. Again. He crosses my mind more often than not lately. My guardian angel. I reach for the charm on my bracelet, running my thumb over it. "I had nothing to do with my escape."

"You don't give yourself enough credit."

"I was twelve. Completely helpless. His son was the one who saved me. He took me to the police station." He didn't want to stay. Will had planned on dumping me off before going back. Back to what, I wasn't sure.

Nothing good.

"You had the strength to testify," Dr. Harris reminds me. "You spoke out in court and helped convict the man who kidnapped and raped you."

Raped. I hate that word. It makes me feel like damaged

goods—maybe because I *am* damaged goods. Who'd want me? I can hardly look a man in the eye, let alone talk to one. "I don't want to talk about this anymore."

"Talk about what?"

"Him. What he did to me. How he raped me. How I'm ruined for any other man," I spit out. It always circles back to this, to him, and what he did to me. They want all the gruesome details. A list of exactly what he did to me, where he touched me, how many times he . . .

I close my eyes and let it wash over me. What he did. What he said. The look in his eyes. The tiny bits of kindness he doled out to convince me he wasn't so bad.

He was the devil.

"Do you believe yourself ruined?" Dr. Harris asks.

"Yes," I whisper. "It's why I sometimes wish I would've died. It would be so much easier, you know? I'd be gone. I wouldn't have to deal with all of this."

"Are you saying you feel suicidal?"

Always the same question, always afraid I'm going to harm myself. "Not at all."

"Do you truly regret doing the interview?"

Opening my eyes, I stare at her. "No. It had to be done. I'm assuming this is part of the process."

"I believe you're right," Dr. Harris says, her voice soft, her expression kind. That tiny glimpse of kindness reassures me and I sit up straight, my thumb still streaking across the silver guardian angel charm. "Talking about what happened after so many years is going to bring up a lot of difficult emotions. You've been taken back to when it happened and you're having to deal with those feelings all over again."

And I didn't deal with them properly the first time around,

not really. I had to pretend everything was okay, even though it wasn't. "I should be stronger," I say. "It shouldn't affect me like this."

"We all deal with trauma differently," she starts, but I cut her off.

"I want to be stronger."

"You'll get there." She smiles, this tight, close-lipped smile that is full of lies. "Someday."

"When?"

"When you're ready."

"But I'm ready now."

"Are you?"

Silence again. Maybe she's right. Maybe I'm not ready.

Maybe I'll never be ready.

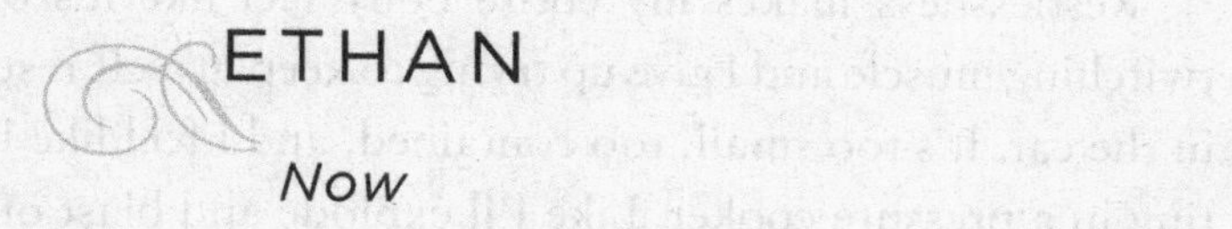

ETHAN

Now

I am a man obsessed.

I sit in my car up the street from Katherine Watts's home, slunk low in the driver's seat, so low I'm eye level with the steering wheel as I watch her house. There's no movement, no car parked in the driveway, nothing happening whatsoever, and I'm antsy. I want to get closer, but not too close. She won't recognize me if she's there, if she happens upon me. I don't want to scare her and I'm sure she's jumpy. She could think I'm a reporter, trying to dig up some info.

It's the perfect cover.

Hell, I shouldn't be here. I promised myself I wouldn't go to her house, that I wouldn't try and catch a glimpse of her.

But here I am, lurking. Waiting. I just want to make sure she's all right. That she's safe. After the interview aired, I'm sure she's had to deal with an overwhelming amount of media attention. It can't be easy. Does she have a solid support system? Friends? Family? From watching her over and over again in that interview, I have the distinct feeling she's lonely. Alone.

I can relate. And I hate that. Does she have that constant ache in the pit of her stomach? Does he haunt her at the darkest moments of the night, when she's alone and vulnerable in her bed, memories wrapped up in a nightmare visiting her every chance they get?

I hope to hell not.

Restlessness makes my entire body feel like it's one big twitching muscle and I give up trying to keep myself restrained in the car. It's too small, too contained, and I feel like I'm sitting in a pressure cooker. Like I'll explode and blast out of it at any given moment.

Patience has never been my strong suit.

So I climb out of the car and slowly start to walk along the sidewalk toward her house. My steps are measured, hands in the front pockets of my jeans, expression neutral, stance casual. I'm wearing a black pullover sweatshirt, sunglasses covering my eyes though the sun is weak. It's quiet. Considering it's just after eleven in the morning, I can assume most everyone is at work. With the exception of the older woman sitting on the front porch of the house that's right next to Katherine Watts's.

Her neighbor.

Shit.

I do my best not to look in her direction, keeping my head averted, though I'm dying to look at Katie's house. I want to check out every detail possible so I can memorize it. Maybe discover a clue, a little glimpse into what makes Katie tick. I want to figure her out.

Desperately.

"Do you need any help, young man?"

Stopping, I turn to find the old lady perched on the edge of the porch swing, watching me with hawklike eyes, looking ready to pounce. I can sense a kindred spirit—she trusts no one, just like me. I bet she's the lone member of the neighborhood watch on this street. "Hi." I wave at her.

Her expression doesn't waver. Not mean, but not overtly friendly, either. "Are you looking for someone?"

I point at Katie's house. "I think I lived there when I was a kid."

Her penciled-in eyebrows lift. "You think?"

"I'm pretty sure." I flash her a friendly smile. "It was a long time ago."

"Uh-huh. You don't look that old."

"Old enough to have some fuzzy memories." I keep my smile planted firmly in place, but she's having none of it.

She keeps studying me, assessing me. Probably thinks I'm up to no good.

That would be correct.

"In the mood to reminisce?" she asks. "Is that why you're here? Don't tell me you're a reporter."

I ignore the reporter remark. It might be the perfect cover, but I have a feeling this woman would drive me away in an instant if she suspected I was here snooping around. "Feeling melancholy." That's not too much of a lie. "Missing my mom." It's easier to pretend I miss her versus dear old dad.

"Aw, did you lose her?" Her expression doesn't change much, so I don't know if she's sincerely sympathetic or not.

I nod, not sure if I'm lying or not. She never came forward, not even when all the shit hit the fan and Dad's name and mug shot were broadcast all over the news. What woman wouldn't reach out and try to contact her only child? I ended up in a foster home until I ran away when I was seventeen, not that my foster parents cared. They only wanted to collect the monthly checks.

Life was hell when I was with my father, and the hell continued on a lesser scale after I was pulled out of his house. I needed a hero. Someone to come rescue me, and I banked on my mother to be the one to do it. The reunion had played over and over again in my head during those years, but it never happened.

She was either a heartless bitch or dead. I prefer to think she's dead.

It's easier that way.

"That's a shame." The old woman's expression never, ever wavers. I'm impressed. "I don't remember any family with a young boy living in that house, son."

"How long have you lived here?"

"Almost twenty years."

Well, hell. She'd know. "Yeah? Well . . . thanks for the info."

"Maybe you have the wrong house," she suggests. "It could be on a different street close by. They all look pretty similar around here."

"Maybe. You might be right." I finally allow myself to stare longingly at the house—Katie's house. It's small, white with pale blue trim and matching shutters flanking the windows, the front door painted a rich, glossy red, which surprises me. Such a bold color, but maybe she likes bright colors. Pots of colorful flowers dot the front porch and a wooden swing hangs from the roof, similar to the one my interrogator is currently sitting on.

If I could, I'd walk into Katie's yard and look through the windows to see how she lives. Her tastes, her furniture, the photos she might have on the walls. But not a one of those windows is bare. Curtains or blinds cover every single one that I can see and besides, I'd look like a damn criminal—a peeping Tom trying to catch a glimpse of a vulnerable woman all alone inside.

No way will I allow myself to share any traits with my father. I hate myself enough already. Any and all comparisons to him would fucking wreck me.

"Who lives here now?" I ask nonchalantly, ignoring the way my heart speeds up. I want just one word about Katie—Katherine. One little fact, a morsel of information I can take back with me to savor later.

Tell me she's safe. Tell me she's happy. Tell me she has friends and a cat and she has a good job and she's seeing someone who might be special. Tell me she's close to her family and she smiles a lot and she's not really lonely. Tell me I'm wrong. Tell me all of that. I need to hear it. I need to make sure she's okay.

That's all I want. To know she's safe.

"Never you mind that," the woman says, like she's scolding me. I take a step back, surprised at the blast of heat that shines from her eyes. Protective. I like that. It reassures me, knowing Katie has someone on her side living so close to her. Not that this frail-looking woman could prevent anything from happening, but . . . she could dial 911. Ward off weirdos who lurked around Katie's house. Like me. "She's a private person."

And that's all she says. All she'll give me.

We stare at each other for a moment and I look away first, letting her win. Wondering if she'll tell Katie that an unfamiliar man came around today. Do I matter that much?

Probably not.

"Thanks for your help," I tell the old woman as I start back toward my car. My disappointment is palpable and I try my best to push it away. I don't know what the hell I'm doing, what I think I might get out of this. Closure? This will never be closed, what happened to me, what happened to Katie. We share something no one else understands. I wish I could talk to her but I can't. I don't want to open up an old wound and make it bleed.

I'll have to be satisfied with the little bits and pieces of Katie that I slowly put together on my own.

For now, that's enough.

KATIE

Then

Lying on a thin mattress for days while chained to a wall left me weak. I hadn't eaten much and I hadn't had much to drink, either. So when Will handed me a bottle of water after cutting the chain off my ankle, I gulped practically the entire thing down in one swallow.

"Take it easy," he warned me, his low, even voice full of concern. I glanced up, saw his furrowed brow and frowning face, my lips still wrapped around the opening of the bottle. "You don't want to puke it all back up."

He was right. I slowed down, taking his advice, my gaze never leaving him as he reached into a backpack he'd brought and pulled out what looked like a folded T-shirt. He held it out to me.

"For you."

I stared at the shirt gripped in his hands. It was navy blue with white lettering, but I couldn't make out what it said. "What is it?" I asked, not willing to fully trust him. What if he had ulterior motives? Maybe he was being kind so he could take advantage of me. I didn't know him. I didn't know why he would want to help me. I didn't understand any of this.

"A shirt. So you can change out of the one you're wearing." He gestured toward me. "I figured you'd want to wear clean clothes, though I don't have any shorts or anything for you. I'm too big and you're uh, too small."

He wasn't that big, but he was taller than me. I took the

shirt from him and shook it out to discover it was a high school football shirt. The name emblazoned across the front, an eagle mascot thrusting his chest out, his expression menacing. "Do you go to this school?" I asked him.

Will ignored my question and glanced around, his eyes narrowed. "You need to hurry. There's not much daylight left."

"I can't change in front of you," I whispered and he moved away from me without a word, his back to me as he bent over the backpack he held in his hands. As he rummaged through it, I watched him for a while to make sure he wasn't going to turn around.

"Hurry, Katie," he urged and I tore my dirty, ripped shirt off, letting it fall to the floor before I tugged his T-shirt over my head. It was too big, the sleeves hitting me at my elbows, the hem about mid-thigh, swallowing up the stained and grungy shorts I wore. I stood on shaky legs, nearly stumbling to the ground because my knees felt like they would give out.

He turned and rushed toward me to grip my elbow, and I jerked out of his touch. "I'm fine," I muttered, my skin burning where his fingers brushed against my skin. It wasn't a bad burn. More like this tingling electricity that felt like a shock to my system.

I didn't understand it.

"I thought you were going to fall," he murmured, his head bent as he looked at me, black strands of hair tumbling across his forehead. Yet again I thought the color completely unnatural and I studied him, really studied him, trying to figure him out.

He wore a black T-shirt. Plain. Faded black skinny jeans, and the most scuffed-up black Vans I'd ever seen covered his feet. His left ear was pierced with a thin silver hoop, and so was the right side of his lip. He was all black, from head to toe, one long, lean line, with hair hanging in his eyes and a defiant expression on his face. He reminded me of the emo kids I went to school with, though he wasn't pale like they usually were. And he had muscles. His arms weren't bulging but his biceps were defined. He looked strong.

Almost intimidating.

"We need to leave," he said firmly, his gaze meeting mine. He sounded like a man, what with that deep voice, but from the look on his face, the nervousness in his gaze, I could see he was really just a kid.

Just like me.

I paused, unsure if I should go with him, and he saw it. Must've seen the reluctance in my gaze and when our gazes clashed, I confessed, "I'm scared."

His expression faltered for the smallest moment. I don't think he knew exactly what to do with me. "You can't be scared, Katie. You have to be brave. You have to come with me."

I wanted to. I really did. "What if he finds us? What will he do?"

The determination that firmed his jaw made him look more manlike. Not so much a kid any longer. "He won't do anything to you. I won't let him."

"You promise?" I asked for too much but I needed to hear the words. Needed the reassurance.

His gaze was solemn. "I promise."

I wanted to believe him. I needed someone to believe in to get me out of here. So I was putting all my faith in him. I had to.

There was no other choice.

Without hesitation he turned and headed toward the shed

door. I followed after him, trying my best to keep up, the mostly empty water bottle still clutched in my hand. He took my other hand to help me down the rickety wooden steps, his long fingers clutched around mine, and I winced when the rough edges of the wood scraped the soles of my tender feet.

"You need shoes," he murmured, reaching for his magical backpack. He pulled out a pair of bright orange Old Navy flip-flops, the cheap ones you can get for under five dollars. "I found these." I wondered who they might have belonged to.

It didn't matter, though. Now they belonged to me.

I slipped them on and though they were a little big, they'd work just fine. He smiled at me. This lopsided, closed-mouth curve of lips that was there and gone, all in a fleeting moment. Then with a flick of his head, he indicated without a word that he wanted me to follow him. I did. I fell into step behind him as we made our escape from the backyard, passing the lone carousel horse propped in the corner of the fence.

"Is that your horse?" I asked him, wanting to know if he lived there. How he played a role in this moment, this situation.

He paused, his head turning toward the horse, a faraway look crossing his face. "Yeah. I found it in a dumpster not far from the park."

The park. The amusement park. It was close. Closer than I thought.

"They usually sell them. Auction them off. People like to buy them. It's like buying a memory, a piece of happiness from their childhood," he continued, and I studied him. Wondered if this horse represented a piece of happiness from his childhood. Though he was still a child, too. Older than me, but definitely not an adult yet.

"But this one, they threw away like it didn't matter. It was broken. Faded and chipped, an ugly brown color that probably didn't look so good with the other brightly painted horses and animals on the carousel. Have you been on that merry-go-round?" His gaze met mine and I nodded. "It's bright and loud, with the bells and the buzzer and music. This guy didn't fit in."

I had this weird feeling he wasn't talking about the horse anymore. He was talking about himself.

"We need to go," he said, sounding irritated. He gave one last, longing glance toward the horse and then we left. He led me to the gate and opened it, indicating I should walk through it first, and I did, my chest tight, my gaze sharp. A tiny piece of me was afraid this could be a trap. He might be leading me to my doom.

We were in a neighborhood, lines of small houses seemingly stacked nearly on top of each other, in neat little rows. The yards were nothing more than weeds; old cars sat parked in driveways or along the street. Rusted metal bars covered most of the tiny windows on the houses, keeping the bad guys out or the good guys in, I'm not sure which.

No kids played outside, no voices carried from backyards or from within the tiny houses. It was eerily quiet, the sun bathing the sky in an orange-pinkish glow as it slowly settled in the west. We trudged uphill, Will keeping his pace even and measured, me trying my best to stay with him, but I was already tired. Exhausted. In pain.

Ready to give up and we'd barely started.

Once we reached the top of the hill, I realized where we were. Not far from the main drag that led straight down to the beach and the boardwalk. I glanced over my shoulder, my breath catching in my throat when I saw the ocean, the sun a yellowish orange ball sinking into the rippling blue. The amusement park was already lit up, the circle of the Ferris wheel a flashing red-and-green beacon, the roller coaster's towering path lit by white lights.

Regret hit me like a punch in the stomach. I never got to ride the roller coaster with Sarah. I never ate a deep-fried Twinkie like I wanted to, either. I didn't get to do much of anything.

But at least I was still alive.

"It's not much farther," Will promised me, and I turned to look at him, saw the guilt pass over his expression. I wondered if he was lying.

Uncertainty rose within me, as well as suspicion. "Where are you taking me?" I asked. More like demanded.

"Police station." He flicked his chin in the general direction, one that was all uphill. I seriously didn't believe I would make it up that stupid hill. "It's closer to downtown."

"How close are we to downtown?"

"Not too far." He dipped his head, his hair falling in front of his face, as if he used it like a shield.

He was lying. I could tell. "Don't you have a cellphone?" I didn't. Sarah did. I wished I had one. I bet Mom and Dad now wished I had one, too.

"No." He shook his head, the slightest sneer curling his lips. "Can't afford it."

Without another word he started walking again and I had no choice but to go after him. We huffed and puffed up the hill—me doing more of the huffing and puffing since he was in perfectly fine shape. He hadn't been shackled to a wall for the last few days, beaten and brutalized and fed nothing but a donut here and a bunch of cookies there, the occasional bag of Doritos accompanied by a Dr Pepper.

I hated Dr Pepper. That I was able to focus on my hatred for a certain brand of soda after everything I'd been through was probably some indication that I was in a state of shock. I didn't know. I'd watched *CSI* with my parents and picked up a few criminal/police terms, but most of the time, I wasn't paying attention.

There were a lot of things I hadn't paid attention to that I wished I had.

"You all right?" Will called over his shoulder and I muttered a *yeah* in response. I winced with every step, the muscles in my calves ached, and I shivered when a cool breeze off the ocean washed over me.

Somehow, he noticed. He noticed everything, and I wasn't sure if I should be afraid of that or not. Out came a light gray sweatshirt from his magical backpack and he handed it over. I took it from him and pulled it on, inhaling deep the scent that clung to the fabric. It smelled of laundry detergent and something else. Something unidentifiable, and I pressed my nose against the neckline, breathing it in. The sweatshirt was soft and warm, the smell comforting, and it swallowed me up, much like his shirt I wore.

"Put the hood over your head," he told me, and I did.

"Why?" I cinched the ties so that the hood fit me tight, molded around my face.

"Your hair. It's bright. He might . . . he might recognize you if he happens to drive by." His voice was hesitant and I saw the wild look in his eyes. "He went in to work. He should be off soon. If he doesn't stop off at the bar first."

Everything within me fell. My stomach tumbled and my mouth went dry. God, I felt like I could throw up. I was foolish to believe I could be free of him. He could find me. He could find us both. For all I knew, this boy was leading me to him and I was idiot enough to follow him wherever he went. "Who is he to you?"

He shook his head, his nostrils flaring. "It doesn't matter."

We trudged on in silence for a few minutes and his answer weighed heavily on my mind. It wasn't good enough. He knew more than he was letting on and I was scared. Scared I was making a mistake. Scared I was walking into a trap.

"The thing is, it *does* matter," I finally said as I caught up to him, so I walked by his side, my breath short, my feet aching, especially my toes. They curled tight into the cheap flip-flops, trying to keep them on my feet.

"What matters?" He sent me a wary, sidelong glance.

"Who he is to you. I need to know before I go any farther." Where the strength came from I wasn't sure, but I lifted my chin, hoping I looked like I meant business.

We both stopped in the middle of the sidewalk, staring at each other, our harsh breaths louder than the otherwise familiar night sounds. A dog barked in the near distance. Cars drove by, their lights passing over where we stood, illuminating us for one brief second before they were gone. A lone seagull flew overhead, its short, harsh cry sad, and I felt like that mournful sound could swallow me up whole.

"It shouldn't matter," Will said grimly. "He's nothing. I'm nothing like him."

I studied him, lights from a passing car highlighting his face, and I realized he vaguely resembled him. My kidnapper. It was the set of his mouth, the angry blaze in his eyes. Though for some reason, calm washed over me, reassuring that I'd made the right choice. I wasn't frightened. He'd saved me. Walked me out of that hellish storage shed like it was no big deal, when it had been my prison for days.

"He's your father."

A muscle in his jaw flexed but otherwise, he never moved. Neither did I. We continued to watch each other until a horn honked, startling us both. "We need to go," he muttered.

"You're not . . ." I reached for him and grabbed his hand, clutching it tight. Too tight maybe, but I didn't care. Looking down, I studied our linked fingers, thankful for the connection, praying that he wasn't trying to trick me. Why this boy calmed me, I didn't know and couldn't begin to understand. Maybe it was the matter-of-fact way he rescued me. Without thought, without worry over what might happen to him. He was putting himself at risk by doing this. Helping me. I couldn't forget that. "You're not—you're not taking me to him, are you?"

He squeezed my fingers and I didn't flinch. I needed his reassurance. I needed to believe he wanted to save me. "No. I wouldn't do that to you."

"You wouldn't?" I peered up at him, never letting go of his hand. I didn't ever want to let it go. I curled my fingers around his, felt his thumb smooth over the top of my hand, and a flutter tickled low in my belly.

"Never," he said firmly, his deep voice in direct contrast to the fear in his eyes. His being scared reassured me as well.

But I still needed to hear his words.

"Promise?"

Will held up our connected hands. And his gaze—so serious—never left mine. "I promise."

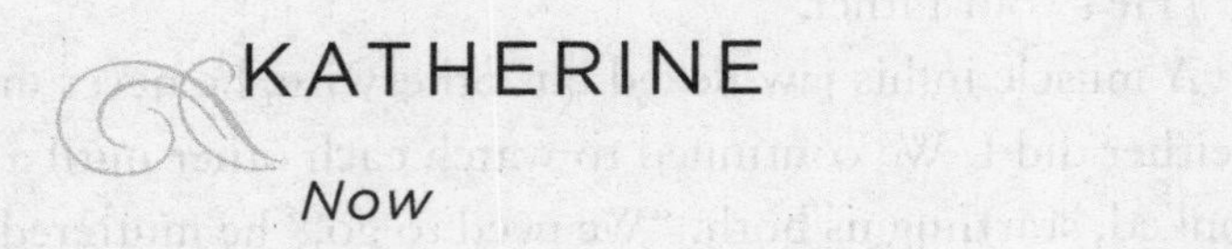

KATHERINE

Now

Confronting your fears.

I looked the words up on Google and came up with a ton of good information, devouring all of it in a matter of hours over the course of one long, sleepless night that morphed into two that turned into three. I read article after article, my eyelids heavy, my brain overloaded with tips and tricks, reassuring words and reaffirming quotes.

My insomnia had kicked in big time and I don't like to take sleeping pills, though I've had some prescribed. I don't like taking any medications. The Xanax, the Prozac, the Ambien . . . I've tried it all.

Hated it all, too. They made my head fuzzy. I didn't feel right, I didn't think right, I didn't act like myself. I'd rather deal with the demons in my head than become dependent on drugs that dull the pain.

My appointment with Dr. Harris a few days ago left me with an uneasy feeling, one I still can't really shed. I felt bad, yelling at her, acting like I did. I sort of came unhinged and took it out on my psychiatrist. I'm sure she's used to that sort of thing, but I emailed her an apology anyway. She reassured me in her reply that it wasn't necessary, but I'm glad I did it. Glad I was adult enough to realize when I threw a tantrum like a child.

Didn't help that I came home that afternoon after our appointment and my neighbor Mrs. Anderson let me know that a suspicious man came "sniffing around my house." I told her it was most likely a reporter looking for me—she knew who I really was, she figured it out pretty quickly after I moved in because she is truly the nosiest person I've ever met—but she didn't appear satisfied with that answer.

Which left me wary.

"Suspicious young man," she'd said. "He wore sunglasses though the sky was cloudy as all get-out. Gave me some cockamamie story about living in your house when he was growing up. I didn't believe him. Didn't quite dislike him, either, but figured he was up to no good." Her eyes had narrowed. "There was something about him that made me think he was harmless. Maybe an ex come looking for you after he saw you on the TV?"

I almost laughed at her suggestion but held it in. "I doubt that," I'd told her, and she gave me a little harrumph in answer, not satisfied, I'm sure.

An ex. That would imply I'd have to be with someone in the first place. I'm as single as they come. I've never been kissed. Never been held tenderly in a man's arms, never been made love to—and anyway, is that for real? What does making love even mean? I don't know what it's like, to be in a relationship.

Lack of sleep has made me anxious. Reading over the countless websites about confronting what's been holding me back has contributed to my anxiety. I've followed some of the suggested steps, though, and I've come up with a game plan.

I'm ready to face my fears.

First, I had to make a list. It was long, but I was able to group together a few things (another suggestion from one of the sites I read), and that helped make my fears list less intimidating. Next, I rearranged my list from least scary to most scary.

The fear I'm hoping I can conquer first? The supposed easiest one? Spending extended time in a crowded public place.

The biggest fear that tops my list? Being intimate with a man.

Since that one seems so incredibly far-fetched and the hardest to face, I figure it'll never happen.

Deciding there's no time like the present, I set out to conquer what I thought would be the easiest item on my list. Going to a place that contains so many of my fears—a place that I can't tell anyone about.

Guilt swamps me as I drive along the highway with the window down, the wind blowing through my hair, the salty tang of the ocean heavy in the breeze. If Mom and Brenna knew what I was doing, they'd flip out. Flip. Out. I'm sort of flipping out just thinking about it. How am I going to deal when I actually get there?

Maybe I've bitten off more than I can chew.

The time of year is all wrong, as is the weather, but that doesn't seem to matter. Once I pull off the highway and start down the road that leads toward the ocean, my heart starts to race. My hands are clammy. I pass the spot at the corner of the road where Will Monroe told me to pull the hood of his sweatshirt over my head and I begin shaking.

I'm at the stop sign, waiting for the other cars to go first, envisioning myself standing on that street corner. The cars going past, the yellowish glow of their headlights streaking across a purplish twilight sky. The faint roar of the roller coaster as it zoomed along the old wooden tracks, the riders screaming in glee.

I always believed I imagined that part. Hearing the roller coaster and its riders. The screaming. It was all in my head, something I made up.

A horn honks, startling me, and I let up on the brake, pressing my foot on the gas. The car lurches forward like a meteor hurtling through space, right in the path of a vehicle that had grown impatient with me and attempted to turn left. The driver lays on the horn and the unexpected sound makes me gasp and curse.

Too late, too late. God, I'm going to die in an intersection mere miles from where I was kidnapped. Mere miles from where I was saved.

How ironic is this?

I dart across the intersection, the wheels of my car never seeming to touch the ground, which is impossible, I know. Glancing to my left, I see the irritated driver give me the double finger, his face contorted with over-the-top rage. I offer him an apologetic look and a wave, but he doesn't care.

I'm sure he thinks I'm a complete idiot. Worse, he looks like he wishes he could choke the shit out of me.

The moment I make it through the intersection, I pull over, my wheels bumping against the edge of the sidewalk. Throwing my car into park, I cover my face with trembling hands, my breaths harsh and loud against my cupped palms.

Did I really believe I could handle this?

I pushed too hard. Too fast. Going to the scene of the crime—literally—was a crazy idea. I want to be cured. I want to be okay. I want to feel strong and carefree and confident that I can do whatever I want without a care. I shouldn't have to worry so much, you know? I shouldn't have to be so afraid.

But I'm none of those things. Confident. Strong. Carefree. Those words belong to the old me. Once innocence is lost, you can never get it back. That's my problem. I lost my innocence at the age of twelve, far too early. And the man who stole it from me will haunt me forever.

Anger surges and I let it wash over me. I'm mad. Irritated with myself. I need to get over this. Live a normal life. Seek out friends. Date guys. Brenna has offered to set me up more than once. Her boyfriend has plenty of single friends whom she approves of. Nice guys. Regular guys.

But something always holds me back. Like I'm waiting for . . . something.

Someone.

I drop my hands from my face and take a deep breath. Glance up into the rearview mirror to see a car parked just behind me. It's nondescript. Black. Could be a Honda, could be a Toyota . . . could be anything. A man sits behind the wheel, his dark head bent, his gaze locked on his lap, though I can't see half of his face considering it's covered by sunglasses.

All the fine hairs on my body rise in awareness. Is he following me? His head is still bent, his dark hair tumbling over his forehead, a white T-shirt stretched across broad shoulders and chest. He looks young. Harmless. But looks can be deceiving. I know this.

I've lived it. Survived it.

Blinking hard, I continue to watch him. In fact, I'm blatantly checking him out in my rearview mirror, my throat dry, my heart picking up speed. Cars rush past, impatient to get to their destinations, but not the car behind me. He waits. Like I wait.

It's disconcerting.

Carefully, quietly, as if he's watching my every move, as if he's literally sitting beside me, I put my car into drive, flick my left blinker on, and slowly pull out into the street.

He doesn't follow me.

ETHAN

Now

She almost caught me.

Panic rises as I drive approximately seven cars behind her. The street is crowded as usual, even though we're beyond the busy summer season. It's a narrow two-lane, usually packed beyond belief in the summer but not as frustrating at the moment.

No, what frustrates me is that she just about figured me out when I pulled my car behind hers. I let her go. I had to let her go. To fall in behind her immediately after she merged back into traffic would have been waving the biggest, reddest flag ever.

Danger. Alert. Stranger following you. Call 911.

Couldn't risk it.

What the hell is she doing here anyway? I think she's flat-out lost her mind. She's going back to the amusement park. I can feel it in my bones, sense it as if I'm sitting in her brain and trying my best to reason with her but she won't listen.

Will she actually go into the park? Or is she seeking the beach? There are plenty of other beaches close by. I would have preferred the ones in the opposite direction, but she's not cooperating.

Tilting my head, I try to rise up in my seat to see which way she's turning. The light is red. Her car is the third one in line. The light is short but not that short, and I hope like hell she turns left. Left means she's leaving. Left means she has no plans on staying, getting out of her car and walking into the park, none of that bullshit.

The light turns green.

She's the second one to turn right.

Fucking hell.

The light turns yellow on the tenth car. Three more turn right after the light becomes red. I'm now the third one in line. I have to wait approximately three minutes, but it'll feel like three hours.

I could lose her. She could park somewhere and walk right into that stupid fucking park and get swallowed up by the crowd. I can't have it. I must find her. What if something happens to her? She doesn't get out much. She admitted that in the interview. That she was a bit of a recluse. She takes college courses online (technology is a great thing), she doesn't have many friends, she doesn't do well in big crowds.

It's a Friday. A perfect fall day and the weather is freaking gorgeous, but there won't be many people at the park because it's so early.

That doesn't matter. I still could lose her.

The light finally turns green and I hit the gas impatiently, smacking my horn when the guy ahead of me starts to turn left, then changes his mind and goes right. He gestures at me in the rearview mirror and I give him a thinly veiled smile, one that feels more like a baring of teeth than anything else.

I'm wild, like an animal. Blood pumps hard in my veins, pounds in my head, adrenaline making me itchy. I'm capable of anything, my gaze skittering over the many cars parked on the side of the road, searching for hers. Earlier this morning I'd parked my car down the street from her house on a random whim; the need to see her, keep track of her, make sure she's safe was almost overwhelming. I gave in to the feeling despite knowing it was a mistake. I shouldn't follow her. I'm no better than my father. Trying to keep tabs on her like some sort of sick fuck.

But that's not my intent. I want to ensure her safety. That's all. She's taken over my dreams. Her face haunts them, the memories twisting and turning, changing into an adult Katie. Katherine. Coming to me, her eyes glowing, a smile curling her lips, her words just for me.

You found me. I knew you would.

She wants to be found, but only by me. That's the recurring theme in my dreams. She trusts no one, wants no one but . . .

Me.

I woke up with my dick hard and my fantasies fueled by nothing but her. Her pretty blond hair, perfect lips, and creamy smooth skin I want to touch. The sound of her voice as she whispers in my ear, her lips touching my skin and driving me wild with lust.

You found me.

All this week, from the moment I wake up, I think of nothing but her. Her name sizzles in my blood and scorches my brain. I can't concentrate. I can't fucking function. So I go in search of her. Keep tabs on her.

And now I could lose her. *Fuck.* I punch the steering wheel with a curled fist, pain flashing through me but not strong enough to overtake the anger.

I'm so pissed at myself I could spit nails.

Losing her wasn't part of the plan. I walked away from her only once, and I've regretted that move my entire life. I remember how thankful I felt at regaining her trust. She'd been so wary that night, so unsure of my every move. She'd had reason to think that way, too.

I'm his son. It doesn't matter if I have a different name, a fictional family background, or a different look. None of it matters because his blood still pumps wildly in my veins, making it sing.

Making me hunt.

Shaking my head, I banish the thought. I'm not hunting anyone. I've never felt like this before about any woman I've ever known. I've dated a handful. Had a semi-long-term relationship with one. She became too much for me. Too loud, too bossy, too demanding, too always wanting more than I could ever give her.

We broke up and she'd railed at me spectacularly. Her anger was like a living, breathing thing, standing between us in a position that mirrored her. Arms crossed in front of her chest, hip cocked out, foot tapping on the ground as if she was waiting for the next answer. An answer I knew nothing about, one I couldn't get right no matter what.

After that last date, I never saw her again. Had no desire to seek her out, either. I've never felt like this, like I feel for *her.*

Possessed. Obsessed. Both bad traits. Both awful, terrible, no-good traits that could end up harming someone, someone innocent. A girl.

Katie.

Lost in thought, I drive right past her, catching a glimpse of her sunny hair as I speed by. I hit the brakes, zipping into the small parking lot of a seafood restaurant, pulling into one of the many empty slots and cutting the engine of my Honda. The giant red-and-white sign posted in front of me says NO PARKING. Another sign states for RESTAURANT PATRONS ONLY, VIOLATORS WILL BE TOWED.

Either way I'm going to end up getting a ticket or getting towed. It doesn't matter. I need to go after her.

I climb out of the car and hit the keyless remote before I cross the parking lot and start heading down the sidewalk, my pace quick, practically a light jog. She's ahead of me, her jean-clad hips gently swaying, long golden-blond hair pulled into a high ponytail, the curling ends bouncing around her shoulders when she walks.

She's moving at a slow pace, her head going this way and that, as if she's trying to absorb every sound, every smell, every taste. The sun is warm as it shines down upon us, bathing us both in bright light, glinting burnished gold in Katie's hair, and my fingers literally itch to touch it.

Fucking itch.

Katie comes to a stop and so do I, staring at the giant roller-coaster track that's right above us. I turn my head toward the entrance to the amusement park, only a few feet away. There aren't too many people inside. The wall around the park is low so it's not meant to keep people out, more of a parameter to let you know you've arrived. I remember seeing that wall as a kid, knowing what magic lay just beyond, and I'd get excited.

I bet Katie was excited, too. Once upon a time. Before my asshole father ruined everything.

Pretending I'm looking west, my gaze is really on her, my sunglasses the perfect shield. She doesn't notice me. She's too caught up in studying the track of roller coaster that rises above her. She's tense, her entire body rigid, like she's waiting for something momentous to happen.

And then it does.

The metal screeches as the roller coaster roars overhead, the smattering of people within the cars screaming their joy and/or terror, their hair flying, various sets of hands held high above their heads. It's there and gone in a matter of seconds, the screams dying on the wind, the track of the roller coaster still seeming to screech and shake, as if a line of phantom cars are still running over the tracks.

Katie remains fixed in place, her head tilted back, her ponytail falling so it hits the middle of her back. I take a step forward, possessed by an urge I can't control. I want to get closer. Close enough to touch her. Smell her . . .

She turns and I freeze, my lungs seizing, but she doesn't look behind her. Instead she approaches the low wall that surrounds the park until she's standing against it, her arms braced on the concrete ledge.

Don't go in there. You're putting yourself at risk. You're not ready yet. Why are you even here? Why are you all alone?

The thoughts race through my mind as I wait for her to make another move. If I could go to her, I would. If I could tell her she shouldn't go inside, I wouldn't hesitate. I'd take her by the arm and steer her away from this place.

She suddenly reaches for her small purse, pulling her phone out of it and pressing it to her ear. I hear her hello carry on the wind, spearing straight through me, and for the briefest moment I close my eyes.

Imagining that she's saying hello to me.

I tell myself I shouldn't listen in on her conversation. It's an invasion of privacy. A violation, and this girl—she's been violated numerous times. An unimaginable number, and all at the hands of my father. His violation ended when I took her out of that storage shed, but the effects of what he's done still linger.

Memories may fade, but they never really go away.

But I've already taken it this far. Following her. All in the name of protection. It's my duty after all. A job she gave me long, long ago. I'm her protector. Her guardian angel. She said so herself and I made a promise.

A promise I refuse to break.

"You will kill me if I tell you where I am," I hear her say, and I wonder who she's talking to. There's no man in her life. That much I've figured out through my thorough investigation, though I believed her when she said it on national TV.

Maybe it's her mother. Or her sister, or possibly a close friend. Any one of them would freak out if they knew where she was. I'm freaking out and I'm right here with her. I could save her, if need be. Interfere if I have to.

"I need to do this, Brenna." Her sister. A pause and I take a step forward, wanting to hear more, needing to hear more. "Brenna, stop. Listen to me. I know what I'm doing. I have to face my fears sometime, right?"

Another pause, her entire body tensing as she stands up straighter. She doesn't like what she's hearing. "You did what? Mom is *tracking* my phone? Are you serious? Oh my God, how old do you think I am? You two can't shelter me forever."

She starts to turn and so do I, pivoting away from her, not wanting her to see me. I face the other direction and start walking, my steps measured, hands in my pockets like I've got all the time in the world. A breeze washes over me, tangy with salt and something darker, almost rotten. It ruffles my hair, whistles against my ears, and I curl my hands into fists. Wishing I could look back, refusing to look back. Conflicted as usual, but I don't want to make her suspicious.

It just about fucking kills me, but I keep walking, slowing my pace, relaxing my stance until finally, finally I glance over my shoulder.

To find she's gone.

KATIE

Then

I should've never guzzled that large soda at lunch. Now I had to pee so bad, but I didn't want to leave the line for the roller coaster. We'd been standing there for the last thirty minutes and it was moving at a snail's pace. Not that Sarah minded. She'd been flirting with the boys standing behind us practically the entire time.

It's like she turned into a different person when she was around the male species. I didn't like it. I was uncomfortable enough, hanging out around older boys. And these boys were definitely older. They were all going to be sophomores in high school with the exception of one, who was a year younger.

Sarah and I were going into the eighth grade. We were babies compared to these guys, but she didn't care. She loved practicing her flirting skills on anyone she could find.

She was mad at me for not flirting along with her, so her back was completely to me as she constantly flipped her hair over her shoulder and laughed at every stupid thing they said. And they said plenty of stupid things, their laughter extra loud, causing other people in line to look our way. They thought they were hilarious but I rolled my eyes more often than not, their lame jokes grating on my nerves.

I hopped from one foot to the other, trying to ignore the pressure against my bladder, but it was no use. I was going to burst if I didn't find a bathroom and since I wasn't in the mood for utter humiliation, I figured I needed to go now. I touched Sarah's arm and she whirled around, her eyes narrowed, the smile on her face false.

My hand fell away from her, surprised at the irritation that came off her in obvious waves. "I need to use the bathroom," I whispered, tilting my head close to hers so only she could hear.

Sarah wrinkled her nose, like the thought of using the bathroom disgusted her when she'd been complaining of the same exact thing right after lunch. What, she gets around boys and suddenly she doesn't have bodily functions?

"The line is long," she reassured me, waving at the people ahead of us. "I doubt we'll move too much while you go to the bathroom."

Thanks. Advertise it to everyone, why don't you. "But my parents don't want us to separate," I reminded her.

She shrugged. "It'll only be what? Five minutes? The bathroom is just right over there." She pointed and I looked in the direction she was indicating.

I did a little dance, but really I was trying to ward off the urge to pee. "I don't know . . ." My voice drifted and she gave me a look. One that told me I was being pathetic. I'd seen that look before.

But not usually directed at me.

"Don't be such a baby," she practically hissed, flicking her head. "Go. I'll hold your place." When I hesitated, an impatient sigh escaped her. "Nothing bad is going to happen to you, Katie. Just go."

"Want me to walk with you?" one of the boys piped up. The youngest one. There was a hopeful look in his gaze and when I caught his eye, he smiled, revealing a mouthful of braces.

He was being nice, but jeez. I didn't need an escort. Sarah was right. It was just the bathroom and it was right over there. "I'm okay." I smiled shyly, hating that I could feel the blush heating my cheeks. "Thanks, though."

"Your loss," Sarah muttered, and I knew then she thought I was stupid for not taking the boy up on his offer.

Whatever.

Maybe I should have. Then I wouldn't have to go alone, but . . . I didn't feel right going with him. Besides, I could handle this. On my own. I was no baby.

"I'll be right back," I said firmly, holding the chain down that roped off the line and stepping over it as agilely as I could, which was really pretty awkward. I ended up hopping on one foot, practically tripping over myself, and I prayed I wouldn't pee my pants in front of everyone.

Sarah would have killed me.

"Don't get lost," Sarah said, making the boys crack up.

Practically making me cry.

Willing the tears away, I stormed off, infuriated at her. More so at my reaction to her cattiness. She was right. The bathroom wasn't that far. They were all painted a hideous bright blue, a spot of recognizable color on the primary spectrum, and I came to a stop when I saw the long line to get inside.

Great. It looked almost as long as the one for the roller coaster.

But it moved fast. Next thing I knew I was in a dirty stall, untying my sweatshirt from around my waist and hanging it on the hook on the stall door. There were no more seat liners, so I grabbed some toilet paper and draped it over the seat before I took what felt like the longest pee of my life.

By the time I'd finished washing my hands, I was sure Sarah

and her new friends would be at the head of the line, just about ready to get on the roller coaster. I needed to hurry before I lost them. Sarah was the one with the cellphone. If I got separated from her, my parents would kill me. I'd be stuck following after them everywhere we went until I graduated high school.

That was the last thing I wanted. I yearned for independence. I didn't even like thinking of myself as twelve. I'd already moved on to thirteen. It sounded so much older, more mature. Twelve is a little girl.

Thirteen is practically a woman.

Once I exited the bathroom, I tied my sweatshirt sloppily around my waist and started back toward the roller coaster, pushing my way through the crowd that somehow had grown thicker over the last few minutes. A man kept yelling behind me, his voice friendly but insistent, saying, "Hey, hey you!" again and again.

No way could he have been talking to me.

"Hey." A big hand clamped over my shoulder, pulling me to a complete stop, and I turned around slowly to find a man standing before me. His face was expressive and his smile was nice. He looked like every other dad wandering around the place, with neatly trimmed brown hair and a slightly wild look in his eye, like he'd rather be anywhere but there.

It was the wild look that filled me with both curiosity and caution.

"You dropped your sweatshirt." He held it out toward me, the obnoxious red fabric bunched in his fingers, and I stared at his hand as if it were a snake preparing to strike out and bite me at any given moment. "It fell off right after you came out of the bathroom."

I don't know why I hadn't noticed that. "Thank you," I said shyly, taking the proffered sweatshirt from him. I must not have tied it on well enough. I wrapped the sleeves around my waist and tied the knot twice before I was satisfied.

"Hey." He flicked his chin at me, all friendly and good-natured. He reminded me of a guy on a commercial trying to sell me lemonade. All sunny and wholesome, the ideal family man. "Do you know where the entrance to the Sky Gliders is?"

That used to be my favorite ride when I was younger. It's kind of lame, but I liked to use it to get from one side of the park to the other. "Over there." I pointed and turned. Started to walk away. I needed to get back to Sarah. "Thanks for finding my sweatshirt," I called over my shoulder.

He followed me. I didn't like that. Increasing my pace, I ignored the erratic throb of my heart and headed toward where Sarah waited for me in line.

"Where you going?" the man yelled after me.

I glanced back over my shoulder and realized he was directly behind me. "The roller coaster. My friends are waiting."

He seemed disappointed by that. Was he hoping to get me alone? My heart started to beat even faster. "That line is always too long."

"Isn't that the truth," I muttered, earning a laugh out of him. He walked beside me and I stepped to the side, putting some distance between us.

"Ah, a feisty one." The smile shifted, became almost . . . predatory. "You tell it like it is, don't you."

Alarm rung through me at the tone of his voice, the way he looked at me. I slowed my pace and started to back away from him. "Nice talking to you," I offered feebly right before I planned on turning and making my escape.

He stepped forward like he could read my body language, grabbing hold of my arm and making me pause. "Wait a minute. You're not going anywhere."

I tried my best to jerk out of his hold but he was too strong. "Stop," I told him as I wiggled against his grip, but his fingers clamped around my arm extra tight.

"Stop what?" Again with the good-natured smile. Like he wouldn't harm a fly. People passed by us, oblivious to my struggle. They probably thought we were a father and daughter having a little squabble. "You're overreacting. Just show me where the Sky Glider is. I can never find the entrance."

He let go of me before I said anything and for whatever reason, I didn't run. Instead, I pointed toward the Sky Glider entrance again, though at least this time we were closer. "There are two," I explained to him. "One on this side, and one on the other side of the park."

"Near the arcade?" he asked.

I nodded. "Yeah." *Run, Katie. Get away from this guy.*

"Show me the entrance over here." When I started to protest he made a face, one that reminded me of a sad puppy dog. "Please? My wife and kids are waiting for me over there and I'm late. They probably already left me. I don't want the wife mad at me, you know?"

He had a family. How bad could he be? "But my friends . . ."

"That line is forever long. You'll be fine," he said, brushing away my words. "It'll take all of two minutes. Please?"

I wanted to help him, but I couldn't put the way he'd grabbed me out of my mind. That had been weird. But now he was so friendly . . . I was conflicted. I knew I shouldn't talk to strangers, but I should help people, right? And this guy, with his wife and kids waiting for him, needed my help. "Come on," I told him with a wave of my hand.

He fell into step beside me once more, the smile on his face . . .

Triumphant.

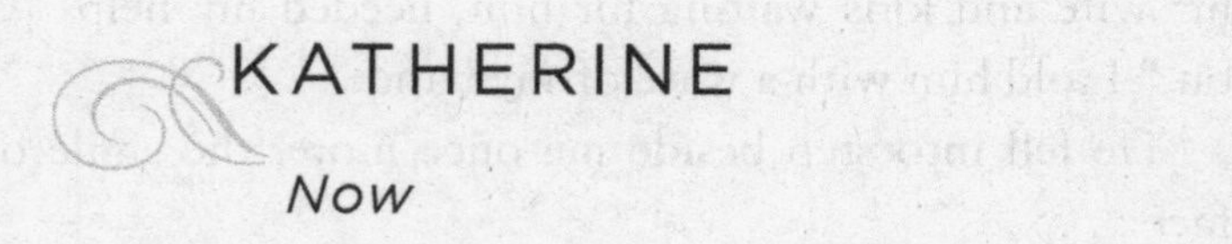

KATHERINE

Now

The memories were so strong the minute I walked inside, so incredibly powerful, that I could feel them rise within me, one after another. The cry of the seagulls, the ever-present scent of fried food lingering in the air, and the screams. The constant screams of the people on the roller coaster, and on that Ferris wheel–looking thing that had individual cages that spun round and round. I never rode it. Was always afraid I'd barf everywhere.

Coming here was a mistake. I'm frozen in place, right at the entrance of the park, remembering vividly the way Aaron Monroe approached me, all friendly with my sweatshirt in his hand, the smile on his face, the pleading way he asked for my help.

I'd fallen right into his trap like the idiot twelve-year-old girl I was. Naïve and stupid and wanting to please someone I didn't even know. I'd shown him the entrance to the Sky Gliders and he'd taken hold of my arm again, steering me right out of the park, right into the giant parking lot nearby. He'd pressed a knife to my side, close to my ribs, the tip of it sharp, piercing through my thin T-shirt, and my legs had almost given out on me right then. Like my bones were made of jelly.

And that wasn't even the worst part of my experience.

I move forward as if in a trance, settling heavily on a bench at the first table I spot at one of the food courts, closing my eyes for a brief moment. This was the place where I had lunch with my family and Sarah and my sister's friend Emily. Where we ate corn dogs and shared fries and I sucked down that large Pepsi like I was dying of thirst. Dad teased me, ruffling my hair, irritating me because he was treating me like I was seven, not almost thirteen. I'd tried to pass my sweatshirt off on my mom but she wouldn't help me out. Said that I was the one who brought it, so I was going to be the one who'd have to carry it for the rest of the day.

It's not my responsibility, she'd said, her mouth thin, her eyes full of irritation.

She'd pissed me off with that remark. I'd griped to Sarah the minute we made our escape. I think of that moment now, how everything would have been different if she'd taken my sweatshirt. I wonder if she regrets what she said, if she ever even thinks of it.

I hope not.

I don't even know what happened to the sweatshirt. It had been left behind in Aaron Monroe's car. I remember that it appeared during the trial as evidence. That they knew I'd been in his car because the sweatshirt was found in the backseat.

It's funny how the park looks exactly the same, like it's hardly changed at all. Even the people who are here at this very moment resemble the ones I remember from eight years ago.

Glancing around, I see a young girl wearing a sweatshirt almost identical to the one I had. They are still popular, with lifeguard written in bold white letters across the front, a giant white rescue cross right below it. She reminds me of a younger me, the same guileless expression and sparkling eyes. Long, thin legs and coltish body. Light brown hair pulled into a ponytail, her face animated as she talks to who I can only assume is her little sister. They look a lot alike.

I want to grab hold of her shoulders and give her a little shake, tell her to never talk to strangers. Don't get separated from your mom and dad. Life is scary. There are predators everywhere.

But I don't. I keep my mouth shut, my butt remaining glued to the bench. I watch people as they enter the park, their heads bent over the tiny map they receive when they pay for the ride tickets or all-day wristbands. Admission to the park is free but the rides cost. A lot of people cut through the park so they can get to the beach, but there aren't many people out there today. It's fall and the ocean is cold. The sun warm but certainly not intense.

A couple walks by; they look around my age. He grabs hold of her hand and smiles at her and she stops, tilting her head back when he delivers a slow, soft kiss to her lips. They break away from each other, smiling, and I turn away, feeling like I'm invading a very private moment. A moment that fills me with an unfamiliar sense of longing. Of wanting to fit in, to find what they have.

For once, the longing overrides the fear and that surprises me.

My stomach growls when a garlicky smell wafts over me and I stand, heading over to the booth that sells garlic fries. I buy a basket of thick-cut fries smothered in garlic and Parmesan cheese along with a bottle of water and sit on the bench I'd vacated a few minutes ago, devouring the fries and sipping my water, enjoying the breeze, watching the people pass by. It isn't very busy and I'm glad. The crowds would have reminded me of the day it happened and I might have panicked more.

I'm panicking enough, thank you very much.

Slowly, as I continue to eat a basket of fries I could probably never finish, my heart rate calms. The throbbing in my head disappears and I sit up straighter, feeling proud. I was doing it. Sitting in the middle of the amusement park where I was abducted, like I didn't have a care in the world. I came back here and survived. I could handle this.

This was the beginning of me handling everything.

Remembering my earlier conversation with Brenna, I frown. I'm trying to grow up and they're just holding me back. Mom has the log-in to the Find My iPhone app on my phone. She figured out where I was and had Brenna call me. I couldn't believe it. They were keeping tabs on me like I was still a child. I don't get it. Yeah, I understand their fear and that they worry about me, but this is taking it too far. How can I ever overcome all of this bullshit if everyone in my life who cares about me is always trying to hold me back?

My appetite leaving me at the thought, I eat as much as I can and then toss a few fries onto the ground, being one of those obnoxious people who feed the seagulls despite the signs they have posted cautioning against it. I sort of don't care. I feel sorry for the seagulls. I know they're just scavengers, that they look for handouts, but that's how they survive. I can either throw the fries in the trash or feed a few seagulls.

I choose the birds.

A food court employee shuffles by me, glaring at me out of the corner of his eye. A teenage kid, his face mottled with acne, his eyes are full of irritation as they slide over me. I look away, gather up my garbage, and stand, shoving it into the nearby trash can before I hurry away from the food court, irritated with myself.

I shouldn't allow some teenager to pass judgment on me. He's probably already forgotten about me and here I am, stewing over it. Quickening my steps, eager to get away, I head toward the end of the park where it happened. Where I was kidnapped. I'm full of righteous anger at the attitude I'd felt radiating from the food court employee and I hope my emotions fuel me. Make this moment easier to deal with, because this is the one I dread the most.

The one I shouldn't have to deal with today if I don't want to. I'm proud enough of the fact that I entered this place. Now with the roller coaster looming ahead, the scenery too familiar, vivid with memories mixed with reality, I wonder if I should leave.

My steps slow as I pass the line for the roller coaster. It's short this afternoon. They don't have much of it roped off like in the past and I'd bet money I could walk right in. Find myself sitting in one of those old carts with the thin cushioned seats, the metal bar coming over my lap, locking me in, filling me with a false sense of security.

The last thing I want. I live with that false sense of security constantly. None of us are safe. Not really. We'll all come upon our little moments one time or another. Some moments are just more severe than others. Most people get off easy. Not me. But they consider me lucky.

Lucky.

I hate that word.

That recognizable bright blue building suddenly appears to my left and I shudder. The restroom. The spot where it happened, where he picked up my sweatshirt and held it out toward me like an offering, that fake smile plastered on his face. I'm sure he hoped like hell I'd fall for it and I did. I tumbled headfirst, wary and vulnerable. Wanting to help and wanting to run, conflicted like every other preteen on the planet.

I should have run.

My breaths are coming faster, I can hear the rasp in my lungs, feel it like a serrated knife tearing at my throat. I try to inhale deeply, to calm myself, but I know. I know without a doubt I'm going to have a panic attack if I don't get it, this—all of it—under control.

Breathe, baby. Breathe.

Mom's voice is in my head. She said those words to me time and again, mostly after I woke from a nightmare, screaming at the top of my lungs. She'd run into my bedroom and flick on the light, the brightness startling me awake, and I'd find myself shaking and crying, tears on my cheeks, my throat raw from the screaming.

That was always her advice. She'd hug me close as she stroked my hair, my face buried in her neck as I inhaled that familiar, floral Mom smell while she whispered, *Breathe, baby. Breathe.* I'd look up, find Dad standing in the doorway, helpless and pale, clad in his standard black T-shirt and pajama pants. I'd catch his gaze, pleading with my eyes for him to come into my room, just touch me once. Hold me. Tell me I'm his little girl.

He'd turn away like he couldn't stand the sight of me and go back to their bedroom. Every single time.

After my ordeal, when I returned home, I became Mom's burden. Never his.

Never again.

I shake the old memories off and start walking again, my steps slow, my head heavy. Doubt plagues me as I draw closer and closer to the bright blue building. I shouldn't have come here. It's as if I'm trying to torture myself.

Haven't I been tortured enough?

It's when I'm reaching into my purse to grab my sunglasses that I feel someone run into me from behind. Something sharp, like an elbow pressing into my back, knocks me forward. A gasp escapes me as I stumble, tripping over my own feet, though thank God I don't end up on the ground. I feel a hard tug on my shoulder, the press of a wiry male body against the back of mine, and I stiffen in fear.

"Give it," a young male voice says, his mouth at my ear. I can smell him, cheap drugstore cologne mixed with excitement and fear, as he presses his fist into the small of my back. The pull on my shoulder becomes tighter and I struggle against it.

My purse. He's trying to take my purse and I grip it harder, crying out when he pulls on the strap so violently I feel the leather cut into my skin through my shirt, pinching the skin of my shoulder.

"Let it go, lady!" he yells and I hear footsteps approach. Rescuers? He'll run. He'll let go of me and run and it'll all be over.

But I realize soon enough that they're helping him, not me, and panic squeezes my throat, cutting off any and all words that might escape. My brain blanks, literally blanks like a whiteboard that's been erased clean of every little mark, and I struggle to scream, to yell, to curse him out, to do something.

Anything but be a weakling—again—and just take it.

"Hurry up, man," one of the others yells. They're young. They're cursing each other out, trying to sound all gangster or whatever but I know they're just stupid kids, stealing on a whim. Or was this planned? *Let's go to the amusement park and rip the tourists off*—was that what they said to each other?

Somehow I manage to jerk out of his hold. I turn to face them, air leaving me in great, shuddering breaths as I assess my situation. Cut and run? What if one of them has a weapon? And why in the world has no one noticed what's going on? I see a couple only a few yards away, but they're so entranced with the Dippin' Dots menu they're staring at they don't even notice my struggle.

Unbelievable. I can hardly wrap my head around the fact that this is actually happening. I don't show up here—the place of my nightmares—for years and I'm at the park for an hour, only to be robbed? Really?

Despite my fear, the irony isn't lost on me. Not by a long shot.

"Hey!" The one who tried to take my purse yells. He takes a menacing step toward me, his eyes narrow little dark slits. He's an older teen, probably can't be that much younger than me, and his expression is fierce. Pissed off. Though there's a hint of fear there, too, lurking deep in his gaze and I start to back away, my fingers curled around the long strap of my purse as I hold it in place. Keep it close to my side.

A jolt of fear moves through me when all three of them step forward as I continue to back away and I contemplate my next move. I should give the purse up. Let them take it. I have one credit card and a debit card in my wallet, plus maybe sixty bucks, tops. No big deal, right? My life is worth more than that. Not that they're threatening my life . . .

But my phone is in there, too. Would it be such a bad thing, letting the phone/newly discovered tracking device that allows my mother and sister to keep tabs on me disappear? I'd have to cancel my cards, get a new driver's license. My car keys are in there, too. I don't want to be stranded here, not after this. Not after everything. I don't think I could stand it.

"Damn it, give me the purse," the kid mutters as he lunges for me, making a grab for the bag, his hands and fingers curled into gnarled little claws. "Hand it over, bitch, and you won't get hurt."

It's the *bitch, and you won't get hurt* line that socks me hard in the stomach. My shaky, sweaty fingers come loose as if they have a mind of their own, slipping away from the strap. I'm about to let him take my purse when out of nowhere a man appears.

He's tall and broad, a blur of movement as he shoves his way in between us, pushing me backward with pure brute strength. I stumble away from him, my fingers somehow miraculously finding my purse strap once more, and I watch him with fascination as he takes over.

"What the hell do you think you're doing?" The man isn't yelling. No, his deep voice is eerily calm as he grabs hold of the front of the boy's T-shirt. The other two run off without a word, ditching their friend, and the man pulls him in close, dipping his face into the boy's so they're only mere inches away from each other. "I should call the police."

The kid shakes his head, stutters out, "N-no w-way, mister. I didn't d-do anything. Please."

They stare at each other, breathing the same air, the man's fingers tightening in the boy's shirt so the fabric strains against his thin chest. I hold my breath, my entire body shaking as I watch them, afraid that they might hurt each other.

"I should make you beg," the man murmurs, the edge in his voice sending a shiver down my spine. "What sort of asshole tries to steal a purse in the middle of the day from a defenseless woman?"

"I-I m-meant n-nothing b-by it," the kid stutters, his voice shaky, his eyes full of fear as he flicks his gaze toward me for the briefest second.

The man jerks on his shirt and the kid's head flops back and forth like he's some sort of old toy thin from lack of stuffing. "Don't you dare even *look* at her."

I stand up a little straighter, a thrill moving down my spine despite my fear. It's the way he says it, all dark and threatening, like he'd tear the boy's eyes out of his head before he allowed him to look at me. It's wrong, the excitement that pulses in my blood, floods my belly. I abhor violence. Of course I do.

But there's something about the way this man handles himself, the way he speaks, so assured, so confident. He makes it all look so easy. Like it's his job, his duty to barrel into the fray and rescue me, ensuring my safety.

"You're not worthy to look at her, let alone fucking touch her." My rescuer lets him go, shoving him in the chest for good measure, which nearly sends the boy reeling. He catches himself before he hits the ground and spins on his worn Converse high-tops so hard I hear the squeak of his soles against the pavement. He runs without looking back, so fast he disappears into the thin crowd within a matter of seconds.

I wait there alone, experiencing the crash. I'm trembling, almost violently, as if the temperature just dropped at least forty degrees, and I wrap my arms around myself. Relief and adrenaline is a heady mixture as it pulses through my blood, and I try my best to calm myself down from the scary high.

"You okay?"

Glancing up, I find myself looking into the kindest pair of brown eyes I've ever seen. A complete contradiction to the dark, menacing man I just witnessed only moments ago.

He tilts his head as he waits for my answer and I stare up at him, at a complete loss for words. He's wearing glasses, so his eyes look even bigger, and his expression is full of genuine concern; I can at least recognize that. Because I've seen it all. Phony, real, every furrow of their brows and purse of their lips, most of it—yes, definitely the majority of it—fake. No one cares about me. Not really. They just want grisly details.

How they hope for the details, sick and wretched humans that we are. Even me, getting excited over a stranger rushing to my defense with a streak of barely contained violence running through him. I found that hint of violence bubbling just beneath his surface strangely . . .

Exciting.

"Hey." His voice is so gentle, a whisper of sound as he reaches out and touches me, and still I don't speak. Dark brown hair tumbles over his worry-wrinkled forehead, his full mouth turned upside down. His cheekbones are sharp, his jaw like granite. Like a gorgeous man you see in a magazine ad staring back at you, all angular planes and smoldering eyes, soft mouth and perfect hair. The flawlessness is ruined by the glasses, though, and I like them. They remind me that he's human.

Imperfect.

Like me.

I look down to see he's still touching me, his fingers curled around my arm loosely, and I don't try and pull out of his hold like I usually would. Normally, I don't allow any man to touch me, especially a strange one.

But this man—for whatever reason—he doesn't feel strange at all.

"Hey," he repeats, a little firmer this time around, the deep sound resonating through me. I watch, transfixed, as he drifts his thumb across the bare skin just above the crook of my elbow, and I shiver. "You're not hurt, are you?"

Slowly I shake my head, my voice just . . . gone. I can't even look at him. I'm so entranced with his hand on my arm, the way he's touching me, like he knows me. Like we've known each other forever. Like he's rescued me before and he'll always be there for me no matter what. It's as if I feel the silent promise radiating through him and pulsing through me.

Fanciful dreams, silly idiot.

I banish the nagging voice in my head to the deepest, darkest corner of my brain.

"You were holding onto your purse pretty fiercely there." I tilt my head up to catch him smiling at me, revealing nice teeth. They're not too white, not too straight. If teeth could be friendly, his are. Which is ridiculous. But I'm starting to think I'm not the most coherent person at the moment. "You probably should've just let it go."

He's repeating exactly what I thought only moments ago. "I-I know, but I couldn't." I clamp my lips shut, hating that my voice is high and breathless and I'm stuttering just like that teenage kid.

Relief crosses his features and he gives my arm a gentle squeeze. I feel it to the very depth of my bones. "She speaks."

He's teasing me and I don't know how to react. So like a zombie, I nod, feeling dumb and completely out of my comfort zone. I don't talk to men. Ever. Not really, not like this.

"Thank you. For coming to my rescue." I still can't believe he did it. I know someone else had to have seen what was happening. Is the world that cold, that callous, that no one wants to reach out a helping hand, especially if the situation could be dangerous?

Yes.

The word whispers through me, defiant and with a hint of snark. Because I knew the answer well before I ever thought the question—I just never want to admit it.

"I, ah, I hope you don't mind that I let him go." His hand drops from my arm and I feel the loss like a sharp prick just beneath my skin. Poking and prodding and reminding me that I might not be good enough, not what he could want.

As if he would ever want me. I'm totally getting ahead of myself.

Realizing that he's waiting for an answer, I offer him a wan smile. "What was I supposed to do with him?" I ask with a shrug, pretending that I'm normal. That what I just experienced is no big deal. I've been almost mugged plenty of times, right? I can handle this. I'm tough. Strong.

Lies, lies, lies.

His expression turns grim. "We probably should've called the cops."

The last thing I need is the police to show up and realize who I am. Where I'm at. They'd connect the dots and most likely crap their pants to be the first one on the phone with the local news. Talk about coming up at eleven—they'd all salivate to have the scoop on this ridiculous story. The media would have a field day with the constant speculation, the questions, the lack of answers.

No thank you.

"Hopefully you scared them enough that they'll never try something like that again." He may not be touching me, but he's standing awfully close, totally in my personal space. Yet I don't mind. My arm still tingles where his fingers pressed into my skin. I take a step backward, suddenly needing the distance, confused by my reaction.

I don't know him. So why am I acting like this? Thinking like this? I shouldn't like the way he's looking at me, the breadth of his shoulders, the scent of him, clean and distinct even with the salty breeze washing over us.

"Are you sure you're all right?" The concern in his deep

voice matches the concern I see clouding his eyes, and I offer him the smallest smile and a quick nod. "You never answered my question earlier. He didn't hurt you, did he?"

Only when he says the word *hurt* do I react. Again. Reaching across my body with my left hand, I massage my shoulder, wincing at the radiating pain that pulsates just beneath my skin. I nudge the loose neck of my shirt away, see the bruise already starting to form just on the outer edge of my shoulder, and he's suddenly there, standing behind me, tall and looming.

Touching the bare skin of my shoulder like some sort of lover or boyfriend.

I'm not comfortable when someone stands behind me, especially a man. It brings back too many memories, ones I don't care to think about. But his fingers on my body act like a balm, calming me from the inside out. Tingles sweep over my skin as they probe gently and I hiss in a breath, my gaze meeting his.

"He marked you," he mutters through gritted teeth, his eyes blazing with anger as his hand falls away from my shoulder.

Excitement fizzes inside of me like soda spouting from the top of a two-liter that's just been violently shaken. His anger over what happened to me is—exciting. There's no other word for it. It steals my breath, makes my chest ache, and I rub at it absently. "I'll be okay. It's just a bruise." I brush it off, not wanting him to do something stupid like chase after those boys. As if he could find them. They're long gone.

Plus, I don't want to lose him. Not yet.

Modesty attacks, reminding me that my plain white bra strap is on blatant display, and I pull my shirt back over my shoulder, covering the bruise. He steps away, giving a wide berth between us, and I wonder if he realized he was standing too close, acting too familiar.

I wonder more if he knows I didn't mind.

"Thank you," I say again because I want him to know just how grateful I am. "For helping me. I, uh, probably didn't handle it right. I'm really thankful you stepped in."

It's his turn to shrug. Those broad shoulders are covered by a thin flannel plaid shirt, dark blue and green, open at the collar and revealing the pristine white T-shirt beneath. He looks—good. Handsome, in that wholesome, strong, virile way, as if he could take two-by-fours and crack them in half with his bare hands.

He's also much taller than me, with the glasses that remind me of his imperfections and the shiny dark brown hair, curving lips, and hint of scruff lining his jaw and cheeks. Other girls would fall all over him, I'm sure. He doesn't break the two-by-fours—he probably needs them to ward off half the female population who want to jump him.

"I did what anyone else would've done in the same situation," he says, all understated modesty.

Right. Because I had so many people running to my rescue just now. Same when I was twelve. No one wants to help. No one wants to interfere. They're all too scared.

Not this man. He stepped right in like it was his calling to rescue me. For that, I will be forever grateful.

"What's your name?" I ask him, the question startling me. I usually don't care enough to learn anyone's name, especially a man's. I don't want people to think we're something that we'll never ever be. I don't make friends.

I don't *want* friends.

He appears just as startled by my question as I am. "Ethan." He pauses, swallows. I see the movement of his Adam's apple and I have the sudden, unbidden image of myself sitting in his lap, my mouth pressed right there, just below his chin, begging him to say something, anything, so I can feel the tickle of movement beneath my lips.

Ethan. *Ethan.* I like it. Oh, God, I really like it.

He clears his throat, startling me from my inappropriate thoughts. "What's yours?"

My what? Oh. My name.

This is hard. What if he recognizes me when I say it? Not that I'm egotistical enough to think I'm famous after being on TV and that he'd know me, know my face and my first name like I'm freaking Madonna or whatever, but . . . the media hounded my mother those first days after the interview aired. My face was plastered all over the Internet. My name was trending on search engines and Twitter that entire weekend.

Trending on Twitter—who can make that claim? My life is surreal, I swear.

But then bright and early the following Monday morning, a scandal rocked the political world. A controversial and extremely conservative senator was accused of having an affair with one of his twenty-one-year-old interns. A fresh-faced girl straight out of a good Midwestern college, and just like that her blond good looks replaced mine on the Web. I'd never been more thankful for someone else's problems.

"I'm Katherine," I finally say, not offering a last name but neither did he, so I'm sure he won't think it unusual. We're not on exchanging-last-name terms.

Yet.

Oh God, did I really think yet?

Yes, I did.

He smiles again. Friendly. Unassuming. My hackles always rise when someone looks at me like this, acts like this. But for once, I feel nothing but calm.

I feel nothing but hundreds of butterflies whirling and spinning in my stomach.

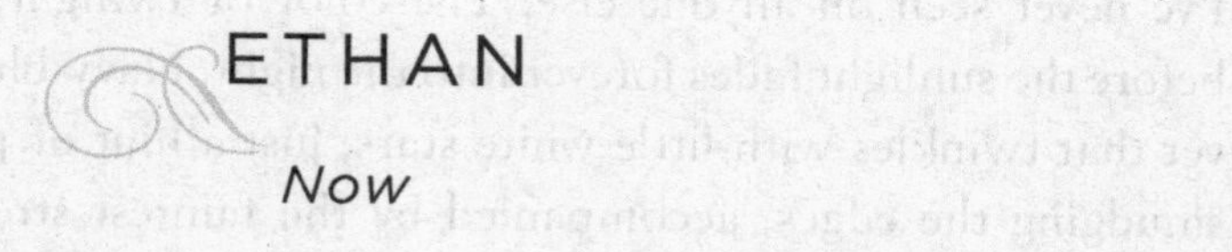

ETHAN

Now

She's standing so close, the sweet scent of her floats in the air, surrounding me, causing my head to spin, my vision getting spotty. I blink hard, needing to see her this close after going for so long without her. I didn't mean for any of this to happen, but I couldn't sit back and let those assholes steal her purse. I did what I was supposed to do and instead of walking away, I'm taking advantage while I can. While I have this moment so I can memorize everything that unfolds and revisit it later. Turn the words we said, the looks we exchanged, around and around in my mind, searching for a sign, a clue that she cares.

That she might recognize me.

Not what I want, though. Not at all.

I'm struck dumb by her beauty. Seeing her on TV with the lights and the heavy makeup gave the illusion that she's this big, grand thing, more than what she really is. Not just Katie Watts but *Katherine Watts*, the poor little girl abducted from one of the happiest places in all of California. A happy place turned into a nightmare by a man who scared the hell out of every parent who lives in this cloying, small, coastal beach town.

I'm veering off track but it's so easy to do with her like this. The memories are there, hovering on the edge, when I'm desperate to savor the here and now. I focus on her. The way she's standing in front of me, achingly beautiful with not a stitch of makeup on, her cheeks rosy, her eyes that beautiful dark blue

I've never seen on anyone else. The color of twilight, right before the sunlight fades forever into the night. Navy-blue velvet that twinkles with little white stars, just a hint of purple smudging the edges, accompanied by the faintest streak of pinkish orange. So faint you think you almost imagined it.

That's the color of her eyes. Like a fucking poem or something. Having her here like this clearly renders me a lovesick poet.

I can't stop staring at her. The sun shines upon her hair, turning the thick strands varying shades of gold and cream, and she's looking at me what feels like every few seconds—God, does she like me? I sound like a stupid kid—smiling at me, so shy and open and vulnerable and curious, it's . . .

Fucking killing me.

This is what I've sought for years. This instant connection that Katie and I share. Energy crackles in the air between us and I wonder if she feels it. I'm drawn to her and she doesn't have to say a word, doesn't have to do so much as look at me, and I want more. So much more than she could ever willingly give.

I'm not walking away now. Hell no. I about lost my shit when those punks tried to take her purse. That she held on so tight, wasn't willing to give it up—I couldn't believe it. The last thing I wanted to have happen—me intervening in her life, the words *too soon, too soon* throbbing in time with my beating heart—but I had to do it. I had to rescue her.

I'm her guardian angel after all. It's my duty to ensure she's safe.

I figured she'd freak out, then thank me in the most coldly polite way possible before she rushed off, never to be seen or heard from again. She's not very friendly. She admitted as much on national TV. She's closed off, doesn't allow people in, is afraid to broaden her social circle for fear people are only curious to know the dirty details in regards to what happened to her all those years ago.

She confessed that on national television, too.

All that vulnerability, the quiet confessions, had about done me in. I knew then I could be there for her. The one who doesn't want the lurid details of what happened to her.

I just want to help. Help Katie.

Because I know what happened. I was there. I lived it. I don't need to hear all the dirty details. I'm an integral *part* of those dirty details. The only thing I'm curious about is . . . her. What makes her tick, what moves her. Does she ever laugh, or is she serious and sad all the time? What's her favorite movie, her favorite color? Does she sigh in her sleep? Does she sleep soundly? Or does she deal with the nightmares every night?

If I'm honest with myself, I also want to know what she might feel like in my arms. Is her hair still just as soft as it was when I first met her? Would I ever get a chance to kiss her? Whisper in her ear how she makes me feel? Discover the way she tastes?

I want all of that. Every last bit. I want all of *her*.

And now she's here. Beautifully simple, confident yet scared. Playing pretend and being real. I get her. I do. I'm the same. We have more in common than she'll ever realize.

Yet all I can do is stare at her like an idiot.

"Um, would you mind . . ." Her voice drifts and she gestures with her hand back in the direction we came. If she knew I'd followed her, she'd freak. She'd have every right to. "This might sound silly, but would you, uh, walk me to my car? It's just, after what happened, I don't know. What if I run into those boys again? I'm not feeling very—"

"Sure, I'll walk you to your car," I interrupt her, my heart flipping over itself when she offers me a soft, pleased smile. "It's no problem. I was just about to leave anyway."

"Okay. Thank you. That's—that would be great." Her voice is shaky, as is her blossoming smile, and it takes everything within me to keep from reaching for her so I can cup her cheeks and smooth my fingers across her skin . . .

She starts walking and I fall into step beside her, noting how small she is compared to me. It doesn't look like she's grown much since the last time I saw her, but I've put on another six inches since I was fifteen. Nothing gave me greater satisfaction than the day I realized I was a head taller than dear old dad. I could pound that fucker into the ground if I was so inclined. Playing sports kept my head straight, kept me fucking alive until I had to give them up. But they made me stronger when I needed it, so I felt as if I could take on anything.

Everything. Including *him*.

Not that it mattered. By the time I could've taken him, he was in jail, locked up tight and with no way out. He was done. I'd ruined him. So did Katie. I helped her escape and for that unforgivable sin, I became his enemy.

I went to his trial, but it was hard to listen to all of that. Those cold, hard facts, repeated again and again. The endless barrage of photos of dead girls who looked a lot like Katie. Blood and gore and slashed throats and violated bodies, flashing on the screen again and again as the prosecuting attorney stood with her arms crossed, her expression grim. She'd made that juicy little slide show, ending it with the infamous image of Katie being led out of the police department wearing the too-large matching gray sweats, teary-eyed and devastated.

The jurors shuddered in their seats. Gasps of horror rang out, echoing as the sound bounced off the tall ceiling. The image of Katie filled me with such violent rage, such overwhelming nausea, I snuck out, ducking low as I slid across the bench, practically crawling out of there on my hands and knees, I was so hunched over.

Even though in the end I testified against him, I didn't want him to see me. Didn't want him to think I was deserting him or worse, that I was some sort of pussy who couldn't handle it.

Pussy, he'd spit at me after a drunken bender. *Fucking pussy who likes to eat dick.*

I'd dealt with those words being thrown at me again and again. I'd come to wonder if *he* was the one who liked to eat dick and projected his feelings on to me. Had to throw that theory out the window when I found out he'd raped, beaten, and murdered a seemingly endless list of girls.

So yeah, he liked females—just young ones. And that's just about the worst thing in the whole damn world, so bad I can't even begin to process it.

Against my better judgment—not that I had anyone to tell me if it was right or wrong; I was so on my own I sometimes had full-on conversations with myself—I visited him once after sentencing. He'd been such a conniving asshole—why I was surprised, I don't know—that I'd vowed never to see him in the flesh again.

He'd already gone jail soft, the weight around his belly stretching his requisite prison uniform of starched white T-shirt and light blue jeans. His skin was pale, an unnatural white tinged with green, his eyes pale, too, and a patch of hair had gone missing right in the direct center of his scalp.

He looked small. Weak. He'd once seemed mighty and powerful, like the Great Oz when I was a kid. The only one who knew how to push the buttons and pull the strings, the one I looked up to and told everyone near the end of third grade, "I'm going to grow up and someday be exactly like my daddy!"

A shiver steals over me at the memory. How I'd idolized him for that short period of time. He went from being the ideal father to the man who slowly, methodically turned into a monster.

Now who's the soft one?

Once he recognized that I had no plans on coming back to visit, he wrote me letters. Five to ten pages of angry, nonsensical ranting, about how I failed him as a son, how the system failed him, my mother, all the whores he'd ever been with, all the little girls he'd touched and disposed of so casually, as if they were nothing but dolls he'd played with for all of thirty minutes before he tossed them aside with disdain.

Letters so full of disgust and hate I'd burn them immediately, though I could never stop myself from reading them first. I had to open every single one. I don't quite know or understand what compelled me. It was like—an obligation. I might not see him anymore but I still needed to read his words. Needed the reminder that this evil, horrible man was *my* father. I come from him. A part of him lies deep within my soul, my bones, my heart and mind.

That scares the shit out of me.

On occasion I receive a letter that reminds me of a different man. The man he was before he became so twisted up with hate he didn't know how to do anything but lash out. My childhood memories are nothing close to pleasant. I can't lie.

But there *was* a hopeful point in my life. A very small period of time where everything was . . . okay, and I was full of innocence. Ignorant innocence, I suppose, but that's better than the cold, stark reality.

God, I've really lost it. Here I am with the girl of my dreams and I'm wasting my opportunity. The minutes are just ticking by. Tick, tick, tick, and soon the girl who thinks I saved her because I'm some sort of good citizen rescuing lost females with a single bound will realize I'm an idiot who can't fucking speak. And she'll shrug her shoulders, get into her car, and take off.

Never to be seen again. Well. I may be watching her like some sort of fucked-up jerk who can't figure out what he wants, but I want this. The closeness, the chance to spend time with her, talk to her, touch her . . .

I knock myself out of the memories, out of my yearnings, and focus on her.

"So. What brought you out here today?" I ask.

She peers up at me for the briefest moment, wariness in her eyes. "I, uh, just needed to get out of the house."

She's lying. But I'm not about to challenge her.

"What about you?" she asks. I see the curiosity in her gaze and I like it. I want her curious.

I need her interested.

Pleasure blooms in my chest despite my brain scrambling for an answer. "I wanted to check out the beach. It's one of my favorite spots."

She turns her head west, toward the ocean, and shields her eyes with her hand, effectively hiding her eyebrows completely. The sun is bright, reflecting off the water, and she squints against the glare. "It's definitely beautiful today."

"The weather's perfect," I add and she nods, flashing me a brief smile as we continue walking.

I shouldn't be doing this. Talking to her. Getting to know her. It's wrong. Twisted. Being honest with her would be best, but how do I bring that up in casual conversation?

Oh hey, want to know who I really am?

Yeah. I can't do it. If I continue on with this charade, with this pile of lies that will only grow taller, I'll never find a way to come clean.

This is the last time you'll talk to her. You got what you wanted—a chance to look her straight in the eye and see that she's all right. Even better? You rescued her. You did your job. Now you walk away. Escort her to her car and end it now.

We exit the park within minutes and I let her steer the course, pretending I don't know where she's parked. We make small talk, discussing mindless topics like the weather, the way the town hasn't really changed in years. She asks me if I live here and I say yes. I ask her if she lives here and she changes the subject, points out a dolphin jumping out in the ocean.

We stare at it for a moment, transfixed. I steal a glance at her, see the way she's watching the sleek gray dolphin leap in the water, her eyes wide, her rosebud lips parted. Damn, she's pretty. The urge to grab my phone and snap a photo of her at this exact moment is strong, but I know she'd freak.

So I'll have to settle with etching her expression in my memory instead.

"My car is close." She smiles and turns to face me. "Just right there." She waves behind her and I look, knowing exactly which vehicle is hers, but again, I'm not supposed to. "Thank you again. For . . . everything."

"You're welcome," I say solemnly, dread filling my gut and

making me feel sick. This can't be it. I can't . . . I can't let her go like this. Not with a "thank you and it's been real but I'll never see you again."

Fuck, I can't do it.

She's turning away from me. Starting toward her car. I watch her walk, drink in her lithe figure, the subtle sway of her hips. She's thin. I don't know if she eats much and I'm suddenly overcome with the need to feed her. Take care of her.

"Hey," I call and she pauses, turning to look at me with curiosity in her dark blue eyes. "Uh, are you doing anything right now?"

She contemplates my question, her delicate brows scrunching downward, her teeth sinking into her lower lip for a brief moment. "I should probably head on home. It's getting late."

"Oh." I nod, swallow. Pray I don't fuck this up. "I was wondering . . ."

Her face—there's no other words for it, it lights up. Like she wants me to ask. "Wondering what?"

"If you wanted to have a cup of coffee with me. Maybe get something to eat." I cock my head, stuff my hands in the front pockets of my jeans. Trying for unassuming. I don't want to push.

But I can't let her walk away from me. Not yet.

"Right now?"

"Yeah." I swallow against the dryness in my throat. "Unless you have somewhere else you need to be . . ."

"I have nowhere to be. Nowhere to go but home," she says, a rush of words that make her clamp her lips shut the moment they escape her, as if she didn't want to admit that.

"There's a little coffeehouse just up the street. We could walk there." I pause. "They have a great view of the ocean."

The smile on her face is nothing short of brilliant. "Okay. Yes. I'd love to."

Despite my instincts screaming at me in protest, I move forward and she falls into step beside me, just like before, when I was someone else and so was she.

As if we were meant to be.

WILL

Then

She was tired. And whiny. Her whimpers and constant sniffling was getting on my nerves, but I dealt with it. How could I be mad when she'd already suffered so much? My father chained her up to the wall like an animal. Something I could still hardly comprehend.

How many others had there been? That was the part I didn't like to think about too much. But it lingered in my mind always, pounding an incessant question through my blood.

How many? How many?

I didn't want to know.

Yet I had to know.

Saving this one was all I could do. I didn't know about the others. From the things Katie had said, the hints my father had given her, I knew without a doubt kidnapping Katie wasn't his first attempt. He had experience. He almost killed her. He'd raped her repeatedly. She never said exactly what he did to her beyond mentioning the choking incident, but I'd seen the bruises on the inside of her thighs, black and purple and huge. I could only imagine him wrenching her legs apart just before he . . .

"Are we there yet?" she asked for about the fiftieth time, sounding like every kid they make fun of on TV. Reminding me of Bart and Lisa from *The Simpsons*. There was an episode I watched where the whole family was going on vacation and that's all they said, over and over.

Are we there yet? Are we there yet? Are we there yet?

Until Homer finally screamed at them and they reluctantly shut up.

"Almost," I said, my rote answer. So tired of her asking that. But I was thankful for the interruption of my thoughts. I don't want to envision what he did to her. Bad enough I saw the lingering evidence.

"I'm so sore. I don't know if I can walk any farther." Her voice trailed off, so weak and pitiful, and I turned around to see her standing there, her body hunched over, my sweatshirt swallowing her up, making her look incredibly small.

"Katie," I started and she shook her head, closing her eyes as the tears slid down her cheeks.

"I can't do it, Will. My feet hurt. My legs. My whole body." The tears were really falling now, multiple little tracks bisecting each other on her dirty face as the sobs started to rack her shoulders. "I don't want to go on. I can't. I can't do this."

I went to her, grabbed her by the shoulders and gave her a little shake. Not too rough, though. I didn't want to make things worse. But she needed to get on board with the plan. "Come on. Don't give up on me now. You can do this."

She cracked open her eyes and peered up at me. "Tell me the truth. How far is the police station?"

I heaved a big sigh and turned my head to stare out at the traffic passing us by. "Almost a mile," I muttered.

"How many miles have we already walked?" She sniffed and it turned into a hiccup. I hated seeing her cry. It made me feel strange emotions I couldn't describe and wasn't comfortable with.

"I don't know," I said honestly. "Two? Maybe three?"

"It feels like twenty." She wavered in my grip, like her legs were about to give out on her, and I shook her again, causing her head to lift so her gaze met mine. "I can't do this," she whispered. "You're strong but I'm not."

"You're strong, too." I slid my hands over her shoulders and pulled her into me, going on pure instinct. I wanted to offer her comfort. I wanted her to feel safe with me and when she went willingly, folding her arms in front of her chest, her forehead landing on my shoulder, it felt . . . good. Her absolute trust in me made me feel like I could do anything for her.

As I slid my arms around her and held her close, I whispered against her hair, "Just a little while longer, Katie. Do it for me, okay?"

She nodded, the barest movement of her head, her body going limp against mine, and I gathered her as close as I could, the sweatshirt bunching between us. I willed some of my strength into her, needing her to pull it together. We were so close and I couldn't have her give up before we got there.

"Okay," she whispered, turning her head as she spoke, and I swore I felt her damp mouth move against my neck. "Just—promise me you'll walk into the police station with me."

I stiffened. That was the last thing I wanted to do. "I can't promise you that."

Katie lifted her head up to stare at me. "Why not?"

"I have to go back home." The words sounded lame, but it was the only excuse I had.

She studied me as if she were ready to call bullshit. Not that I could imagine her saying the word. "Go back to what? *Him*? Your father? Are you going to warn him that you let me go? Then the two of you can go on the run or whatever?"

"Hell no," I said vehemently. "I'm not telling him shit."

"Then why go back there? And to what? Your life can't be

that good, can it? He's a monster, Will." Her voice dropped to the barest whisper, her eyes wide and full of fear. "Does he hurt you?"

I remained stiff, even my lips immobile. I couldn't admit to her my darkest secrets.

"Does he?" she probed as she disentangled herself from my grip. Like I might be so disgusting she could catch a disease from me if she stood too close. I guessed I deserved that. I'm his son, after all. "Tell me."

"He doesn't hurt me," I mumbled, tearing my gaze from hers so I could stare at the ground. I could feel her watching me, her gaze moving over me from my head to my toes and everywhere in between. I could only imagine her wondering exactly what he did to me. How he hurt me. I hadn't felt his fists in a while, but he used to smack me where no one would notice. In the ribs, my back, my stomach. When I was nine he had a habit of pinching my inner thighs, twisting the skin until I yelped and cried and screamed, begging him to stop. Leaving ugly purplish bruises there that seemed to fill him with satisfaction when he'd notice them later on.

Those same wounds he used to give me reminded me of the bruises on Katie's thighs.

"You're lying." It wasn't an accusation, just a statement of fact, and I felt like a shit for not coming clean. But what could I say? How could I reveal to her what he did to me? What he forced me to do, what he made me watch? I hated it, was ashamed of him and what he did.

"I don't want to talk about it." I took her hand and tugged on it, indicating that I wanted her to start walking. She did so, reluctantly, the expression on her face nothing short of frustration. Petulant.

"You can't keep it inside you forever, you know," she said

as we headed down the sidewalk, me maintaining a slow pace so she could keep up. She practically walked on tiptoes, wincing with every step, and I considered picking her up and hauling her in my arms the rest of the way but decided I'd better not.

"Are you my counselor now? What do you know about life? How old are you, anyway?"

She lifted her chin, somehow looking dignified despite the matted hair, tearstained cheeks, purple bruised smudges on either side of her neck, and the giant sweatshirt that nearly swallowed her whole. "Almost thirteen."

Meaning she was fucking twelve. *Twelve*. God, my father was disgusting.

"You don't know shit," I muttered, immediately pissed at myself for talking to her like that. I was supposed to be the one who saved her. I needed to watch my mouth.

"I know enough to tell you it's hopeless, going back there, going back to *him*." She squeezed my hand, reminding me that I hadn't let hers go. Our fingers were linked, palms pressed together, and I liked it. Holding on to her like this, despite my sweating hand, made me feel good. Safe. "Come into the police station with me."

I kept walking, stifling the groan of frustration that I wanted to let fly. She was still young. Probably sheltered, not so innocent anymore but enough so that she believed the world could still be inherently good. No bad intentions allowed. She had parents to go back to, who wanted her. A safe home, a place where she felt loved and supported.

Me? I had nothing. No options. A father who kidnapped and raped little girls for sport and a mother who abandoned me long, long ago. "They'll just put me in a foster home."

"Wouldn't that be better than being with him?"

What was that old saying? The devil you know is better than the devil you don't? How messed up was that?

But that was my life in a nutshell.

When I didn't say anything she continued. "What about your mom?"

"What about her?" I sounded hostile and I pressed my lips together, fighting tears. Fucking tears. For a woman who ditched me the first moment she got a chance. I'll probably end up having serious mommy issues when I'm older, swear to fucking God.

"Where is she?"

"Not a part of my life." That was all I wanted to say. I sent Katie a look, one that said no more questions, and I was fairly certain she got the hint.

We came upon a red light and waited for it to change so we could cross the street. The police station was close by, on the street we were about to approach, and we'd need to turn right once we crossed. A few more blocks and we'd be there.

A few more blocks until I let go of Katie forever.

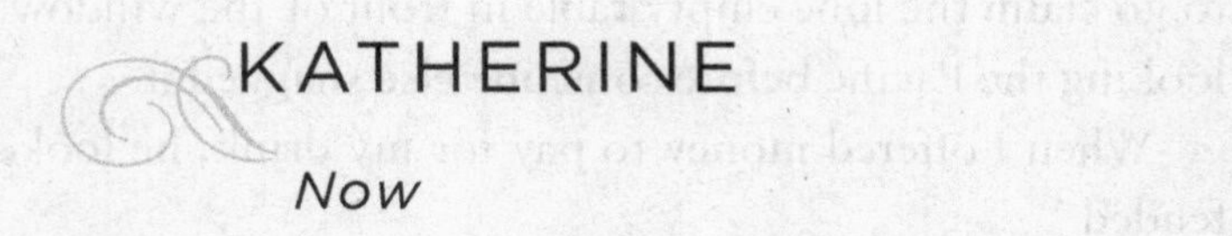

KATHERINE

Now

I accept my vanilla latte and watch him from across the table, marveling yet again at his good looks, at the fact that he asked me to go for coffee with him and I accepted. We're on some sort of weird date—I can't imagine calling it anything else—and he'd instigated it. Meaning he wanted to continue spending time with me.

Me. Katherine Watts. Poor, pitiful Katie.

I didn't know what to make of it.

As usual, I ran through the gamut of possible explanations. He's really a reporter. He knows exactly who I am and is trying to get close to me. My new favorite theory—he was sent by Mom and Brenna to trip me up. As a test to see if I'd be dumb enough to fall for his tricks.

If these theories are wrong and he doesn't know who I really am, as soon as he finds out he'll bolt. Not that I could blame him. I'm not easy. My past is difficult. Who wants to be with a girl who was repeatedly raped and beaten at the age of twelve, only to never allow herself to be touched by another man again? Who wants to follow that up?

No one, that's who. Not even this guy, not if he's normal. Any guy my age or close to it would cut and run.

We'd stood in line together, me checking the giant chalkboard menu that hung on the wall behind the front counter. Ethan made a few recommendations, letting me know what he planned on ordering, and once I made my decision, he told me to go claim the lone empty table in front of the window overlooking the Pacific before someone else snagged it.

When I offered money to pay for my drink, he looked offended.

I scurried over to the tiny table and settled in a chair, staring at the wide blanket of blue topped with whitecaps. The wind was vicious, whipping the ocean into a froth of choppy waves, and there weren't many boats out there. Most of them had already come in for the day.

Staring at the ocean could sustain me for only so long and I tilted my head, checking out Ethan as discreetly as possible while he stood patiently in the long line. The place was busy, the interior quaint, with exposed brick walls and rough-hewn wood planks. The glass case gleamed beneath the lights, full of delicious-looking pastries and cookies, and a tray of chocolate cupcakes topped high with thick vanilla frosting that looked extra tempting. But I wasn't hungry and besides, I was too nervous to eat.

Two women passed by, heading toward the doorway, and they blatantly checked out Ethan, who was completely oblivious considering his back was to them. I watched as they did a slow perusal of his backside, the two of them falling into fits of giggles before they hurried out of the coffee shop.

I couldn't help but look at his backside, too. The first time I'd ever done something like this. The dark jeans he wore were loose but not baggy, so I could make out his butt beneath the denim. It had a nice shape. What impressed me the most, though, were those shoulders. They were so broad. Capable looking. As if he could fight wars and ward off evil monsters all while I clung to his side.

A ridiculous fantasy, but one I couldn't help but entertain.

He smiled pleasantly at the cashier and handed her a

twenty, nodding his thank-you when she gave him back his change. He slipped the loose bills into a slim black leather wallet and shoved it into his back pocket, striding over to the other counter where the drinks were delivered. I watched him the entire time, my elbow propped on the table, chin resting on my curled fist. He didn't notice, and I was glad because it allowed me to study him unabashedly.

I feel like a preteen nursing a crush. This was what Sarah referred to all those years ago. Why she went so boy crazy and wanted to flirt with all of them. I'm not ready to do anything like that, but just watching Ethan stand there waiting for our drinks and checking his phone, his head bent, seeing his hair falling across his forehead, filled me with the sudden urge to push it back . . .

He glanced over his shoulder, his gaze meeting mine, and a knowing smile curved his lips for the briefest moment. I lifted my head and dropped my arm to the table, my cheeks heating at getting busted, and then I was saved by the barista calling out his name because our drinks were ready.

Could I make more of a fool of myself? I didn't have a chance to experience all the dating bumbles and mistakes through middle and high school. I didn't deal with any of that, and now I have to figure all this stuff out years later.

I take off the lid of my coffee, watching the steam rise off the thick head of foam. He does the same, popping his lid off, taking the stir stick he must have grabbed when he picked up our order and twirling it in his hot drink, making the light brown liquid swirl.

"They always make their drinks extra hot here," he says. "Just a tip."

I smile, liking that he said that. It almost implies that he might want to bring me here again someday.

Maybe. Hopefully.

Something settles over me; I don't know how to explain it. This moment just feels so normal, so everyday, and I'm savoring it. I sense that he has no idea who I am. And I'm so fine with that. I don't want to see the flicker of dismay in his dark brown eyes. Don't want to watch as sympathy pulls his mouth into an automatic frown and he makes one of those tsk-ing noises. You know what I'm talking about. The ones all of us make just before we say something like . . .

That's so awful.

Or:

What a tragedy.

And my favorite one of them all:

You're so strong. So lucky you made it out alive!

I've never felt truly lucky. I'm a survivor, yes. Never a victim—God, I hate that word. But lucky? Luck is for those who narrowly miss a car accident or win the lottery, or get a job because the first candidate backed out at the last minute.

That's luck. Me suffering through an ordeal no child should ever have to endure only to continue on with her life a shadow of her former self, a sad little adult who feels broken inside? Who's lonely and craves companionship but doesn't know how to talk to a stranger, especially a man?

I don't consider that lucky. Not at all.

"How's your coffee?" Ethan asks and I glance up to find him watching me, his eyes almost owlish behind the glasses. I may be shy and awkward, but I'm not dead.

The man is gorgeous. That he asked me to have coffee with him is sort of mind blowing.

"Really good," I answer with a slight smile, lifting my cup so I can take another sip. I can feel the foam lining my upper lip and I lick it away nervously, feeling like an idiot.

His gaze darkens, if that's even possible, and I wonder if it was because he saw my tongue. My heart pounds like a slow, primal throb against my ribs and I wonder . . .

Could he be attracted to me?

Am I attracted to him?

I've never been so aware of someone before. It's like all I want to do is stare at him. Or ask him an endless amount of questions. Then stare at him a little more.

I'm being ridiculous.

"How about yours?" I ask, nodding toward his cup. His long fingers are curled around it and I remember how they curled tight into that kid's T-shirt, trembling with barely restrained violence.

Another shock of excitement courses through me and I watch in shaky silence as he takes a sip from his white chocolate mocha and smiles at me. "It's good. I haven't been here in a while, so I was hoping they wouldn't disappoint."

"I'm definitely not disappointed," I say with a soft huff of laughter. Am I flirting? I didn't think I knew how to do that. Maybe it's just coming naturally.

"Good." His eyes squint a little when he smiles and I can't help but find it attractive. *He's* attractive. And large, so broad and tall, with long legs and arms, the muscular shoulders, the wide chest. The round table we're sitting at is small and his legs seem to sprawl everywhere, taking up every inch of his allotted space and some of mine, too.

But I don't scoot my chair away from him. I don't try to withdraw. I stand my ground, enjoying the way his foot seems to nudge against mine every few minutes, the brush of our jeans-clad legs sending a spark of fire across my skin when it happens. It's weird, but he feels both familiar and new, comfortable and thrilling, all at once. I don't get it.

"So how long have you lived here?" I ask, trying my best to make small talk, something I'm not very good at.

His eyes slide away from mine to stare out the window at the ocean spread out before us, and he works his jaw. "Um, we came here when I was nine. My family and I."

"Oh." I nod, wondering why he doesn't seem very comfortable. Have I already blown it? Pried when I shouldn't have? God, I don't know how to do this, how to be casual and talk to a guy. I'm freaking pitiful. "Can I ask how old you are?" I'm sure that's a faux pas, too, but who cares. I'm too curious to worry about it.

"Twenty-three." His gaze meets mine once more and he leans across the small table, putting himself into my personal space yet again. It's like he can't help himself and I don't mind, because now I can smell him. Feel the warmth radiating from him in palpable waves. For some reason I want to get close to that warmth. I can't explain why. "How old are you?"

"Twenty-one," I answer. *And never been kissed. You're my first real date and you probably don't even count this as one.*

"A legal adult then." He leans back in his chair, his gaze still locked on mine. "It's not all that it's cracked up to be, is it?"

I shrug. Take another sip of my drink before I answer. "I don't feel like an adult, if that's what you mean. But I'm thankful I'm not a child any longer, either."

The light dims in his gaze and for a panic-stricken moment, I wonder if I said too much. "Didn't have a great childhood?"

"It was okay when I was really young. Once I hit my teen years . . ." I don't finish the sentence. I don't need to. For some reason, I think he might understand. Does anyone think their teen years were easy? Probably not.

Mine were just abnormally awful.

"I get it," he says with a nod, and relief hits me square in the chest when I hear those three words. "Most of the time, being a teenager fucking sucks."

I burst out laughing, shocked and pleased by his blatant description. "Well, you don't mince words."

"What's the point?" He shrugs those broad shoulders. "I'm just being honest."

"Are you always honest?" The pointed question makes him pause and I realize that I'm not good at this. Not at all. I ask invasive questions or ones guys don't want to answer.

"I try to be," he says after a moment's pause. His eyes darken, as if an ominous cloud drifted past them, and I wonder why. "As best that I can."

I say nothing. It's not my place to judge, to have expectations. We're two people who met over strange circumstances and are now having coffee together. That's it. Once we're finished I'll get in my car and drive back home. Never to see him again. I'm fine with that.

Really.

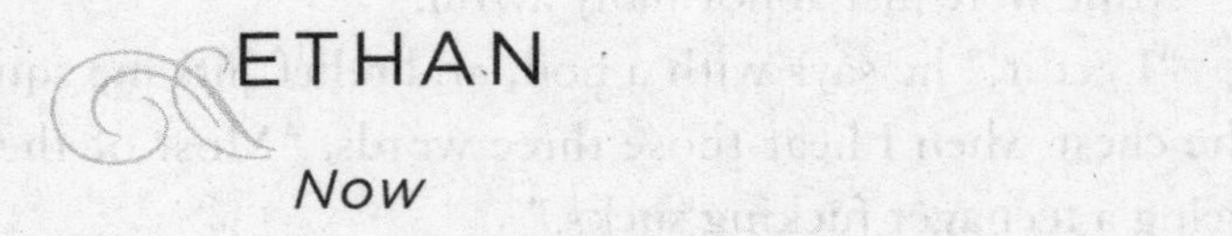

ETHAN

Now

An hour later, I walk her back to her car. The wind had whipped up almost violently while we were inside the coffeehouse, and now it knocks into us as we head down the sidewalk, our heads bent, our bodies leaning forward. She wraps her arms around her middle, a visible shiver racking her body, and I wish I could slip my arm around her shoulders and pull her into me. Share my warmth, hold her close.

More like I just want to hold her close.

She stops directly in front of her car and turns to smile at me tentatively. "Thank you again for the coffee. And the conversation."

We'd chatted easily, though at times she'd seemed uncomfortable. She also asked me questions that were tough to answer, which in turn made me uncomfortable. I tried my best to brush it off. Blame it on her not dating much because I know she hasn't. Being with her, spending time with her one-on-one like I've been doing, I can tell.

It was her question about being honest that got me. Has stuck with me no matter how much I've tried to shake it. I'm an asshole for giving her some bogus answer. I'm an asshole liar.

I should come clean, but how? That's why I need to walk away and end this. I got what I wanted. Hell, I even rescued her. Saved her from getting her purse stolen. Talked with her, got to know her a little bit and see that she's doing all right. She *will* be all right. I know it.

"Thank you for agreeing to come with me," I say, taking a step back like I desperately need some space between us, glancing across the street where I parked my car in front of the Mexican restaurant. Like a miracle, it's still there, though I think I see a ticket clamped under the driver's-side windshield wiper, fluttering in the wind.

"Thanks for the coffee. And thank you for helping me earlier, with the purse situation." She sinks her teeth into her lower lip and I want to groan. It's like she's so damn sexy and doesn't even know it. I *know* she doesn't know it. That's part of the reason she's so damn appealing. "That could've gotten really . . . ugly. I can't say enough how grateful I am that you did."

I take a step closer, forgetting my earlier thought about needing space. Fuck that. I *need* to be close to her. "I wasn't going to let those guys hurt you," I murmur, taking her hand and squeezing gently. It's like a jolt of electricity passes from my palm to hers and I know she feels it. I see it in the widening of her eyes, the way her fingers curl around mine and tighten just the slightest bit. Like she can't help herself.

When we're around each other, that's exactly it. We can't seem to help ourselves. The need to touch her, stand near her, breathe her in, is so strong I can't fight it. I don't think she can either.

She tilts her head back, her gaze meeting mine. She doesn't say anything and neither do I. We just look at each other, the wind swirling around us, golden-blond tendrils slipping from her ponytail and flying about her face. The sun is lower in the sky, casting her in a pinkish-orange glow, and the words slip past my lips without thought.

"Can we exchange numbers so you can text me when you're home safe?"

Her hand doesn't stray from mine. "Yes," she whispers.

I slowly—reluctantly—release my grip on her hand, reaching into my front pocket to pull out my phone. I open up a new text message and she hesitantly repeats her number to me, which I enter into my phone along with a quick message before I hit send.

Her phone dings and she pulls it out of her purse, smiling when she sees the message.

Hi.

Her fingers flash over the screen of her phone as she sends a reply, and my phone chimes within seconds.

Thank you. For everything.

My heart cracks. This girl. She's burrowed right into it. She tucked herself in the depths of my heart years ago, when I first found her on that dirty mattress, bruised and filthy and so scared. It tore me up, what my father did to her, and I wanted desperately to help her, as if my good deeds could make up for that.

I don't think it came close to making up for what he inflicted on her, but I tried my best. I rescued her, yet I was still somehow made out to be the bad guy. Is that what she thinks of me—the old me? That I was involved in my father's sick, twisted games? That I played a part in all of it? Theories abound over what I did. One is that he used me as a way to lure the girls in. Another is that I gave my dad up so I wouldn't have to go down with him.

Those two theories hurt the most. To think she might believe it?

Just about tears me apart.

"Enough with the thank yous," I tell her out loud, making

her smile. "You'd better get on the road. How long does it take for you to get home?"

She hesitates as she returns her phone to her purse, almost like she doesn't want to tell me. I wait patiently, shoving my hands in my front pockets, watching her. "A little over an hour," she admits.

It still blows me away that she lives so close to the so-called scene of the crime. It's as if she wants to test herself on a daily basis.

"Then you'd better text me in about ninety minutes." I give her a stern look and her smile doesn't waver. In fact, it grows even bigger. "Okay?"

Katie rolls her eyes in exaggeration. "Okay, I will."

"Promise?" The word slips out of me, the one word she always used to repeat to me, and her eyes widen as shock washes over her face.

"I promise," she murmurs solemnly, her gaze as wide and blue as the ocean behind us.

I know without a doubt she won't break that promise.

WILL

Then

"So let me get this straight." The detective paused, his gaze locked on mine with cool blue eyes that reminded me of ice.

His attitude was icy, too. We'd been going at it for a couple of hours. Question after question, the same one asked a different way, again and again, until I felt like I was going to break. Which was exactly what they wanted to do.

Break me.

I refused. I might have been exhausted and mentally brain dead, but I tried my best to be completely honest. It was like they were dying for me to confess I was involved with my father's crimes. As if they were waiting for it, wanting that confession so damn bad they were downright breathless with anticipation.

But I had nothing to confess beyond bringing Katie to them. I thought they'd be happy, you know? This girl—I saw her on the news just that morning. A missing child report, stating that she disappeared three days ago at the amusement park down on the boardwalk and they believed she'd been abducted. She'd been seen with a man that they described in the most general terms it was almost laughable.

Three days gone. I found her on the second day. Brought her to the police station on the third day. What the hell happened to her on that first day? How had I missed it? While the detectives left me stewing in my own thoughts when they first brought me here, I pondered the question.

Where had I been? How had I missed this?

I racked my brain until it came to me all at once. I'd gone to football practice as usual, then hung out with a friend for a while. We smoked pot and got the munchies, so we raided his kitchen and then watched TV—old-school cartoons that made us laugh hysterically—until his parents came home from work, ruining our good time.

It was a typical house, typical family, all of it so nice and normal despite our smoking a joint and eating most of their food. Hell, I guess that part was normal, too. What wasn't normal was having a dad who, while you were taking care of a case of the munchies, kidnapped a twelve-year-old girl and raped her.

Fucking *raped* her.

Remembering the fear in Katie's eyes, the way she cowered from me when I first entered the storage room, imagining what he did to her, made me want to puke.

Worse? How realization slowly dawned. The police didn't see my bringing Katie to them as a rescue. They wanted to believe it was a confession. Dad, of course, was their number-one suspect. I quickly realized I was their second suspect. They believed we were co-conspirators.

"Get what straight?" I asked wearily. I was so tired of their questions. Well, the one detective's questions. The other officer sat quietly, taking notes on a yellow legal pad. His writing looked like chicken scratch.

"That you have no idea where your father is."

I slammed my hand on the edge of the table, startling the other detective so bad his pen dragged across the legal pad in a jagged line. "I've already told you, I don't know where he's at. I left the storage shed with Katie and brought her here." I paused, wishing I had something to drink, but I'd drained the soda they brought me over an hour ago. "Is she okay?"

"She's as fine as she can be, considering what she's been through," the detective snapped. He leaned across the table, his gaze narrowed, his tone menacing. "Let's cut the bullshit, shall we?"

I went completely still. They'd been toying with me since they'd brought me in here. Never coming right out and saying it, but I knew what they believed. They had no plans on letting me out of this crappy little room with the beige walls and no windows anytime soon. I'm surprised they hadn't tossed me in a jail cell already.

Not like they could send me home. I'd probably get sent to foster care, and that was the last thing I wanted. My house had been roped off and was officially considered a crime scene, overrun with police officers. And my father was nowhere to be found.

"Just say it," I murmured, tired of the repeated questions, the irritation that radiated off the both of them in waves. They hated me. Judged by a jury of two, I'd already been tried and convicted by them.

"Fine. You want to know what we think? Here it is. We believe you were an accessory to the kidnapping and rape of Katherine Watts." I flinched at the word *rape*, and at hearing her full name for the first time. "And we're going to dig and dig and badger the fuck out of you until you finally come clean and tell us exactly what happened. Because you know. We know you know. You're just a punk asshole, a replica of your dad."

"I didn't do anything." My voice hitched and I clamped my lips shut. I felt like crying but damn it, I wasn't a kid. I needed to suck it up. "I brought her here. I wanted to save her."

The detective threw back his head and laughed like I'd just said the funniest thing ever. *Asshole*. I sat on the edge of my chair, tense with anger, my hands clenched into fists, and I lifted them up, resting them on the table. "You didn't want to save her. You wanted to save your own damn skin. You knew your father was taking too long with her and that something needed to happen before he blew it. So you panicked. Decided the best thing would be to bring Katherine to us, look like the supposed hero and get yourself off the hook. Throw your dad to the wolves and you end up looking like a damn saint."

I said nothing. There was no point in defending myself. No one cared what I had to say; no one was listening to me.

So it was best I kept my fucking mouth shut.

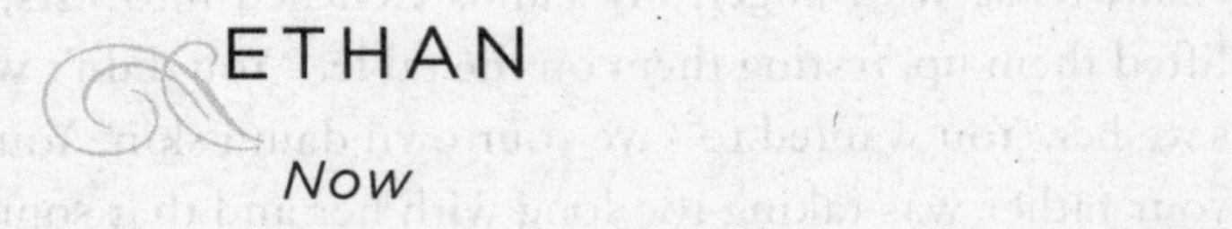

ETHAN

Now

I wait.

I pace.

I want to tear my hair out, and end up running my hands through it so many times I'm sure it's standing on end and looking like shit.

Like I care. Who's going to see me?

I'm alone. As always.

Pacing one end of my living room to the other.

My head is filled with . . . thoughts. Worried thoughts. Crazed thoughts. Lust-filled thoughts.

Wrong thoughts.

It finally comes through approximately one hundred minutes after she last left my sight. What I was waiting for.

> Made it home safe and sound! Had a great time this afternoon despite the almost purse snatching. ☺

The relief that floods me at seeing her text makes me weak. Makes me feel like a fucking baby. With shaking fingers I answer her.

> Thanks for letting me know. I had a great time too.

I pause, my fingers hovering over the screen. I tell myself not to do it. I have no right. I'm fucking with her by doing this.

Fucking with myself. I'm mental enough. Damaged enough. So is she. I don't want to hurt her.

But I can't let her go. Not yet. I need more.

I want to see you again.

I hit send before I can second-guess myself.

She doesn't reply for so long I'm afraid I blew it. I pace again as I wait. Just about wearing a path into my living room carpet. What the hell is wrong with me? What the fuck am I doing? I run my hands through my hair yet again, gripping the strands on the back of my head and giving them a hard tug.

When my phone finally buzzes I can't even care if I'm supposed to play it cool. I'm desperate to see what she says.

I'd like that.

The smile that stretches my mouth wide is painful. I want to laugh with relief. Collapse in triumph. I respond as coolly as I can.

I'll call you tomorrow?

She replies without hesitation.

Okay.

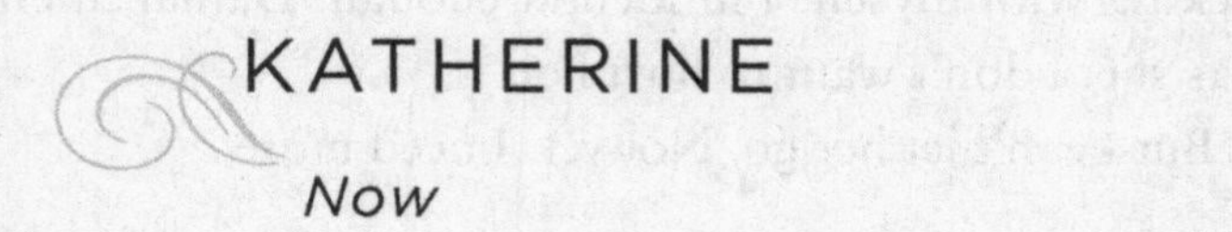

KATHERINE

Now

I am giddy with anticipation after answering Ethan's final text. He wants to see me.

Me.

Silly, messed-up me.

I can't focus, can hardly think straight. That sign, KEEP CALM AND CARRY ON? I couldn't do that if I tried.

I know what's going on, though.

I understand.

I think.

I have a crush. A real-life, bona fide crush on a sweet, good-looking guy who I think is also interested in me. He must be if he said he wanted to see me again, right?

I can't believe I'm so comfortable with him. It's so unlike me. Nothing like this has ever happened before. Men make me nervous, and with good reason. I've been hurt too many times to trust a man who is a virtual stranger.

Ethan didn't feel like a stranger at all. He felt like someone I've known for a long time. He's comfortable—and not in a bad way. In a good, exciting way, if comfortable can even feel like that, which I think it can. I caught him watching me more than once, and every time our gazes connected, I experienced butterflies breaking free in my stomach, making my breath shuddery and my entire body quake.

Ridiculous.

Thrilling.

I toss my phone on the couch and dance around my house in my socks, my feet sliding on the hardwood floor. I almost fall but catch myself, giggling as I twirl around in a circle, making myself dizzy.

Or maybe I'm dizzy from Ethan. A man whose last name I don't even know.

But for once I don't care.

I just want to get to know him. Find out more.

Find out . . .

Everything.

KATIE

Then

My head hurt. My eyelids were heavy as I slowly pried them open, immediately slamming them shut with a moan when the bright sun seemed to pierce straight through my sensitive eyeballs. I lay there for a moment, trying my best to recall what happened. My body ached and the smells, the sounds, all of it was completely unfamiliar.

And then I remembered. The park. The long roller-coaster line. Going to the bathroom. The man. Dropping my sweat-shirt and how friendly he was when he handed it back. Helping him find the line to a ride so he could meet his wife and children. Realizing too late that there were no wife and children. He'd lied to me.

Tricked me.

Taken me.

Tears squeezed past my tightly closed eyelids, though I hadn't noticed them until they were already streaking down my cheeks.

Taking a deep breath, I attempted to open my eyes again, turning to the side so I wouldn't face all of that bright sun. My head throbbed with the movement and I whimpered, unable to help myself, hoping no one would hear me.

"You're awake."

Fear made my throat constrict. I recognized that voice. It was him. The man who took me.

"Look at me," he demanded when I didn't say anything.

I turned my head toward the sound of his voice, my entire body beginning to shake. My foot shot out and I heard a noise that sounded like chains clanking against each other, felt the heavy weight around my ankle, and I knew he'd chained me up like a dog.

God, what did he plan to do to me?

"Aw, shit, don't start that," he grumbled as I started to cry harder. I wouldn't look at him. I couldn't. I looked away, staring at the pale wall that was really no color. Not quite white, not quite beige, I didn't know what to call it.

Ugly. It was ugly. Wherever he'd put me was awful and when I glanced down, I could see the edge of the thin, dirty mattress that I was lying on. I shifted my leg again, the chain loud as it rattled against the bare floor. The chain was hooked around a rusted pipe that seemed to lead nowhere.

"Stop crying!" he yelled and I squeezed my eyes shut, willing myself to stop.

But I couldn't. I couldn't stop. His yelling made me cry harder. He shouted again and I pressed my lips together, containing the sob that wanted to escape. I held it in, felt it grow bigger and bigger like a balloon full of too much air until I couldn't take it anymore and I opened my mouth, the sound like a sad sort of pop that only made him madder.

"Shut up!" Without warning he slapped my face and I cried out in shock, scrambling back on the mattress, trying to press myself against the wall. "Shut the fuck up and listen to me!"

I was shaking. So terrified that I clutched at the wall, moaning low in my throat, begging for my mommy like I was a baby.

I'd have given anything to be a baby at that moment, back in my mother's arms as she cradled me and kept me safe. I could feel his hands on me as he grabbed me by the waist and threw me down onto the mattress like I was a rag doll. He was strong. So much bigger than me. I lay there, my eyes closed, my head turned to the side, and he drew closer, his breath wafting across my face, hot and sour, as he whispered, "You sure are pretty."

No, no, no.

He drifted his hand across my cheek and I recoiled from his touch, whispering the word that was like a chant inside my head.

"No."

No acknowledgment of what I said. "I wish I could keep you."

Oh God, oh God, what did he mean? Of course he couldn't keep me. That meant he'd have to . . .

Eventually get rid of me.

No way could I think of how he might do that.

I sobbed. I wailed. I sounded like someone else, like a character from a scary movie, and for one quick moment, it all felt so unbelievable, so incredibly crazy, I couldn't wrap my head around the fact that this was real.

That this was really happening.

To me.

"Shhh," he whispered as he cupped my cheek. His fingers were gentle but they made my skin crawl and I shook my head, wishing he would stop touching me. "Be quiet. I can't let anyone hear you."

That meant someone *could* hear me. Hope lit a small flame inside my chest and I yelled louder, repeating the same words again and again.

"Help me! Help me, please! Please help me!"

He slapped me, so hard I saw stars, which I'd never believed was a real thing. I immediately went quiet and he placed his hand over my mouth. Despite my keeping my lips as tightly sealed as possible, I tasted him. Salt and dirt and whatever else he'd touched that I couldn't identify.

I wanted to throw up.

"Look at me." He pressed his hand harder on my mouth, his fingers nudging against my nose, and I inhaled sharply, my nose wrinkling as I caught his distinct scent, a mixture of sweat and something else, something that reminded me of—excitement. He was excited by all of this.

I hated him.

Opening my eyes, I found his face so close to mine I could count every tiny eyelash that lined his eyes, every hair in his eyebrows. His eyes were wide, his pupils huge, and a weird, exaggerated smile curved his mouth.

"Keep your mouth fucking shut, you hear me? I don't like it when girls are loud. When girls fight." He paused, and his smiled faded. "I suggest you don't fight. It's much easier when you let me do what I want."

A noise left me, painful and raw. My eyes burned from unshed tears and my head felt like someone had taken a hammer to it. I gave no answer, but he didn't care.

"You swear you'll be quiet?" His hand clamped my mouth like a vise.

I nodded, my entire body quaking. He shifted, I could feel him looming over me, his knees on either side of my waist as he straddled me. Fear coursed through my blood, turning it to ice, and I felt it happen before I could stop it, the warmth spreading immediately.

I peed myself.

"Jesus." He leapt away from me as the sharp scent of urine hit the air and he removed his hand from my mouth only to slap my face again, his wide palm cracking against my skin and knocking me so hard my head swung to the side. "Fucking dirty bitch. What the hell is wrong with you?"

That was when he tore off my shorts and my underwear. I closed my eyes, his hands pressing against the inside of my thighs and spreading them wide. He wiped at me with my own underwear and I heard them land on the ground with a damp plop.

I cried. I cried so hard my chest hurt and my throat was raw. He rose above me, his hand settling on my mouth to keep me quiet, his lower body wedged between my legs. He watched me, I felt his eyes on me like a hot, sweeping laser, and my skin crawled.

Everything else disappeared and I floated out of my body. I couldn't feel what he did to me. I couldn't hear it. I couldn't see it. It was happening to someone else.

It wasn't, though. It happened to me.

I wished for death. Anything to save me from what he was doing.

But it never came.

WILL

Then

The phone call was unexpected. Late in the evening, just after I got off shift at the discount store where I worked. The number was unfamiliar and I almost didn't answer, but something compelled me to do it anyway.

I was glad I did.

"Will." The soft, slightly breathless voice was familiar, and I knew in an instant who it was.

"Katie?" I stopped in my tracks and glanced around, half expecting to see her magically appear like some sort of ghost from my past.

"How are you?" She paused, a hesitant sound escaping her before she continued. "I've missed you. You haven't sent me a letter in a long time."

On the advice of my attorney. Yeah, I had a lawyer, but only because of what was going on with my father's trial. For my own protection, he told me I shouldn't remain in contact with Katie Watts any longer. As much as it killed me to do it, I stopped writing her.

And I'd felt like I had a hole in my heart ever since.

"I've been busy with school and work and stuff." I paused, wondering if I should be an asshole and just end this. I didn't want to be mean, but it would be a surefire way to hurt her feelings enough that she'd leave me alone.

Not that I wanted her to. Not that I wanted to end whatever this friendship was that we shared. I couldn't stand the thought of hurting her, but it would be best. I wasn't good enough to be her friend and she needed to let go of her past.

That's all I really was to her—a dark and ugly reminder of her past.

"Too busy to write?" She sounded hopeful and hurt, a horrible combination that made me feel like a jerk.

"Sort of."

We both said nothing and for once it was awkward between us. I started to walk, headed back to that shitty group home I was close to leaving for good, and I was craving a cigarette.

Anything to help ease the pain that was wrapping itself so tightly around my heart.

"You're mad at me," she finally accused, and I immediately denied it.

"No way, Katie. I could never be mad at you. It's just—it's me." And that was the truth. It was all on me, never on her.

"What about you? You don't want to be my friend anymore?" Her voice trembled. She sounded like she might cry at any moment and my heart felt like it was being strangled.

"I will always be your friend," I whispered, reaching into the pocket of my coat and withdrawing a pack of smokes. I pulled out a cig and held my phone between my neck and my shoulder, lighting up and taking a deep drag before I started talking again. "It's just—shit is bad right now, with the trial and all. It's probably best if we didn't talk."

"Whatever, Will." She was full-on crying now and she sounded angry. "You were my only friend. The only one who understood what happened. And now even you won't talk to me. Thanks. Thanks a lot."

"Katie, wait—" I started, but the call ended and I was left listening to nothing but silence.

I shoved my phone into my back pocket and started walking once more, my strides long, my anger flowing like liquid fire through my veins. I just pissed off the only girl who ever meant something to me.

And I didn't know how to fix it.

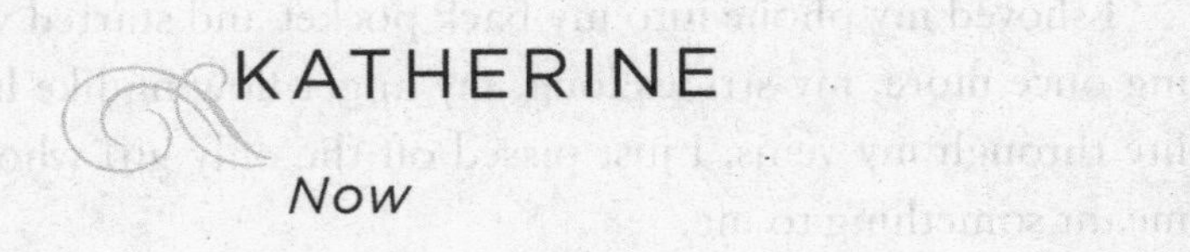

KATHERINE

Now

I wake with a jolt, my eyes flashing open as remnants of the dream—nightmare, take your pick—still cling to me. I lie completely still, my heart racing so hard I feel it roar in my ears and I wait for it to calm, listening for the normal middle-of-the-night sounds that will reassure me I'm where I should be.

In my house, alone, with no one standing over me.

A dog barks. The house creaks, settling as it does. I've always wondered how long it takes for a house to completely settle. I hear a car's engine in the distance and I wonder if they're leaving or coming home. Where are they? Where are they going? What are they doing?

I imagine a man leaving his girlfriend's house. Maybe they're not fully committed yet and that's why he's not spending the night. Perhaps he doesn't even consider her his girlfriend. But they do boyfriend/girlfriend things. She invited him in after a night out and he agreed willingly, thankful she asked. He'd been thinking of only one thing the entire night.

He couldn't wait to get his hands on her. And she couldn't wait to let him.

An ache starts deep inside me and I roll to my side, facing the bedside table with my alarm clock on it. The time glows back at me, red digital numbers that say 1:09. I've felt this ache before, after I read a particular book or watched a certain movie. I experienced it when I went out to dinner with Mom and Brenna and saw a couple sitting at a nearby table exchanging longing glances and holding hands.

I finally figured out that the ache I felt was desire.

Desire for human touch—for a man's touch. Something I believed I would never want. The feeling has always been fleeting. There and gone in a matter of minutes, and I would forget about it. Move on with my life and tell myself, *That didn't really happen. You don't want that. You don't need it.*

I feel it now. Dark and warm in the pit of my stomach, maybe even lower, a trickle of hot liquid through my veins, slowly touching me everywhere, reminding me that I have a body. A body I don't use, I don't understand, I don't touch.

I don't allow anyone to touch.

Closing my eyes, I concentrate harder. The tingling. The heat. My muscles feel languid, my skin sensitive, and I know why I'm experiencing this. I understand the cause.

Meeting Ethan. The violence that brought us together and how he charged right in and saved me. I'm ashamed that his brute strength, the way he handled the situation, aroused me. Ashamed at how scared and flushed and excited I felt when I saw him grab the boy by the shirt. I thought he would hurt the kid. Hurt him for me. And God help me, I liked it. I wanted it. I shouldn't have.

But I did.

The contradiction of his sweetness, how protective he was of me, a virtual stranger, aroused me further. Intrigued me. He touched me and I didn't flinch. His fingers were like a hot brand on my flesh and just remembering the moment, I want more of it.

More of him.

A sigh escapes me and I let my mind drift. I blame the

dreamy state of consciousness I'm in for the odd thoughts. And the nightmare. Why, after experiencing what ended up being a pretty good day, would I dream of Aaron Monroe?

Because you were at the place he abducted you, dummy.

True.

I reopened old memories. That's all. I went to the amusement park to overcome my fear and I did something else. Something I never believed could happen.

A man touched me and I let him. A man asked me out for coffee and I went. A man asked me for my number and I gave it to him. The man texted and said he wanted to see me again and I agreed.

Maybe I really am on my way to conquering my fears.

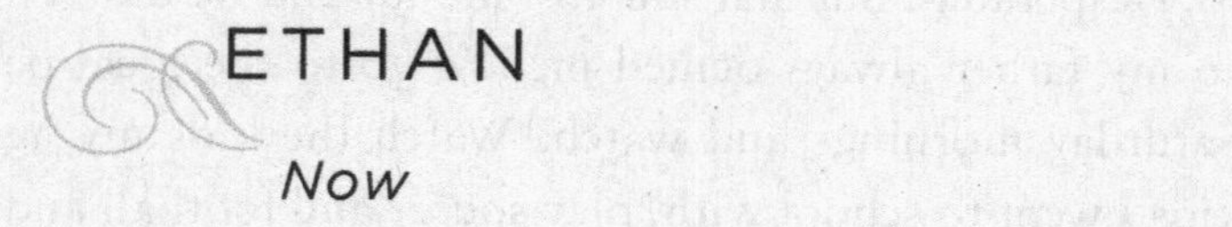

ETHAN

Now

I'm proud of Katie. When I called her a few nights ago and finally asked her to go to dinner with me, so damn nervous I was afraid my voice was shaking, she agreed—reluctantly. She said she'd do it only if we met each other in a public location.

Fine by me, I told her, and she sounded relieved.

That she didn't fully trust me pleased me only because I want her safe. She shouldn't easily place her trust in me—in anyone. She's been through so much and she has every right to be wary, especially now that she's told her story to the entire nation. I have no idea how many people watched, but I bet it was a ton. Everyone's fascinated with a story like Katie's.

I'm fascinated with the woman, not just her story. Not just her path. I was there. I lived it. Was a part of it and contributed to her survival. Yet a part of me—almost the entire whole of me—wants to forget that. I crave the past connection with Katie but I don't want to remember the details. The whys and the wherefores.

It's like I'm starting fresh and new with her, though I have an advantage. I know all about her, but she doesn't know me. Well, she doesn't know the new me. Ethan.

Even the old me, she didn't know that well. She probably wouldn't have liked him much anyway. I hadn't been the best kid, given the terrible example I had growing up. No mom, a dad who used yet was useless. When I was little I could never play Little League baseball or peewee football, and I wanted to. Desperately. But that shit cost money and we didn't have it, so my father always denied me. I'd go to the local park on Saturday mornings and watch. Watch the kids my age, the kids I went to school with, play soccer and football and baseball. Envy ate at me, made me angry and frustrated, but no one cared.

No one.

I practiced, though. Whenever I could. Played sports during elementary school during P.E. and recess. Kicked balls around, threw them, made baskets, idolized my third-grade teacher, Mr. Elliott, who let us play flag football pretty much every day, rain or shine. God, I loved flag football. At school no one bothered me, no one picked on me or told me I was worthless. All that happened at home.

School was my refuge.

I threw myself into sports in middle and high school as an escape. I was so damn thankful when I could start playing on teams and didn't have to pay for any of it. I put in the time and the work, kept up my grades, and reveled in my athletic success. I wanted something to lose myself in, wanted to hear someone tell me *good job,* because I sure as hell never got that from my father.

And I got that. All of my coaches loved me. I played every sport they let me, minus wrestling. Never could get into that. Reminded me too much of home. Someone trying to pin me down, encourage me to fight, to break free.

Hated it.

I might have run away from my foster home when I was seventeen, but I remained in school because hell, I was on the baseball team and we were going to the division championships. I couldn't abandon them. I wanted that title. I had scouts sniffing around me for a while, but my playing abilities combined with my grades were never quite enough. I wanted to finish out my senior year, though. By that time no one was allowed to call me Will anymore and I was going by Ethan. No one questioned the change, not even my teachers. It was as if they knew.

They probably did.

I stayed with my friend Daniel, crashed on the floor of his bedroom and thanked his hot mom over and over again, though she always told me it was no bother. She'd blush furiously, like she knew I thought she was hot and she was trying to discourage a crush.

Never did anything with Daniel's mom, though I wanted to. Back then I was ashamed of any sexual feelings, afraid I would turn into some sick asshole like my dad. That scared me. I think I fixated on Daniel's mom because I didn't have one and she was so nice to me. I just . . .

Wanted someone to love me. Accept me.

If I were honest with myself, I'd know I was seeking something more with Katie than just reassuring myself that she's safe. I want to watch over her, and it's not just because I feel it's my duty.

I want her. As wrong and twisted as I know it is, I can't deny it. I want her, all for myself. When I think like that, in such possessive terms, it scares the shit out of me. Makes me feel like I'm turning into my father.

The last fucking thing I want to happen. I know I'm nothing like him. I get angry, yeah, but I don't have rage issues. I don't want to brutalize women or exert my power over them. And I definitely don't want to do that to little girls.

Dear old dad is a sick fuck. I'm just a warped individual with an unhealthy fixation on a girl from my past.

Regret and guilt course through me and I shove both feelings aside. One dinner, I tell myself, making yet another empty promise I will no doubt break. One dinner won't hurt anyone or anything. I'm playing with fire, I know. The more I get to know her, the more I talk to her, text her, fucking *think* about her, the more I want her. There's no use denying it. I may as well embrace the want.

No matter how much it might get me in trouble in the long run. If she figures me out . . .

I'm fucking done for.

I'm here now, waiting for her in the location of her choosing. Not in the town where she lives, which surprised me but again, made me proud. She's being cautious, not allowing me a deep glimpse into her personal life, though I'd give anything to know what she's thinking, specifically about me.

Katie keeps me at arm's length while we get to know each other and I understand why. It's the right thing for her to do. She's being safe.

Safe is good.

And I'm being reckless. Insane. Fucking around with something—someone—I shouldn't. Though I know it's wrong, it's as though I can't stop. I want her, all for my own. I want her to belong to me.

Have you ever experienced something that you know is so fucking wrong it only ever feels . . . right? That's what's happening right now. Talking with her on the phone—though the conversation had been brief—I'd almost fallen apart at just hearing her voice. The voice of my dreams, the same sweet voice that haunts me in my nightmares.

I hold on to that voice like a lifeline. There are so many things I want to hear her say to me, whisper to me in my ear. Forbidden, dirty things she'd probably find terrible. She's not that kind of girl. She's good and sweet and pure, a girl who's been damaged by a man who violated her and tossed her aside like yesterday's trash.

The sick cycle of what I've become isn't lost on me. I want what I can't have. I have no right to do this, to think like this, to act on this. I followed her like a stalker. Found her address after much investigating and skulked around like the asshole I've become. My behavior reminds me of . . .

My father.

Fuck.

I run a hand through my hair, pushing it off my forehead as I wait. I dressed up for her and I dress up for no one. I don't have to considering I work from home, safe at my desk, behind my laptop, on various website development projects. I took a few courses at the local community college and somehow fell into the profession. I don't make a ton of money, but it's enough. Plus I had money left over from the sale of our house. The new owner tore it down, but the area became a hot commodity considering its close location to the ocean.

So yeah, I'm not wealthy, but I'm not struggling. And I can dress up on occasion to impress a girl, though I haven't done that in a long, long time.

I'm wearing a pair of black pants and a white button-down shirt untucked, the sleeves rolled up to my elbows since it's so damn hot. The air is close, unusual for this time of year, and sweat dampens my forehead as I pace in front of the restaurant, ignoring the others who are waiting to get a table. They're all couples. Younger, older, they're chatting and laughing, sounding like they're having a good time, and I feel like I'm about to be dumped. Maybe Katie chickened out. Had second thoughts. Worried I might be something I'm not.

She'd be right.

Glancing at my phone, I check the time. She's almost ten

minutes late. Is this normal? I don't know considering I haven't closely studied her habits. I hadn't followed her around long enough to know. Since we'd started talking, I'd stopped following her, lingering in her neighborhood. I cut it all out. It felt like a violation and she's been violated enough through the years. Plus, she could recognize me. Bad enough that I have to live with what I'm doing to her. I don't need to add fuel to the fire.

I start pacing again and glance toward the parking lot when I spot her. The relief I experience at seeing her walk toward me is almost overwhelming. The lust I feel at knowing she's come to meet me is almost as strong.

As she draws closer, I notice the faint smile curving her lips. Lips that are pink and full and welcoming. Her hair is down, falling about her shoulders in casual waves, and she's wearing a dress. A dress that wouldn't be considered sexy or revealing, that covers her almost to the point of being modest, but the dark pink fabric seems to cling almost lovingly to her slight curves. The slope of her shoulders, her small, round breasts, the dip of her waist and flare of her hips.

I'm sweating, and not just from the heat. I'm sweating because the most beautiful woman I've ever seen is approaching me, offering me a shy wave, and I wave back, wanting to shout in triumph that I've got her.

I've got her.

KATHERINE

Now

The restaurant is nice, the food amazing, and the company wonderful. Our conversation was stilted at first and I blame myself. I'm not used to this sort of thing. Spending time with someone new, learning about him, being willing to allow him to try and learn about me, it's difficult.

I'd texted Brenna before I left, telling her where I was going but not telling her it was a date. It feels too new, too fresh, and I didn't want to share it. What if this dinner ended in disaster? As in, he hates me and never wants to see me again. I'd be too embarrassed to admit it, even to my sister.

Brenna swore she and Mom took the Find My Phone app off my cell, but who knows if they're telling the truth or not. I'd rather be somewhat honest with them and let them know where I'm going than receive a hysterical call from Mom in the middle of my date.

Who are you going with? Brenna had texted back when I told her my evening plans.

A friend.

I'd kept it simple, chewing on my lower lip, waiting for her to dig. She likes to do that. She knows I don't have many friends, but she's been wrapped up in her own life lately. I think she's having trouble with her boyfriend, though she'd never, ever admit it. She prefers to pretend everything's perfect between them. They have the ideal relationship, whereas I'm the damaged one who will most likely never give Mom grandkids.

Such a depressing thought, more so because we all know it's true.

Have fun! had been her reply minutes later. I could tell she was distracted. She only ever uses exclamation points when she's distracted.

"Do you have any siblings?" I ask, more like blurt out of nowhere. We're halfway through our meal, Ethan and I, and the conversation has lulled since we started to eat.

He has his fork in his mouth when I ask my question and he sets it down on the edge of his plate, chewing thoughtfully and swallowing before he answers. "No, I don't." He pauses, those rich brown eyes studying me, seeming to sparkle behind his glasses. I've never found a man who wore glasses attractive before, but when had I ever found *any* man attractive before? "What about you?"

"I have an older sister." It's my turn to pause as I consider whether I should say her name. "Brenna."

"How many years?"

I frown. "Excuse me?"

He takes a sip of water before he repeats himself. "How many years? Between the two of you?"

"Oh, about two and a half." I smile as I remember our adolescent hatred for one another. That was before. My life has been divided into two parts, the first one happy, the second one not so much. I'm hoping to turn that around. "She's my best friend."

"Whether she likes it or not?" He's teasing me, and I laugh.

"Back when we were younger, our parents used to say that. Tell us that we needed to get along because when we were older and everyone else in the family was gone, we'd only have each other. We never believed that would happen, that we would actually want to count on each other. We used to fight all the time and it drove our parents crazy."

"And now you don't."

I shrug. "She really is my best friend. I tell her almost everything."

"Did you tell her about me?"

Would the truth hurt him? "No," I admit, my voice soft. "I didn't want to explain exactly how we met."

"You mean the near purse snatching."

I nod. "I didn't want to worry her. She would . . . freak out."

"Does she do that, your older sister? Worry about you a lot?"

The truth is there, sitting right on the tip of my tongue, and I'm tempted to let it all spill out. But I can't admit everything. Not yet. He still doesn't know my last name. I don't know his. I want to keep this part of myself quiet for now. Maybe for as long as I spend time with Ethan, because I know this won't last. It can't. He'll find out what happened and bail. He should. I'm not worth sticking around for. My problems are such a heavy burden, I don't expect anyone to want to deal with them.

But it's liberating, spending time with someone who doesn't know about all your baggage. There's a freedom in just being me versus the girl who was kidnapped, held captive for days, and raped repeatedly. No pitying looks, no hesitation. I'm not easy to be around.

It's not easy being me. This is why I'm so reclusive, why I have such a hard time pushing myself out of my shell. All the therapy in the world won't really help. What's done is done. I get it. Having a father who refused to talk about what happened to me didn't help matters. We were a solid family who became dysfunctional in a matter of days. Who remained dysfunctional for years, until my father died. We're still not perfect.

Most of the time, I blame myself for our falling apart, for losing that sense of normalcy I so needed when I came back. I didn't ask to be kidnapped, but I felt responsible just the same.

Easier to blame yourself and start down a path of intense self-loathing for the rest of your life.

"Sometimes," I finally say nonchalantly. "Just like I sometimes worry about her. It's what sisters do. We watch out for each other."

"It must be nice, to have someone you can always count on." His voice sounds almost wistful. "No matter what, she'll be there for you."

"It is nice." I want to ask him if he has someone to count on but I don't. It feels too personal, too invasive, and I don't know him that well yet.

"So do you work? Have a job you love? Or are you in school? What do you do with your days?" He pushes his plate away slightly, indicating that he's finished, I guess, and my appetite flees, too, at the tone of his questions. We've only made general small talk, nothing too personal, revealing nothing too intimate. Just the way I prefer it.

But now he wants more details and I guess that's natural. I shouldn't throw up a wall, but it's such a natural defense mechanism for me, I almost can't help it. "I'm a full-time college student." All online, so I don't have to interact with anyone else in person.

He sends me a look, one I can't quite read, but it's almost as if he doubts me. "What's your major?"

"Graphic design." When I was little I loved to create things.

Draw and make crafts with lots of glitter and glue and paint. Create scrapbooks with all of Mom's stuff that she never used. She'd get so mad at me at first but after a while, she gave it all to me since she wasn't using it. I became the one who made the family vacation scrapbooks every year until the summer I turned thirteen.

We all know why I stopped. There were no more summer vacations after that year.

"Really?" His face lights up. "I'm in Web design."

"You design websites?"

He nods. "I went to community and took some courses, met this guy who was trying to start a band and wanted a website for his so-called fans, of which he had maybe, I dunno, ten? He firmly believed he was going to be a huge star. I designed his website for him and he loved it, told all of his friends about it. Turned out the guy had a lot of friends. Like, a ton, and they were all starting up businesses and wanted websites and banners for social media. My business sort of grew from there."

"That's amazing," I breathe, impressed. "You're so lucky."

"I consider myself pretty lucky, that I'm able to make a living out of something I love to do."

"So it keeps you busy."

His expression turns almost bashful. "I have a two-month wait list."

"Wow, you must be very good at your job." Now I'm definitely impressed.

"When I find something I enjoy, I throw myself into it wholeheartedly. It's like I almost become . . . obsessed." Now he looks guilty. It seems odd. "I probably shouldn't admit that to you."

"Why not?"

"I sound like a freak."

"No, you sound like someone who is passionate." My cheeks burn at saying the word and I tell myself to get over it.

"When I was in school, it was sports," he admits. "I was obsessed with any sport that ended in *ball*. Baseball, football, basketball. It's all I wanted to do."

That explains his athletic build. "Do you still play any of them?"

"Nah, not really. I had to quit so I could work. I, uh, I needed the money, so I had to give up all of my after-school activities. Every waking hour that I wasn't in school, I tried to fill with various jobs." He presses his lips together, like he didn't want to just admit that, and I know the feeling.

"Sounds like you eventually found something else to shine in, then," I say, wanting to reassure him, make him feel better.

"Yeah, I guess so." He takes a drink of his water and I study him, noting the way the light from the candle sitting in the middle of our table casts him in golden shadow. He's incredibly handsome in a raw-boned, rough-hewn way. All those sharp angles and the solid jawline, offset by that glorious mouth of his. And it really is glorious, soft and full looking. I've never really stared at a man's mouth before. Never really knew one could be so beautiful, almost feminine in the midst of masculine features. Not that he's feminine, not at all, but I like the softness. It draws me in. Makes me wonder what it might be like to . . .

"What kind of music do you like to listen to?" he asks, interrupting my thoughts.

My cheeks feel hotter and I hope he doesn't notice. Thank goodness the restaurant is relatively dark. "Are we playing twenty questions now?"

He shrugs, looking faintly embarrassed. "Just trying to get to know you."

I immediately feel like a jerk. I shouldn't be so defensive. He's not out to get me. Not out to dig up any lurid facts, and I have a ton of them. "Is it wrong to admit I like anything that's popular on the radio?"

"You still listen to the radio?" He's teasing. I can tell by the glint in his eyes.

"Sometimes." When he just looks at me I admit, "Fine, I love the iHeartRadio app."

He laughs. "Who's your favorite band or singer?"

"Don't laugh," I warn him, and he holds his hands up defensively. "You're going to laugh."

"I won't," he says solemnly.

"Promise?"

"Promise." He swallows, I see his throat move, and something washes over me at his words, the way he's watching me, his expression serious, his eyes so incredibly dark. I feel like we've said these words to each other before, though in a much more serious manner. I'm having a total déjà vu moment.

It makes me think of Will and for some inexplicable reason, I feel almost unfaithful to him, sharing this night, these words, with Ethan.

"I really, really love . . ." My voice drifts as I draw out the moment. "Katy Perry."

His lips twitch, like he's trying to hold in the laugh that wants to escape, and I point at him. "You promised."

Again he holds up his hands defensively. "I did. No laughing allowed."

I shake my head and drop my hands into my lap, clutching at the white cloth napkin still lying there. "It's lame, right?"

"Never." His lips twitch again.

I ignore the twitch and decide to tell the truth. "I just find her songs so empowering. Like 'Roar.' She wants people to hear her roar, you know?" Now I just sound ridiculous, but I really do find power in words. Written words. Books and poems and songs. Since I've always felt like I have no power, I like to look for it in other places. That way I do feel strong, at least for a little while.

However temporary it may be.

"Has anyone ever heard you roar?" he asks, his deep voice low and quiet, sending a scattering of goosebumps across my skin.

I slowly shake my head. "Not really. I'm pretty quiet."

"You're not quiet with me."

His observation makes me ponder. He's right. When I'm with him, he asks just the right things to open me up. I came into this tonight on the defensive, too. I had no plans on revealing so much. I figured we could eat dinner, talk about the weather and current events, and be done with it.

This is what happens when you've never been on a date before. You have no clue what you're supposed to do, what you should say, what the other person will say. I have no control over this moment and panic licks at my belly, reminding me that the very last thing I want to do is lose control.

I decide to ignore what he said and talk about my other favorite Katy Perry songs. "'Dark Horse' is a total favorite, too."

He cocks a brow, looking a little arrogant, a little skeptical. It's a good look for him. "Really."

I nod. "And I really loved 'Teenage Dream.'"

He frowns. "What?"

"Katy's song from a few years ago. 'Teenage Dream.'"

God, did I love that song. I would sing it at the top of my lungs when I knew I was alone, which wasn't often. I'd sing it in the shower, murmur it under my breath as I sat with Brenna or Mom in the car. The words just got to me, because even though I was a teenager when it came out, I was in no way close to living the teenage dream of letting a boy put his hands on me in my skintight jeans.

I yearned for something like that whenever I heard that song, even though the idea scared me to death.

"Ah yeah, I remember that song." He smiles. "They played it to death."

"I still love it."

"Did they used to call you that? When you were younger?" When I frown, he continues. "Katie."

"Oh." I haven't heard anyone call me that in a long time. I didn't even put it together, that Katy Perry and I share the same first name. "Yes, when I was a child."

"No one calls you Katie now?"

I shake my head.

"Kat?"

I wrinkle my nose.

"Kathy?"

"Ew. No." I laugh.

"So everyone calls you Katherine."

"Usually."

"That seems so formal." He studies me and his eyes seem to see everything. I don't know whether to squirm uncomfortably or sit up straighter and let him really see me, battle scars and all, roaring into the darkness. "You look like a Katie to me."

I like the way he says my name. His voice softens over the word, making those ever-present butterflies take flight within my belly. "You can call me that, if you want." I can't believe I just said that. Katie is part of before. It took forever to get everyone to break the habit. I didn't want to be Katie Watts anymore. Everyone knew me by that name, the entire world.

I preferred Katherine. It sounded like someone else—so sophisticated, so grown-up, so unlike me. I didn't feel like me anymore. I became someone new instead.

"I do want." The way he says *want,* it's almost . . . sexual, and sends a shiver down my spine. His expression is so serious, though there's an unfamiliar light in his gaze, like he's just won a magnificent prize and he's feeling triumphant. "I like that a lot." A pause. "Katie."

My skin warms at the tone of his voice, the way he watches me. I could get used to this.

Who am I fooling? I *am* getting used to this. Too soon. He'll hurt me if I don't watch it. That's what Brenna would say. She'd warn me to be cautious, to not let this man get too close.

But for once I'm tempted to let go of some of that control I keep myself so tightly cloaked in. Throw some of that caution I'm always holding on to to the wayside and just . . . see where it takes me. Where *he* might take me.

I want that more than anything else.

ETHAN

Now

There's nothing like a slap of reality to ruin my not-so-good intentions. I'd been on a high after my dinner with Katie. I got her to open up; I got her to be real. Our conversation might have bordered on silly—that she's a Katy Perry fan is sort of adorable—but she was honest. She allowed me a glimpse of herself and that's all I ever wanted.

Was I satisfied with only that? No. I'm a selfish bastard. Now that I've had a taste, been given that tantalizing glimpse, I want another one. I want to get closer. I want her open and raw and completely willing to give me everything that I want.

Which is her.

It's the morning after our dinner and I'm eager to text her even though it's barely eight o'clock. Ridiculous. I need to be patient, take my time. Rushing gets me nowhere, and I need to remember that. If I come on too strong I might freak her out, and that could be detrimental to our tentative friendship.

I'm at the local post office, where I keep a secret P.O. box, one for a certain William Monroe. He doesn't exist any longer, I'd made sure of that, but right before I had my name legally changed, I purchased a P.O. box with my William Monroe ID. Just in case, I told myself. I figured it was the best way to allow my father to contact me without him discovering the new me. He has no idea where I really live, or that I've changed my name.

I made sure of that.

And it's worked. It's worked for over five years, ever since I had my name legally changed. The P.O. box is not that expensive and it's well worth the money I've spent. Yeah, I get the occasional letter from prison. I also receive letters from reporters seeking me out. Once a publisher wrote me, wanting to hear my side of the story.

I ignored them all. How they found my address, I'm not sure. The P.O. box address isn't made public that I know of, but I don't necessarily make it completely private, either. And no one knows Ethan Williams is William Monroe.

No one.

Approximately once a month I stop by the post office and clean out my mailbox. I go during off times when I think no one will be around so I can sneak in with relative anonymity. I haven't received a letter from my father in over six months, maybe even closer to a year. Hell, I can't remember the last time he wrote me. It's been a relief, not hearing from him. His ranting, rambling letters are exhausting.

I pull out a pile of junk mail—newspaper mailers, postcard advertisements, the car insurance letters that are addressed to "resident." But nestled among the miscellaneous junk mail, there is a letter waiting for me. I'd recognize that scrawling handwriting anywhere.

Dread consuming me, I toss the junk mail into a nearby garbage can and stare at the letter, the return address mocking me. I slam the metal door shut, turning the key with a hard yank before I pull it out. Shoving the key into the front pocket of my jeans, I clutch the letter so hard, it crinkles in my fingers as I stride out of the post office. My head down, my breath coming fast.

I don't want to read the damn letter. But I have to.

I have to.

Waiting until I get inside my car, I tear open the envelope with shaking fingers, cursing under my breath at my nervousness. I know what made him write. I can sense it.

He saw the interview.

He saw Katie.

I pull the lined white paper out of the envelope and unfold it, surprised that it is only one page. His writing is small, every word tightly packed on each line, and I squint, trying to decipher it.

Dear Will,

It's been a long time. I haven't seen you since I don't know when and it hurts that you don't come around. I miss you. I wish you'd visit me and I try my best to understand why you don't, but it's hard. Can't say that I enjoy the way you ignore me. A man gets lonely up here without any family around. No son to smile at and see how he's doing.

It's tough in here but I stand my ground. Not that you care. Why can't you even write me? I don't know what you do, where you live. Why all the secrets? I've found God, you know. He's my savior, the Man who now guides me and has taught me right from wrong. I know what I've done is something I have to live with for the rest of my life but I've forgiven myself. Now I am in search of forgiveness from the people I've affected with my rash decisions. I hope that maybe someday you can forgive me for all the wrongs I've done to you throughout your life.

Did you see the interview with Katherine Watts? I watched it, every last awful minute of it. She lied. She makes me sick, with all of her lies. I was kind to her, as best as I could be considering at the time, I was sick. I kept her in a safe place. I was going to return her to her family. That she accused me of such filthy, horrible things . . . it hurts. What hurts worse? Because she's pretty and so young and sincere, everyone believes her. That bitch Lisa Swanson ate up every word she said. It makes me sick.

With a few choice words I look like a disturbed predator, thanks to Katherine Watts. Yes, I had issues, but I wasn't some evil monster. I wish that bitch Lisa Swanson would talk to me. I could change her mind about what kind of man I am. I'm not as bad as they make me out to be.

Katherine Watts is no pure, sweet angel either. She's a silly little whore, just like every other woman out there. Wish everyone could see that.

Hope you see it. Hope you come see me. A man needs his family, son, and you and me, we're just alike. We're all we've got.

Don't ever forget that.

Love,
Dad

I crumple the letter in my hands until it's a tight little ball pressed against my palm, my fingers curled into a fist around it. Closing my eyes, I hit the back of my head against the car seat once. Again, harder this time, like I can knock sense into my brain, but it's not working. Nothing works. His words replay on a loop in my head, taunting me, making the feeling worse.

Silly little whore. I look like a disturbed predator. I miss you. You and me, we're just alike. We're all we've got. Don't ever forget that.

He makes me feel like shit. Worse, he makes me feel wrong. Reminds me that what I'm doing with Katie, it's wrong. Seeking her out, following her, even rescuing her at the park, I should've never interfered with her life. I walked away from her before and I should have stayed away.

I took my need to find her too far. I became obsessed. I *am* obsessed—with Katie. With seeing her, with the way she makes me feel, how my heart twists when she smiles, how her eyes light up when she looks at me. It's all fucked up, a mixture of memories and fantasies, the past and now. I've made a mess of things. Like usual.

Like always.

Like my father.

The ultimate in taking it too far was meeting her for dinner, like we were on a real date or something. Making conversation, revealing little bits and pieces to each other, like we were strangers and how we met was completely random.

It's all a lie. She's such a part of my life, my past, it's like she's permanently imprinted on my heart, seared into my fucking soul. Her words are on my skin and she has no idea. No fucking clue. I sat across from her and smiled and nodded and gently teased her about her love for anything Katy Perry and I'm the ultimate liar.

Reaching out, I grip the steering wheel so tight my knuckles turn white. I grit my teeth, exhale through them, and stare out the window at nothing. My heart is thundering as though I just ran ten miles and no matter what I try to do, no matter how hard I try to forget, all I can think about is her.

Katie.

I'm sick of the lies I tell. My entire life is a lie. I need to do right by this girl, no matter how much it hurts me. I need to leave her alone. Never contact her again. It's what's best.

I'm obsessed, but I know better. I'm bad for her. I'll ruin her. Because I'm just like him—and he will never let me forget it.

KATHERINE

Now

"I met a man."

Dr. Harris glances up from the iPad where she takes her notes—I would never, ever want to see those notes about me, *God no*—and smiles faintly. "Did you now? Was that on your list of goals? Meeting a man?"

She sounds so neutral, like it's no big deal that I met someone. When it was the absolute biggest deal ever for me.

Until it wasn't—at least for him.

I nod, anger firing my blood as I launch into the entire story. How he saved me from the potential purse-snatchers, though I don't mention where I went. Why I keep my visit to the amusement park a secret, I'm not sure, but I don't really want a lecture about moving too fast. So I keep it to myself, burying yet another dirty little secret deep inside.

Stupid.

Dr. Harris remains quiet as I talk, eventually abandoning her tablet to concentrate solely on me. I pour out my heart, as hard as it is to do. I tell her how I felt instantly connected to Ethan as we talked over coffee, that he asked me to text him when I arrived home so he'd know I was safe and we exchanged cell numbers. That we even met for dinner.

How I haven't heard from him since and it's been over a week.

"You feel abandoned," she states after I finish my story.

"Of course, I do." I throw my hands up, giving her the universal *duh* expression. "For the first time in my adult life I show interest in a guy, actually go out on what I thought was a date with a man. I thought he liked me, too. He said he would call me. And he hasn't."

The pain from Ethan's apparent rejection is almost unbearable and I hate that I'm so focused on it. I know it's silly and I feel like a dumb teenage girl, but I thought . . . I truly thought he liked me.

Dr. Harris sets her iPad on a nearby table and folds her hands in her lap. "Who does Ethan remind you of?"

I frown. "What do you mean?"

"How he's treating you. Does his behavior remind you of anyone?" She's prodding. Fishing. I'm supposed to figure this out on my own because she's already put it all together.

We're quiet as I mull over her question. The minute it clicks, I don't want to admit it. "My father," I confess reluctantly.

"That you realize this so quickly is good," she says, sounding pleased. "You're making progress."

Here we go. "I suppose."

"Beyond his looks—he is handsome, I assume?" When I nod she continues. "What else attracted you to him? How he jumped in and protected you without hesitation?"

Yes. Absolutely. But that trait is nothing like my father, considering he did nothing to protect me after everything that happened.

"He became your hero. And I think you'd like one. You *want* a hero."

I *had* a hero. My father was my hero throughout my childhood. For a very brief, very dark period of my life, Will Monroe became my hero. I craved his attention, so much that I think I drove him away. And now . . . what? Ethan is my new hero?

Ridiculous.

"I don't want a hero," I retort.

"But you like it when someone steps in and rescues you," she points out, and I don't deny it. I can't. "Were you scared when those boys tried to take your purse?"

Terribly. All the fear had turned into something else when Ethan stepped in. Excitement. Arousal.

Shame washes over me. I don't dare admit that. Do I?

"Did Ethan scare you?" she asks when I still haven't answered her first question.

"Yes. I didn't know who he was. He just—he immediately took charge and shoved me out of the way. I almost fell and at first, I wondered if he was with them. But then he grabbed the boy's shirt and threatened him. He looked so incredibly angry, it was frightening."

"Did it also excite you? Seeing his anger? How he wanted to hurt those boys who were trying to hurt you?"

I bend my head, not wanting to face her. "Yes." My voice is shaky. "And that's the last thing I should feel, right? Me? Excited by violence?"

"There's no right or wrong in the way you feel, Katherine. If you were excited, no one will judge you. And if you're angry now because he hasn't contacted you, I can't blame you. Your feelings are valid. They belong to you and no one else. Remember that," she says gently.

It's hard to remember when you've been filled with shame over what happened to you most of your life.

"I haven't been angry in a long time." I look up, casting my gaze out the window. It's a gloomy day, cloudy and cold, fitting nicely with my mood. "I've been sad and depressed and cautious and overwhelmed. I can't remember the last time I was mad."

"How does it feel?"

"Liberating." Our gazes meet and I start to laugh. "Empowering."

"That's good," she encourages. "There's nothing wrong with a little anger now and then."

"He should be afraid if he tries to call me now. I might go off on him." Laughter still tinges my voice but it sounds kind of . . . sad. And I doubt I would really go off on him, but it seems like the right thing to say.

"When was the last time you were happy?"

My laughter dies and I become quiet. Too quiet. My mind flips through memories as if they were flash cards, one after the other, going back years. "That morning, before it all happened," I say, tears springing to my eyes. I've been on an emotional edge ever since I did that stupid interview. "I was normal then. Nothing bothered me. I had my mom and dad and my best friend with me and they didn't think I was a freak. They didn't treat me like damaged goods, like something they should be ashamed of, you know? Well, Brenna acted like she hated me half the time but I didn't care. I hated her most of the time, too."

"Is that really the last memory of when you felt genuinely happy?" Dr. Harris asks.

"Yes." I squeeze my eyes shut, trying to stop the tears, but it's no use. They flow down my cheeks and I wipe them away. "Any happiness that I experience now is so fleeting it's hard for me to hold on to. Or it's always overshadowed by another emotion. You know what I mean? I can be happy, but there's always something else lingering. Pure happiness feels like a myth."

"I find it interesting that two such warring emotions happened within such a short time," Dr. Harris says. "You were happy and terrified, both in one day."

A fact I've never realized before. "No matter how much I try to forget that day, I can't. Both the good and the bad memories cling to me. The joy of being at the park, one of my favorite places to go, there with my best friend, is a good memory. But it becomes tainted by—him. Those days he held me captive, what he did, they're always front and center in my brain. Telling my story on TV didn't purge it all away like I hoped."

"Did you really believe you'd be able to purge it all that quickly? You only just did the interview, Katherine. It will take time, like everything else. Your quest to finding your true self is a process. We discussed this before."

If I could punch my counselor, I so would. I'm sick of everything taking time. I want the instant fix, no matter how unreal my expectations are. I want it.

I deserve it.

I keep my phone off during my appointments with Dr. Harris, not that anyone reaches out to me beyond Mom and Brenna. I've given up on Ethan—as much as I can. I compartmentalize my emotions; I always have. Dad's disgusted by me? Put him away in box one. My best friend, Sarah, ditches me at school and won't be my friend anymore? Shove her into box number two.

Ethan won't talk to me? No problem—I'll just stash him away in box number three and never deal with him again. His loss, I tell myself.

I'm tired of dealing with emotions triggered by the actions of the people in my life. I did nothing. He's responsible for this mess. Not me.

Irritating as it is, hope still lights the tiniest flame in my chest when I turn my phone back on and see the usual junk emails load up my in-box, the class assignments under the email address I use for school.

Imagine my surprise when I see a text from the very person I'd been secretly hoping for.

> I'm going to have to cancel our meeting this afternoon. Sorry. Hope we can meet tomorrow at the same time instead?

Okay, clearly that message wasn't meant for me. Could it be a work thing and he sent it to me by accident? That wouldn't be good. I should reply. Let him know about his mistake.

Yet jealousy rears its nasty head. What if that message is for another girl? Not like we had anything close to a commitment. I have no business feeling this way. There could be a long list of women he texts throughout the day.

Irritated, I shove the phone back into my purse and stalk across the parking lot, heading toward my car. The clouds are low, creating a mist that I can feel dust my skin, dot my hair, and I glance up at the sky, wishing I could do things differently. Do them over and take a different route, though it's pointless to think like this. There are no take-backs in life.

My real problem is I'm emotionally exhausted after my appointment with Dr. Harris, which is typical. Facing all my demons, talking about the bad stuff leaves me drained.

No matter how much I want to, I can't change my past. Not even what happened between Ethan and me. What's done is done. Though I wish I knew what ruined it. I believed we had a connection. I felt it. Did he? Maybe not. Maybe it was all me? It had to have been me. Maybe he discovered who I really am. All it would take is a simple Google search, though he'd have to figure out my last name. If he did discover who I am, that would turn off any normal guy.

Too much baggage, he'd think. Too damaged.

I've turned the night of our dinner over and over again in my head and I still can't figure out where everything went wrong.

I'll probably never figure it out.

Unlocking the car, I climb into the driver's seat and slam the door, jam the key into the ignition, and start the motor. But I don't move. It's like I'm consumed with thoughts of that stupid text that wasn't even meant for me. I should ignore it. He doesn't deserve to hear from me ever again. He's a jerk who lost his chance.

Right?

He's a jerk I wish I could see again, as stupid as that sounds.

Unable to stand it any longer, I pull my phone out of my purse and type Ethan a reply.

I think you meant to send this to someone else. ☺

I agonize over that stupid smiley face like it's the most important thing on the planet. Finally deciding against it, I hit the back button, delete the too-cheery symbol, and hit send.

And pray I don't look like an idiot.

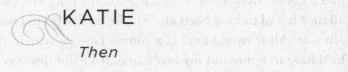

KATIE

Then

"Why can't I see him?" I was in a hospital bed, all bandaged up, and Mom sat by my side. They wrapped my ribs and my wrist, which I somehow sprained during my days in captivity. The cut on my mouth still throbs, though they said it wasn't bad enough for stitches. The bruise on my cheek—the one he caused when he slapped me so hard that first day—is already fading.

They decided to keep me in the hospital for a few days—for observation, they called it. They'd already poked and prodded me in every way conceivable, so I couldn't imagine what more they wanted to observe. Maybe they were afraid I would lose my mind and try to kill myself.

Too late. I already feel dead inside.

"See who?" The confused expression on Mom's face wasn't a surprise. She'd looked that way from the moment we were reunited, when they first saw me in that tiny interrogation room in the back of the police station. My parents had clung to me and we all cried together for what felt like forever.

There were no more tears at the hospital, only confusion and questions. Lots and lots of questions, ones I had to answer again and again, to the point where I felt like I was on constant repeat.

"Will," I whispered, irritated that she wasn't really paying attention to me. She was too distracted by some suited-up guys that stood in the hall outside my hospital room. Men who would probably come in here at any minute and ask me yet another set of questions.

I was so sick of it.

Horror filled Mom's eyes and she shook her head, her mouth thinned into a tight line. "Absolutely not," she said vehemently. "You can't talk to that boy ever again."

My heart cracked. Beyond my family and Sarah, Will was the only other person I wanted to see. I needed to know he was all right. He took care of me and it was my turn to take care of him. "Why? I just want to thank him for helping me." I was whining but I didn't care. "He's not the enemy, Mom."

"He's the son of that—that horrible man, so he is most definitely the enemy," Mom said with a nod of finality. One that read *over my dead body will I let you see that boy.*

"I just want to thank him," I said again. I sank my head into the pillow, closing my eyes. No one really listened to me when it came to Will. They wouldn't tell me what they were thinking, but I figured them out. They hated him. The police. My parents. The detectives and the doctors and the nurses—I could tell by the way they all exchanged knowing glances when I brought up his name. They believed he had something to do with this. It was like they wanted me to confess that he hit me and raped me, too, even though I denied it over and over.

They didn't care. They wouldn't listen.

"He didn't help his father," I told Mom, speaking to her back. She stared at the doorway, wringing her hands in her lap. "He helped me. He saved me. The only reason we're together right now is because of him. Because of *Will*."

She glanced over her shoulder, her eyes clouded with worry.

"You're confused, darling. Please, just . . . stop talking about him. He's not worth your time or energy. The cops say that he's been in trouble before but they can't say how because he's a juvenile. He's no good. You need to forget he even exists."

I couldn't give her what she wanted. "But I *can't* forget that he exists. He's the reason I'm alive." My entire body ached. My arms, my legs, my back, my throat, between my legs . . . it all hurt so bad and I didn't know how it could be fixed. Time, the doctor had told me. The bruises would eventually fade. The sprained wrist would soon be as good as new. The broken ribs would heal.

Would my broken heart ever heal? I wanted to ask but I remained quiet. I'm pretty positive he wouldn't have the answer.

"You're alive because of *you*," she said, turning to face me once more. "You're a survivor. No one helped you. You did it all yourself."

Was my mother delusional? She hadn't been there, I had. And Will Monroe was the one who got me out of that storage shed, no one else.

"Mom, you sound crazy," I whispered, and she glared at me. "I don't know how many times I have to tell you this. The cops said it, too—Will was the one who saved me."

Her gaze flickered, like she couldn't stand the fact that I would even dare say his name. "Then write him a letter," she suggested, as if that were the perfect solution. "Write him a nice letter and thank him for all that he did for you. That should suffice."

"I don't know his address." A letter wouldn't be enough to express my gratitude. I couldn't come up with the words to tell him how much it meant, what he did for me. It wasn't just about me thanking him, either—I needed the connection with Will. He was the only person in this entire world who knew what I went through. He understood what happened. He saw me at my worst, in stained, old clothes, chained to a wall, lying on a filthy mattress after I'd been beaten. And still he took care of me.

"Someone will know," she said as her head swiveled toward the doorway again. But the men in suits were gone.

Good.

"No, I don't think they will. I think they're going to put him in foster care, since his—father is missing and his mom isn't around." My mother looked shocked that I knew so much about Will, but she couldn't understand. People bonded when they spent time together trying to survive.

"Katie, you're being difficult." She sighed and pinched the bridge of her nose. "Send the letter to the police station. I'm sure they'll forward it on to him."

"It's silly to have a letter forwarded to him when he's probably in this hospital right now, getting checked out, like me." I leaned forward. The sudden movement made my head swim, and I lay back against the pillow carefully. "I don't want to send him a letter, Mom, I want to see him. I want to talk to him. Just for a few minutes. Do you know if he's here? Are they keeping him like they're keeping me?"

"He's not in the hospital. He wasn't even hurt," Mom sniffed. Like this was some sort of contest and I took first prize for the ugliest wounds. "They were holding him at the police station, but they've probably already let him go. For all we know he could be in jail. They might've found out some information we don't know about."

Dread trickled ice cold down my spine. No way would

they put him in jail. He was just a kid. He didn't do anything wrong. "Ask the detectives over there. I bet they know where he is." I waved my hand to try to get their attention and Mom lunged from her chair, pinning my arm to the hospital bed, her face in mine. I reared back, startled by her reaction, uncomfortable with her closeness. My heart was racing as I blinked up at her.

"*No.* I'm sorry, Katie, but I refuse to let you see that boy ever again." She stared at me, her eyes wide and full of fear and disgust and a few other emotions I didn't recognize. "He's not—he's not good for you. I don't want you spending time with him."

"He's my friend." Tears fell down my cheeks and I wiped at them furiously, not even aware I was crying until I felt them dampening my skin. "Doesn't that matter?"

"You need no reminders of what happened." She stood and wrung her hands together, like she'd just rid herself of all that unpleasantness. "It's time to move on. Not relive what happened to you again and again."

"Well, the detectives aren't helping me with the reliving part, what with their constant questions," I retorted, crossing my arms in front of my chest. But the movement only caused me pain and I winced, letting my arms fall to my sides.

She sent me a look. "Stop being obtuse. You know what I mean. That boy." Her lips screwed up into the ugliest pout I'd ever seen. At this very moment, she looked so vulnerable, so old. When did she get so old? There were wrinkles around her eyes, her lips were thin, and her hair—I could see gray mixed with the dark blond strands. I felt bad. Really bad. Did what happened to me age her that quickly? "There's no hope for him. Believe me. Seeing him will only dredge up unpleasant memories and I want you healing, not trying to relive everything."

"So you're not going to let me see him." My voice was more breath than sound and my heart hurt at the realization that I might never see Will again.

She shook her head, her expression firm. "It's pointless."

According to her.

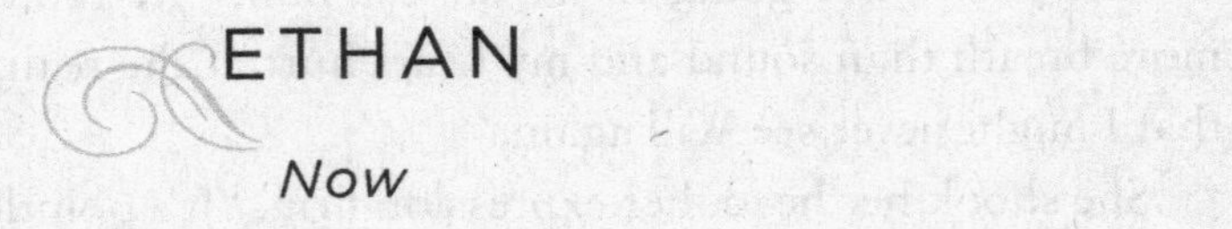

ETHAN

Now

I think you meant to send this to someone else.

I stare at the text on my screen from Katie, nerves eating at my gut. Last night I'd been feeling lonely and read over our few text messages like a lovesick idiot. I never got out of the text conversation with Katie when I sent the message to my client Linda, asking if we could reschedule our afternoon meeting for tomorrow.

Instead of texting Linda, I'd texted Katie.

If I ignore her I'm a dick. If I answer . . . I'm still a dick, because I've avoided her for over a week. I had no plans to contact her again. After that letter from my father, I knew I couldn't keep this up. Toying with someone's emotions when the person is already so fragile is dangerous and cruel.

I'm not sure if I'm talking about Katie or myself.

I text my client first, resending her the message that I can't meet today, and she immediately replies saying that's fine. I've fallen a little behind on projects and I can only blame it on my twisted feelings for Katie. Despite not seeing her for the last nine days, I still think about her. Constantly.

Too much.

Her text haunts me and I switch to that conversation, staring at what she wrote. I can hear her voice, sweet and hesitant. I can see her face, those big blue eyes, her slightly pursed lips.

I don't know how to reply without looking like an asshole, but not saying anything is worse, so I decide to keep it short.

Thanks for letting me know.

I hit send before I can add anything else and pray like hell she doesn't reply right away. Or ever.

My phone buzzes and I close my eyes. Breathe deep. Open my eyes to read Katie's reply.

You're welcome.

That's it. I exhale in relief. In disappointment. What did I expect? A warm greeting? A pissed-off "where have you been"? She wouldn't do that. She's too sweet, too hesitant, too unsure. She doesn't date, she's never had a relationship, and here I am toying with her like a complete prick.

But I can't resist her. I don't want to resist her. It's like I have this need inside me that keeps growing and growing.

The need to see, to touch Katie.

I clutch my phone tight, stare at the screen. Start typing before I can stop myself.

How are you?

Good.

A pause.

And you?

She's being polite. I need to stop communicating with her. I'm just getting myself in deeper and soon I won't be able to climb out of the hole I've dug myself. I'm already in too deep.

I feel like shit.

Her reply is immediate.

Why? Have you been sick?

I haven't called you or texted you.

My fingers hover above the keyboard. *Fuck it.*

I'm sorry.

I wait for her reply and it feels like forever before I finally get it.

For what?

For ignoring you.

Is that what you were doing?

Running my hand through my hair, I contemplate what to say next. I shouldn't say a damn thing. Leave it at the apology and quit this conversation for good. But . . . I can't. It's so damn hard. I want more. When it comes to Katie, I always want more. It's killing me that I haven't seen her. I want to see her. Talk to her. Make her smile, make her laugh.

I finally answer her.

Yeah, I was. And I'm sorry about that. It was a dick move.

My phone rings, startling me, and . . . *fuck.*

It's her. Of course.

The moment I answer she starts talking.

"Why would you ignore me? I mean, maybe I shouldn't ask this sort of question, but I have to know. Did you—did you find out something about me that you can't deal with? Because if that's the case, I can totally understand why you're ignoring me. *I'd* ignore me if I could." She laughs, like it's so hilarious, but it's not. It's sad, her making jokes about what happened to her. How she's afraid I discovered her truth and ignored her because of it.

If she ever discovered mine, she'd freak the hell out.

"Katie." I say her name quietly, my voice low and measured. She immediately quiets. "What are you talking about?"

She sighs, the sound so wistful it goes straight to my dick. *Jesus.* I need to get a grip. "I should've never called you."

I clutch the phone tighter, as if I'm holding on to her. "I'm glad you did."

"Did I do something wrong?" Her voice sounds so small, so far away. "I'm not very good at this sort of thing."

"What sort of thing?"

"This dating thing. This boy/girl thing. God, I sound like a child." She sighs again, though this time in irritation. "There's so much I should tell you."

"You don't have to tell me anything you're not comfortable with," I say, not ready to play true confessions. If she starts talking, that'll make me feel like I should start talking, and I can't tell her who I am.

I just . . . I can't.

"Then I won't tell you a thing. My entire life is a blank slate." She laughs again, the sound raw, like it's scraping her throat. "I've—I've been through a lot, Ethan. It's not pretty."

I close my eyes and lean back in my chair, making it rock gently. I'd given up on pretending to work a while ago. Now that I have Katie actually on the phone talking to me, I won't get shit done the rest of the day, I can guarantee it. And hearing her allude to her past just about rips me apart. "We all have." It sounds lame, but it's the truth.

"I've been through more than the average person. I'm . . . broken. A mess." Her voice cracks and she clears her throat. "I have serious hang-ups."

"What sort of hang-ups?"

"I . . ." She blows out a harsh breath and laughs yet again, this time nervously. "I can't believe I'm about to say this, but maybe it's easier because I don't have to see you, you know?"

"I do know," I say gently. "I get it, Katie."

She's silent for a moment and I forget that no one calls her Katie anymore.

Except me.

"I have issues . . . sexually." She squeaks out the last word. "And it all stems from a traumatic experience in my past that was really—it was really bad."

I blow out a harsh breath. This is an impossible conversation. The guilt that threatens to overtake me darkens all my edges, making me feel like a complete shit. "How bad?"

"On a scale of one to ten? Twenty."

This is the last thing I want to hear. How my father—my fucking *father*—brutalized her to the point that he completely ruined her life. That she calls herself broken. That she has sexual issues. All because of him.

I hate him. I need to right his wrongs. I need to make this girl feel wanted. Needed. Strong. Beautiful. Sexy.

Because she is. She's all of those things. She just doesn't know it.

"Yet here you are, brave enough to call and ask why I was ignoring you," I point out. "That's pretty ballsy, Katie."

More laughter, though it's genuine this time. "I was feeling brave. I just left my appointment with my therapist and was a little irritable. A lot angry."

At me, I can only assume. I deserve her anger. She should

remain angry with me forever, for how I'm tricking her. But maybe . . . maybe I can help her. "You want to take your anger out on me?"

"I took it out on Dr. Harris instead." She still sounds the tiniest bit irritated. "I'm glad you didn't ignore my call, Ethan," she murmurs, her soft voice curling through my veins, simmering under my skin like warm, fragrant smoke.

The urge to see her pushes me to the point that I can't even think straight. It's like she consumes me, and I say the first thing that comes into my head.

"Can I see you tonight?"

She hesitates and for a moment, I think I've blown it. If she tells me no, I won't ask again. I might want to help her find the confidence my father destroyed, but I know I'm walking a fine line here. I say one wrong thing, I give away one clue that reveals who I really am, and I'm done for.

So it's now or never. She says yes, I'm in. She says no, I walk.

"I'd like that," she finally says.

I'm in.

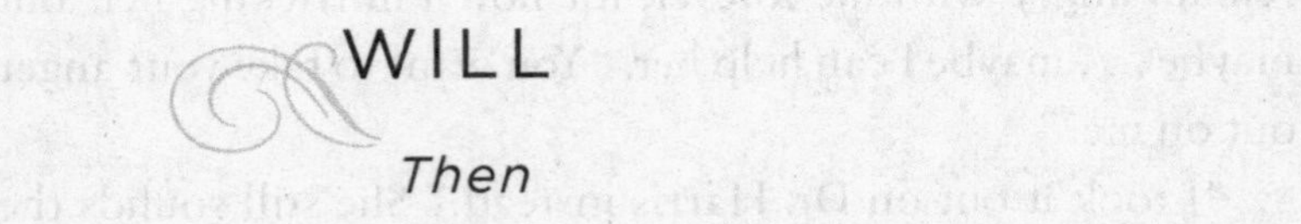

WILL

Then

"You won't give me her address." I glared at the detective, the one who'd taken pity on me and showed me some kindness, unlike the rest of them. They all hated me with the exception of one Detective Ross Green. Somehow, he saw something no one else noticed.

That I was telling the truth.

"I can't. Her parents won't allow it. We have to respect their privacy." Detective Green smiled gently at me, his eyes full of sympathy. "Why do you want it? It's probably not a good idea, trying to contact her right now. Her parents won't talk to anyone, not even the media."

"I have something for her. A—a gift." My cheeks were warm and I figured I was blushing. I'd never bought a girl a gift before, so this was embarrassing. "I just want her to know that I'm thinking about her."

I couldn't stop thinking about her. I worried. Was she dealing with everything okay? Did she feel safe? Was her reunion with her parents all she hoped it would be? Were the cops treating her all right? They wouldn't stop asking me questions. They were mean as shit toward me most of the time. Treated me like I was the damn criminal, taking it out on me since my dad had gone on the run.

"You're thinking about her." Green watched me. We were at a fast-food place not far from the station. I'd asked him to meet with me and my temporary foster mom had dropped me off a few minutes ago. She thought I was meeting with the detective because he wanted to ask more questions about the case. My dad was still on the run; it had only been a week since Katie and I showed up at the police station and the police were in almost constant contact with me.

But really my sole purpose was to dig up information on Katie. I missed her like she was a part of me and now I'd lost a limb. I dreamed about her; her voice and face haunted my thoughts, and I didn't know what that said about me.

All I knew was that I was dying to see her. Talk to her. Make sure she was all right.

"Yeah. I just—I need to know she's okay," I admitted, clearing my throat. I squirmed in my chair, uncomfortable with my confession. Did this make me a freak, that I worried about her? What we'd been through together—it wasn't normal. No one else understood. Only Katie and I did.

"She's doing fine," Green finally said as he rested his forearms on the edge of the table. He hadn't ordered any food for himself, just a drink, but I was devouring a double cheeseburger and a large fries, paid for by the detective, like he knew I was starving. My foster parents were typical beachside vegetarians. It sucked.

Relief flooded me but I tried to act cool. "Good." I shoved a wad of fries into my mouth.

"I shouldn't be telling you this but her parents aren't dealing with this very well, especially her dad." Green paused, his gaze meeting mine. "He thinks you're to blame."

I about choked on my fries at Green's words. Grabbing my soda, I took a sip to get the food down before I could speak. "What are you talking about? How am I to blame?"

"They think you had something to do with abducting Katie. At the amusement park," Green explained. "That you lured her in."

I set my cup down on the table, frustration making me wish I could tear something apart. "You've all thought that about me at one point or another. You know it's not true."

"I do. I've convinced my colleagues that isn't the case, too. The Wattses? They still believe you're involved. They're not satisfied with us letting you go."

It was difficult to comprehend what Green was telling me. "Are you serious?"

He nodded. "They want someone to blame. They want your father behind bars. Because he's still on the loose, you're the next best thing. That's my theory, at least."

I glanced out the window of the restaurant to watch a family of four as they exited their car and made their way to the front entrance. Smiling parents, two girls, one who looked close to my age, the other a little younger. They looked nice. Normal. Without a care in the world.

I envied them with every fiber of my being.

"Do you guys know where he's at?" I asked, my voice low, my appetite gone. I didn't like thinking about him, where he might be. What he might be doing. What if he was grabbing other little girls? What if he'd killed another one? They went through the storage shed and our house. There was enough evidence to arrest him for the kidnapping and rape of Katie and the murders of at least three other girls.

That had shocked me, when Green revealed that information to me the second day that they called me back to the police station. I had no idea he'd done this to other girls. That he'd . . . killed them.

My dad. The killer. I couldn't wrap my head around it.

"We've had some leads." Green's lips went thin. "You know I can't reveal too much."

"Sure. Yeah." I nodded, tapping my foot against the leg of the table. "He's not gonna—he's not gonna come after me, is he?"

"We don't think so, but we have surveillance on your foster family's home, just in case."

My jaw dropped open. "Are you fucking serious?" I sat up straighter when he glared at me. "Sorry. I'm just . . . I had no idea."

"I'm serious. We take your safety seriously. There's also surveillance on Katie, in case he decides to come after her again."

"He won't do that," I said with such confidence Green looked at me oddly. "He doesn't want the trouble. That's why he ran."

"We'll find him, Will. I promise," Green said with a slight nod.

I said nothing. Promises were made to be broken. I tried my best to keep the promise I made to Katie and I think I somehow fucked that up. I got her to safety, got her out of that storage shed, but did I really help her?

I don't know.

"If I give you my gift for Katie, will you make sure she receives it?" I pulled the envelope out of the back pocket of my jeans and slid it across the table.

Green picked up the legal-sized envelope and shook it. "Can I ask what's in there?"

"Jewelry." I shrugged, uncomfortable. "A bracelet. I liked the charm on it."

"A charm bracelet?"

"Sort of. There's a guardian angel on it. Someone to watch

over her since I can't be there to help her any longer," I explained, dropping my head so I could study what was left of my burger. I didn't want to see Green's eyes, the expression on his face. I felt weird, telling him this. I didn't want to share my feelings for Katie with this guy.

I couldn't even understand them myself.

"That's nice of you, Will. Real nice." Green's voice was gentle, and I glanced up to watch as he slipped the envelope in the inside pocket of his jacket. "I'll make sure Katie gets this, okay? Even if I have to hand-deliver it myself."

Relief poured through me and I leaned against the back of my seat. "Okay. Yeah. That's cool. Thanks. I appreciate it."

KATHERINE

Now

"Where are you going?"

I glance up to see Mrs. Anderson standing in her front yard, watching me as I walk down the steps from my porch and head for my car, which is parked in my driveway. A low fence divides our property and she's standing on her side, an empty plastic watering can dangling from her fingers.

"Hi," I say as I make my way toward her. Both Mom and Brenna find my elderly neighbor completely annoying, what with how nosy she is, but I like it. Her nosiness means she cares, at least a little bit.

"You look pretty." She gives me a critical glance, taking in my outfit. I'm wearing a pair of black leggings with black ankle boots and an oversized midnight-blue sweater, my hair up in a bun. Nothing special, but I know this particular shade of blue looks good on me. "Doing something special tonight?"

"Sort of." I want to hop up and down like a little kid, but I keep myself contained. "I'm going on a date."

Mrs. Anderson's eyebrows rise. "Oh really? I figured you didn't do that sort of thing. Or you kept your love life a secret because maybe you were a lesbian or something."

I burst out laughing and shake my head. "I just haven't really ever met anyone who interested me before." That was the truth. And despite the fact that Ethan ignored me for the last few days, I appreciated his honesty when we talked earlier. I can only wonder if he appreciated mine. But my excitement overrides my nerves because I get to see him tonight and I can't . . . I can't wait.

"I like that. You're picky. I was picky. Took me a long time to find my Mr. Anderson. But when I met him, I knew." She nods, her gaze turning wistful. I knew she lost her husband a few years ago to cancer and that she still missed him terribly.

"You knew what?" I ask.

"That he was the man for me. Once I set eyes on him, I saw no one else. He was *it*." Her gaze narrows. "Where are you going? Why isn't he coming here to pick you up like a proper gentleman?"

"I don't know him that well and I don't want him to, uh, know where I live yet." I wince, feeling silly. My privacy issues aren't normal. I know this. "I'm a very private person."

"That's good. Real good. There are too many creepy guys out there. You didn't meet this boy on one of those dating websites, did you?"

"No, nothing like that." I smile. "I should get going. Have a good night, Mrs. Anderson."

"You too, Katherine! You should come over tomorrow morning for coffee and tell me all about your date!" She waves after me as I go to my car, and I turn around and smile.

"I'll try." I slip inside my car and shut the door, smiling like an idiot as I start the ignition. If Brenna were here, she'd be going off about my nosy neighbor who's only offering up coffee so she can dig info out of me.

But I don't mind. Who else am I going to talk about my date with? I can't tell Mom and Brenna I've met someone. Not yet. It feels too new, too uncertain, and I want to keep him my secret. At least for a little while.

I start the car and let the engine warm up as I pull my iPhone out of my purse and check the maps app. I put in the address of the movie theater where we are meeting and I hit start, ready to be guided since I've never been to this particular theater before. I push my sleeves up, the angel charm on my bracelet snagging on the fabric, and I carefully remove the thread that got caught on my angel.

Rubbing my thumb over the bowing guardian angel whose giant wings are spread over her in protection, I think of the person who gave this bracelet to me. Wonder yet again if he's all right, if he's happy, wherever he is.

I hope so.

"Do you like popcorn?"

I'm standing next to Ethan in line at the concession stand, staring up at the menu, trying my best not to stare at him. It's so difficult because for whatever reason, he's extra attractive tonight and he smells so good. The scent of popcorn fills the air but I barely notice it.

All I can smell is the woodsy, clean scent of Ethan.

"I love popcorn," I say, turning to smile up at him. He's watching me, a crooked smile curving his lips, and my breath hitches in my throat. "With extra butter," I add weakly.

"And M&Ms?"

I frown. "M&Ms? What do you mean?"

"I always like to buy a box of M&Ms and dump them into the popcorn," he explains as we move forward in the line. It's long. I blame the weather. It started raining as I drove over here and I figure everyone else wants to get out of the rain, too.

"It's good?"

"The best," he says with absolute authority. "That mixture of salty and sweet? Delicious."

"Then let's try it," I say, making his smile grow.

"You won't regret it." His gaze locks with mine, those dark

brown eyes soft and melting, and I sort of lose myself in them for a little while. I'm loving this, loving how normal it feels. A bona fide movie date where we talk about popcorn and candy like two regular people.

I can't remember the last time I felt regular.

When we finally get to the front of the line, Ethan won't let me pay for a thing. He wouldn't let me buy my movie ticket, either, though I tried. In the end, I help carry the giant soda we're going to share and he grabs the bucket of popcorn and box of candy. I make sure to stuff a pile of napkins in my tiny purse because I saw the girl behind the counter pump all that extra butter over the popcorn. Our fingers are going to be a greasy mess.

I don't mind, though. I'm not counting calories or worried about eating a bunch of junk food. Tonight, I'm having fun. I'm not Katherine Watts, kidnapped girl. I'm just Katie, watching a movie with Ethan.

"I hope you like action films," he tells me as we walk into the hushed quiet of the theater. "I hear this one has lots of car chases and shoot-'em-up scenes."

"I don't mind." I didn't. My father and I used to watch these sorts of movies all the time when I was little. *Die Hard* was his favorite movie of all time and he could quote almost all the lines, which used to make me laugh.

But that was before. One of the few fond memories I have of my dad.

"I hear this one is funny, too." We pause at the bottom of the stadium seating and I notice there aren't a lot of people in the theater tonight. The movie has already been out for a few weeks and there are a couple of more recent and very popular films playing tonight, so I figure that's where everyone is. "Where should we sit?"

"I like to sit high and in the middle," I suggest, and he nods his approval.

He follows me as we walk up the stairs, and I feel really self-conscious. I tuck a few stray hairs behind my ear and clutch the giant soda in my other hand, hoping like crazy I don't drop it. His closeness makes me nervous. I can feel him just behind me, his body heat radiating toward me. I sort of want to snuggle up against all that warmth and I never, ever want to do that.

I pick an empty aisle and we settle into seats in the exact center. I pull the armrest down and set the soda in the slot. Ethan looks at it, then looks at me. "I hate these armrests."

"You do?" I frown.

He nods, pulls the soda out of the slot, and takes a sip. "I don't mind if you want to hold it on the other side, if you don't mind me asking for a drink every once in a while."

"Um, okay. Sure." I take the soda from him and stare at the straw, where his lips just were. I didn't even think this through. We're going to share a drink, which means my lips are going to rest on the spot where his lips just were. Which is the stupidest thought ever, because right now I sound like a thirteen-year-old girl with a massive crush. It's just that I've never done this sort of thing before and it makes me feel giddy and stupid, and I . . .

I love it.

I sip from the straw, glancing up to find him watching me, the dim lights above causing a slight reflection on his glasses so I can't quite tell how he's looking at me. He's hard to read sometimes. I probably am, too.

The moment I slip the soda into the slot on my left armrest, Ethan's lifting up the one that divides us, smiling at me. "That's better. I always feel like my elbows constantly bang into these things." He lifts up the one on the other side of him, too.

All I can think is how much closer we can get without the barrier between us. This is only our second official date, third if you count the afternoon we had coffee, but I'm anxious. Excited. I want to be closer to him.

He rests the bucket of popcorn in his lap and tears open the box of M&Ms, sprinkling them over the top and then shaking the bucket so the candy sinks deeper. He does this a few more times, emptying the entire box of candy into the bucket before he thrusts it toward me. "Try it."

I dig around and grab a handful of popcorn and M&Ms and munch away, enjoying the salty sweetness, the way the chocolate is already a little melted from the heat of the popcorn. "It's delicious," I say after I swallow.

"I knew you'd like it." He starts eating and the lights dim, the darkening theater signaling that about twenty minutes of previews are about to start up.

We watch silently, our hands bumping every so often as we both make a grab for more popcorn. My sticky fingers tangle with his and I offer a whispered "sorry," which only earns me a cute smile in return. I don't think he minds that our hands are touching. I know I don't.

During the fourth preview he bends his head, his mouth right at my ear as he whispers, "Can I have a drink?"

I shiver at his nearness, thankful I put my hair in a bun. I can feel his warm breath on my neck and I almost want to die from how close he is, how good he smells, how good he looks.

I have it so bad for him, I don't know what to do with myself.

So I try my best to play it cool. I pass him the soda when he requests it. I don't apologize anymore when our fingers meet in the popcorn bucket. Who knew munching on snacks during movie previews could be so . . . romantic?

I didn't. I hadn't a clue.

One of the movie previews leaves me squeamish. It's a horror movie, bloody and violent, and I wince at a graphic scene, turning my head to the right so I don't have to see it. The music is scary, the sound of a knife slicing skin awful, and I close my eyes, dipping my head so my forehead touches Ethan's shoulder for the briefest moment.

He turns. I can feel his eyes on me and I hope I'm not being too forward, but I couldn't watch that for another minute. "You okay?"

I nod and slowly lift my head, meeting his gaze in the darkened theater. The flickering blue from the screen casts Ethan in interesting shadows and I wish I could touch his face. "I'm fine. That preview was gross."

"Yeah. I don't like horror movies either." Then he does the craziest thing. He reaches out, tucks a tendril of hair behind my ear, his fingertips brushing my skin, and I tingle . . . everywhere. "I think the movie's starting," he whispers.

I don't bother looking at the screen. I'm too enraptured with his expression, the way he's watching me. "Good," I whisper back. "I can't wait to watch it."

He smiles and taps my nose with his index finger before he turns back toward the screen and settles into his chair, his long legs sprawled in front of him, the now half-eaten popcorn bucket still in his lap.

This is probably going to be two hours of pure, agonizingly delicious torture.

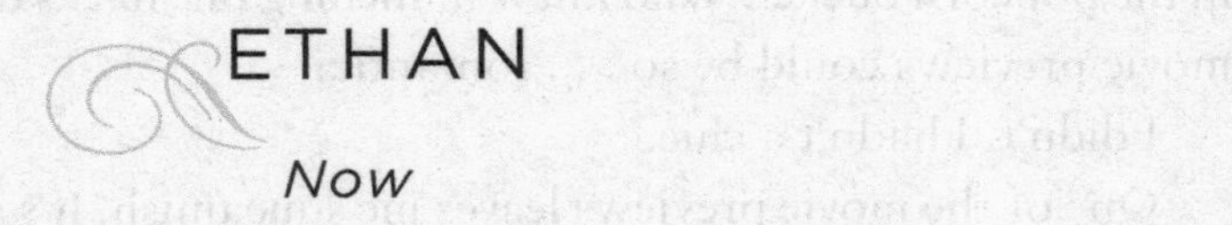

ETHAN

Now

I can't concentrate for shit. Having her this close, with really no barrier between us while sitting in the dark of a mostly empty movie theater, is a slow form of torture. Our hands constantly touching while we reach for popcorn makes me insane—which is the craziest thing ever because, come on. We're grabbing at popcorn.

But every time my fingers brush against hers it's like I touched a live wire. I'm jolted into awareness—as if I wasn't aware of her enough already. She has her hair up in a bun like a ballerina, and little wisps of blond strands lie against her otherwise bare neck. I want to press my lips there, right behind her ear, breathe in her scent and slowly kiss her neck, her cheek, her mouth . . .

Katie jumps at the loud boom from a car crash on-screen, her shoulder bumping against mine, and I lean in close, taking advantage. "That scare you?" I whisper close to her ear, stating the obvious. Any excuse so I can get near her.

She nods and turns toward me, her face so close to mine it would take nothing to lean in and kiss her. "Yeah," she whispers shakily, her gaze lifting to meet mine.

I glance around. There's no one near us. They're all paying attention to the movie anyway. I'm tempted. So damn tempted.

Reaching out, I touch her. Drift my fingers across her cheek. Hear her inhale shakily, her gaze dropping from mine. I trace the delicate line of her jaw with my thumb, slip it just beneath her chin to tilt her face up, putting our lips in perfect alignment.

I shouldn't do this. But I have to know. The need to taste her, just once, overwhelms me completely, and I give in to the urge and brush her lips with mine.

A little sound escapes her at first touch. The softest "oh" I've ever heard, as if I surprised her, which I might have. I pull away from her slightly, my hand still cupping her cheek, my thumb beneath her chin, and she lifts her lids, her dark blue gaze meeting mine.

We say nothing. My heart is racing so fast I wonder if she can hear it, but I don't care. I want to kiss her again. That first brush of lips was nothing. A tease.

Her lips part and her eyelids fall shut, an open invitation for me to kiss her again. So I do. I move closer and so does she, and then my mouth is on hers. Our mouths cling, break apart, cling again. Kiss after kiss. Simple, no tongue, but our lips are parted and we share breaths, mine fast, hers shaky.

The movie is forgotten. I'm making out with Katie in a movie theater like we're kids, though I never bothered doing this with girls when I was younger. First, I couldn't afford to take them to the movies. Second, we'd just find some dark corner at a party. That's where I always made out with girls before I would usually drag them to an empty bedroom and fuck them.

It never meant anything, though. Ever.

This entire night has been like a teenage date straight out of a cheesy movie, nothing I ever experienced the entire time I was in high school. My life was shit then. Getting lost in the foster system, treading water with classwork, and throwing myself into any sport I could play. Girls weren't a priority, but they were there and easy to lose myself in for a while.

What I'm sharing with Katie is something completely different. And though I have no fucking business leading her on like this, kissing her and treating her like this is a real date when I should walk away the minute this evening is over, I know I won't.

I should, but I won't.

She breaks the kiss first, dropping her head forward so my chin rests close to her forehead. I stroke her cheek and tuck a few stray hairs behind her ear, my fingers lingering when I hear her whisper, "I'm not good at this."

"Good at what?" I shift away so she lifts her head and our gazes meet once more.

Her expression is pure embarrassment. Torment. "Kissing."

"I'm going to have to argue with you on that." I lean down and kiss her again, savoring the little sigh that escapes her when I do so.

Katie pulls away. "Remember what I told you earlier?" I nod at her question and her gaze skitters from mine. "I'm, uh, not big on dating. As in, I've never done it."

I remain quiet. Trace her jaw with my thumb, streak it across her bottom lip. Now that I've touched her like this, so intimately, I can't stop.

"I haven't done much of anything," she continues. "There's—there's so much I should tell you, but I'm afraid I'll scare you away." Her voice is the rawest whisper, touching something deep inside of me. She couldn't scare me away if she tried. Makes me think that maybe we *are* meant for each other, as crazy as it sounds. Her horrible past doesn't bother me, not in the way it might bother other men, because I'm a part of that horrible past. I can help her, not hurt her.

Would she see that, though? Would she agree, especially once she finds out who I really am? I don't know, and it's the doubt that troubles me. Worries me.

Makes me think I'm doing the wrong thing when Katie deserves only the absolute best.

"It's okay. You don't have to tell me," I start, but she's already whispering, cutting me off.

"You keep saying that, but you deserve the truth about what happened to me. And it's awful. Like, really awful." She pauses, her eyes seeming to glisten in the dimness of the theater, almost like she's about to cry. My heart cracks at the possibility. "So I totally get it if you don't want to see me again after tonight."

As usual she's killing me with her words. "Jesus, Katie." I glance around, thankful no one else is really close to us. We're talking in whispers, and the movie is so damn loud they can't hear us anyway, but still. A movie theater isn't the best place to have this sort of conversation. "You honestly think I'd walk after you say something like that?"

Katie lifts her head, her watery gaze filled with the faintest bit of hope. "You should. You should definitely walk. I'm a mess," she whispers. "I already warned you."

"What are you saying? That you should come with a warning label?" I ask incredulously as I reach out and rest my other hand on her hip. She jumps beneath my palm and I'm tempted to let her go.

But I don't.

She nods. "Probably."

Without a word I pull her as close as I can and settle my mouth on hers once more. This time, though, I'm not gentle or slow. I'm a little more aggressive, kissing her harder, tilting my head so I can take the kiss deeper. She doesn't really respond, her moves so tentative, so inexperienced, that when I finally break away from her lips, I whisper, "Kiss me back."

She blinks up at me, her lips swollen and damp from mine, and I move toward her, ready to make another attempt, just before she leaps to her feet.

"I'm sorry. I just—I can't," she mumbles, her purse dangling from her fingers before she turns and leaves, running down the stairs and toward the exit door that leads to the back parking lot.

I sit in stunned silence, shocked that she bailed on me in the middle of the movie theater, before I spring into action. What the hell just happened? Why did she leave? I pushed too hard. I demanded too much. This is what I get, what I deserve.

I shouldn't follow her outside. I should do Katie a favor and run in the other direction. I won't help her. I'll only hurt her.

Instead of doing what I should, I follow her, hoping like hell she hasn't got away. Kissing her, pushing her like I just did, was a mistake. I wasn't fucking thinking.

That's the theme in regards to Katie, though. I flat-out don't think. I feel. I want. I hurt.

I need.

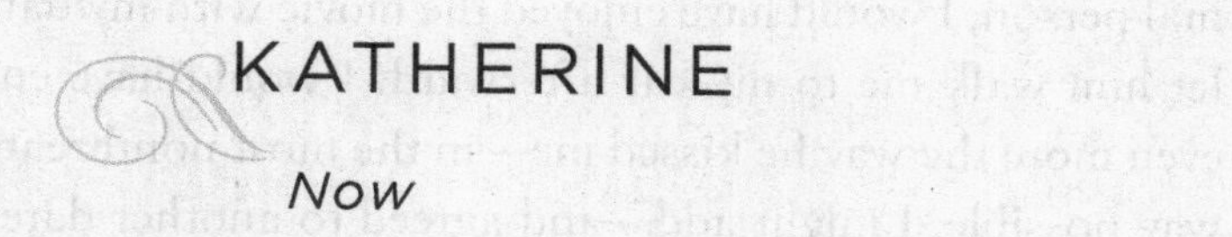

KATHERINE

Now

My legs are shaky as I run out into the dark, cool night, the theater door slamming with a heavy thud behind me, the sound jarring in the otherwise quiet. I come to a stop on the sidewalk that fringes the parking lot and glance around, my breaths fast, as I try and gather my bearings.

Like a coward I ran. Fear made me do it. Fear makes me do everything. It's the driving force in my life and God, I hate it so much. Why can't I stand up for myself? Why do I always get so scared?

At first, I liked the way he kissed me. Soft and sweet, his warm, firm lips on mine churning up all sorts of unfamiliar, yearning sensations that seemed to radiate throughout my body. I wanted to melt; I wanted to grab hold of him and cling tight. Savor the feeling of his arms wrapped around me.

But then he became bolder, his mouth more insistent, his hands seemingly everywhere, though truly, he was always respectful. Always a gentleman. When he demanded I kiss him back, I don't know what happened. I didn't . . .

I didn't know what to do. I got scared.

And I ran.

Glancing around, I look for any sign of life, but no one's out here. It's cold and cloudy, the sky dark and threatening, and the ground is damp, like it's already rained. I parked far away and I'm a little spooked being out here alone, but I tell myself to get over it. It's all my fault anyway. If I were a normal person, I would have enjoyed the movie with my date and let him walk me to my car afterward. I would have enjoyed even more the way he kissed me—in the most nonthreatening way possible, I might add—and agreed to another date if he asked me.

But he won't ask me, ever again. I've ruined it. I ran out on him like a complete freak, so why would he go after me? He won't. I don't care how nice he is, how he says all the right things and looks at me like he cares and kisses me like he's interested; once he finds out the truth . . .

He'll leave.

Stiffening my spine, I head out into the parking lot, my steps hurried as I walk toward my car. Raindrops fall on my cheeks and I bend my head down, quickening my pace when it starts to steadily drizzle. I only have on a sweater since I left my coat in my car and the air is freezing, made worse by the rain.

Gloomy and cold, much like my mood.

"Katherine!"

I recognize his voice, hear him call my name—my full name—and I slow my steps and glance over my shoulder to see Ethan coming toward me. I contemplate running the rest of the way to my car, I'm ashamed to admit, but I remain rooted where I stand, waiting for him. The rain starts falling in earnest and I blink against the drops hitting my face, wishing I could wipe my eyes but knowing that will smear my mascara.

Not that it matters. It's probably all smeared anyway.

"Come back inside," he says as he draws closer.

I shake my head. "I just want to go home."

"Let me take you home."

"No." He stops just in front of me and for one fleeting moment, I want him to grab hold of me and pull me into his arms. Never let me go. "I should—I'd rather be alone. I'm sorry." Why did I apologize? That was one thing I had to work on years ago, with one of my many therapists. I apologized for everything. I had to realize that not everything is my fault.

Most everything I apologized for was never my fault. I hate that I'm falling back into old, bad habits.

We stare at each other, the rain falling down upon us, drenching us completely. His expression is uncertain and he looks . . . different. Is it his hair as it becomes plastered to his head, water dripping from the ends? Or is it the way he frowns at me, like I've disappointed him for the millionth time?

Slowly I realize what's different about him—he doesn't have his glasses on. I see them peeking out of the front pocket of his shirt, the dark fabric molding to his chest the wetter it gets. Despite all the moisture in the air, my mouth goes dry at the sight of it, at the sight of him.

He's broad. Muscular. Strong. He could snap me like a twig, not that I believe he ever would. All that restrained strength contrasted with the gentle way he just touched me, kissed me . . .

My head grows light and my breathing accelerates. There's something very awe-inspiring about a large man who restrains himself. Who is kind and caring yet fierce in his defense of someone who needs protecting.

Like me.

"You have nothing to apologize for. I'm the one who should be sorry," he finally says, his voice so low I have to take a step closer so I can hear him. "I pushed too hard, and . . ."

"It's okay." I cut him off. I have a bad habit of doing that with him, yet I never do that with anyone else. It's like I'm in this rush to say things to him, as if I want to convince him of something else. I don't like how I do this. "Really. It's all on me."

A crack of thunder sounds in the near distance, making me jump, and he steps toward me, his hand going to my elbow and giving it a squeeze, like he can't not offer me comfort. My skin warms where he touches me and I both want to withdraw and throw myself at him. What I feel for him, how I react when he touches me, looks at me, it's confusing.

Conflicting.

Exhilarating.

"You should go to your car," he murmurs, his deep voice plucking at my nerve endings, making me achingly aware of how close he's standing next to me. "You're getting wet."

"So are you." A shiver moves through me, causing a tremor in my voice, and he slips his fingers around the crook of my elbow, steering me around. "What are you doing?"

"Where's your car?" He ignores my protests as we start walking, Ethan taking command and leading the way. "I'll take you to it. Make sure you get in safe."

Always a gentleman, always polite and protective. I run from him like a fool and he still treats me kindly. I'd think any other guy would have given up on me by now. "I'm okay, really . . ."

"Stop." He gives my arm a gentle squeeze. "Where did you park?"

I point and he steers me toward my car, his long strides eating up the pavement as I try my best to keep up with him. The rain is falling harder now. My clothes are sticking to my skin, my leggings and sweater clinging heavily. I blink hard against the water coating my eyelashes and wipe away the rain that dots my skin, my other hand shooting out with my keys clutched in between my fingers as I hit the remote to unlock my driver's-side door.

Ethan opens it for me and I dive inside, turning my head so I can look up at him. He looms above me, a dark figure against an even darker night, his scent mixed with the damp, stormy air intoxicating. "You okay?" he asks. "You seem a little shaky."

I nod, not wanting him to leave yet. Reaching for his hand where it rests on top of my car door, I grab it, clutch his cool fingers in mine. "I'll be fine. Thank you."

"You sure about that?" He's watching me, his long fingers curling around mine and giving them a squeeze. I squeeze back, thankful for the way his touch anchors me, confused by the tight feeling in my chest, my breaths coming in shuddery exhales, the quivering that moves just beneath my skin. It's not from the cold, though.

It's from him, from his touch, from the way he studies me, like I'm the only woman in the world, like it doesn't matter that I ran out on him. He's okay with it.

He's okay with me.

"I'm sure." I nod firmly, turning so I grip the steering wheel, sticking the key into the ignition and starting the car. "Thank you again," I say when I look back up at him.

Ethan smiles, pushing his damp hair away from his forehead. "Drive carefully."

"I'll text you when I get home." I pause. "Or you text me when you get home, whoever makes it first."

"I will." He starts to shut the door. "Good night, Katherine."

I hate how he's calling me Katherine. Like we've gone back to formalities, now that there's a boundary between us after my freak-out in the movie theater.

"Wait a minute." I withdraw from the car, causing him to step back, his hand still gripping the top of my car door, his arms boxing me in.

"What—" he starts but I wrap my arms around his neck, slide my hands in his rain-wet hair, and press my mouth to his in a lingering, soft kiss.

One strong arm comes around my waist and he pulls me closer. I let him, go to him willingly, my arms tightening around his neck, fingers clutching at his hair. I hope he understands what I'm doing, why I'm kissing him in the rain. My kiss is an apology, a request for his forgiveness, a hope that he'll give me a second chance.

He growls softly against my lips as we break apart and everything inside of me flutters at the sexy sound. "What are you doing to me?" he asks, his voice pained and so low I can barely hear him above the rain.

"I could ask you the same thing," I murmur close to his mouth just before I withdraw from him, letting my arms fall from around his neck. He lets go of me and I slide back into my car, smile up at him, and offer a little wave before he slams the door shut for me, enclosing me in the quiet darkness, alone with my thoughts once again.

My lips tingle the entire drive home as I relive the moment again and again. The exact moment when I grabbed hold of Ethan and kissed him. Me. The girl who's terrified of men.

Ethan doesn't scare me. More like it's my body's reaction to him that terrifies me—and fills me with curiosity. He touches me, kisses me, and I want . . . I want to melt. I want more.

As I spend more time with him, he also makes me feel safe. Protected. There's something about him that I find so incredibly comforting and I can't quite put my finger on it.

I frown, wishing I wouldn't overthink so hard. Worry so much. Maybe I'm not supposed to understand. Maybe I should just go with it. And I've never just gone with anything in my life. Not anymore at least.

The one time I did . . .

It cost me. Almost everything.

KATIE

Then

The nice detective came on a Thursday, twenty-six days after my rescue. The reason I knew was because I kept count on a calendar, marking off each day with a red slash, wishing for some sort of sign that he wanted to reach out and talk to me.

But no sign ever came.

Detective Green appeared in front of our house in the afternoon, before Brenna came home from where she volunteered at the community pool. Dad hadn't wanted her to go when I came back. He was too afraid something might happen to her and Mom finally had to put her foot down, explaining to him that lightning rarely if ever struck twice.

Great. So they referred to what happened to me as lightning. How . . . weird. They didn't seem to know how to talk about it, what to say about it. I didn't either.

So none of us did. Not as a family. We pretended everything was back to normal. Or as normal as we could make it. No one came over. Brenna tiptoed around me like I might shatter and I sort of loved it. She'd never treated me that nice before.

Dad, on the other hand, refused to look at me. I didn't know why. I didn't know what I'd done to make him hate me. I'd already cried enough tears at night to soak my pillow straight through, which was exhausting.

In the daylight, though, I acted like everything was fine.

When she answered the door, Mom was flustered to see Detective Green on our doorstep. I thought she found him handsome, because he was. I also thought any detective made her nervous, because she was always afraid they were going to deliver more bad news.

The good news had already come a week ago, in the form of one Aaron William Monroe being apprehended in Nevada. Las Vegas to be exact, hanging out in front of the Circus Circus Casino and trying to entice a cute teenager to go with him. She got uncomfortable and reported him to a nearby security guard. He took off in chase of Monroe, who fled the scene immediately, but the guard caught him, tackling him right there on the Strip in front of approximately one hundred spectators.

Quite the catch. Hard for me to believe he was actually in jail. Not that I felt better knowing he was locked up . . .

"Nice to see you again, Mrs. Watts. But actually, I came to see Katie." Detective Green's warm gaze lit upon me and I turned away, uncomfortable. I knew he meant no harm, but it didn't matter. All men made me uncomfortable after what happened. The bruises had faded and my ribs felt a lot better, but I hadn't forgotten.

I would never forget.

"Oh. Really?" Mom twisted her clutched hands in front of her as they stood in the living room. I was at the entrance to the hallway, watching the two of them, wondering whether I wanted to talk to the detective or not. "What's going on?"

He offered Mom a reassuring smile. "Don't worry, Mrs. Watts. Everything is okay. I just have a few things I'd like to discuss with Katie. Privately of course."

"Of course." Mom turned to look at me, the strained smile

on her face almost painful to look at. She hated that he said privately, I knew. She loved nothing more than to hover around me, making sure I was all right. "Katie, come over here and talk to the nice detective."

We ended up outside in the backyard, the sun warm upon our backs, and I wondered how Detective Green hadn't broken out in a complete sweat yet, what with wearing his dark blue detective suit. The summer air was stifling and I wished I had something to drink.

"How are you?" he asked, his voice soft, his concern . . . genuine.

I met his gaze for the first time since he arrived. "I'm all right."

He raised a brow. "Really?"

I shrugged. He was too perceptive. "I'm trying."

"That's all you can do." He reached into his suit and withdrew a white envelope from a secret pocket he must have had in there. "I have something for you."

He set the envelope onto the table between us and I stared at it like it was a poisonous animal about to strike. "What's inside?"

"Open it and see."

I grabbed the envelope and studied the unfamiliar writing. My name was on it, nothing else. I glanced up at Detective Green in question, but he didn't say a word in response, merely tipped his head toward the envelope, waiting for me to open it.

So I did.

I tore into the envelope carefully, withdrawing a folded piece of white paper. Something heavy wrapped in white tissue fell out and I grabbed it, giving it a shake. It had weight, and I heard something jangle, but I had no clue what it was.

Curiosity filling me, I set the tissue-wrapped object on the table and opened the letter first, frowning at the writing, which looked like it was scratched across the surface of the paper, black and slashing, almost aggressive.

Dear Katie,

I'm just going to come out and say it. I miss you. A lot. And I never miss anyone, trust me. I've had no one in my life that I want to miss, you know?

Until I met you—and helped you. No one understands what we went through together and I feel like everyone's trying to keep us apart. I get it. You've been through a lot, way more than I ever have, and they think I'm bad so I know that's why they don't want us to see each other.

But I wish I could see you. Make sure that you're okay, that you're healing and that you're not mad at me. I never wanted to hurt you. I hope you know that. I only wanted to take care of you and make sure you were safe. It just sucks that the person I was trying to save you from was my dad.

I don't know how to feel about it, how to talk about it, so I just don't.

I'm in a foster home with a bunch of other dudes my age while I wait for them to place me. I don't trust anyone. It's awful. But it was worse living with my dad, so I guess I can't complain.

There's a little something with this letter for you. I wanted to find you a gift, for you to remember me by. I hope you like it. It's not much, but when I saw it, I knew I had to get it for you.

It would be great if you can write me back but I understand if you can't. Just know that I miss you a lot and I hope you're okay.

I hope you'll always be okay.

Will

I stared at the letter, tears blurring my vision, blurring his words, his wonderful words that I wanted to read again. Later. When I was all alone and could savor exactly what he said to me.

"There's something else for you, too," Detective Green reminded me.

Refolding the letter, I set it on the table and reached for the tissue-wrapped gift, carefully undoing the tape and peeling back the layers of white paper. A silver bracelet lay nestled within, the band thin and solid, a tiny charm hanging off of it.

I lifted the bracelet from the paper and turned it this way and that, admiring the charm, my heart aching when I saw what it was.

A guardian angel sitting on the ground, her head bowed over her bent knees, her giant wings folding over her as if protecting herself from . . . everything.

I turned the charm over. Two words were engraved on the back.

Healing. Strength.

Without thought I slipped the bracelet on and shook my arm, the charm twisting back and forth. "If I wrote him a letter, would you make sure he got it?" I asked the detective, not meeting his gaze. What if he said no? I would be devastated.

He paused for a moment, hesitation shimmering in the air,

and I closed my eyes and held my breath until I heard his answer.

"Yes."

Opening my eyes, I studied Detective Green, saw that there was an ally sitting in front of me, and relief flooded through me, making me weak. "Let me get a piece of paper and a pen."

WILL

Then

I tore into the letter, my hands freaking shaking I was so eager to read what she wrote. Disappointment crashed into me when I saw there was only one page. It was unfair to have so many expectations on her when the letter I wrote her was barely one page, too.

But I couldn't help it. For whatever reason, when it came to Katie, I wanted more. I wanted . . . all of her. It made no sense but the connection between us was so strong, I still felt it. Tethering me to her, an invisible string that tied us together no matter how far apart we were.

Completely insane, but undeniable.

Detective Green dropped off the letter at the foster home with a smile and an apology not even fifteen minutes ago. He couldn't stick around, he said. Had somewhere to be, a case he needed to work on. Guess I wasn't important to him anymore.

Again, I was being unfair. I should have been glad he brought me the letter from Katie. He took the time out to help me and I appreciated it.

Dear Will,

Thank you so much for writing me. It meant a lot that you did this. It was such a nice surprise to hear from you. I've thought about you a lot, wondering where you were, how you're doing, and I was worried.

No one would tell me anything when I asked about you. I asked about you a lot.

I'm okay. Doing the best that I can. My family treats me weird. I haven't seen any of my friends, not even my best friend, and I don't know why. It's like they're all scared to see me, like they don't want to look me in the eye because they know what happened to me and they don't want to face it.

So I sit at home and watch a lot of TV. I read a lot. Spend time with my sister, which is nice because she always ignored me before. My mom won't let me go on the Internet and that sucks. I'm already bored and wish I could go back to school, but then again, I don't want to go back.

I'm scared. Scared of everything. Scared of what people might say, what they might think. That's why it feels good to wear your bracelet. It makes me feel strong and I need that right now. So thank you, Will. The bracelet means a lot to me and I really love it. I'm wearing it right now and plan on wearing it forever. So I will never forget you.

I don't want to forget you, Will. Ever. I wish I could give you a gift but I don't have any money and I wanted to get this letter to you right away before Detective Green left my house. My mom would be suspicious, so this is the best way for me to communicate with you.

That means I might not be able to write you again. I hope not. I hope we can keep in touch. Like you said, no one else understands what happened. Only us. You're the only person who I fully trust, who knows what I've been through and doesn't care. Everyone else, they don't know how to treat me.

But you do. You're my friend, Will. I wish you were here right now. I'd give you a big hug as my thank-you.

Instead, I'm going to draw you a little picture. This is what reminds me of you.

Love,
Katie

My fingers were still shaking as I studied the picture she'd drawn. A set of angel wings—the intricate details were there despite the rough sketch. I could make out the individual feathers in the wings, was impressed by her drawing skills, and I glanced up, saw the word *love* before her name, and had an inexplicable pang in the vicinity of my heart.

I rubbed at my chest, glaring at the pack of idiots that walked by me as I sat outside in front of the house. They lived in the same foster home, angry guys a little older than me and always looking for a fight. I refused to play their games, kept to myself, and they didn't mess with me.

Fairly certain that was because they knew who I was, who my dad was. They thought I was guilty, too, as guilty as him.

For once, I really didn't give a shit.

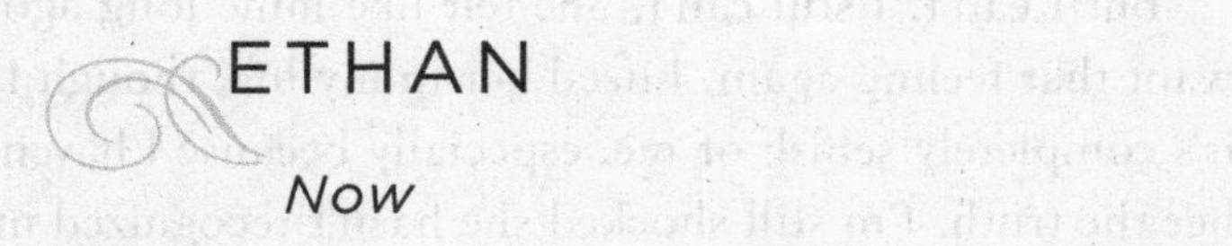

ETHAN

Now

I fold the letter and slide it back into its battered envelope. I've handled this letter a lot over the years. Unfolded and refolded it, reading over the words she wrote me, her girlish, curling script that's faded over time, the paper thin and worn from my constant handling. I still stare at how she wrote *Love, Katie* at the end of the letter and the words *only us*. Those words, they hit me like a punch in the gut every single time I read them.

And I've read them a lot.

There are other letters we shared over the years, but the first one means the most to me. It felt the rawest, the most emotional, and I know the first letter I wrote her was in the same vein. As time passed, I became more guarded, until I finally had to give her up completely.

I still have so much regret over that.

Placing the letter back in my top dresser drawer, I shut it quietly and stretch my arms above me, my knees popping. The minute I got home from the movie theater I shed my soaked clothes, leaving them in a heap on the bathroom floor. I took a hot shower, warming my chilled skin after driving for over an hour in the pouring rain, my head filled with thoughts of Katie. The taste of her lips, her slender arms curled around my neck and holding me tight, the sweet smile she offered me before I shut her car door and watched her drive away.

All are thoughts I shouldn't have. Thoughts that are wrong. I need to stop. I need to let her go and live her own life.

But I can't. I still can't. She felt like mine long ago and I want that feeling again. I need her in my life, though I know it's completely selfish of me, especially because I haven't told her the truth. I'm still shocked she hasn't recognized me, but I'm a totally different person now.

I barely recognize myself most of the time.

I stare at my reflection in the mirror that hangs over my dresser and turn to the side, lifting my arm. I'm only wearing a pair of sweats, my chest is bare, my rib cage covered in black swirling ink. The tattoo isn't very large, the image I brought into the tattoo shop and demanded they duplicate imprinted on my skin forever.

It's a pair of angel's wings, roughly sketched but each individual feather in fine detail, accompanied by two simple words written below them.

Only us.

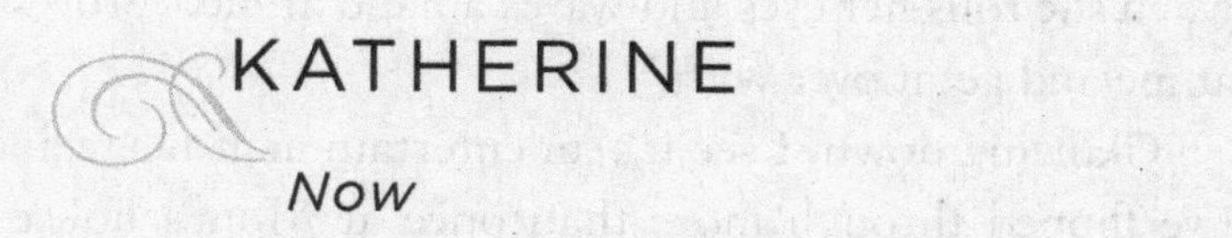

KATHERINE

Now

"I thought I should be the one to show you this first. You haven't mentioned it, and Mom fished around when she last talked to you but you seemed completely unaware." Brenna hands over an open magazine, folded to show the page I assume she wants me to read.

I take the magazine from her. We're at my house. She came over bearing vanilla lattes and cinnamon rolls from a little shop not too far from me that's well known with tourists. I don't live directly on the ocean, but my town is on the way and people passing through make frequent stops—at the Old Time Cinnamon Roll Shop, specifically.

That I'm so focused on stupid cinnamon rolls is an indication that I don't want to know what Brenna's about to drop on me.

"What is it?" I ask warily. I almost don't want to look at the magazine. It's an article she wants me to read, I'm sure, about my tragic past. Most likely a mention of the interview, considering lots of entertainment magazines covered it, including *People,* who still contact me once a week asking if I'd like to tell my story to one of their reporters for a possible cover.

No thanks.

"Just read it." Brenna flicks her chin, her expression composed.

I'm clutching the magazine, my gaze fixed on Brenna,

when she rolls her eyes and waves a hand at me. "Stop staring at me and get it over with."

Glancing down, I see it's an entertainment magazine that I've flipped through more than once at Mom's house since she's a subscriber. The page has a variety of articles and the headline near the bottom of the page catches my eye.

TV Movie About Kidnap Victim Katherine Watts in the Works

My mouth drops open as I read the short but succinct article. "They can't do this," I murmur, my eyes skimming over the blurry words. A network is mentioned; the script is being written. Much of it will be based on my interview with Lisa Swanson.

Brenna nods. "Looks like they're doing it." I know what she's thinking. We must face this head on, accept it, and move on.

But maybe I don't want to move on. Maybe I want to fight it. I only just recently got my life back—somewhat. I don't need to relive this short period of time again and again.

"How can they make a movie about me without my permission?" I look up at her and she just shakes her head.

"They do it all the time, K. Seriously, think about it. How many crazy docudrama movies have we watched on Lifetime? Other networks made movies about you after the kidnapping. We've already dealt with this, right? Besides, this is all about money. Your story will make any network advertising dollars. The interview you just did proved that."

I don't answer her as I finish the article, thinking back to the other unauthorized bio movies made about kidnap victims—excuse me, *survivors*—over the years. Most I've never watched, their stories too painful, too familiar. I never watched the ones they made about me, either. I couldn't bear to see a reenactment of the abduction.

"I wonder if I should try and stop them. Find a lawyer or something. I'm sure someone would run to my defense." I toss the magazine on the coffee table in front of the couch, already wishing for a moment alone so I can process this new discovery.

But Brenna only just got here and it's not fair, me taking out my frustration and anger on her. She's only the messenger in this situation.

"I think it would just be a waste of time." She snatches the magazine up from the table and stuffs it into her purse, which rests by her feet. Like she wants the stupid magazine out of sight, out of mind. "Want your coffee?"

I nod and she hands it to me. I take a grateful sip, my appetite long gone, and I shake my head when she offers the white paper bag with the cinnamon roll we planned on splitting inside.

"Are you sure?" she asks incredulously. She knows how much I love them.

"I'm not hungry anymore," I say with a shrug.

She rolls her eyes again and opens the bag, pulling out the cinnamon roll, its warm, sweet scent drifting toward me and immediately making me regret my decision. "Mom was dying to be the one to tell you about the movie, you know. I had to put my foot down and insist I be the one to break the news to you."

"Why did she want to tell me first? So she could give me a lecture about the big, bad world and how I should've never done that interview?" I've already heard it, more than once. Mom went along with my decision to talk with Lisa Swanson but I know she didn't like it. She's tried her best to be supportive, but after all, she's a mother. *My* mother. And she wants to protect me.

Plus, she'd been trained by my father over the years to never speak of what happened to me. She's so conditioned, she flinches if she so much as hears Aaron Monroe's name. And when she hears my name and his together, along with words like *kidnapped* and *raped*? Forget it. She can hardly take it.

"Probably. I warned her off." Brenna takes a sip of her drink. "I told her I wanted to do it because I also come here with ulterior motives."

I frown, unease slipping down my spine. "What do you have up your sleeve?"

"Oh stop. I always have your best interests at heart." She smiles and sets her drink on the coffee table, then tears into the cinnamon roll. "I have a proposition for you," she says after she takes a bite.

"What is it?"

"I work with this guy." I part my lips, ready to protest, and she cuts me off. "No, listen to me! He's really sweet. His name is Greg and he's a speech therapist for the school district. Quiet and calm and so incredibly patient with the kids, they just adore him. And he's cute."

"Brenna . . ."

"Stop. I think a date is in order, Katherine. You deserve a fun night involving dinner and conversation, no pressure. I told him about you."

My jaw drops open. "What exactly did you tell him?"

"Nothing about—that, but if he wanted to find out, he could. Google exists, you know. There's nothing we can do to prevent anyone from looking you up."

I slump down on the couch, lean my head back against it, and stare up at the ceiling. She's hitting me with too much information all at once. "I know you mean well, but I don't need you setting me up on dates."

"If I weren't already taken, I'd go after Greg big time. He's adorable. Twenty-six, he dresses nice, and I like his hair. He has friendly eyes." Brenna is rambling on, not even paying attention to what I'm saying. "Look, if you're nervous we could double-date the first time. That'll probably help you feel more comfortable with Greg."

She looks so hopeful and I know she means well. "I'm sure he's a great guy and I appreciate you looking out for me, Bren, but I'm not interested." I pause. Should I tell her? "I, uh, I've sort of . . . met someone."

It's as if Brenna didn't even hear what I said. "Though I'm sure for your first date, while you're getting to know each other, you don't want us there as a third wheel. Well, third and fourth wheel—you know what I mean." She stops talking, her eyes going wide. "Wait a minute, what did you say?"

"I met someone," I admit again, my voice quiet, my thoughts all over the place. My heart pounds hard against my chest at the mere thought of Ethan and all of a sudden I feel like I could burst. "His name is Ethan and he's . . . I like him."

She stares at me as though I've grown three heads. "Where in the hell did you meet a *guy*?" she practically screams.

"Um, the day you called me? When you and Mom were tracking me?" At least my sister has the decency to look embarrassed. "I met him there. At the park."

"In the amusement park?" Brenna squeaks out.

"Well, yeah." I pick at a loose thread on the couch. I'm not going to tell her the circumstances that surrounded our meeting. She might freak out, or worse, tell Mom about the almost purse snatching and that's the last thing I want to happen. "We started talking and the next thing I knew we were at a coffee shop, and it was—it was nice. He's easy to talk to."

Brenna looks stunned. "Give me more details. Where does he live? What does he do? How old is he?"

I give her a brief rundown, telling her we went to dinner, the movies. Leaving out the part where I ran out on him. That was a few days ago. We've texted off and on, nothing major, but he's wrapping up a website project and warned me he'd be busy.

Funny how I barely know him yet I still miss him.

"I want to meet him," she says vehemently the moment I stop talking.

"Not yet." I shake my head. "You'll scare him off."

"I will not!" She appears indignant as she tears off a chunk of the cinnamon roll and shoves it in her mouth.

"You will," I say calmly. "You and Mom both will come at him with an endless list of questions and freak him out. We've seen each other only a few times. I don't even know if he likes me like . . . that." I'm lying. I'm pretty sure he does like me like that, but I don't want to ruin things before they really start. "Let's wait a while before I bring him around, okay?"

"So you're going to see him again." She sounds skeptical. Protective. And I love that, I do. But I also need freedom. A chance to figure out what I'm doing and if I really want it, want *him*.

"I hope so." God, I really do. I dreamed about him last night. We were kissing in a dark room with no one else around us, no movie playing, just the quiet stillness making me acutely aware of him. Of me. Of us.

Together.

In my dream, I wasn't hesitant. Instead, I was fully engaged, enjoying it, wanting more. Sighing and moaning and whispering his name, hearing the sounds of our mouths connecting, clothes rustling as hands moved and shifted, my fingers sinking in his hair, his fingers curling around my waist . . .

I woke slowly, my body hot, my bones languid. I wanted more of that. More kissing, more touching, more Ethan. I wanted to take it a step farther.

But would he?

I still feel restless from that dream, from the turbulent feelings he causes within me. I know that's why I mentioned him. The need to talk about him, say his name out loud, prove to someone else that yes, he does exist, he's not a figment of my imagination, was so incredibly strong, to the point of almost overwhelming me.

"So tell me. Is he cute?" Brenna smiles, reminding me of the old Brenna, the teenage girl who only cared about hot guys and if she could get their attention. How she ended up with the dud she's living with now, I'm not really sure, but she claims Mike makes her happy. That he's safe and steady and doesn't leave her feeling lost or lonely.

I feel like she's giving up. Twenty-four years old and she's settling. That's awful.

"Yes." Embarrassed, I start to laugh and so does she. "Very."

She wants security, not excitement. I get that. I do.

But I'm starting to think maybe security and excitement can go hand in hand.

At least, it seems to with Ethan.

"Does he know—who you really are? What happened to you?" Brenna asks, then shakes her head. "Of course he does. You've been everywhere lately. He's had to figure it out."

"I . . . I don't know if he has. I told him I went through a traumatic experience in my past but I didn't give him any details." We haven't even exchanged last names, but no way am I going to tell Brenna that. She'll rip into me, not that I can blame her.

I'd rip into me. And maybe that's part of the excitement. That unknown quality, that there are so many things I don't know about Ethan at all. He's mysterious. A puzzle I want to put together.

"Something to consider, if you keep seeing him and it becomes serious," Brenna says, a gentle reminder that I can never forget my past and neither can anyone else.

I hate it. My past follows me, leeches itself upon me like a shackle and chains. Like the very chain Aaron Monroe wrapped around my ankle so he could keep me hooked to the wall like some sort of animal.

That's my past. Attached to me so tightly I can never, ever let it go.

No matter how much I want to.

ETHAN

Now

I want to make you dinner tonight.

But just thinking about it makes me nervous.

What if I screw it up?

What if you don't like my cooking?

My house?

Me?

(forget I said that last line)

What if you leave my house hungry?

What if you never want to see me again? All because I can't boil water and make a decent meal?

These are the things that run through my head on a Saturday morning when I wake up too early and can't sleep.

When I contemplate inviting you over and second-guess my every decision.

And now I can't take these thoughts back because I already hit send.

No matter how badly I want to.

Hope you'll say yes. ☺

I woke up to a list of texts from Katie that made me smile. Then made me realize she wakes up at an ungodly hour on a Saturday morning. It's barely eight o'clock and I'm pissed at myself for not sleeping in later, but what's done is done. I'm up.

And Katie wants me to come over tonight. I can't believe it.

Once I handle the usual morning stuff and get a few swallows of coffee in me, I answer her, keeping it short and simple.

I would love to come over for dinner. Tell me what to bring.

She answers me almost immediately.

Just yourself. That's good enough.

I smile. I can do that.

What time then? And let me know if you really do want me to bring something.

She doesn't reply and I wonder what she's doing at this exact moment. I've been busy all week and haven't talked to her much. I hope she doesn't think it was because of the movie incident, though I was giving her a bit of distance, too. Seemed like she needed it.

What's currently blowing my mind is how she hasn't mentioned who she really is. We haven't exchanged last names. We haven't shared intimate details, not that I would expect to, considering we've seen each other less than a handful of times. I shouldn't be surprised she doesn't want to lead with the sort of information that would rock any normal man's world.

My name is Katherine Watts and I survived a horrific kidnapping and rape for three days. Until I was finally rescued, and my captor is now in prison for the rest of his life.

Yeah. That's a complete bombshell.

My phone buzzes and I check it.

Come over around six.

I answer her quickly, not bothering to play the game and make her wait. Screw that. When it comes to this girl, I don't want to play games. I just want . . .

Her.

I'll be there.

She gives me directions and I pretend I've never been there, reassuring her I can find it with my phone's GPS, no problem. She seems excited, nervous, even via text and I wonder if she can sense the same excitement and nervousness in me.

I arrive at her house at ten to six, feeling like an idiot for showing up early but thankful I'm not late. I park directly in front, quietly closing the driver's-side door, not wanting to alert her next-door neighbor. The nosy old lady who gave me the third degree a few weeks ago when I'd been lingering on Katie's street like some sort of fucked-up stalker.

I'm still not proud of that moment, though I can't take it back. Don't necessarily regret it, either, but come on. I took it too far.

You found her, though, right? And that had been your goal all along.

I ignore the voice in my head and start up the sidewalk that leads to her front door, a bottle of wine in one hand, a bouquet of fall-colored flowers in the other. I climb the three steps to her porch and knock on the door with the bottom edge of the wine bottle.

She's there in an instant, her slender frame filling the doorway, an expectant look on her face. Her hair is down, falling in soft golden waves past her shoulders, her lips subtly shiny, cheeks pink. She's dressed in black, a soft oversized sweater and tight jeans that make her legs look long.

Endless.

"Hi." Her gaze drops to my full hands. "I told you that you didn't need to bring anything."

"I wanted to." I hold the flowers out to her. "For you."

She takes them from me, her eyes dancing as they meet mine, her entire face . . . glowing. I've pleased her with the flowers. That I made her so happy with such a simple gift reminds me that I need to keep this up, just so I can see that smile on her face. "Thank you," she murmurs as she dips her head and inhales. Her eyes fall closed for the briefest moment, her lips parted, and I've never seen her look more beautiful.

I want to, though. See her look even more beautiful than at this simple moment. Like when I have her naked and lying beneath me . . . or right after I make her come. Will she let me? Can I take it that far between us or will she throw up her walls?

Something I'm determined to find out.

"Come in," she says as she takes a step backward, shifting to the side and holding the door wider so I can enter. "You brought wine, too."

"I hope it works with whatever you're making for dinner." I have no clue about wine. I'm not a wine guy. I drink beer. Vodka on occasion. For the most part, I avoid alcohol. It reminds me of my father, the dirty, fucked-up drunk. He started drinking, then he started doing drugs, bringing various women into his bedroom, dragging me into his bedroom . . .

Yeah. I push him firmly out of my mind for tonight.

Katie looks at me as if she has no idea what I'm talking about and then she starts to laugh, the sound soft, almost musical. "I'm not much of a wine expert," she says as she closes the door behind me, turning the lock. Trapping us inside together.

There's nowhere I'd rather be.

"Me either," I admit with a smile.

Her laughter dies as she blatantly drinks me in. "You look nice."

"Thanks," I say casually, allowing my gaze to drift over her in return. "So do you."

No answer, just a sweet smile as she tears her gaze from mine. Despite the usual hesitancy, the typical shyness that is Katie, she seems different from the last time I saw her. More confident somehow, yet also carefree. No darkness clings to her tonight; it's as if she's shed her nervousness. As if that panicked moment at the movie theater never happened.

"Then I hope your wine goes well with chicken, since that's what I made," she says as she walks through the house toward the kitchen.

"I'm sure it'll work. I deliberately chose something uncomplicated." I try to take in her place, see if I can catch a glimpse of Katie nestled among all the little details that are on the bookshelves and the coffee table, the color of her couch, the patterned rug, the walls, the photos and art on her walls. But I'm too entranced with the swing of her hips, the scent of her, light and airy, that lies just beneath the heavier smells coming from the kitchen.

I could inhale her forever.

"I made chicken Marsala," she announces as she goes to stand behind the tiny island in the center of her kitchen, setting the bouquet of flowers on the counter. "And salad and garlic bread."

I've never eaten chicken Marsala in my life. I grew up on ramen noodles and fast food. My father hadn't been a big believer in eating healthy and we sure as shit didn't eat anything that sounded fancy, with words like *Marsala* in the name.

"Sounds great," I say as I come to a stop on the other side of the island. She still needs the barrier between us and I'm fine with that. Whatever makes her comfortable. I'm in her space, so I won't push. She's calling the shots tonight. I've handed over the power to her and she probably doesn't realize it. "Smells even better."

"I hope it tastes okay. This is the first time I've tried this recipe." She blushes and looks down at the flowers, rubbing a velvety burgundy petal with her fingertips. "I should find a vase for these." Turning around, she opens a cabinet, then takes a step back so she can look at the very top shelf. I glance up, catching sight of the lone vase sitting on the shelf, and know there's no way she can reach it.

"Let me help you," I start as she protests she can reach it when we both know she can't. I stop just behind her, so close my front presses against her back as I reach around her and grab the vase and hand it to her. I don't move away, my arm still curved in front of her, and she takes the vase from me, our fingers grazing, electricity sparking where we touched.

"Thank you," she says breathlessly. She remains in place, as if she's almost afraid to move, and now I reach for her, tease the strands of hair close to her right cheek with my index finger before I slowly tuck them behind her ear, my finger lightly tracing the curve, teasing the pearl earring she wears, before my hand drops.

"You look pretty tonight, Katie," I tell her, my voice low,

my thoughts complete chaos. I'm strung tight. I've been here less than five minutes and all I can think about is exactly how far she will let me go tonight.

Because I want to touch her. Kiss her.

Desperately.

KATIE

Then

"Okay." Will stopped in front of the low, nondescript building that looked like it was built sometime in the sixties or seventies. It was ugly, with a squat, flat roof, the walls constructed of brick that was painted a washed-out green. It reminded me of what a prison should look like. "We're here."

My thoughts weren't too far off. "This is the police station?" I rubbed at my gritty, stinging eyes like I was a little kid.

I was tired. My brain wasn't firing right and I couldn't wrap my head around . . . anything. I just wanted something to drink. To find somewhere to lie down so I could close my eyes, at least for a little bit. I wanted Mom and Dad. I wanted to go home.

"Yeah. So go." He pushed at my shoulder, kind of roughly, and I stepped away from him, turning so I could face him. "What are you waiting for? Get out of here."

"What do you mean, 'get out of here'? You're not walking in with me?" I asked incredulously.

He shook his head, all that raven hair falling in his eyes, his mouth thinning into a straight line. I could still see the hoop of his lip ring, his tongue darting out to tease it, and I waited breathlessly for his answer. It took forever and when the words finally came, haltingly, a little shaky, I closed my eyes, knowing he would say something I didn't want to hear.

"I . . . I can't, Katie." I opened my eyes to see him staring at me, his expression pained, his eyes so dark. Bottomless, really. "I go inside with you and my entire life will change."

"And that's a bad thing?" I couldn't understand why he wouldn't want his life to change. How good could it be, having that—that horrible, disgusting man as his father? Did he do things to Will? Did he abuse him and force him to do . . .

"I don't know—it scares the shit out of me." Will's voice was harsh. "I'd rather just avoid my dad and not have to deal with anything, you know?"

"No. I don't know." I was angry. Mad he wouldn't come into the police station with me. Mad he'd pushed me like I didn't matter. I didn't get him. He was a contradiction, a confused, scared, lonely boy who figured it was better to stay with his monster of a father than try and get help. "You have to come inside with me."

He rushed toward me, gripping my shoulders and giving me a slight shake. His touch didn't hurt, and his face in mine didn't scare me because I could see the fear in his eyes, feel it in his shaking hands as they held me. "Your life is perfect, do you realize that? You have a mom and a dad. A sister. A family who loves you, probably a lot of friends who think you're nice and teachers who care about you. You don't know what it's like to go hungry because your dad spent all the money he had on booze and drugs. You don't understand when kids make fun of you when your clothes don't fit and your shoes have holes in them. You have no idea what it's like to have your dad drag you into his bedroom and make you watch when he . . ."

His words came to a complete stop, his breathing ragged. I stared up at him, horror filling me at those final words he just said. At everything he just said. My life had changed. I knew this without a doubt. But he was right. I had no idea what it was like to be him.

I'd dealt with his dad for only a handful of days. Will had been dealing with him for a lifetime.

"Things will get better," I told him as I reached up to touch his forearm. He flinched beneath my hand, his fingers loosened their grip on my shoulders, and eventually his hands dropped away from me. I felt oddly cold without his touch. "You've suffered for a long time. They'll help you."

"No they won't," he said bitterly. "They'll probably think I had something to do with this."

"You're just a kid," I pointed out. A kid like me, but he really wasn't. His life was nothing like mine. He'd seen and done too much, things that couldn't be taken back. "They'll take care of you."

"I'll be thrown into the foster system and they'll forget about me. Or they'll accuse me of raping you and toss me in jail."

It was my turn to rush toward him. I clutched at his hands, held them in mine as I stared into his eyes. "I won't let them. I'll tell them the truth. They'll believe me. Just please, Will. Come inside with me."

He stared at me, hesitancy written all over his face. I had him. I knew I did and I tugged on his hands, turned us so we were walking toward the front door of the police station together. I steered him toward those double glass doors, knowing that men and women who would help me find my parents were just beyond those doors, and I hurried my steps.

Will broke free, his expression full of remorse as he shook his head. "I can't, Katie. I just . . . I can't. I'm sorry."

"Hey!"

I turned to see a uniformed officer standing in front of the doors, holding one of them open. He frowned at me as he started walking in my direction. I glanced over my shoulder and saw the way Will was frozen in place, like he wanted to bolt but couldn't.

The officer jogged toward him, huffing and puffing as he drew near, his gaze hard as he stared at me. "Aren't you that missing Watts girl?"

"Yes." Relief flooded me and I nodded, tears stinging the corners of my eyes. "I am. Please, please help me."

"Who's that?" The officer flicked his chin toward Will and he ran. Just flat took off without a backward glance and the officer followed after him, telling him to stop or he'd shoot.

Panic rose within me. "Don't shoot him!" I screamed, my entire body trembling violently. "Please! He brought me here! He saved me! Will, stop running!"

Will was young and fast. He could have easily outrun the older, overweight police officer, but he slowed his pace. Came to a complete stop. Turned around with his hands held high, his T-shirt riding up with the movement and offering a glimpse of his flat, pale stomach.

I didn't remember much after that. A swarm of officers—both uniformed and plain clothed—came outside to surround me. A woman wrapped her arm around my shoulders and led me inside, her voice calm and soothing as she informed me she was going to contact my parents right away. Saying what a miracle it was that I was there, safe and sound. In one piece.

I couldn't tell her that I was actually splintered into many pieces and that I doubted I could ever be put back together again.

Glancing over my shoulder, I spotted Will. Saw the way the officer grabbed hold of his arm and escorted him behind us. I saw the sullen expression on Will's face, how grown-up he looked, with his tall body and long arms and legs. Yet his expression was vulnerable, scared, and my heart cracked when our gazes met.

"I'm sorry, Katie!" he yelled above the din, his voice pleading. Broken. "I broke my promise."

I couldn't answer him. The female officer wouldn't let me, jerking on my shoulders as we entered the cool, quiet sanctuary of the police station. She turned so we went down a darkened hall, her arm still around my shoulders as she mentioned my parents, my family, the need for me to go to the hospital so I could be examined. The words blurred, as did everything else, and I was so overwhelmed, so tired and shaky and hungry and thirsty, I couldn't concentrate on any of it.

All I could think about was Will. Would he be all right? Would this be the last time I ever spoke to him? Did he think I hated him?

That was the last thing I felt for him.

The very last.

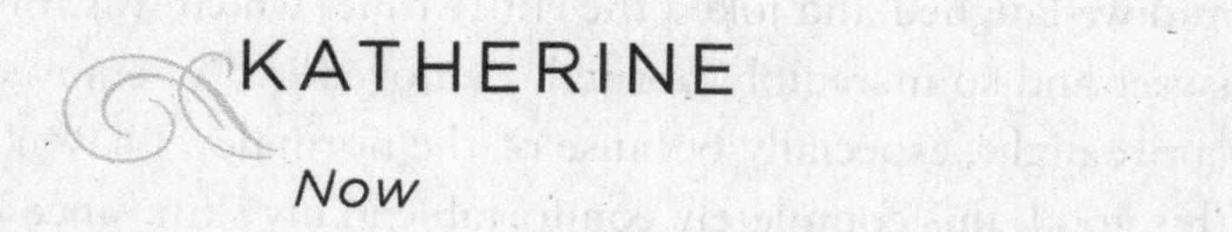

KATHERINE

Now

I'm so nervous I'm practically shaking. We ate dinner and he actually liked the chicken Marsala. It was a dish I'd never made in my life, but I remembered how much Dad loved it when Mom would make it. That was a long time ago and I wanted the memory to fuel me. Help me create a new memory.

It worked.

During dinner he didn't talk about anything personal and neither did I. We talked about the weather and current events and pop culture–type stuff, which made me nervous because I'm fairly certain I was front and center pop culture–wise only a few weeks ago. I mentioned growing up in the Bay Area and he said he grew up in the very town where the amusement park was. I told him I was home schooled and that my parents were overprotective—a complete understatement.

He didn't say much at all about his family. Made vague mentions of his dad, said his mother took off when he was small and he has no recollection of her. He changed the subject every time I tried to ask him a personal question and I wondered if he was trying to hide something.

Snippets of his past were few and far between. I wanted to know more, but considering I wasn't ready to volunteer everything yet either, I kept my mouth shut.

It was easier that way. At least for now.

Once we finished dinner, Ethan helped me wash the dishes

and we laughed and joked the entire time, which was fun and sweet and so incredibly normal, I enjoyed it. I've enjoyed the entire night, especially because of the normalcy. I haven't felt this good, this completely comfortable in my skin, since I was twelve.

How sad is that?

But I'm not comfortable anymore. Though my discomfort isn't necessarily a bad thing. Ethan's on the couch, his arm slung across the back of it, his legs spread wide in that way men sit. I'm not used to how much space he takes up, how he seems to eat up the atmosphere when we're in the same room together. It's overwhelming, exhilarating, and I come to a stop in front of the couch, two cold bottled waters clutched in my hands.

"Should we watch something on Netflix?" I ask as I round the coffee table and sit on the couch, setting the bottles on the table.

"Do you want to?" he asks. His knee nudges against my thigh and I wonder if he moved it there on purpose. If he can feel the electricity crackle and flame between us, even when our bodies barely brush against each other.

We're practically combustible.

"I suppose," I answer with a shrug.

We both remain quiet for a moment and I glance over my shoulder to see he's watching me, his gaze drifting down, seeming to linger on my backside as I sit on the edge of the couch before he lifts his head, his gaze meeting mine once more. "I'm not in the mood to watch a movie tonight," Ethan says. He studies me almost hungrily, his gaze roving over my face, and my heart flutters at the look in his eye.

"Okay." I turn away and face forward once more, swallowing hard. Almost afraid to look at him again. I'm being ridiculous. I know it. But I have no clue how to behave, what to do. My mind races and I hope he doesn't think I'm hopeless. "What do you have in mind?"

His hand drops from the couch and lands on my lower back, slowly smoothing upward, his fingers spread wide, seeming to touch all of me, all at once. My eyelids waver and I force myself to keep them open, savoring his touch. I bend my neck forward, a rush of breath leaving me when his fingers slip beneath my hair and circle around my nape, gently holding me there.

"I don't want to scare you," he murmurs, his deep, rumbling voice seeming to vibrate deep within me.

"You're not," I whisper, sucking in a breath when his thumb streaks across the side of my neck.

"I've wanted to do this all night," he continues in this low, hypnotic tone that lulls me. Seduces me. My limbs feel heavy, as does my head. My blood is languid as it moves sensuously through my veins. His thumb sweeps back and forth, so light I almost don't feel it, causing goosebumps to rise.

I don't answer him, don't want to turn around for fear he'll stop touching me. I'm perched on the edge of the couch, my entire body softening with his every touch, and when he runs his fingers through my hair I almost want to purr in pleasure.

No one has ever touched me like this before.

"Come here," he whispers and I finally turn to look at him, his fingers tightening on my neck, pulling me closer. I go willingly, he doesn't have to force me to do anything, and the next thing I know I'm fully encircled in his arms as he draws me into his warmth. His hand still around my neck, his other hand resting on my back, our mouths are perfectly aligned.

But he doesn't kiss me, not yet. It's as if he wants to torture me. Like he knows exactly what he's doing to me, and I ache.

I ache so bad I curl my fingers into a fist, my nails biting into the palm of my hands. His lips hover above mine and I can smell his breath, warm and fruity from the wine we consumed earlier. The very wine that makes my head buzz the slightest bit now. He licks his lips, as if anticipating my taste, and something hot and foreign begins to throb low in my belly.

A matching throb beats between my legs.

"Tell me if I'm moving too fast, okay?" He touches my cheek, that same thumb that stroked my neck only moments ago now on my face. Caressing me, driving me insane as he runs it across my skin. Everything he does is slow. Deliberate. He doesn't ask, though he's cautious. He makes sure I'm all right, that I'm good with whatever is about to happen between us.

And then he just . . . does it.

My eyes close with absolute trust as his mouth falls on mine. I feel like I'm still falling at the first touch of his lips. A free fall into open air as my stomach rolls and turns, everything inside of me going loose and making my head spin. All from the subtle shift of his firm mouth as he steers the kiss and it becomes more determined. I part my lips and he swallows my shuddery exhale, just before he touches the tip of his tongue to the center of my bottom lip.

I go still at the sensation and he does it again. Tentative yet assured. Bold yet inquisitive. I don't react when he slips his hand into my hair, his fingers curling around the strands and giving them a gentle tug. I reach out and rest my hand on his chest, feel the accelerated beat of his heart beneath my palm, and I shift closer, wanting to feel more of his warmth, his strength.

Wanting to feel more of him.

He ends the kiss and pulls away to study me, his brows

drawn down, his lips damp. With my other hand I touch his face, my fingers drifting across the line of his jaw, his prickly stubble abrading my thumb. He watches me, his glasses gone, and I don't remember him taking them off but I like him like this. Open and warm and vulnerable, quiet and calm and . . .

Sexy.

He closes his eyes and presses his lips together, his jaw going rigid. It's like he's trying his best to control himself, control his emotions, and a thrill courses through me that *I* have enough power to make him react this way.

Me. The girl who's felt so powerless for so long.

"You know exactly what you do to me, don't you." He says it as a statement, not a question, and my entire body goes warm at the tone of his voice, the look in his eyes. I don't remove my hand from his face, letting my thumb streak across his bottom lip, and as he parts his lips I feel a gust of warm breath against my skin. A shiver moves through me.

"What am I doing to you?" I want to hear him describe my effect on him. It's a heady feeling, realizing my feminine power for the first time in my life. I want to revel in this moment.

"Driving me insane." He grabs hold of my wrist, circling his fingers around it as he brings my fingers more fully to his mouth. He drops kisses on my knuckles, his lips light as a feather, damp and hot and leaving me an aching, confused mess. "I don't want to push you."

"You're not," I say quickly, my voice shaky. His lips on my skin send shock waves pulsing through my veins. It's like nothing I've ever experienced before and I'm unusually greedy. I want more.

His smile is gentle though his gaze is somber. "You've mentioned more than once that you've dealt with something terrible in your past." He kisses the top of my hand, his gaze never leaving mine, intense and searching. The achy, fuzzy feeling inside me slowly dissipates, replaced with a slow trickle of dread. "I'd like it if you told me about it. You don't have to tell me everything—I'm sure you're probably not comfortable sharing the details—but I want to know. So I can understand."

I go completely stiff. How? How can I tell him? Not now. Not like this. There's just . . . no way. Not yet. I don't know him that well. What if I scare him away? "I . . ."

His expression is immediately contrite. "If you don't want to talk about it, I get it." He squeezes my hand. "We can wait."

Frustration rolls through me and I disentangle my hand from his. I definitely don't want to talk about what happened to me but I also don't want to wait. I want more of what he has to offer. Being with Ethan is . . . a revelation. He doesn't treat me like I'm made of glass, like I might shatter and fall apart at any given moment. That's one of the reasons I enjoy spending time with him. He doesn't know who I really am, what happened to me, and I like it.

I can act normal, act like a regular woman who's becoming involved with a gorgeous, thoughtful man. I might have blurted out a thing or two when I panicked the last time we were together but for the most part, he only knows who I am now, not the broken girl I was, and I love that.

I want it to stay that way. I just don't know how to put it all into words, how to ask for what I want.

So I don't ask. I do what Ethan's done all evening.

I just take.

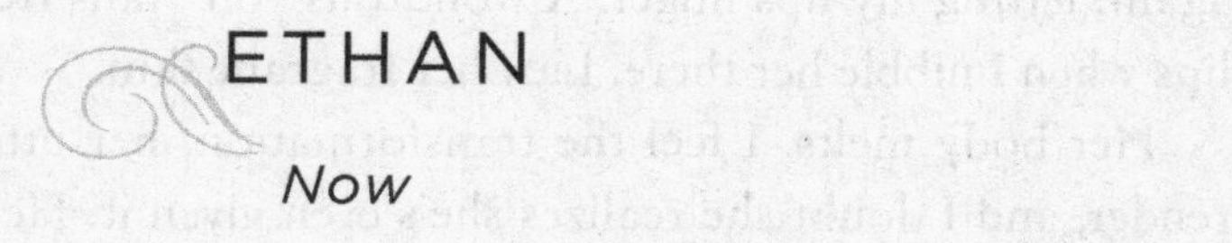

ETHAN

Now

One minute she's looking sort of pissed and conflicted as she watches me and the next, she's in my arms, her slender body pressed close to me, her arms around my neck and her lush mouth finding mine. She gave me no warning, never said a word, just jumped into my arms and is now straddling me, her bent legs on either side of my hips, her chest pressed against mine as we kiss.

I slowly wrap my arms around her, anchoring her to me. She's warm and soft, her mouth insistent, frustration seeming to vibrate from her directly into me. I feel like I can absorb her tumultuous emotions and all I want to do is calm her.

Claim her.

Reaching for the back of her head, I cup her there, my fingers in her hair, tugging a little so I can separate our mouths.

"Slow down a little," I whisper, my lips moving against hers as I talk. *Christ,* it feels good, having her like this. Eager and willing and unabashedly greedy. A man could get used to this. *I* want to get used to this, but I refuse to push. I tried my damnedest to get her to confess, but she wasn't having it.

Guess I can't blame her.

"I don't want to slow down," she murmurs, a little sound of frustration escaping her lips. This girl is wound up tight, her body tense, her heart rapidly beating. I can see the gentle throb in her neck and I dip my head, run my lips over the spot where her pulse pounds. She's so soft and I kiss the same spot again, letting my lips linger. A wondrous "oh" falls from her lips when I nibble her there. Lick her fragrant skin.

Her body melts. I feel the transformation, her utter surrender, and I doubt she realizes she's even given it. Her arms loosen around my neck and I release my grip on the back of her head, my hand falling to her lower back so I can press her closer.

"Ethan." My name falling from her lips twists my insides, makes my cock twitch. For a brief, absolutely ridiculous moment, I wish she were saying my old name. My *real* name.

But I'm not Will anymore. And I will never be him again. Ever.

William Aaron Monroe is dead and gone.

Lifting my head, I stare at her and she blinks up at me, her eyes falling closed right at the moment our mouths connect. Yet this kiss is like no other we've shared. I slide my tongue into her mouth, tangle it with hers, and she responds tentatively at first. Within seconds she becomes bolder, the kiss turns carnal, and then she's gripping my hair, her hips shifting against mine as if she's trying to burrow herself inside me. Her legs squeeze my hips and these sexy little soft sounds come from deep in her throat.

Hottest thing I've ever heard. She's so responsive. As if she were made for me. I pull her in as close as I can get, tempted to just grind up on her so she can feel exactly what she's doing to me, but I know I can't. Not yet.

I don't want to end this before we've even really started.

Hungry kisses gradually turn into slow, deep kisses. I cup her cheek and guide her. She's an eager student, following my lead, her hands sliding to my shoulders, down my arms, her fingers seeming to memorize everything as she touches me. I return the favor and run my hands over her. Down her arms, along her waist, resting them on her hips for a moment before I slide them in, touching her stomach. Going higher. Higher still. Until my thumbs are brushing the underside of her breasts and I can feel the satiny-smooth texture of her bra just beneath her sweater.

Back and forth I barely touch her, keeping it light, waiting for her to pull out of my embrace, or say something. Tell me to stop.

Katie should definitely tell me to stop.

But she doesn't do any of that. She moans softly against my lips. The sound emboldens me and I lift one thumb, drift it across the generous curve of her breast for one lingering moment before I let it drop.

She breaks the kiss this time, her breaths fast, her lips swollen and wet as she looks down at me. My hands go to her sides and I hold her there, spreading my fingers over her rib cage as we continue to watch each other and catch our breath.

"I should go," I tell her, because I should. Damn it, I should leave her and never look back. I take it too far every single time I see her and that's half my problem. More than half my problem.

Because I'm possessed with the need to push it even farther. With the need to see her again, touch her again, kiss her, see how far I can take it when we're together . . .

I'm playing with fucking fire. And we're both going to end up burned.

"Okay," she whispers with a little nod, surprising me. I figured she wouldn't let me leave, but this is good. This is what I want.

Or so I tell myself.

I lift her off my lap and she tumbles onto the couch beside me, her breathing still accelerated, her hair a mess about her head. I must have run my hands through it at one point, though I hardly remember anything beyond her mouth on mine, her tongue circling, her hands gripping my shoulders . . .

"I'm glad you came over," she says, not looking at me, staring straight ahead. She almost seems embarrassed and I don't want her feeling that way. "I hope . . . we can do it again sometime."

Leaning over her, I cup her cheek and tilt her head so she's looking at me. "We will," I promise solemnly. "I can guarantee it."

She smiles, a little laugh escaping her as she murmurs, "So serious," and I capture her laughter with my lips, silencing her. The kiss turns deep in an instant, our tongues tangling, heat growing between us, and I break away as fast as I kissed her, rising from the couch, running my hand through my hair as I try to tell my hard dick to settle down.

It's damn tough, though, when I see Katie sitting on the couch, warm and pliant, with swollen lips and flushed cheeks. I want to swoop in and gather her in my arms. Carry her back to her room and sprawl her across the bed. Strip her naked, stretch her arms above her head, spread her legs and have my way with her. Feast on her, lick and nibble and kiss every inch of her skin, touch her, fuck her with my fingers, my tongue, my mouth, my cock . . .

You're taking this too far. She's still petrified of you, of what you represent, even though she wants it. Wants you. But if she found out who you really are? She'd flip the fuck out. You'll never have a taste of her again.

Reluctantly I head to the front door and Katie springs up from the couch to follow behind me. She zips in front of me at the last minute, her hand on the door handle as she reaches up and undoes the deadbolt.

"Thanks for dinner," I murmur, stopping just in front of her.

She leans against the door, her hands tucked behind her perfect ass. Which I should have touched only a few minutes ago, but I blew my chance. "Thank you for coming over. Sorry we didn't get to watch a movie."

"I had a much better time doing what we just did." I kiss her. Drop the lightest, most chaste kiss possible on her lips because I can't fall into that trap again. It's one I never want to escape.

"Me too," she whispers when I break away from her.

I touch the tip of her nose, drift my finger across her cheek. "I'll call you? Text you?"

She nods, no hesitancy, no coy games from my girl. She's painfully straightforward—with the exception of talking about her past. "Please. I'd like that."

"Good night, Katie." She steps out of the way and I reach for the handle, opening the door. I'm about to leave when she's tugging on my sleeve and I turn toward her, bracing myself when she plasters her body against mine and gives me one last, soul-searing kiss before sending me off into the night.

"Good night, Ethan," she murmurs as I jog down the steps of her front porch.

Her sweet voice echoes in my head the entire drive home.

WILL

Then

It was her voice that came to me in my dreams, even a year later, after everything that happened. Not so much her face anymore, and I missed that, though I didn't like reliving the way she looked the last time I saw her. Bruised throat, bruised and scraped face. Knowing what caused those wounds—and who.

He came to me in my nightmares far too often. Katie though? Not often enough.

She haunted me in the darkest part of the night with that sweet, melodic voice as she called my name, like she was lost and in search of only me. As if I were the only one who could save her, and the pressure was enormous. I felt it pressing down on me, like a weight sitting on my chest that I couldn't push past no matter how hard I tried.

I heard her say my name again and again, her voice rising, the sound panicked as the distance grew between us. It was always dark in my dreams, so dark I could barely see anything as I went in search of her, scared because I couldn't find her. I never could.

More than anything I was afraid my dad would kill me because he told me to watch over the bitches, that they were sneaky and would do whatever it took to slip away from him. Words he'd never spoken to me in real life, yet I dreamed them anyway. I was even guiltier by association in my dreams.

I always woke up sweaty, gasping for air as my heart

pounded an incessant beat against my ribs. Those dreams twisted and writhed in my brain, fucked me all up because just when I thought I had things under control, that my life had stabilized and felt relatively normal, he'd come back to haunt me.

And so would she.

I never blamed her for what happened. Getting tossed in the foster care system was some straight-up bullshit and really, if I were being honest? It *was* her fault. If she'd let me walk like I wanted when I took her to the police station, I wouldn't be where I was right now. I was fucking miserable in this group home. The other guys living here were a bunch of fucked-up mental cases who preferred to start fires, steal shit, and fuck every girl they could get to drop her panties over anything else.

Me? I stayed focused. I tried to keep up with my homework so I could stay in sports. Which was the only thing that cleared my head and made me feel like someone else. Not like myself.

I really fucking hated myself.

Though I guess it could have been worse. I could've been with my father, living the same dreary, hellish routine that we'd had together for years. Pretending everything was fine when I knew it wasn't.

No matter which way I looked at it, my life was total shit. Sometimes . . . sometimes I wasn't so sure it was even worth living. What sort of existence was this anyway?

But then I thought of Katie and what happened to her. What my father did to her. How fucked up her life must be as she tried to recover. Would she ever find peace? Would she ever be all right? Ever feel whole and alive and normal?

When I compared myself to her, I had no reason to complain. None.

The trial was starting soon. After all the stays and the rescheduled hearings and the protests against biased jury selection—hell, his lawyer had tried to change venues, wanted the trial held in a different county, but that request was denied—it was happening. I had to testify. Katie was planning on testifying as well, from what I understood.

Turned out, she was my father's only surviving victim, at least that they knew of. No one else had stepped forward and the investigation had revealed only three other victims. He'd killed three girls, all under the age of twelve.

Fuck me.

Hanging my head, I tugged the last cigarette out of the pack that was resting on the grass near my feet and settled it between my lips. I brought the lighter to the end of the cig and lit it, taking that first satisfying drag before I blew out smoke. Everything turned peaceful the second I felt the nicotine hit my system.

Fucking nasty habit, but my stress level was through the roof most of the damn time and besides, I never smoked when I was playing a sport. But I snuck a few cigarettes on the weekends or at a party. I couldn't completely let the habit go, despite my knowing full well it was gonna kill me.

I sort of didn't care. About anything.

Least of all me.

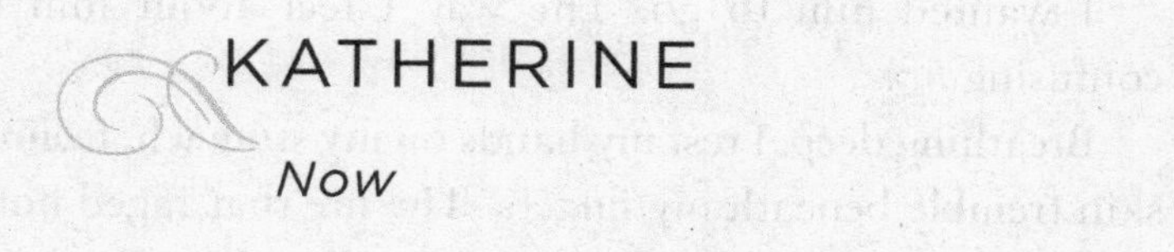

KATHERINE

Now

The moment he left, I went through my normal routine. Locked the front and back doors, cleaned up what was left over in the kitchen, which wasn't much, turned off the lights, went to my bedroom, and brushed my teeth in the adjoining bathroom, but I changed up my final task for the night.

I strip, methodically taking off all my clothes and leaving them in a pile on the floor until I'm left in only my cotton panties. The bedroom light is already off and I crawl onto the bed and lie down in the center of it on top of the comforter, my entire body still vibrating from our kisses, the way he touched me, the look in his eyes, the way his tongue curled around mine.

Adrenaline still flowing through me, I close my eyes and remember the feel of his mouth, his hands, the way he whispered my name, the quiet moan that escaped him when our mouths connected. I wish we could have kissed for longer but it also scared me, the intensity between us every time our lips met. It would lead to more. He touched me in a way that no one ever has and I know what he wanted.

Me. Kissing me, touching me. Sex. With me. And I wanted that, too, I did, but it also scared me.

Scared me so much I was almost relieved when he said he should leave. I'd agreed but then immediately regretted it. I wanted him to stay.

I wanted him to go. The way I feel about him is so confusing . . .

Breathing deep, I rest my hands on my stomach, feeling my skin tremble beneath my fingers. The fire that raged hot earlier when Ethan had his hands on me has calmed but it's still there, lurking just beneath the surface. I smooth my hands up, over my stomach and ribs, stopping just beneath my breasts. I recall the way his thumbs traced the underside of them, so lightly, like a tease, like a promise for more. I slowly cup them, their weight heavy against my palms, my nipples growing hard. A shuddery breath escapes me when I touch them, circling the hard points, feeling the bolt of sensation that shoots from my breasts and lands between my legs.

Never have I touched myself like this. My body is sexually numb. Completely inexperienced. I want to feel more, know more, learn more, and I want Ethan to show me. Touch me.

Teach me.

A sigh escapes as I slip my hands over my belly once more, skimming sensitive, rarely touched skin with my fingertips, trailing them down until they're teasing the thin elastic waistband of my panties. Pausing, my heart races, and slowly I spread my legs, the soft comforter abrading my skin. I tilt my head back at the same exact moment I slip the tips of my fingers beneath my panties.

If I can't be bold with Ethan, I can at least be bold by myself.

I bend my knees and plant my feet on the bed, keeping my shaky legs still spread. Hesitatingly, I push my fingers down, until I'm touching my pubic hair. I go farther, tracing my slit before I slip my fingers in between and encounter creamy, hot wetness. A hiss escapes me and I close my eyes tight, lifting my hips as my fingers go deeper.

It feels . . . good. I can only imagine how much better it would feel if it were Ethan's fingers touching me between my legs. Just thinking of him sets off a pulse inside my core and I know without a doubt that I'm completely and totally aroused.

And it's all because of him.

I allow my fingers to search further, learning myself, sucking in a breath when I touch a certain spot. I brush over it again, the tingly sensation so good a little murmur falls from my lips, and I wonder what it would feel like to have Ethan's fingers touch me here. This particular spot that feels so incredibly wonderful.

The tingling grows at the image of *his* hand between my legs, *his* mouth locked with mine, our bodies pressed close. Never before have I wanted something like this. Have wanted a man to touch me, learn my body, kiss my lips, stir my soul.

I circle the spot with my thumb, going completely still when the pleasure builds. It's so foreign, this feeling. That I've never allowed myself to experience this is such a shame, and I vow right then and there that I won't hold back. That I want this, I want to explore this more. But not just by myself.

With Ethan.

A smile curves my lips as I turn my head, my cheek resting against the pillow. I've got Ethan in my head, my hand in my panties, and the ghost of his mouth still pressed against mine and I've never felt so . . .

Alive.

ETHAN

Now

My name is Katherine Watts.

I study the text I received from Katie earlier this morning, before I woke up. The girl is an early riser, way earlier than me, and I scrub a hand over my face, staring at the words, my gaze dropping to the next text bubble.

Have you heard of me? I sound presumptuous but I have to ask.

Leaning back against my pillows, I slump into the mattress, wondering how I should handle this. I'm still half asleep but I can't forget the way she felt in my arms last night, how she was so responsive. To acknowledge I know who she really is might ruin the tentative connection we've formed; I don't know.

I don't want to risk it.

Are you famous?

I'm an asshole. I toss my phone to the side and scrub both my hands over my face now, as if I can scrub the shitty feeling I have over lying to Katie away. The longer I keep this going, the deeper the hole I'm digging. I'm going to bury myself so deep I'm eventually never going to be able to get out of this unscathed.

Pretty certain I've already hit that point.

But hell. If she finds out who I really am, if I tell her now, she'll be so fucking angry over my lie. I've deceived her. I'm still deceiving her and she'd view it as the ultimate betrayal. I can't blame her. What started out as me watching over her and making sure she's okay has turned into so much more. More than I ever bargained for. Not that I'd change what's happened between us. The connection we share can't be denied. It was formed years ago and the fact that I'm able to explore it, spend time with her, touch her and kiss her and hold her close, makes me a lucky bastard.

My phone dings and I grab it.

I don't know if I'd say famous but I've been in the news off and on for years. It's hard to explain.

A normal guy would be curious. He'd Google her in a heartbeat, with or without her permission. I don't need to Google her, but I think she likes believing that I don't know anything about what happened to her. In her eyes, her past doesn't matter to me because I'm oblivious. If she only knew that her past still doesn't matter even though I know everything, because I was there, how would she feel?

I'm not sure.

Shoving my problems deep, I text her back.

Maybe you could explain it to me. In person.

She responds quickly.

It's just really hard. So much easier to text you.

I get it. I do. The last thing I want is for her to be upset. Sharing her past, what happened to her, is bound to be upsetting. She'll worry about my reaction. I'll worry about hers. All the while I'm holding on to my secret, feeling like a supreme jackass while she's being so honest and open.

I could Google her all I want yet she wouldn't find out anything about me. I blow out a harsh breath. Ethan Williams has no secrets, no social media accounts, nothing. He's boring as shit online and I made sure he's always been that way, from the very moment I created him five years ago. He's my front, my security, the wall I throw up to keep the outsiders away.

But a few wrong moves and a person can fuck everything up. This is me. And you're only as sick as your secrets, or so I've been told. If that's the case, I'm one ill motherfucker. Katie's got nothing on me.

Absolutely nothing.

I finally answer her.

This is probably something we should discuss in person.

You're not going to let me get away with this, are you, she says.

Then she sends me a smiley face with hearts for eyes.

Hell.

I scrub a hand over my face, trying to figure out how to answer her.

I don't want to force you to do anything.

There's a pause and I roll over on my side, scrolling through my phone, checking my in-box. I still have one for Will, a Gmail account I never closed and still have access to on my phone. Hardly anyone ever reaches out to me there, so I'm surprised when I see I have an email.

I open up the in-box and my mouth drops open when I see who the message is from.

Lisa Swanson, network news queen.

Sitting up, I click it open and wait for it to load. Of course, it takes forever. Katie's text reply is flashing at the top of my screen, but I ignore it.

I want to see what Lisa has to say first.

Finally it finishes loading and I scan her message, my heartbeat roaring in my ears.

Dear Will,

I hope I'm able to reach you through this email address. Detective Ross Green gave it to me when I contacted him a few weeks ago and he said it was your last known email address but that he hadn't heard from you in years.

Grimacing, I shake my head. Given up by good ol' Detective Green. I always thought that guy had my back.

Don't know if you saw it, but I interviewed Katherine Watts a while back and it aired on television recently. We talked off camera about you and I wanted to find you. Let you tell your side of the story. You were there. You helped Ms. Watts escape. And then were put under horrific scrutiny that I'm afraid I participated in as well.

Look at her admit she did something wrong. Unbelievable.

I was wondering if you'd be willing to talk, if not in person then perhaps by phone or email? I understand you might wish to keep your privacy and I completely understand. What you went through, who you're associated with is, I'm sure it's a constant struggle. I do hope you'll consider my request.

I hope this email finds you well.

Best,

Lisa Swanson

Talking to her would be begging for trouble. She'd been such a bulldog all those years ago chasing after a big story with utter ruthlessness. Always digging for information, badgering me, just like all the rest of the media who followed me around, pushing for a chance to talk. She'd do the same now. Act all sweet and thoughtful—that's her way of luring me in. Once she had me, she'd do her damnedest to find out all my dirt, investigate me and eventually figure out who I am now. I know she'd figure it out.

Without a doubt I know it. And if that happened, I'd be ruined.

My finger hovers over the button and I finally think *fuck it*.

Quickly, before I change my mind, I delete the email.

I check Katie's text with shaky fingers, mentally telling myself to get a grip. Lisa reaching out has rattled me and I don't like it. I had no idea Detective Green still had that old email address of mine. I don't remember giving it to him, but that doesn't mean shit. How did he get it? And is that the way Lisa really got it? Or is she full of crap?

Pushing Lisa Swanson and her conniving ways out of my mind, I concentrate on Katie's texts.

You're not forcing me. You're right, what I need to tell you is better said in person. It's just hard to share. I'll need you to be patient with me.

So . . . I had a good time last night. I was hoping we could see each other again soon.

Like real soon.

As in what are you doing tonight? ☺

She's getting bold. Only a few minutes ago her texts would have made me smile and I would've agreed to see her, but now with Lisa sniffing around, I'm feeling nothing but pressure. This is a reminder that what I'm doing is all sorts of screwed up. I shouldn't see Katie right now.

What if Lisa wants to talk to her again? Hell, what if she wants to reunite me and Katie? Talk about a story—one that she won't get, but still. And not that I think Lisa would recognize me if we were ever to meet—I look totally different than my fifteen-year-old self, so different that even Katie doesn't recognize me. But Lisa's like a fucking bloodhound and she'd probably sniff me out, no problem.

That woman scares the shit out of me.

I need to back off. Back away from Katie and put the brakes on this—whatever I'm doing with her. I don't want Katie to think I'm doing this because of what she's trying to reveal to me. That would devastate her.

How else can I handle this, though? I've dug myself a hole and can't climb out of it. Most of the time I don't want to. But that's me being selfish. Dealing with what my father did to her, listening to her confession and having to pretend I know nothing about her past . . .

I don't know if I can do it.

Staring at my cellphone screen, I force myself to come up with an excuse. It's what's best. I should let her down gently and eventually fade from her life. She'll move on and eventually forget all about me.

But I'll never be able to forget her.

I hate to tell you this, but I have another big project due in a few days and I need to bust my ass to get it done.

Not necessarily a lie but not completely true, either. It's not due till the end of the month.

Oh, I understand. I have a paper I need to write for school anyway. So I guess that means you're busy tonight?

Yeah, I am. I'm sorry. I'd really like to see you again and I know we need to talk, Katie, but it might take a few days.

It should take fucking forever if I were being truthful with myself.

She sends me a reply filled with various emoji accompanied by the words Maybe some other time, and I crack a smile.

Though it disappears in an instant. I hate what I'm doing. It's all a bunch of fucked-up trickery. My motives are selfish, my behavior is shady, and she's blissfully ignorant of all of it. I'm living a lie. But I've lived a lie for so long you'd think I'd be used to it by now.

Turns out I'm not.

WILL

Then

"Your father wants to talk to you."

I shook my head, pissed at this stupid lawyer who was supposed to be watching over me instead approaching me with the craziest statement I've ever heard.

"Tell that asshole to go to hell," I muttered, feeling on edge. I was here at the courthouse to testify against the bastard, not have old home week and reunite with him. He'd probably try to tear my throat out if I got too close. He had to be furious with me. I was going on the stand for the prosecution.

His own son. His only flesh-and-blood relative in this world was speaking against him.

"Will." My father's lawyer gave a deep sigh and shook his head. "Just give him a few minutes. Please. It'll make him look like more of a family man."

"Family man." I snorted. The last thing I'd ever call my father is a family man. "Sure he is." So the jury wavers and eventually decides to let a killer free. I don't think I could live with myself if that happened. I turned to look at my lawyer. "I shouldn't do this, huh."

"You shouldn't." He paused and took a deep breath.

My father's lawyer looked at me. "He misses you, Will. He told me so himself. Just give him this chance," he pleaded, his eyes watery, like he might break out in tears.

Give me a break.

I crossed my arms in front of my chest. "Bullshit. What does he want to talk about anyway? How much he hates me for turning against him? Maybe offer up details about what exactly he did to those girls who died?"

"Will," my lawyer chastised—I couldn't even remember his name half the time—but I was just warming up.

"He may as well give me those details considering I supposedly worked with him, you know? I just didn't want to get caught. That's why I brought Katie Watts to the police station. So I'd look like a shining hero instead of a scumbag who likes to rape girls along with his father."

"That's enough." I glanced up at my lawyer—his last name was Stone, and when I saw the steely look in his eyes, I couldn't help but think his name was extra fitting. "My client is not willing to talk to Mr. Monroe."

Curiosity got the better of me. "I want to talk to him."

"I advise against it," Stone started, but I shook my head.

"Just for a few minutes. I want to hear what he has to say." It would probably be a mistake, but I had to know.

Within minutes I was escorted to another small room, this one in the depths of the courthouse, where the air was cool and still, the dull buzzing of people milling about and talking dimmed, almost nonexistent. I was surrounded by deputies, two in front of me, two trailing behind me, and my lawyer walked by my side, my father's lawyer leading the way.

Nerves ate at my gut and I tried my best to ignore the uneasy feeling that slipped over me. I could end this conversation whenever I wanted. I had no obligation to the man. He may have raised me, but he fucked me over in more ways than I could ever count and for that, I would never be able to fully forgive him.

I didn't want to forgive him. Everything he had done was unforgivable. The man was a monster.

What frightened me the most? The possibility I could turn into a monster, too.

We stopped at a nondescript door and one of the deputies pushed it open, leading the group inside. A long table sat in the middle of the room, my father on the other side of it. He wore the requisite county jail orange jumpsuit, his wrists and feet shackled, his skin pasty with an almost green tinge, caused by a lack of sunlight.

He smiled when he saw me and lifted his wrists in a sort of greeting. "Will."

I said nothing as I sat down across from him. Stone sat to the right of me. The deputies all hovered behind me and I saw the two that stood behind my dad. Though I didn't trust the police, given the way they treated me after I brought in Katie, I was still reassured by their heavy presence. They weren't messing around.

"You look good," Dad said with a smile. A smile that I noticed didn't quite reach his eyes.

"I can't say the same for you," I muttered, making him laugh.

"I always did appreciate your honesty." He paused, and I glanced up to find him watching me with an almost nostalgic spark in his gaze. "I've missed you, son."

Everything inside of me tensed up. I really hated when he called me that, especially now. I didn't want anyone to know who I was, that his blood flowed in my veins and we shared the same features and practically the same name. I hated that I was forever linked to this man. A serial killer. A rapist of little girls. God knew what else he'd done over the years. Those were only the things he got caught for.

When I said nothing, he continued on. "Are you all right? They treating you okay in the foster system? You only have a year or so left, kid, and then you can skip out on your own."

Like that was going to be easy. I could work. I was working now, part time, so I could have my own money and not have to rely on anyone else. But the thought of being completely on my own still scared the crap out of me, not that I'd admit it to anyone.

Not even my old man.

"You think you're going to beat this?" I asked him because I had to know. He'd always been an arrogant bastard, even at his lowest points. Drunk and jobless with a raging meth problem and he'd strut around town like he was king stud. I'd never seen anyone with such a healthy ego. I realized even when I was a little kid that his behavior wasn't normal.

"I don't know." He shrugged. His shoulders looked small. He'd shrunken in size since he'd been in jail. He'd always been larger than life to me until I finally got some inches on my frame and eventually grew taller than he was. Stronger, too. My size and strength eventually had saved my ass from having to do things he'd tried to force on me.

I couldn't help but wonder more than once if he'd gone on to rape and murder little girls because he could no longer take out his rage on me. Yet another dose of guilt my father's actions had heaped upon me.

"What do you mean you don't know?" I wanted insight into his thoughts.

"The evidence they have on me is pretty bad, with that Watts girl talking. Did you hear her testimony?" He peered at me, his eyes narrowing, going black like they did just before he started yelling. Ice-cold memories slipped over me and I fought against them. I refused to let him scare me. This man couldn't do anything to me without six deputies jumping on his ass. "Are you really going to testify against me?"

Straight to the point. Gotta love dear old dad. I ignore his second question. "I didn't hear her testimony."

"Didn't even see it on the news? You know those lawyers are going to see if your stories match up."

Anger rumbled just beneath the surface and I leaned across the table, glaring at him. "Our stories will match up considering we're both telling the truth."

He glared right back, never missing a beat. "You so sure about that?"

"I can't even believe we're sitting here talking about this."

His lawyer stepped forward. I hadn't even realized he was there. "Aaron, I would suggest—"

"Shut the fuck up." Dad smiled, his gaze never leaving mine. "Lawyers. They can't stop suggesting things."

"You should probably take his advice." We were in a roomful of deputies and lawyers. What he said could be used against him if he didn't watch it.

"I'm thinking you should probably take *my* advice." His smile was eerily pleasant. I could imagine him leaping across the table and wrapping his hands around my neck so he could choke me out. The only reassurance I had that he wouldn't do it was the presence of all the menacing deputies surrounding us. They'd pull him off of me in seconds.

"And what's that?" I asked warily.

"Don't talk about that day. Any of those days you saw Katie Watts. Say you don't remember what happened."

I gaped at him. Couldn't believe he had the nerve to say something to me like that. "Like they'll believe me," I scoffed.

"They can't make you testify. If you can't remember, you can't, you know?" The silence between us, between everyone in the room, was downright deafening. "I would suggest it's best if you don't remember, if you know what I mean."

"What, like that's going to help get you off, my faulty memory? I don't think so."

"It'll help, damn it." He banged his fists on the table, his handcuffs clanking, and two deputies shifted forward, ever ready to pounce. "Not that you give a shit."

I pushed back in my chair and stood, staring down at him. "You're right," I said through clenched teeth. "I don't give a shit. Just like you never gave a shit. Did you care what happened to me? You were too busy fucking all your whores or snorting crank or whatever you did. Stalking and murdering little girls."

He smiled again, serenely. Like he hadn't a care in the world. All while I was seething inside, filled with rage and so tense I felt like I could shatter. No one else said a word—not the lawyers, not the deputies. The only sound that filled the room was my harsh, ragged breaths.

"You never cared about me," I finally said. "I was always a burden, or a toy for you to play with when you felt like it. So fuck you." I looked at my lawyer, who was already scrambling out of his seat. "I'm done."

"Let's go." Stone grabbed hold of my arm and started to escort me out of the small room, the deputies falling into step beside us.

"I won't forget this, son," my father called, his voice ringing with an almost manic-sounding false hope. I couldn't begin to understand him. I never could. "I'll never forget you turned against me. Someday you'll pay for this. Karma is a bitch."

"You should know, old man." Pausing at the door, I glanced at him from over my shoulder. "Considering where you're going to spend the rest of your life. And don't call me 'son.' You lost that right a long time ago."

With those final words, I walked out, headed straight to the courtroom . . .

And sat on the stand for over two hours as I testified against my father.

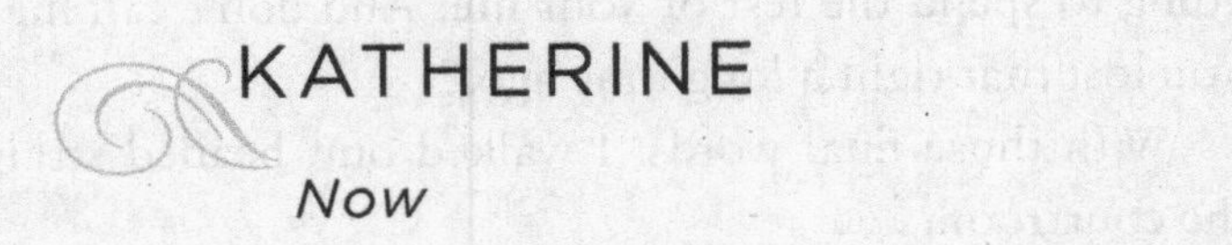

KATHERINE

Now

"I feel like I did something wrong."

My therapist—she keeps insisting I call her Sheila, and so now I finally am—watches me with her ever thoughtful gaze, her lips pursed as if she doesn't like what I just said. She probably doesn't. "Why do you feel like that?"

I shrug. It's hard to put into words, my disappointment. How all-encompassing it's been these last few days while I've been telling myself over and over I'm being too dramatic. I've been rejected. I spend one incredibly romantic night with Ethan, I tell him my last name via text, we discuss having a serious talk about my past, and now . . . nothing. No word from him. Crickets. That's it.

Clearly he wants nothing to do with me.

"Because I told him who I was and I haven't heard from him since. He probably Googled my name and found out all the dirty details of my life. That would scare any guy away," I explain, blowing out a breath of frustration once I'm finished.

"Then he wasn't the man for you," Sheila says, as if that's an acceptable answer.

But it's not. Not to me. I truly thought Ethan and I had a connection. The chemistry was definitely there between us. I know he felt it, too. That night when we made out, if I hadn't been so nervous, I would have let him take it farther. If he showed up on my front doorstep right now I'd probably let him take it farther.

Well, I'd want to punch him first. I'm sure he could persuade me with his lips, though, and make all of that anger melt away with just a few kisses. Not smart on my part. I shouldn't be so easy, but I don't want to let this go.

I don't want to let *him* go.

"I want him to be the man for me," I say with a sigh. "I like him. But maybe he doesn't like me. Maybe he thinks I'm too damaged."

"Who says you're damaged?"

I blink at Sheila, irritated by her calm demeanor, the surprised tone to her voice. "I am. It's pretty undeniable, right?"

"No, it's not. If you think of yourself as damaged, broken, whatever word you want to use, then guess what? That's all anyone who knows you or meets you will see."

I contemplate her words. As reluctant as I am to admit it, they make sense. "I guess I've always assumed the role of damaged girl," I say.

"Not a surprise considering what you've been through. But don't forget how offended you become whenever someone refers to you as a victim. You hate that word," Sheila points out.

"I despise it," I say in agreement.

"So you call yourself a survivor yet claim you're damaged."

"I think a survivor can still be damaged," I admit. "Don't you?" We all have things we need to overcome, some worse than others. It's okay to be hurt, to be damaged and a little broken and still consider yourself strong. Not that I'd ever considered myself strong before, not until recently . . .

"I truly think a survivor wouldn't want that word associated with her. *Damaged* implies permanence. Don't you want to stand tall above what happened to you? Not let it define you?" Sheila cocks her head, watching me.

"He kissed me."

"And you liked it."

There's no point in denying it. "I loved every minute of it." Just thinking of his lips on mine makes me shiver. "I think I scared him by mentioning I wanted to talk to him about my past."

"Do you think you moved too fast?"

"Maybe." I shrug. "I don't know how to maneuver in the dating world. This is my first attempt and honestly, I don't want to deal with a bunch of crap."

Dr. Harris raises a brow. "What crap are you referring to?"

"Game playing. Coyness. Putting on a front. It all feels like lies if I do that. I just want to be open. Honest. Real."

"And you want the same from him."

"Definitely." I nod.

"Then tell him that. Maybe he is nervous. Maybe he really is busy. But you should be open and honest and real with him, just like you want him to be with you. You might be surprised by your results."

"Pleasantly surprised?" Now it's my turn to raise a brow.

"You deserve happiness, Katherine," Sheila says, her voice soft. "Finding a nice man who cares for you, engaging yourself fully in a romantic relationship, learning how to be comfortable with your body, with your sexuality. Finding pleasure with a man. You deserve every bit of that."

She lays it out on the line and normally I'd be embarrassed. In the past I didn't even like to hear the word *sex*.

But now, I'm curious. It sounds ridiculous, but I want to find myself. I want to become a woman. A normal, regular woman who has sex and isn't scared to say the word out loud.

"I want to have sex with Ethan," I blurt, making Sheila smile. "But I'm scared."

"That's natural." She nods.

"I like it when he touches me. When he looks at me, it's like he's trying to see beneath my clothes and it's not in a gross way." I sigh and shake my head. "I'm not making sense."

"You're making perfect sense," Sheila reassures me.

"So what do I do? Sit by the phone and wait for him to text me? Make the next move? I don't know how to do this." I lean back against the chair, irritated with myself. Irritated with Ethan.

"You do what you feel most comfortable with. And if you don't want to do anything at the moment, that's okay, too."

I nod, not willing to speak. I'm tired. Feeling drained. I haven't slept much, too worried over what happened between Ethan and me, which is stupid. I'm sure he hasn't lost a lick of sleep over me.

He's probably already forgotten all about me.

"Do you have any regrets, Katherine?" Sheila asks after a few quiet minutes tick by.

"About what?" I ask warily.

"Going on a date with Ethan. Letting him kiss you. Inviting him to your home." I'd told her all the details and she hadn't so much as batted an eyelash. Now she was making me doubt my choices. "Are you thinking that maybe you shouldn't have done that?"

"I'm glad I did it," I say truthfully. "I can't stay cooped up in my house forever, letting life pass me by."

"Good answer." Sheila sounds proud. "How about the interview? Still okay with your decision?"

"You heard about the movie," I say, my voice flat.

Dr. Harris nods but otherwise doesn't say a word.

"I don't like the idea of another cheesy TV movie being made about my kidnapping, but I can't stop it." I sit up and shrug. "What's done is done."

"Your attitude is very healthy." Sheila smiles. "Much healthier than it was only a few weeks ago. I think you've made progress."

Hope lights within my chest. I need to hear this. Need to see that someone else believes in me, not just a family member who has to. I'd hoped Ethan could give me the same support, but I'd been wrong.

Taking a deep breath, I launch into the last subject I wanted to talk about during our session.

"I've been thinking about someone." I finger the bracelet Will Monroe gave me, rubbing my thumb over the guardian angel charm, along every ridge of her wings. "Someone from my past."

"Who?"

"Will Monroe."

Her expression remains neutral but I see the slight flare in her eyes. No one understands why I'm so interested in Will, why I feel the need to talk about him. I think they all wish I'd forgotten him. "What about him?"

My family never understood. Sheila probably won't understand either.

"He's the real reason I'm alive. It's not because of me, or anything I did. I feel like I owe him something. I wish I knew where he was, so I could see him. Talk to him."

"You shouldn't feel like you owe him anything. You played a big part in your return," Sheila points out, and I send her a look. It doesn't even faze her. "Perhaps you're giving him too much credit."

"Perhaps I don't give him enough. That's the biggest problem. His name is rarely mentioned because of who his father is. That's not fair. He didn't choose his family, his father. No one should blame him for this. He's a hero. Will Monroe is *my* hero."

I bite my lip, not quite willing to express my deeper concerns. That I'm so interested in Will lately because of meeting Ethan. They remind me of each other. Their features are vaguely similar but not quite. The Will I remember was lanky and average height, with long black hair and piercings, with a somber expression and intense gaze, as though he saw everything and hated it all. A boy who rarely smiled.

A boy with no reason to smile.

Ethan had a different attitude, a better attitude, but he was a rescuer. Like Will. If Sheila ever realizes that I compare the two of them, she'll just try to overanalyze the entire situation and I'll be opening up a whole new can of worms.

I can hear her tapping away on her iPad and I wish I'd never brought Will up. He's a sensitive subject. He'll always be a sensitive subject.

And I hate that.

Regret washes over me and I pull so tight on the charm of my bracelet I feel it give, the guardian angel no longer attached to the bracelet but now lying in my palm. I stare at it helplessly, upset that I so casually broke it, after all these years. I should have known better, taken care of it better. The angel charm is fragile.

Like my heart.

"Have you spoken to him at all?" Sheila asks.

"Will Monroe is nowhere to be found." Tears prick the corners of my eyes as I stare down at the pretty angel who represented so much to me. "He gave me this." I hold up the charm to her. "I just—I just broke it."

The words pass my lips and it's my turn to break. To cry. I

bend over my knees and sob, letting the tears fall without care, my chest aching, my head hurting as I clutch the charm so close I can feel the edges of it press into the thick skin of my palm. I cry for me, for my family, for that stupid, ridiculous man Ethan who ignores me and doesn't deserve my tears.

The person I cry the most for, though, is Will Monroe.

And he has no idea.

KATHERINE

Now

The text comes three days later, seemingly out of nowhere.

I want to take you out tonight.

Gnawing on my lower lip, my fingers hover over the keyboard of my cellphone, unsure of how to reply. I should tell Ethan to go to hell. The best action would be to not reply to him at all.

But I can't ignore the longing I feel at just seeing his words in a text bubble. Clearly I'm weaker than I thought.

Weak for Ethan.

What do you have in mind?

He immediately replies and I smile at his answer.

Concert for a Web client. Small band playing at a club. It'll be fun.

Totally out of my element. I've never been to a concert. I don't always do well in crowds. This could be a recipe for disaster. I should say no.

I don't.

What time are you thinking?

It's like my fingers have a mind of their own.

I'll pick you up at your house say around 8? Concert doesn't start until 10 and the club is here. Downtown.

Say no. Tell him you have other plans. Tell him you have no interest dating a guy who runs so hot and cold. You deserve more. You deserve better. You can resist him. Really you can.

Sounds good. What should I wear?

His answer not even a minute later makes me smile so hard it almost hurts.

Something sexy.

And this is why I can't resist him. Why I allow him to play with my emotions despite his bad behavior. I like him. Allowing him into my life wasn't easy, and I wasn't going to kick him out because he isn't perfect. That's just ridiculous.

Absolutely ridiculous.

He picked me up when he didn't have to and I appreciated it. Appreciated even more the way he looked when I found him on my doorstep. Black long-sleeved Henley that somehow defined every muscle in his arms and chest and dark-rinse jeans that were slightly baggy yet molded to his strong thighs. His hair was freshly cut though left longish on top and he had about two days' worth of scruff lining his cheeks. A total contradiction.

A very sexy contradiction.

His appreciative gaze as he drank me in set a flurry of newfound butterflies free in my stomach and blood rushed to my cheeks when he murmured, "You took my suggestion to heart, didn't you, Katie?"

I'd never dressed sexy for anyone before and I was unsure

if my outfit was sexy enough. I wore the tightest jeans I owned and a simple black tank top, though I threw on a hoodie before we left considering it was cold. I left my hair down so it fell in natural waves down my back and slipped silver hoop earrings on, jewelry my sister gave me two Christmases ago that I'd never worn.

I felt like a different person. A new me. A woman who dressed for a man and was able to chat with him for the entire ninety-minute ride with ease. Who laughed and joked and didn't once ask why he hadn't texted or called.

The night had started on such a positive note, I didn't want to ruin it.

"What sort of music does the band play?" I ask as we head toward the entrance of the club. The parking lot is packed and I can already hear music coming from within, the throb of bass and drums, reverberation as someone sang into a mic. The night air is cool as it washes over my skin, making me shiver, and I regret leaving my hoodie in Ethan's car.

But I knew I'd get hot wearing it inside, so I really had no choice.

"They have a nineties grunge sound. They borrow heavily from Soundgarden and STP." At my blank look, Ethan continues. "Stone Temple Pilots. Don't tell me you've never heard of them."

I slowly shake my head. "I didn't listen to much nineties grunge. Way before my time. Kurt Cobain died the year I was born."

He laughs. "Before my time, too, but I discovered them when I was around fourteen, fifteen." A shadow crosses his face, his lush mouth forming into a frown. "Dark music for a dark kid."

"Were you a dark kid?" I step in closer to him, drawn in by

his warmth. His body heat radiates, calling me like a siren, and I wish I were brave enough to wrap my arm around him and absorb some of that delicious heat.

"Yeah." His mouth turns tight and he glances down at me, coming to a stop. "Cold?"

Another shiver passes through me at the exact time he asks. "Sort of," I mumble.

He does exactly what I wished I could do. Without thought he slips an arm around my waist and pulls me into him, fitting me perfectly under his arm. "Luckily enough there's no line at the door. Once we get inside, it'll be like a sauna. You'll be glad you wore the tank."

Within minutes we're in the club, Ethan taking hold of my hand as he leads me through the bar area in the front, pulling me close to murmur in my ear, asking if I want anything to drink. I don't drink much alcohol and I want to keep my head clear tonight so I say no. He orders himself a beer, reassuring me he'll only have one since he has to drive me home.

I say nothing. Just glance around the bar, taking in the variety of people surrounding us. Young and old, some dressed like us, others wearing such outrageous clothes I wonder if they're in costume. One girl has a giant hoop hanging from beneath her nose. Two guys are standing in a corner, their hands as busy as their mouths. Another girl walks by, she looks around my age, and the dress she has on is so short I can guarantee I'll see the back end of her underwear as she passes.

Nope. I actually see the bottom half of her butt cheeks. As in, she's wearing no underwear. Swallowing hard, I shake my head.

I've never seen anything like it. I feel like a gawking little kid.

The opening band has finished their set and Ethan's clients

are already up onstage, tuning their instruments, the riffs on the guitar loud and screeching. I wince, my gaze clashing with that of a man who's standing not even twenty feet away from us. My hand is still clasped in Ethan's, I'm clearly with him for the evening, but the flirtatious wink and devilish smile the man sends me fills me with irrational fear.

I turn away from him, pressing my cheek against Ethan's biceps as I close my eyes and breathe deep his intoxicating scent. I didn't like the way that guy looked at me. Like I was a piece of meat on display just for him. Maybe this dressing sexy for a man isn't all that it's cracked up to be . . .

"You all right?" I glance up to find Ethan watching me, his dark brows furrowed with concern, the beer bottle clasped in his hand. I don't answer, just offer him a reassuring smile. He smiles in return, though I still see worry in his eyes. "Let's go see if we can find a table."

Without a word I let Ethan lead me into the back half of the club, where there's a section of round tables and chairs, every one of them full. The open area in front of the stage is crowded with onlookers, most of them female, many of them scantily clad and yelling obscene things to the guys onstage.

"They have a strong female following," Ethan says, his mouth twisted into a wry smile, just as a shrill female voice screams out, "I want you to fuck me, Marty!"

"I can see that," I murmur, gasping out loud when a girl lifts her top and flashes her braless breasts at the stage.

Ethan slips his arm around my shoulders, his mouth at my ear. "You're okay with this, right?"

I'm uncomfortable. I can't deny it. But being at this concert, watching girls throw themselves at a bunch of sweaty guys who play instruments and sing decently, isn't going to kill me.

Doing something different is good. Sheila would be proud of me. She'd call it part of my growth process or whatever.

The drummer counts, his drumsticks tapping out a beat before the band launches into a song that is heavy on the guitar, the lead singer's moody voice filling the room. We're standing on the edge of the open area, Ethan having removed his arm from around my shoulders as people stream by us, crowding all around us. He's drinking his beer, his body moving slightly to the beat, and I can only stand there awkwardly, feeling unsure.

What do I do, what do I say, how do I move? I've never been much of a dancer, at least publicly. I've never been much of anything really. It's as though my life came to a complete standstill at the age of almost thirteen and I didn't allow myself to experience much of anything.

How sad is that?

I remember all the times I skipped around in the privacy of my bedroom, shaking my hips to the sound of Katy Perry songs. I'd never been to a school dance, but I'd watched enough music videos on YouTube to pick up some moves. I could do this if I could just let go. Drop all the worry and the misgivings and the self-consciousness and just . . . be.

Resolve slowly fills me and I stand up straight. If I want to dance, I should dance. And if I want to feel a man's hands on me as I move to the beat, I shouldn't feel ashamed. I'm a grown woman with—needs.

Yeah. Needs.

The song ends and the crowd roars their approval. The band doesn't hesitate, just launches into another song, and I turn to face Ethan, excitement pulsing in my veins as I step closer to him, my hand on his shoulder. "Take me to the front of the stage," I yell at him, hoping he can hear me above the din.

"What?" He frowns, looking confused, his eyes narrowed behind his glasses.

He's so adorable. Bringing me here tonight is quickly making up for his earlier awful behavior.

"I want to get closer to the stage," I yell again, emphasizing each word.

He glances toward the crowd lining the front of the stage. "It's packed."

I shrug. "So?"

"Hot. Sweaty." He sniffs the air. "And someone's passing around a joint."

Drugs and alcohol, all while listening to a live band play. Tonight is like nothing I've ever experienced in my life. "I don't care. Not like I'm going to smoke it."

He starts to laugh. "You sure you want to go out there?"

I nod, my hair sliding against my damp neck. The heat is already getting to me but I don't care. I want to experience this. Want to immerse myself completely into this night and I want Ethan by my side while I do it.

He takes me by the crook of the elbow and leads me into the fray. "Then let's do this."

ETHAN

Now

I've never seen Katie like this before. She's open and warm, her lithe body swaying to the beat as I stand behind her, glaring at every motherfucker who gets too close. We're standing as close to the stage as we can get, right in front of a speaker, so the music is extra loud. There's no point in talking—we couldn't hear each other anyway and besides, there's no need for words.

Our bodies are talking loud enough.

I'm an ass for reaching out to her like I did, as if nothing ever happened between us a few days ago. But the need to see her, smell her, touch her was so strong I couldn't resist. Going so many hours without talking to her was pure torture. Having her like this now, my hands resting on her hips, her scent wrapping around me and making me as high as those assholes passing around the joint a few feet to our left, I'm in heaven.

Or hell. I can't quite tell which yet.

The set is almost over and the band saves one of their most popular songs for last. The crowd goes crazy with their approval when they hear the song begin and Katie hops up and down, yelling along with them. She glances over her shoulder, sending me a sweet smile, and I don't remove my hands from her hips. In fact, I pull her in closer, her back flush with my chest, her ass nestled against my groin. Her body stiffens the slightest bit, I can sense her discomfort, and then slowly, she relaxes.

Her trust in me is humbling.

The crowd goes wild around us but I don't move. I brush Katie's sweat-dampened hair away from her nape and press my mouth there. A brief yet lingering kiss on her smooth, soft skin that's never been touched by another. Just me. A tremble moves through her and she bends her head forward, as if asking for more, and I give it to her.

More kisses, soft, hungry presses of my mouth against her fevered skin. A sound escapes her; I hear it even with the band playing and the people yelling. A sexy hum as she tilts her head to the side, allowing me a glimpse of her face. Her eyes are closed, her lips parted, her cheeks flushed.

Sexy.

My tightly reined-in control slips. The need for her grows and I get hard. Hell, I don't want to scare her. Don't want to push too fast, but she's so unbelievably gorgeous like this. I've wanted her for what feels like forever and now that I have her, the two of us playing at normal, I don't want to let her go.

Despite the warning bells clanging in my head, despite my knowing I'm tempting trouble and could end up hurting the both of us, I can't stop. This has been years in the making.

A lifetime of wondering. Of wanting. Of needing.

I let one hand slide from her hip to her front, splaying my fingers wide as I rest my hand on her stomach. She shifts against me, the sensation of her backside brushing against my erection nearly making my eyes cross. I toy with the hem of her tank, deciding to hell with it, and slip my fingers beneath the fabric, encountering nothing but the hot skin of her belly.

She sucks in a breath, her stomach muscles contract, and she glances over her shoulder at me, our gazes clashing. I'm asking her permission without saying a word, needing this moment with her, wanting the connection of skin on skin. If I could I'd touch her everywhere. Strip her of her clothing, search her body, use my mouth and hands to bring her pleasure. Make her forget every ugly thing that's ever happened to her.

Katie's still watching me and I lean in, press my mouth to hers in a brief kiss. She turns toward me, her hands going to my chest, her body nestled against mine as she kisses me this time. Our mouths are hungry, our hands clutching as the crowd shifts around us, the heavy beat of the song seeming to keep time with our kisses.

I break away first, needing to catch my breath, calm my thoughts, and she pulls away, taking my hand to lead me through the crowd.

I follow blindly, not sure where she's taking us. Screaming applause erupts around us as the lead singer—Jay—announces that they're done for the night. It's a lie. I've watched them before. They'll play an encore, maybe two, before they finally retire for the night. The crowd knows it and not a one of them moves a muscle.

This gains me time. Time alone with Katie.

We somehow end up in a darkened hallway, the bathrooms nearby. I press her against the wall, my hands at her waist, her hands in my hair, as we continue where we left off. Mouths open, tongues wild. She whimpers, sexy little sounds low in her throat that drive me insane with wanting her, and my hands are beneath her shirt again, gripping bare skin, moving up, greedy as always.

Katie makes me greedy. Makes me want what I shouldn't have.

She murmurs my name against my neck after we come up for air, her mouth against my skin, her hot breath radiating through me. I clutch her close, my hands falling to the back of her thighs so I can lift her up. Her legs automatically go around my hips, as if it's the most natural thing in the world, and I pin her to the wall. I lean my head back at the exact moment her eyes open and our gazes meet, mine full of questions.

Hers full of uncertainty. Desire.

Katie licks her lips and I bite back the groan that wants to escape. She's inherently sexy and doesn't have a clue what she does to me.

"Do you want me to stop?" I ask, sounding tortured. I'll do it. I'll stop for her. Whatever she wants, I'll give her, no questions asked.

She slowly shakes her head and I move in closer, triumph making my heart light, the sensation of her body pressed so close to mine making my head spin. "No," she whispers.

That's all the permission I need. I kiss her, drown in her, search her mouth with my tongue, search her body with my hands, and she arches against me. Doesn't stop me when I should be stopped. Doesn't tell me no when I should hear that word again and again.

What I'm doing is wrong. But it feels so damn right I know I'll never be the same again. I'll always want this, need it, crave it. Crave her.

Minutes pass. Long, drugging minutes filled with kisses and touches and gasps and sighs. People pass by but we don't pay them any mind. She stiffens once, twice, aware that we're in public and putting on a show, but we're deep in the shadows at the back of the hall. Not out in the crowd in front of the stage.

The band is finished, I hear Jay scream out an enthusiastic good night, and the air shifts. Changes. Fills with the sharp scent of sweat and booze, perfume and cologne as the crowd disperses, many of them making their way toward the bathrooms, which we're not too far away from.

Katie ends our kiss, her breathing erratic, her chest rising and falling against mine, her breasts tempting me. But I restrain myself, play it cool, hope like hell this isn't it for the night.

"That was . . ." Her voice drifts and she nibbles on her swollen lower lip, her gaze almost reluctantly meeting mine. Her cheeks are flushed, her expression shy, and I want nothing more than to gobble her up.

"Awesome? Amazing? Unbelievably good?" I offer up as suggestions, pressing my mouth to hers in another lingering kiss.

I can feel the smile that curves her sweet lips. "Insane," she whispers. "There are so many people here."

"They didn't notice us." Her legs are still loosely wrapped around my hips, our bodies pressed close. I pull away from her mouth and touch her cheek, drift the back of my fingers along satiny-smooth skin. "I should take you home."

Her eyes change color, if that's possible, turning a deeper, darker blue. "Yes," she agrees. "You should."

I glance toward the end of the hall, which leads backstage. "I should go tell Jay they put on a hell of a show. Want to go backstage with me?"

She slowly shakes her head. "It's okay. I, um, need to use the restroom before we go."

Unease slips down my spine. I don't want to leave her alone. Not even for a minute. Talk about overprotective. "Are you sure? I can wait for you."

"The line is mega long for the ladies' room." She waves a hand at the line, which runs down the hall and out into the main room of the club. "By the time you're done talking to your friend, I'll barely be inside the restroom."

I cup her cheek and tilt her head back so our gazes meet. "Are you sure?"

She nods, smiling. "I'm a big girl, Ethan. I can use the restroom by myself."

The details of exactly how my father abducted her fill my mind. The similarity of this situation doesn't go unnoticed, but . . . she's right. She's a twenty-one-year-old woman who's fully capable of taking care of herself. Not a naïve kid who believes every lie a creep tells her.

"Okay. I'll be right back." I kiss her, our mouths lingering. "If you're ready before me, wait right here. This will be our meeting spot."

She nods, her gaze stuck on my lips. The need to kiss her again is overwhelming. "Okay," she murmurs.

I don't move until I see her get in line for the restroom and then I slip down the hall, toward the backstage area. The bodyguard stops me and I tell him who I am, knowing that I'm on their list. He lets me back and I go in search of Jay and the rest of the guys, ready to give them a brief compliment and thank-you before I hightail my ass out of there and go back to Katie.

The change in her tonight has been amazing. Mind blowing. She's so open and warm and sexy, willing to do just about anything I want. To the point of shocking me, if I'm being honest with myself. She should be angry with me, what with the way I ignored her. Trying to do what's best for her never seems to work, though, not when it comes to me.

I can't resist her. The need to be close to her, to see her smile, to hear her voice, to bask in her presence, is just too overwhelming to deny. I know it's wrong, but I'm tired of denying myself. I'm tempted to go after what I want.

And what I want is . . .

Katie.

In my arms. Beneath me. Naked. In my bed.

Forever.

KATHERINE

Now

The line to the ladies' room moved surprisingly fast and I finished before Ethan returned. I even made friends with some other women while in line, all of us chatting about the band, the girls comparing notes over how sexy they thought the lead singer was.

When I told them my date actually knew the lead singer, I thought they would explode with envy. They kept going on about it, even calling me an idiot when I said I'd turned down an opportunity to go backstage.

But I don't care about the lead singer. The only man I find remotely sexy is Ethan.

I'm waiting for him now, standing in the exact spot where he had me pressed against the wall, his mouth fused with mine. Memories flooded me, one after the other, and I knew the flush in my cheeks wasn't caused by the hot air swirling in the building.

I can't believe how uninhibited I acted, but then again . . . it was exactly what I wanted to do. Let go, be free, be normal. This is what twenty-one-year-old girls do. They go out to concerts at nightclubs and dance. They let their dates put their hands on them and kiss them. They might even make out in dark corners and get lost in the taste of a man's lips and tongue.

A smile curls my lips and I touch them, brush my fingertips

over my swollen mouth. Giddiness rises in me and I wonder if I should invite Ethan inside when he takes me home. I don't know if I'm ready for all that, but I'm close. So incredibly close . . .

"Hey beautiful."

I jerk my head up at the unfamiliar male voice, glancing around when I see no one. My heart trips over itself as it starts to race and a man steps out of the shadows. The same man that winked at me when Ethan and I first got here.

Uneasiness slips down my spine as I watch him warily.

The smile never leaves his face. "Not going to say hi?"

I lift my chin, hoping he doesn't see the fear that's starting to eat me up inside. "I don't even know you."

"Doesn't mean you can't say hello to a stranger." He steps closer and I press myself against the wall as discreetly as possible, wishing Ethan were here. But he's nowhere to be found. "What's your name? Don't think I've seen you around here before."

I say nothing, contemplating my next move. I could dart around him and make my escape, but what if he stopped me? Now that he's closer, I can see the redness rimming his eyes, the slightly slack look to his jaw and mouth. He's drunk. And eyeing me like I'm the best thing he's seen in a long time.

"Want me to get you a drink? You look a little lonely." He slurs his words, stumbles over his own feet and chuckles. "Whoops."

I seriously need to get out of here. "I'm waiting for someone."

"Who?" He frowns. "The four-eyed dork you came in here with? I could take that guy."

I doubt it. Ethan's got a few inches on this creep, plus he's not drunk.

"Besides," the man continues as he draws even closer, "he's not here. So I'm guessing you're fair game."

He talks about me like I have no say in this. Deciding to make a break for it, I push away from the wall, skirting around him, ready to make my dash to freedom, but he's quicker than I thought. He grabs hold of my arm and pulls me close to him, his alcohol-laced breath in my face as he speaks.

"Don't move too fast there, pretty girl. You're not going anywhere."

Terror nearly freezes my heart. "Let me go." I try to jerk out of his hold, frustrated that I keep finding myself in this type of situation. Like I ask for it or something. Am I a magnet for creeps or what?

Ethan's not a creep.

He's about the only non-creep I know. But he's going to be regulated to creep status if he doesn't show up and soon.

"Come with me to the bar." He's completely unfazed. Like he doesn't notice how I'm desperately trying to break free of his hold. "I'll buy you a drink."

"I don't want a drink," I start, but the guy lets go of my arm in an instant and drops to the ground with a resounding thud, landing at my feet.

I scream. I can't help myself. It happened so fast, with barely a sound, and I glance up to see Ethan standing in front of me, his expression one of pure rage, his hands clenched into fists at his sides. The man lies on the ground, clutching his face, and I gape at Ethan, unsure exactly where he hit the guy.

"Keep your hands off her," Ethan says, giving the guy a kick in the legs. The man groans and rolls to his side, his hands falling from his face as he glares up at Ethan.

"Didn't have to hit me, dude," he wails, the sensitive skin beneath his eye already starting to swell.

"Then you should've respected the lady's wishes. She told you to let go." Ethan grabs my arm, his touch much gentler than my assailant's, his voice low and full of concern. "Are you all right?"

I nod, unable to speak. I'm in shock. I can't believe Ethan just ran to my defense again. Popped the guy in the face without hesitation, and did it so quickly, so quietly, I still can't believe it happened.

"You want to go?" His thumb streaks across the bare skin of my arm and I shiver, offering him another nod. "Then let's get out of here."

Better words were never spoken.

Shock hits me full force during the ride, when we're almost home. I start to shiver uncontrollably and I wrap myself up in my hoodie, but it's no use. It doesn't ward off the cold or the worry or the fear.

That man touched me. Said creepy things to me. He might have been harmless, but I'd been instantly assailed by fear. Yet again I put myself into a situation I found difficult to get out of, and I can't expect Ethan to rescue me every single time.

I chance a look at him, see the way he's gripping the steering wheel as he drives, his jaw like granite, his usually lush mouth drawn into a thin line. He looks mad. I hope he's not mad at me.

An irrational thought, I know, but I can't help it.

"I feel terrible, Katie," he finally says. We've been silent most of the drive, making unnecessary small talk until finally I pretended to doze so I wouldn't have to talk anymore. It's not that I'm mad at him or blame him for what happened. I just don't know how to react. How to behave.

Everything's a big, jumbled mess and I feel like it's my fault.

"Why?" I ask, my voice small.

"I should've never left you alone, not even for a minute." His tone is grim, as is the set of his mouth. "That jerk pounced only because he thought you were by yourself."

"I have to deal with the occasional jerk pouncing, Ethan," I tell him. "It's a part of life."

"I put you into that situation." He sounds tortured.

"No, you didn't."

"I brought you to the club. I left you alone."

"I told you I would be all right," I counter.

"But you weren't," he says, pointing out the obvious.

"I could've handled it," I say, hating the uncertainty in my voice. Could I have handled it? I don't know.

And I hate that. The doubt. It hangs over my head constantly.

"You really think so?" He sends me a look, full of skepticism.

My blood starts to boil. Now I'm mad. He has no faith in me. Though I shouldn't be surprised, considering I have no faith in myself. "You can't run in and be my hero every time, Ethan. I don't always need to be rescued."

"Could have fooled me," he mutters.

Anger has me nearly sputtering. I clamp my lips shut and cross my arms in front of my chest, my mind a constant whirl as we remain silent for the rest of the drive. If he thinks I'm inviting him in after that particular discussion, he has another thing coming. I'm too angry, too upset at his doubt, at my own doubt.

As we draw closer to my house, I think of my therapy sessions with Sheila. How she believes I want a hero in my life. Is that true? Am I drawn to Ethan because he shares those same hero-type qualities with Will? Guilt engulfs me and I press the back of my head against my seat, closing my eyes. That's not fair, comparing them. Feeling guilty over my feelings for Ethan. My lingering feelings for Will. Those lingering feelings mean nothing; they're only based on old memories I should store away for good. I reach for my bracelet, then remember that I broke it, and disappointment crashes over me.

I think I've bitten off way more than I can chew.

The moment Ethan pulls his car in front of my house he turns it off, the warm engine ticking in the otherwise quiet of the night. I feel him watching me and I open my eyes to find his penetrating gaze seeming to see right through me. "You never did tell me what happened to you. In your past."

I gawk at him. He's going to bring this up now? Really? Well, maybe the truth will set us both free.

"You didn't look me up?"

Ethan slowly shakes his head.

I'd half hoped he would, just so I wouldn't have to say anything. But then again, with me in control of the information, I don't have to tell him everything. He may search for more info later, but at least for this first conversation, I am in control. Taking a deep, shaky breath, I decide to be done with it. "When I was younger, I was—I was raped."

The word falls into the air, settling between the two of us, and I press my lips together, thankful I just said it, that it's out there. I wait for the repercussions, wait for him to say what everyone thinks are all the right things, but he says nothing.

Nothing at all.

He turns away from me, his jaw still tight, his hands resting loosely once more on the steering wheel. I decide to forge on.

"I was almost thirteen. It happened at the amusement park, where we met. That's where he—he took me." He turns then, his gaze on mine once more, and we just watch each other. "It was—it was awful, what he did."

Pain flashes across his face and he releases the steering wheel, almost as if he wants to reach across the car and touch me. I lean back into my seat, not wanting to feel him, not wanting anything from him as I continue to talk.

"But I'm okay now. Mostly. I'm trying. To deal, to move forward. It's been a long time, but it's not an easy thing to get over."

"I-I'm sure it's not." His voice is a croak, his gaze dark. "Katie, I—"

I hold up my hand, silencing him. "Don't say anything. Don't tell me you're sorry, don't think you need to offer me comfort or anything like that. It happened. There's nothing we can do to change it. It's in the past and I'm trying to focus on the future."

"How are you doing with that?" When I look at him strangely he clarifies. "With moving on?"

"It's a day-by-day process," I admit. "Some days are good. Others, not so much."

He nods, seemingly satisfied with my answer.

"Will this make you even more overprotective of me?" I ask, needing to know. Wondering at his reaction. I've never told a man what happened to me before. I'm treading in unfamiliar territory.

He stares at me, as if unsure how to answer.

"Because you're already pretty overprotective. Always running in and saving me."

"Is that a bad thing?" His brow furrows.

I shrug. "It is if I become too dependent on you." He starts to say something but I cut him off yet again. "I'm scared this might be too much for you to deal with, Ethan."

"Let me be the judge of that," he says.

The relief that sweeps over me is fleeting. I don't know if he really can handle this. I still don't know if *I* can handle this. A relationship after everything that happened to me seems so far-fetched, so hard to imagine.

"Maybe we need some . . . time. Some distance," I suggest, hoping he'll argue with me. Deny my wishes.

Stupid but true.

"Is that what you want, Katie?" He reaches for my hand and clasps it loosely in his. Too loosely. I want to feel his palm press against mine, our fingers intertwined. I want him to pull me in close and kiss me like he did against the wall in the club.

But he'll treat me differently now. Like I'm a piece of fragile glass that could shatter at any moment.

"It might be best," I say tentatively. "Just for a little while. I know you're busy and you might need some time to wrap your head around this. What I told you."

He stares at me, his lips parting, his fingers circling around mine. "I'll give you all the time you need. Whatever you want." As if he knows I might be the one who needs time, not him.

I think he might be right.

ETHAN

Now

I hear Lisa Swanson's voice on my television and it's like a moment of déjà vu.

Exclusive interview with Aaron Monroe! Hear his side of the story.

Disgust fills me as I watch the commercial in a state of semi-shock. Flashes of old photos appear in rapid-fire succession. Ones of Katie, of my father, *shit,* a couple of me and my father together, and it ends with a photo of my dad now. I haven't seen him in what feels like forever.

He looks old. Thin. Worn the fuck out.

"I have things to say." He puffs out his chest, trying to look important but failing. He just looks like a ragged old man who's been locked up for a long time. "No one has wanted to hear the truth. It's time I set the record straight."

I think I'm going to throw up.

Lisa appears in one last shot, that thoughtful expression on her face as she nods and listens to what my scumbag of a father has to say, as she does a voiceover telling us the date and time of this shit show she's so proudly put together. She's working it. Working it hard. I wonder if the network is going to give her a promotion for all of these exclusive interviews she's nabbing. I bet she'd crap her pants if she heard from me, if I'd actually replied to that email she sent me. If she got me to tell my side of the story, which no one has ever heard.

Ever.

Can't happen, though. William Monroe is dead and buried. I bet she's given up on trying to find him, frustrated at her failure.

I get a little thrill out of that particular fact.

Seeing the commercial for the upcoming interview does spring me into action. I need to reach out to Katie and make sure she's okay. I know I said I'd give her time, but fuck that. This news had to send her reeling. She could need me during this difficult moment.

If she needed you, don't you think she would've reached out by now?

I ignore the shitty nagging voice in my head.

I'd backed off for her sake, granting her request, or so I tell myself. I've gone over that night at the club again and again, wondering if I came on too strong and scared her. Afraid my punching that guy who had his hands on her with no warning might have turned her off. She most likely abhors violence. Was probably disgusted by my primal behavior that night. I'd had my hands all over her, kissing her like I wanted to devour her whole.

I'd wanted to. My plan had been to get her back to her place and pick up where we left off. Until that asshole had to come along and ruin everything.

Maybe *I'm* the asshole who ruined everything. I truly thought I'd never know.

But now I'm an asshole who wants to make sure she's all right. Forget all that we-need-time business. My father's interview could hurt her. Devastate her completely, and I can't have that. I vowed I would protect her all those years ago and I'm trying my damnedest to keep my promise.

I haven't kept tabs on her in what feels like forever and I open up Google on my laptop to do a quick search, icy shock washing over me yet again when I read one of the first articles that comes up in the search for Katherine Watts.

Unauthorized Movie Planned Based on Katherine Watts's Abduction

Shit.

Distance. I promised to keep my distance and I truly believed it was the right thing to do. She thought I would freak over what happened to her. I know she would freak if she knew who I really was. Our situation has gotten completely out of hand and I don't know how I can fix it. I feel helpless.

But I can't let this go on any longer. I need to make sure she's all right.

Grabbing my phone, I send her a quick text asking if she's okay, but she doesn't reply.

Over two hours later and she still hasn't replied. Which means she's not okay and she most likely hates my guts. I should be happy with this. It's what I wanted. What I should've done from the very start. I didn't need to interfere with her life so much. But one touch and I was a goner. Spending time with her, making her smile, making her laugh . . . I wanted more of that. Learning her taste, finding out what makes her feel good, what gives her pleasure . . .

I want all of that.

But from the moment I walked into her life, I've brought her nothing but turmoil. I had nothing to do with the movie and my dad's interview, but I feel like I did. It almost feels like I'm responsible. Yeah, she opened herself up to all sorts of scrutiny after the interview with Swanson . . .

Including scrutiny from me. Seeing her on TV broke open all the memories, all the forgotten longing and need. So much need. Having her in my life once more, the both of us consenting adults, I knew from the moment our gazes first met what I wanted from her. More than just friendship. More than just me watching over her and ensuring her safety.

I wanted her, body and soul, as much a part of me as breathing.

No matter how wrong my feelings are, I can't resist them. Knowing all the potential consequences, knowing what I'm doing isn't right, that if she found out the truth she'd be crushed, it doesn't stop me. My intentions might be good.

My methods are horrible. Dishonest. And I hate liars.

Yet here I am lying my ass off to Katie. The one I want to protect. She doesn't know it yet, but she's mine.

And despite how fucked up I am over this, I can never let her go.

Frustration rippling through me, I grab my phone once again and fire off another text, not caring how abrupt I sound. Hoping like hell she'll do what I ask.

> The coffee shop we first went to—meet me there tomorrow at 3.

If she doesn't, I will have to let her go once and for all. I won't have a choice. But if she responds—or even better, shows up—then I need to tell her the truth.

Even if it kills me.

KATHERINE

Now

"Don't you dare go meet him at that coffee shop," Brenna sniffs, leaning away from my phone after I show her the text. "Who does he think he is, anyway, bossing you around like that? Demanding that you meet him somewhere without a please or thank-you. Texting you out of the blue after you don't hear from him for days, acting like the concerned, caring boyfriend. It's a bunch of crap if you ask me."

I stare at my phone, half listening to my sister's tirade on my behalf as I contemplate whether I should answer Ethan or not. Everything inside of me is screaming to not say a word. Or to tell him I have other plans. After all, I'm the one who told him we should take some time apart. It's my fault he hasn't contacted me.

And I truly thought it best that he wasn't a part of my life anymore. I was setting myself up for disappointment. Surely it would have ended sooner or later, so why not end it now? Before I can get too hurt?

But I'm already hurt. I miss him so much my body aches. I can't move on with my life if he's not in it. I just . . .

I can't.

That secret, dark part that both wants and fears his touch is begging to see him, to hold him. Kiss him. To just go to that coffee shop, stare at his handsome face, and listen to what he has to say. Then dig up some courage and tell him I miss him.

That I need him in my life. That I can't go on like this without him.

Would I, though? Was I brave enough to reveal my true feelings to him? I want to be, but I don't know if I can. I hardly know him, yet he has this hold on me I can't explain. I'm not ready to give him up, no matter how many times he pushes me away.

And that makes me feel weak. Yet pushing him away this time around doesn't make me feel any stronger, either.

"You'd better not answer him," Brenna says, her firm voice breaking through my conflicting thoughts.

With a sigh I set the phone down on the table between us, snatching it closer when Brenna makes like she's going to take it away from me. "I won't answer him, I swear." At least, I won't answer him at this very moment. Can't promise I won't answer him later, though . . .

Ugh. I sort of hate myself for even thinking that.

"Don't go to that coffee shop to meet him, either." Brenna reaches out and settles her hand over mine, making me flinch. Funny, how I pull away when someone casually touches me, even someone like my sister. That little whisper of panic washes over my skin, the one that makes me want to recoil and hide. Except with Ethan. With Ethan it's been the exact opposite.

You'd think I wouldn't have a problem with it after all this time, but every once in a while, an unexpected touch can almost make my skin crawl.

"I find it weird that after all the crazy stuff that came out over the last few days, he's suddenly texting and asking if you're okay. That he actually wants to meet with you," Brenna continues.

"I don't think it's all that strange. I briefly told him what happened to me, and he has my full name. All it takes is a quick search and he can figure everything else out." I shrug, trying to act like it's no big deal, but inside I'm dying of curiosity. And fear. Lots and lots of nervous fear. *Did* Ethan Google me? And if so, how accepting will he be of my past? The details I gave him were completely glossed over. The truth of my abduction and rape is almost too much for anyone to deal with.

"Right, so when he Googled you, he probably saw the news about the unauthorized movie, then the upcoming television interview with that dickwad who kidnapped you." Brenna shakes her head. "Maybe he thinks he'll become famous because he hangs out with you or something stupid like that."

I almost want to laugh, but I hold it in when I see how serious my sister is being. She's defending me. Worried about me. How can I fault her for that? "I doubt it has anything to do with that. Not like I have much money or anything."

"You own your own house," Brenna points out. "Not many women in their early twenties can say that."

The house was purchased with money I inherited when our father died, so I've lived there only six months. Brenna is holding on to her share until she finds the perfect house for her and Mike to move into once they get married.

"He's not after any sort of fame or fortune, Brenna. You're being ridiculous."

"Am I, Katherine? Do you really know much about this guy? You haven't been seeing him for very long." I know she's being protective, but I'm tired of it. Tired of everyone trying to lock me in a cage and never let me live.

"I'm a big girl, Bren. If I want to see this guy, meet with him, then I will. Not even you can stop me. I have to live my life, not walk around in constant fear all the time," I say, letting all my anger and frustration show.

Brenna gapes at me, like she can't believe I just let loose like that. "I just want to make sure you're safe. I don't—I don't trust this guy."

I roll my eyes. "You won't trust any guy that comes into my life."

"That's not true," she starts, but I send her a look and she shuts up. I wish we already had our dinner in front of us. Or even better, that we had finished dinner so I could leave. Going out with my sister tonight was a huge mistake.

We say nothing for a while, and the quiet slowly drives me crazy. I can't take it anymore.

"What am I supposed to do? Huh? Pretend it never happened? Never tell a guy I'm interested in my last name and hope like crazy he doesn't find out the truth? I have to be honest. Open. That doesn't mean I need to dump everything on him during the first date, but if a man is really interested in me, he deserves to know the truth. I can't hide forever."

"You've been in hiding for years, ever since it happened!" She's yelling and I glare at her, hating how loud she is. A few nearby diners glance at us, and my cheeks heat with embarrassment. She's making a big deal out of nothing. "Then you meet a hot guy who finally gets your hormones going and you're not acting normal. It's like you don't even care anymore about your safety, your privacy. None of it. You're reckless and quite frankly, making some stupid moves. You won't listen to me and you won't listen to Mom either. We don't know what's going on with you and all we want to do is help."

I don't know what to say. Her words make me mad, but worse? They hurt. A lot. So much that I take my napkin from my lap and throw it on the table directly in front of me. "I didn't realize your opinion of me is so low." I stand and grab my purse from where it hangs on the back of my chair. "I'm leaving."

"Oh, come on, Katherine," I hear Brenna call, but I ignore her and hurry through the crowded restaurant, hoping no one is paying attention to me. My entire face is hot and I keep my head down as I exit the restaurant, exhaling loudly once I'm outside. The cool night air wraps around me, pulling me into its icy embrace, and a shiver passes over me as I tilt my head back and stare at the silvery moon above.

I'm tired of being scared. Of giving up before I should. Of never attempting something I want to do. That's been my life since I was almost thirteen. Always giving up, or worse, never going after what I want. I remained in this fragile little protective shell, my head bent forward, my shoulders hunched, pretending I was invisible.

I try to come out of my shell and it still doesn't seem to work. I don't know what to do anymore. Don't know how to act, how to feel.

How to live.

I reach for my wrist, sadness filling me when I realize yet again the bracelet isn't there. It sits on my dresser, the broken charm lying next to it. I need to get that fixed. Or fix it myself. I bet I could if I just worked on it for a few minutes.

"Katherine." I turn to find Brenna standing there, flushed and looking irritated. "They didn't even serve our dinner yet."

"I'm not hungry." I sniff, turning my head so I don't have to look at her. Thank goodness we met at the restaurant. I don't think I could have handled being dependent on her to get a ride home, or having to give Brenna a ride back to her place. Talk about tense.

"You're being ridiculous." I send her a pointed look and

she sighs. "I'm sorry. You know what I mean. Just . . . come back inside, K."

"Why? So you can continue telling me how stupid I am?" I turn my back fully to her and cross my arms in front of my chest. I'm sick and tired of everyone voicing their opinions and basically insulting my life choices out of concern for my well-being. It's a crock of shit.

The only one who treats me like I'm normal is Ethan. And half the time he ignores me, so I don't know where I went wrong with him.

I curl my arms around myself and frown. Maybe this dating thing won't work. Maybe this living-in-the-real-world thing won't work either. Perhaps I'm better off living in that little protective shell, staying at home and never actually doing anything.

"We'll talk about other stuff, okay? I'm sorry." I hear Brenna's heels click on the sidewalk and then her hand is on my shoulder, giving it a squeeze. This time I don't flinch. Slowly I glance over my shoulder at her and offer a wan smile. My heart just isn't in it.

"Let's go inside," I say wearily, giving in.

Like always.

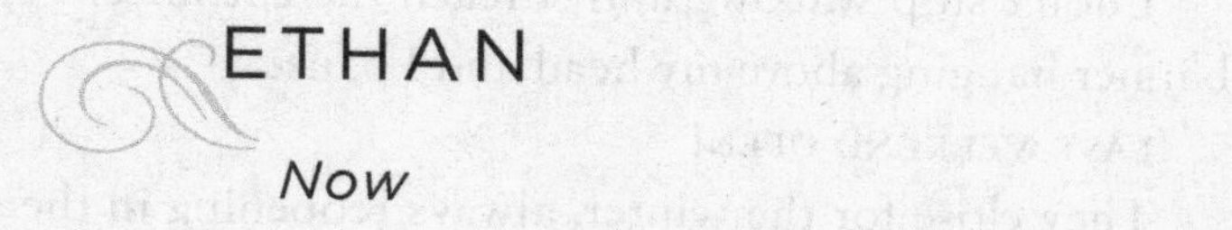

ETHAN

Now

I wait for her outside the front of the coffee shop, pacing as I try to keep warm. It's a Friday afternoon, one that started out sunny and bright but became cloudy around noon, leaving the sky dark and gray.

Depressing.

It's a quarter after three and she's still not here. I text her but there's no reply. I've been stood up. I told myself if she didn't show, I'd have to let her go once and for all. So I need to stand by my promise and let her be.

No matter how much it kills me.

Another ten minutes pass by and I finally give up, pissed off as I storm away from the busy coffee place. All sorts of people have been walking in and out of the shop, smiling and happy as they clutch their paper to-go cups. I want to knock all of those cups out of their hands, I'm so angry. So bitter at their happiness when I have none. I fucked up. I royally fucked up, let myself get too close to Katie, and now that I know what I'm missing, now that I can't have her . . .

I'll never be the same again.

Frustration fueling me, I keep walking, my gaze straight ahead, my strides long. I'm heading toward the boardwalk amusement park, surprised when I see a few of the rides running, hear screams coming from the roller coaster as it goes roaring overhead. I thought the season was over.

I don't stop walking until I reach the entrance. I spot the banner hanging above my head and I pause.

LAST WEEKEND OPEN!

They close for the winter, always reopening in the spring. This was their last hurrah before they shut down for the season and without thought I enter the park, almost like I can't help myself.

The scent of fried food lingers in the air, sweet and pungent. A seagull squawks and swoops down, picking up a piece of discarded soft pretzel on the ground nearby and flapping its wings wildly as it flies away. As I watch it go, I see a balloon drift in the sky, its bright pink color vibrant against the slate-gray clouds. Hear the crash of the waves against the sand and know there probably aren't any families out there sitting on the beach. There's no point. It's too damn cold.

Like my heart. It's cold. Like ice. It's been that way for years. It was my only defense against my father when I was young. If I didn't feel anything then he couldn't hurt me, right? That's what I told myself.

Sometimes it worked. Sometimes it didn't.

Katie melted that ice within me twice. When she was young and I was a different person, and now. I wish she were here. I wish she were by my side, smiling and asking for a corn dog or maybe some cotton candy, a funnel cake. Something we could share. Maybe she'd tell me she wanted to ride the roller coaster or the merry-go-round. This place isn't so bad. I have a lot of fond memories of coming here when I was a kid, despite my shitty dad and my shitty circumstances.

We could create new memories, Katie and I. Banish those old ones once and for all and remember only the good times here. Good times we create together.

But I guess it isn't meant to be.

I stop at a concession stand to buy a soda and immediately regret it, wishing I'd picked up a coffee when I had the chance. It's damn cold outside, the wind has started to pick up, and I walk around the park aimlessly, along with an assorted lot of other aimless people, all of them not seeming to fit in. Fit together. Where are the families, the kids? Most of the kids are in school. There are teenagers here, and they all remind me of myself, when I was their age. They look like trouble.

Like me.

I also see quite a few tired-looking mothers pushing strollers full of loud, bratty toddlers, looking for a distraction, and I feel for them.

I'm in need of a distraction, too—from Katie. From my fucked-up, confused feelings for her.

Heading toward the Sky Gliders line, I see that it's short and I'm thankful. I'll hop on a glider and it'll take me across most of the park, dumping me off not too far from where I parked. Then I can get the hell out of here and head home, away from the memories of Katie.

Back to nothing but loneliness.

At first I don't believe it when I hear my name being called. I feel like it's all in my head, that I'm losing my mind, which I wouldn't doubt. The shit I've been through over the years . . . I think people would understand if I went crazy. Hell, I should've gone crazy long ago.

But I hear my name again. And again. Until I finally turn around at about the fifth *Ethan* and my jaw drops open in shock when I see who's standing there.

Katie.

She's frozen, her eyes wide, her hand falling at her side, like she was trying to wave me down. We stare at each other and all the sounds, the scents, the people, everything seems to fade until it's just me and her standing in this park. The both of us too scared to approach the other first.

I spot a garbage can nearby and dump the half-full soda inside, wiping my damp hands against my jeans as I start to walk toward her. She still doesn't move. She looks scared and I ache to take away her fear. Offer her comfort. Tell her I'm sorry.

Tell her who I really am and hope like hell she can forgive me.

"Ethan," she breathes when I'm finally close enough to hear her. "I found you."

"What are you doing here?" I stop just in front of her, wanting so badly to reach out and grab her I have to curl my hands into fists to prevent them from doing so.

"I came to meet you just like you asked, and . . . chickened out at the last minute." She drops her head so I can't see her face anymore. "I don't know what compelled me to come to the park."

"I did the same thing." When she lifts her head and her gaze meets mine, I continue. "You didn't show and I was . . . mad. I started walking, wishing you were with me. Next thing I knew, I was here."

Her lips part, her eyes full of sadness. "I don't know what we're doing anymore," she whispers.

I step closer, grabbing hold of one of her hands. Her fingers are cold and I interlace them with mine, squeezing her tight. "I don't either."

She tilts her head back, her pretty, dark blue gaze meeting mine. Her eyes are full of pain and confusion and the tiniest flicker of hope. "You know what really happened to me, don't you."

"It doesn't matter." I shake my head. I don't want to talk

about the past. I want the here and now. I want to be with Katie. "Come home with me."

Her eyes widen, I swear she's about to jerk her hand out of my grip, but I tighten my hold on her, not wanting to let her go. If I had my way, I'd never let her go. The connection we share, the one we formed when we were just kids, it hasn't gone away. If anything it's become stronger and I'm sick of fighting it, sick of fighting my feelings for her.

"Please." I bring our connected hands to my mouth and brush my lips across her knuckles. Her audible gasp tells me everything. That our chemistry, our attraction for each other, isn't just one-sided. She feels it, too. She always has. It's been there, ever since the first moment we laid eyes on each other so long ago. "Ride the Sky Glider with me and you can follow me home."

"I-I don't know." The panicked look on her face nearly does me in. I've scared her and I hate that I made her feel this way. Her eyes are full of such fear and I'm not sure why. "This is the ride that the man who abducted me asked me to take him to. I don't know if I can ride it."

God, I'm such an idiot. How could I forget? Her pain is bringing me pain, making my heart feel like it wants to crack in two. Taking a deep breath, I grimace, hating myself. "I'm an asshole."

The smile that curves her lips is faint. "No, you're not."

"Yes," I say, my voice firm. "I am. I didn't even think about this ride, how you're able to deal with the memories when you're here in this park. It can't be easy. And I've been a total jerk to you and I'm sorry. I'm going through my own shit. It has nothing to do with you but unfortunately it's affected you, and I hate that." A half-truth. It has everything to do with her, but I can't tell her that. Not now. Not yet.

But soon.

"I need to be stronger. I know it, but it's so hard. I just—I need time. I think you do, too. Maybe we aren't meant to be. Maybe this won't work. I'm too new at this, too . . ." She closes her eyes and shakes her head once before she looks at me once more. Her words are about to give me a fucking heart attack and I try my best not to react. "I'm not equipped for this, Ethan. Not yet, at least. So you need to tell me if you're in or not. I need to know."

I don't even hesitate. Leaning forward, I press my mouth to hers, whisper against her lips, "I'm in."

And I mean it.

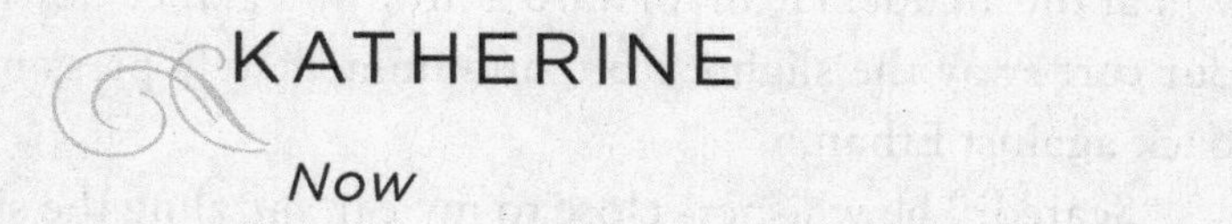

KATHERINE

Now

We head up the stairs that lead to the Sky Glider together, Ethan by my side. It's surreal, how we found each other, how he just kissed me and told me he's in. We're holding hands and he escorts me to where they seat us, waiting for an empty glider cart to appear so we can back our butts up into it and the attendant can lock the bar across the front of us.

I push past the fear, shove the memories far, far away. Even laugh a little as the bar comes down and the teenage kid working the ride gives our car a push so we swing on the wire. The Sky Glider used to secretly terrify me when I was a kid, stuck in that car with what felt like too much room between the bar and the seat. Usually sitting with my mom, who would clutch the back of my shirt as if she were truly afraid I would slip out and fall to my death.

The Sky Glider skims across most of the park, a great shortcut to use when you want to get to another ride—or the other side of the park—fast. That had been Aaron William Monroe's excuse. That he needed to get across the park quickly to meet his family. A lie, like everything else he said.

I refuse to think of him now. I don't want to taint this memory of Ethan and me together.

Ethan slips his arm around my shoulders and pulls me close to his side as we glide quietly above the park. We pass a tall concession stand that sells ice cream, its rooftop littered with the flip-flops, hair accessories, and plastic bracelets kids win at the arcade. I lean forward a little and glance down, feel our cart sway the slightest bit, and immediately press myself back against Ethan.

"Scared?" he whispers close to my ear, nuzzling the side of my face with his nose.

I shiver, but not from the wind. "No. Not when I have you to keep me safe." I want him to always keep me safe. Help me feel secure.

I think Ethan could be the one to do that for me.

I feel him smile before he kisses my cheek, his mouth lingering, making me shiver again. I still can't believe I'm here with him. I'd come to meet him at the coffee shop against my better judgment, hating the inner voice nagging at me, telling me to turn around and go home.

That voice sounded just like Brenna.

The moment I started walking toward the coffee shop, the inner voice got louder. More insistent. Like it was screaming at me to turn around and go. Just leave. So I did. And somehow ended up at the park, where I wandered around, looking for . . . something, anything to ease the dull ache inside of me, but unable to find it.

Until I spotted Ethan and the pain disappeared, replaced by a glimmer of hope.

I thought I was seeing things. I truly believed he was a figment of my imagination. But there's no mistaking his dark hair, that beautiful masculine face, the glasses and the broad, capable shoulders. The way he moved through the waning crowd was so familiar to me, so dear, that I automatically shouted his name.

He didn't hear me. I shouted again, and again, my voice louder with every call of his name until finally he turned around. The moment he spotted me, from the look in his dark eyes, the expression on his face, I knew.

There was no turning back. Not for us. Not today. And I don't want to turn back. I want him. Every time I'm near him I feel greedy. Like I want to grab hold of him and tell the world that he's mine. That he belongs to me.

I've never wanted anything before the way I want this. Never wanted someone as much as I want Ethan. It's like I'm addicted and I can't give him up. I don't want to. I want to take what's mine.

The wind whips over us, my hair flying in my face, and I reach up to push it out of the way. The guardian angel charm bracelet dangles from my wrist, the sleeve of my sweater falls down my arm to reveal it, and Ethan grabs hold of my wrist, his gaze jerking to mine.

"What's this?"

"It's a-a bracelet." I fixed it last night, determined to do something on my own, to prove I can take care of myself. And I did take care of it. It might've been small, but hey, it's something.

And fixing that bracelet felt good, no matter how small the accomplishment might be. Made me feel like a grown-up when I hardly ever feel that way.

The only other person who makes me feel like an adult is the very man I'm sitting next to, who's got an odd expression on his face as he studies my bracelet.

"Who gave it to you?" he asks, his voice quiet. So quiet I almost don't hear him, what with the music playing down below, the clatter of the roller coaster as it roars nearby.

"A boy I used to know," I admit, sinking my teeth into my lower lip. "He was a—friend."

Ethan frowns, toying with the charm with his index finger. "A friend?"

My heart starts to race. I don't know why. His voice sounds strange. The expression on his face is dark. There's no other word to describe it. He's reacting to my bracelet in such a weird way and I don't know why.

"He helped me, saved me." I wave my hand, the bracelet sliding down my arm. "It's complicated."

His gaze meets mine, his fingers still circling my wrist. "It happened a long time ago." He talks as if he knows who gave it to me and why.

I nod, a shuddery sigh escaping me when his thumb sweeps across the inside of my wrist. "It helps me when I feel lost."

"A guardian angel." His voice is flat and he fingers the charm again, pressing the flat backside of it, the metal cool against my skin. "Does it watch over you?"

"Always," I whisper at the exact moment he releases his hold on the charm . . .

And it detaches from the silver circular bracelet, falling to the ground.

"Oh!" I lean over the bar, causing the cart to sway, and Ethan clamps my shoulder with his hand, trying to pull me back. "It fell off!"

"What did?"

"The charm!" I turn to look at him, trying to swallow past the panic clawing up my throat. "I can't lose it, Ethan. I just . . . I can't."

He glances down and scans the ground below. "Maybe we could find it once we get off this thing."

"How?" I ask incredulously, my gaze following his. We'd just flown over a cluster of concession stands. For all we know the charm could've landed on one of the roofs, and there's no way we'd find it if that happened. "That charm is so small. It could be anywhere."

"We'll find it," he says firmly, his unwavering gaze meeting mine. His jaw is tight, his eyes incredibly dark and oh so serious. "I promise."

His words, the sincerity in his voice, the way he's looking at me, reminds me of another promise made to me years ago. I'm taken aback at the similarities and I stare at Ethan for a long time, searching for a glimpse of Will in his features.

No. I shake my head. I'm being ridiculous. Crazy. Will Monroe is gone. Maybe I'm so drawn to Ethan because of the similarities they share. Who knows how Will turned out, anyway? Circumstances weren't on his side. For all I know he's locked up in prison somewhere, following in his father's footsteps.

My heart breaks just thinking that.

The moment we disembark from the Sky Gliders, Ethan takes off and I follow after him, glancing up at the gloomy sky in irritation when it starts to rain. The weather doesn't deter Ethan, though. People scatter as the rainfall picks up in intensity, most of them going for shelter, but Ethan keeps walking, pushing himself into a slow jog as he heads toward the spot where we think the charm fell from my bracelet.

I try to hold back the overwhelming disappointment and sadness that threatens, but it's so hard. I don't know how we're going to find it. I'm not sure exactly where it fell. It could be anywhere.

I'm fairly certain it's lost forever but I don't want to discourage Ethan from looking for it, either. That he wants to help means more to me than he'll ever know.

"Ethan." I call his name but he ignores me, stopping in the

spot where the charm might have fallen. He starts looking, pulling his phone out of the back pocket of his jeans and turning the flashlight on so he can see better. I watch helplessly as he searches everywhere, around the buildings, along the sidewalk, the light from his phone creating a silvery glow that seems to highlight the raindrops falling from up above and make them sparkle.

"Help me, Katie," he says and I leap into action, feeling like an idiot for not doing so sooner. We scan the entire area, at one point Ethan falling to his hands and knees, grimacing as he looks through the discarded trash that lines the gutter of the sidewalk. I imagine all the many feet that have passed over the very spot where he's kneeling through the years.

I can't believe he's doing this for me.

"There's no point," I tell him when he finally stands and brushes his hands against the front of his jeans. I blink away the rain dotting my face, obscuring my vision. "It's gone." A sob falls from my lips at the last word and I cover my mouth with my hand as I start to cry.

He approaches me, his expression despondent, his eyes full of so much sadness and worry. All of it for me. "Katie. Baby, don't cry. We'll find it, I promise. I'll do whatever it takes to find that charm for you."

"It d-doesn't m-matter." My teeth are chattering and I'm having a hard time catching my breath.

Ethan grabs hold of my upper arms and pulls me in close. Even with the cold rain falling, his clothes drenched, I can still feel the warmth of his body reaching toward me, consoling me. I try my best to absorb it. "It matters to you," he says, his voice quiet and earnest. "I'm so sorry I lost it."

"It wasn't your fault." I shake my head, press my lips together. "The charm fell off a few days ago and I thought I fixed it. But I guess I didn't." Another sob escapes me and I lean forward, pressing my face against Ethan's damp hoodie sweatshirt. "I can't believe I lost it."

He strokes my wet hair, his mouth close to my temple as he murmurs, "I'll find it. I swear to God I'll . . ."

His voice drifts and he pulls away, disentangling himself from me. I watch in stunned disbelief as he walks over to a nearby building, a small stand that sells ice cream. A bright red counter lines the front, where they keep napkin holders and cups full of spoons. Ethan reaches out, scoops up something into the palm of his hand, and approaches me, opening his hand to reveal what he's found.

My guardian angel charm.

"Oh my God," I whisper just before I tackle him. He clenches his fist around the charm when I throw myself at him, my arms wrapped around his neck, my mouth on his as I give him a quick, grateful kiss. "You found it."

He smiles, his face wet from the rain, his arms tight around my waist as he pulls me into his embrace. "I promised you." Another kiss, this one a little longer, a little deeper, and a sigh leaves me when he pulls away. "I'll never break a promise to you, Katie."

His words . . . are another echo of Will. It's eerie, how they're suddenly reminding me of each other. I blame it on my thoughts drifting toward Will lately. I'm just superimposing old feelings I had for Will on Ethan. Memories and emotions that are heightened because of what we went through, what Will and I suffered together.

It's nothing. The two of them are nothing alike.

"Thank you." He kisses me before I can say another word, his lips soft and clinging to mine. I open for him, feel that first sweep of his tongue, and I meet it with my own, my fingers curling around his neck, my lower body pressing into his. I'm in the cold, misty rain, out in the middle of the very amusement park where I was kidnapped, where horrible things happened to me, and it's okay. I'm creating new memories, ones that wipe away the old.

And strangely meld two people together, one a boy.

The other a man.

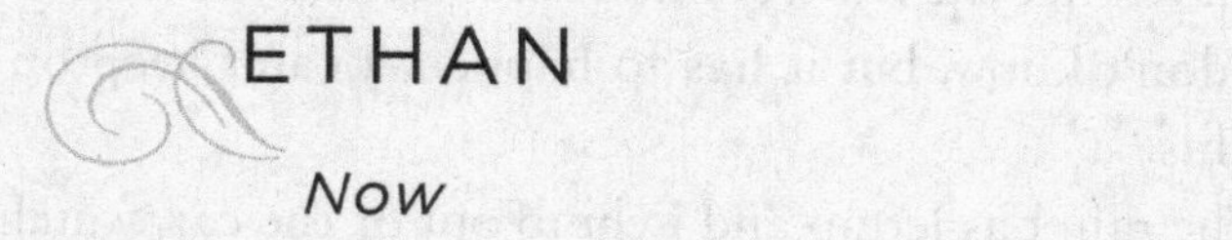

ETHAN

Now

She follows me back to my place, her car right behind mine as I drive slower than usual so I don't lose her. My mind races the entire drive, my thoughts chaotic as I navigate us through shitty traffic, the rain only making things worse.

All I want to do is get her back to my place in one piece. Where I then plan on taking her completely apart. Bit by bit, piece by piece, until she's a trembling, naked, incoherent mess. And the only one who can satisfy her needs is . . .

Me.

Seeing her wearing the bracelet I gave her all those years ago tore me up. Knowing that she kept it all this time, hearing her describe who gave it to her—*me*—shredded my soul. I meant something to her. After all this time believing I was worthless, that Katie hated me and believed I had something to do with her kidnapping, to find out that she considered Will a friend. That she kept the bracelet I gave her and was devastated when she thought she lost it . . .

I scrub a hand over my face as I pull into my driveway. *Fuck*. I don't know how to feel anymore. She deserves the truth. I know that. But I don't want to ruin what tonight can bring. I need her. I want her. I tell her who I really am, I blow her mind with the truth, and I'm putting everything at risk.

Everything.

And I can't do that. Not tonight. I need one night with her. Just one.

I'll tell her the truth soon. Tomorrow maybe.

I don't know, but it has to happen. I can't keep on living like this.

The rain has let up and I climb out of the car, watching as Katie exits her car and runs toward me. I take her hand and lead her into the quiet, dark house. The blinds and curtains are still drawn, and with the storm coming in, everything's shrouded in darkness, hushed and still.

I push her against the door the minute it's shut, bracing my hands on either side of her head. Though it's dark, I can still see her and she lifts her head, her wide-eyed gaze meeting mine. "Katie," I whisper as my head descends and my mouth brushes against hers once, the touch of her lips on mine electrifying me from the inside out.

A trembling sigh gusts across my lips and I capture it, kissing her again. Then again. She reaches for me, her fingers curling into my damp sweatshirt, her head tilted back, her lips parting beneath mine. I sweep my tongue into her mouth, tangle it with hers, and I reach for her face and cup her cheek, holding her there as I devour her mouth.

I'm holding everything back and it's killing me. Fucking slaying me dead. I want her. So bad. My clothes are wet from the rain, heavy and uncomfortable, and when I finally break the kiss I whisper, "We should take our clothes off."

Her eyes pop open, wide and full of hesitation. "Wh-what?"

"They're wet." I chuckle. "I don't mean we get naked." Yet. "I just think we should get out of these soaked clothes."

"But I have nothing to change into," she protests.

"I can fix that," I offer.

So I do. I hand her an old, soft T-shirt and a button-down flannel, along with a pair of thick socks. None of my sweatpants or shorts would fit her since she's so slender. I let her change in the bedroom while I use the living room, giving her privacy. I change into dark gray sweats and a long-sleeved white T-shirt, then wait for her on the couch, on edge and wishing she'd just come out already.

When I hear my bedroom door open I sit up straight, my hands perched on my knees, feeling like I'm poised and ready for flight. She enters the living room, her feet encased in the thick socks I wear only with a certain pair of boots, wearing the T-shirt and the flannel halfway buttoned over the shirt, looking sexy as fuck with her hair piled into a sloppy bun on top of her head, her cheeks flushed a rosy pink.

Adorably sexy.

"You okay?" I stand and go to her, feeling incredibly protective toward her. She looks so small wearing my clothes, her unsure expression, her bare legs and scrubbed-clean face reminding me of when she was younger.

When I first met her.

Katie smiles, the sight of it like a zing straight to my already shattered heart. "Yes. Much better after getting out of those wet clothes."

"Where'd you leave them? We can toss them in the dryer."

We go about doing exactly that, acting like a domesticated couple who've just come home from a long, hard day. She follows me into the tiny laundry room that's just off my garage, her clothes in her hands. I open the dryer for her and she throws them in along with my own, and I shut the door, push the button, and hear the dryer roar to life.

She meets my gaze, a little smile curling her lips. "Now what?"

Does she really have to ask? Every primal instinct tells me to grab her. Haul her up onto that vibrating dryer and kiss her. Put my hand between her legs and see if she's wearing any panties—which she can't be, because I saw them land in the dryer only a few moments ago. She's bare under my clothes. No bra, no panties, just skin.

My fingers itch to touch her, stroke her. Figure out what she likes and do it again. And again. Until I have her arching against me and begging for more.

"What do you want?" I ask, my voice husky, my brain short-circuiting when she reaches out and curls her finger around the drawstring of my sweatpants. Her hand is way too close to my dick, which is already hard and aching.

"You were my hero today, Ethan," she whispers as she tugs on the string. I stumble toward her, feeling like a bumbling idiot with her hands on me, her body so close. I press my hand against the top edge of the dryer and lean in, sniffing the floral sweetness of her hair, the heady, rich scent of her skin, a combination of the lotion she must use and her perfume. I want to eat her up.

Her words remind me of things said to another boy long ago and I close my eyes, slip my other arm around her waist. She's backed up against the dryer, and I lift her with one arm, her ass perched on the edge for a brief moment before she scoots back.

"What are you doing?" she asks breathlessly, her hands resting on my shoulders, giving them a brief squeeze.

"Spread your legs," I demand, and she does so automatically. I step in between them, my hand still braced on the dryer, fingers brushing against her outer thigh as I readjust my other arm around her waist. "You look good in my clothes, Katie."

She blushes and tilts her head down. "You sound rather possessive, Ethan."

"I feel possessive." Leaning in, I press my cheek to hers and close my eyes for a long, quiet moment, breathing her in, absorbing her. "I want you. So damn much. Being apart from you just about killed me."

She sighs as she runs her fingers along my shoulders. God, her touch feels good. "I-I want you, too."

Triumph surges through me at her admission. "After everything you told me, I think I understand where you're coming from. And I don't want to push you. I know you're scared, but I won't hurt you. I promise."

"I know." She nods. "I trust you."

My heart sinks. I don't know if I'm worthy of her trust. I want to be. God, how I want to be. But I've lied to her for so long and I feel like a total asshole for that. Will she ever forgive me once she finds out the truth?

I'm willing to take the risk.

"Will you let me, Katie? Let me touch you?" I move my hand from the warm, rumbling dryer to rest it on her outer thigh. Her skin is smooth, like silk, and I run my fingers down the length of her leg, curve my fingers over her bare knee. "Or do you want me to stop?"

She shakes her head, her lips parting on a sigh when I smooth my hand back up, my fingers tracing along her inner thigh. "N-no."

"You want more of this?" I'm torturing her. Torturing myself. And damn, it feels so good to finally let go, to finally give in to my need for Katie and let her know what she does to me. "More of me?"

"Mmm-hmm." She nods, her eyes falling shut when I skim my fingers down the top of her thigh. She's open and willing and I swear I smell her. Wonder how wet she is for me, if she's confused and scared or if she really wants this.

Wants me.

I kiss her and she reaches up, her fingertips splayed across my jaw, her lips clinging to mine. Her touch makes my skin tingle and I deepen the kiss, my tongue thrusting, and she slips her other hand beneath the hem of my shirt.

She's bold tonight. Not hesitant at all. As if she knows what she wants and she's going after it.

Breaking our kiss, I push into her neck and lick her there, feeling the movement of her throat as she gasps, dragging my lips over her delicate skin. Her hand moves from my face to wrap around my nape as she holds me to her. I taste her, nibble on her skin, feel her shiver, and I rest my hands on her hips, holding her still. I want to strip her naked but not yet. Not here while she sits on my fucking dryer in the middle of my laundry room.

"Ethan." My name is a breathless plea but I don't answer her. Continue to lick and suck her skin instead, my hands slipping beneath the hem of my T-shirt that she's wearing, touching her flat belly. It contracts and flutters beneath my palms and I finally pull away from her neck to stare down at her. "You'll be—gentle with me, right?"

I nod, my gaze never wavering from hers. "I'm going to take you to heights you've never even dreamed of, Katie," I solemnly promise.

She closes her eyes. "Oh God."

Those are the last words she utters before I swallow them with my lips, lick them away with my tongue. I remove my hands from beneath the shirt to undo the buttons of the flannel slowly, one by one, my fingers brushing against her unbound breasts as I continue to kiss her. She pushes her chest against my hands, a whimper sounding low in her throat, and a wave of possessiveness hits me so strong I swear my knees grow weak.

She's been through so much, has endured too much at such

a young age. That she trusts me, is allowing me to touch her like this, kiss her like this, is humbling.

Nearly brings me to my knees.

I finish unbuttoning the shirt and practically tear it off of her, throwing it on top of the washer, reaching up to cup her face as I continue to kiss her. I could kiss her like this for hours, her knees bracketing my thighs, one arm wound around my neck, the other hand slipped beneath my shirt and skimming my side. Her mouth open, her tongue busy, everything about her sexy and warm and every inch of her belongs to me.

And I'm not giving her back. Not again.

Not ever.

WILL

Then

The realization hit me like a sock to the gut after about the eighth girl I fucked in high school. They all had a similar look, a sameness to them that I hadn't noticed until the night I hooked up with Maddie Whitaker. Flirtatious, blond Maddie had attached herself to my side from the moment I entered the party celebrating the end of school my senior year. I knew what she wanted.

I wanted it, too. And gave it to her good back in a guest bedroom, right after she blew me.

"I knew you'd fuck me," she'd said almost triumphantly as she pulled her clothes back on. We were already finished and I just wanted the hell out of there. "Everyone said you would, since I'm your type."

I paused in buttoning my jeans, glancing across the room to find her watching me. "I have a type?" I asked.

She nodded, buttoning up her shirt. "You like girls who are petite and blond. Blue eyes. Innocent looking." She blinked her eyes at me and I saw nothing innocent about Maddie's face. After all, her lips had just been stretched wide around my dick not even fifteen minutes ago.

"Really." My voice was flat as I tugged my T-shirt over my head.

"Yeah. Rumor around school is some pretty, innocent blond totally broke your heart."

Maddie slipped out of the room soon after she said that

and I sat on the edge of the bed, lost in thought. No pretty, innocent blond had ever broken my heart. My heart was unbreakable. Hell, half the time I figured I didn't even really have one. Not a normal heart, in any case.

Mine was impenetrable. Lots of girls at school had tried to get me to be their boyfriend but I wasn't interested. Hooking up? I was all for it. A steady girlfriend who I had to make time for?

Fucking forget it.

Disturbed by Maddie's observation, I ran a hand through my rumpled hair, wondering if she spoke the truth. They really talked about me like that at school? I swear half the time the girls liked the dangerous aura they believed I had. I was the son of a known serial killer. I couldn't escape my reputation if I tried.

Lord knows I'd tried. Tried like hell.

The truth dawned on me about ten minutes later as I sat in the guest bedroom of a house owned by people I didn't even know. Only one girl had ever touched me, broken me, lingered within me like an intense longing. I had no idea what happened to her, where she was. She'd cut me off, though I never forgot her. No matter how much I tried.

Katie Watts. Pretty. Blond. Innocent. Sweet and trusting and needing me so damn bad. She was the one I kept chasing like a drug.

She was the one I could never have.

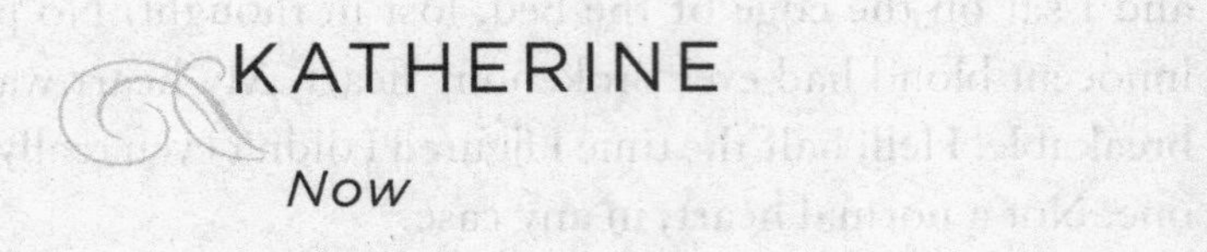

KATHERINE

Now

He picked me up as if I weighed nothing, his big hands sprawled across my butt, my legs automatically going around his hips. I wore no panties and he held me so close, my bare skin pressed against his flat stomach, that I wondered if he could feel me. If he knew I wasn't wearing underwear. If he thought I was too forward, too . . . much.

Stupid thought. He was a man. He was attracted to me and I could feel his erection, but it didn't scare me. More like I became excited. My blood pumped hard, my heart pounded, and I throbbed between my legs. His hands rested over the cotton of his shirt I wore but I'm sure he could feel me.

I wanted his hands on my bare skin.

After delivering a lingering kiss that left me breathless, he carried me to his room, deposited me on the edge of the bed, and now stands before me, shedding his shirt, revealing his bare chest to me for the first time. I stare unabashedly, mesmerized by his masculine form. His shoulders, his defined arms, his chest, his pecs, his flat stomach. He's muscular without being over the top, and my palms tingle I'm so anxious to get my hands on him.

There's a tattoo on his side, along his rib cage, and I tilt my head, wanting a good look at it. Two short words written in elegant script say *only us,* with a set of angel's wings beneath them.

Weird. And oddly familiar. I wonder what it means. I wonder who meant enough to him that he'd tattoo such romantic words on his body for that person. A girl. A girl that may have held his heart at one point in his life. A wave of jealousy flashes through me and I shove it away.

Lucky her.

I'm wearing only his T-shirt, nothing else—well, and the socks—and I rub my thighs together, unsure of the unfamiliar sensations flowing through me. I'm anxious. Edgy. I want his hands on me, yet . . . I don't. I want his mouth all over my skin but I'm afraid. Will he push me too far? Will he get mad if I don't let him do certain things? I don't even know what those certain things are, but I might not be up for them and I don't want to make him angry.

"You okay?" His deep voice knocks me from my thoughts. He touches my cheek and I lean into his hand, closing my eyes, absorbing his warmth, his kindness. "Katie."

I open my eyes and look up at him. He took off his glasses when we changed out of our wet clothes earlier. His eyes are incredibly dark, the muscles in his face and neck visibly strained, and I know he's holding back for my sake.

What would it be like, though, to have all of that restraint unleashed on me? Would I like it? Become lost in it? Or would all that focused intensity frighten me?

It was time I found out.

"You don't have to hold back because of me," I whisper, my gaze locked with his. His brow furrows, as if my declaration confuses him, and I continue on. "I want you, Ethan. I want . . . all of you."

He doesn't say anything for a few seconds until he finally clears his throat. "I don't think you know what you're asking for."

Now it's my turn to frown. "What do you mean?"

"Seeing you like this, knowing you're completely naked beneath my shirt." He clamps his lips shut and shakes his head, seemingly overcome. Pleasure slips over me, warm and liquid, as that sensation of unbridled feminine power returns. I love that I can make him react so strongly. "You're going to make me lose control, Katie. I know it. I've wanted you for so long."

"So long? We haven't even known each other—"

He kneels in front of me, startling me and cutting me off mid-sentence. "From the first moment I saw you, I knew."

I take his hands, his fingers curling around mine. "You knew what?" I ask, my voice trembling.

"That you would be mine." He leans in and kisses me, softly. Slowly. "That I would make you mine and there would be no going back once I did." Another kiss, his tongue tracing the inside of my lips, making me gasp. Making me shiver. "Do you want to be mine, Katie?"

"Yes," I whisper against his lips. "That's all I want. To be yours."

He says nothing, just pushes me onto the bed, his large, warm body over mine, our hands still clasped. He lifts them, brings them up over my head as he continues to kiss me, our tongues tangling, our bodies rubbing. His erection is nestled between my legs and I spread them wider, the shirt riding up, baring me, and I can feel the direct contact of his cotton-covered erection brushing against my core.

I tense up and he senses it, his entire body going still for a long, quiet moment, and then my moan breaks the silence.

"You feel so good." I don't sound like myself. God, I don't even feel like myself. My skin is hot, my entire body throbbing in time with the frenzied beat of my heart, and I lift my hips, deliberately rubbing against him. It's his turn to groan, the low, masculine sound rippling through me, making me insane.

Making me wish I could hear him groan like that again.

Without a word he lifts away from me, letting my hands go so he can rest his at my hips, his fingers pressing into my flesh. I wait with held breath as he slowly lifts my shirt, exposing my body inch by inch, until the shirt is above my stomach, bunched just below my breasts. I close my eyes with a sigh as he stares at me, his fingers drifting across my stomach, one finger circling my belly button.

"Your skin is so soft," he murmurs reverently.

I say nothing, just bask in his compliments, in the way he touches me. He pulls the shirt up higher, over my breasts, the fabric catching on my erect nipples, and I suck in a breath when the cool air hits my sensitive skin. He cups them both, engulfing my breasts in his big hands, his thumbs smoothing over my nipples, and I press my lips together to keep from whimpering.

"I want to hear you." I open my eyes to find him staring at my chest with an almost dazed fascination. "Don't hold back, Katie. Does this feel good?"

I nod, unable to speak. Too entranced with the way he seems entranced with me. It's fascinating.

Thrilling.

"Let's take this off," he urges. I lift my arms above my head, lift my head away from the mattress, and he tugs the shirt off, tossing it onto the floor. I'm completely naked beneath him. The only barrier between us is his sweatpants and they're just thin cotton. I can feel every inch of him press against me and though I'm a little worried about how exactly this is going to work, I'm also excited.

"Fuck, Katie." I close my eyes once more at the guttural groan that escapes him as he lifts away from me. I can feel his hot gaze rove over me, as if it were a physical caress. "I don't know if I can hold back much longer."

"Then don't." I reach for him blindly, my fingers tracing over the hot, firm skin of his chest. I want to feel all of him against all of me. "Please, Ethan."

I think it's the use of the word *please* that gets to him. He's on me in seconds, his mouth devouring mine, his hands wandering everywhere. I arch into his touch, moan against his mouth, entwine my tongue with his. Urging him on, wanting more, pushing past my fear because this is Ethan who I'm with.

I trust him. I care for him. Despite his earlier hot-and-cold attitude, I can't deny the connection between us. It tethers me to him whether I like it or not and when he's not with me, I feel a little lost. A lot alone.

And I'm so incredibly tired of feeling alone.

He moves down my body, his mouth blazing a trail over my skin. Along my neck, my throat, my collarbone, my chest, the tops of my breasts. The valley between my breasts, his lips lingering, his hot tongue darting out for a lick, making me gasp and hold him close. When his mouth rains kisses on my left breast, then my right, I bury my fingers in his hair. When he draws a nipple into his mouth and sucks, his tongue swirling, I pull his hair and cry out.

The attention he lavishes on my breasts leaves me mindless with pleasure. My entire body shakes, my stomach clenches, and between my legs, I'm wet. Incredibly wet. I want him to touch me there. I want his mouth on mine again. I love the almost forceful way he uses his tongue. His gentle approach drives me wild, too, and I pull on his shoulders. I want him closer. I want more.

Ethan gets the hint and he's there, touching my face, his mouth fused with mine. He shifts so he's directly on top of me, his erection between my legs, his chest hot against mine. I stroke him everywhere I can reach, our mouths open, our tongues wild. His hand wanders across my belly and lower, and I tense beneath his touch. I can't help it. My fears still drive me and though I trust Ethan, it's hard to break those old habits.

"Let me," he whispers, his fingers barely grazing my pubic hair. "I want to make you feel good, Katie. I want to make you come."

I melt at his coaxing words. Slowly I nod and his hand moves lower so he's cupping me, his hand covering the entirety of me. I pulse beneath his palm, my breath lodged in my throat. One long finger presses against me, gains entry, and then he's searching my delicate folds, his touch feather light.

"You're so fucking wet." He sounds as if he's in agony, and a matching pain pulses in my blood. "God, Katie what you do to me."

More like what he does to me. He shifts to the side, gaining a better angle so he can stroke me, and I rise up against his hand, my legs spreading wider, and moan. He leans over me and takes a nipple into his mouth, sucking it deep as he slips one finger inside my body, and I stifle the cry rising in my throat.

I'm . . . overwhelmed. And the slightest bit ashamed. It shouldn't feel so good, should it? My worry, my guilt, is such a burden, unable to let me go, seeming to dig its claws deeper inside me every time I think I've shed it for good. I hate it. I hate it so much and I don't want my issues to ruin this night with Ethan.

But here they come. Engulfing me. Reminding me of who I am and what happened to me.

"Relax, baby," he whispers against my breast, his breath blowing across my nipple and making me shiver. "Let go."

"I-I can't," I admit, my voice practically strangled with frustration.

"Don't think about the past," Ethan urges as he lifts up to watch me. "Don't let any of that shit hold you back. Just focus on me. Focus on my touch. Focus on how I can make you feel."

I try my best but it's no use. The pleasure that had zipped through my veins only moments ago feels like a distant memory now. His mouth returns to my skin, his fingers shift and move between my legs, but I can feel only a small measure of excitement. It's faded to almost nothing and I squeeze my eyes shut, forcing the tears away.

But they fall despite my wishing them gone.

KATIE

Then

By the time I was sixteen, my expectations of romance had turned into complete Fantasy Land. I was a walking, talking Disney princess, alone in my castle.

I awaited my mysterious, handsome prince to come and rescue me from my lonely tower. I read romance books, sweet young adult stories with plenty of longing and covert glances and enough dreaming of kissing to fill an entire teenage girl's secret diary. All that wishing and hoping and praying was my favorite part. Once the kiss happened, once the confirmation of boyfriend/girlfriend status was in place, I was totally over the story.

The unrequited love was what spoke to me. I could understand that. That was me. Actually having a boyfriend, dealing with the issues that came with a relationship, talking and hugging and kissing a boy on a regular basis?

I could barely wrap my head around it. I was sixteen and completely isolated. Completely alone.

I hated it.

Boys never paid attention to me before everything happened, and they sure as heck didn't pay attention once I returned to school. I think I scared them.

I know they scared me.

Everyone scared me. That was half the reason Mom decided to homeschool me despite the protests from my guidance counselor and my teachers. They wanted me in school; they wanted me experiencing a normal life.

But I couldn't deal. Neither could Mom.

My therapist was desperate for me to have a breakthrough. She wanted me to realize who my fantasy boy was. My hero. My rescuer. I was in denial. I knew, deep down inside, who he was. But so much time had passed. Almost four years. I should've been over him, right? No way was he coming to rescue me ever again. He'd done it once. He'd met his obligation.

Our moment together was done.

I brushed my fingers across the guardian angel charm, then slowly withdrew the bracelet from my wrist. Went to my dresser and grabbed the old jewelry box I received from my grandma the Christmas I was seven. Opening the top, I set the bracelet inside, then slowly closed it.

There. No more physical reminder of Will.

It was the emotional reminder, the way he lingered in my mind and came to me in my dreams, that was going to be so much more difficult to shut off.

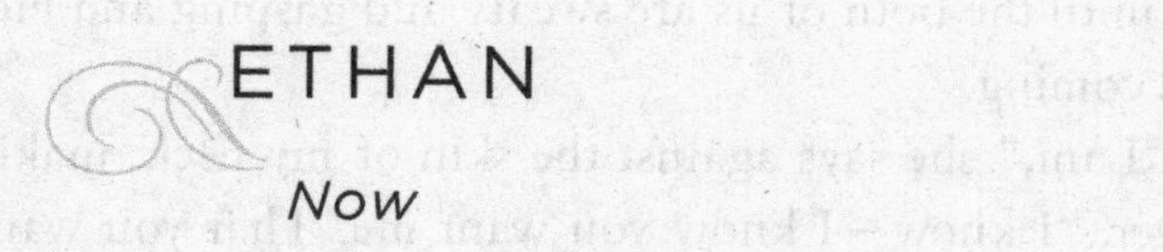

I lost her. She was so close, too. I know she was into it. Enjoying it. Deriving pleasure from my touch, from my mouth, my words.

"Hey." I shift up, aligning our bodies, and see the tears flowing down her cheeks. They make my heart stutter almost to a complete stop. I hate seeing her in pain. I always have. "Baby, what's wrong?"

She cracks open tear-filled eyes, blue and so intense. "I don't know if I can do this, Ethan."

"What happened?" I stroke her cheek, gathering up every tear I can with my thumb. "I pushed too hard."

"N-no." She shakes her head. "It's all me. My problems. My issues. I'm a-a m-mess."

I pull her in close and wrap my arm around her back, letting her press her face against my chest. Her tears wet my skin, her shoulders quietly shake as she cries, and my heart splinters into what feels like a million pieces.

What if I can't help her? What if she'll never be one hundred percent comfortable with sex? I don't want to think that could happen, but it's a distinct possibility.

"You're not a mess," I reassure her, my fingers drifting up and down the silky-smooth expanse of her back. Every naked curve is snug against my side and my cock could pound fucking nails, I swear. But I have to restrain myself. Pretend that I'm not all worked up and dying to push deep inside her. Fuck her until the both of us are sweaty and gasping and moaning and coming.

"I am," she says against the skin of my neck, making me shiver. "I know—I know you want me. That you want this. But I don't think I can give it to you."

I draw a single finger along the length of her spine, stopping perilously close to her perfect butt. "You don't want this? Me?"

Her entire body goes still as she lifts her head, her gaze snagging with mine. "I-I do."

"You're just scared." I kiss her. Just a soft press of lips, completely innocent. No tongue. Her lips part beneath mine, but I break away from her before we can take it any farther. "I understand."

"I'm not scared. I'm not really. I just . . . I don't know." She trembles as I continue to stroke her back, and I know she's not as unaffected by my touch as she believes.

"Sshh." I roll her onto her back and she stares up at me, her eyes wide, her entire body shaking. "Just listen to me, Katie. Close your eyes."

She takes a deep breath and her eyes fall shut, her entire body tense, as if she's afraid I'm going to do something awful to her. I reach out and gently touch her face, my fingers skimming her cheeks, her eyebrows, the length of her nose, her plump lips. I touch the line of her jaw, the point of her chin, the skin just beneath, her throat, the side of her neck, her ear. Her other ear. Trace the shell with my fingertip, then pull on her lobe, my hand falling to her shoulder.

"Do you like it when I touch you?" I ask.

She nods, her lips curving into the faintest smile. I wonder if she's even aware that she's smiling. "It feels good."

"Made even better because you know it's me touching you,

right?" When she nods again I drop my head close to her ear and lower my voice. "I feel the same exact way. When your hands are on me, when we kiss . . . it feels fucking incredible. And that's because it's you."

I skim her shoulders, her chest. Drift the back of my fingers across her nipples and make her suck in a harsh breath. She's on fire for me, whether she can admit to it or not. I know she is. She wants me. I want her. I need to get her over this fear. Again, I feel like it's my duty to rescue her, to help her overcome this. The man who gave me life ruined this for her.

It's my job to save her.

"Ethan." My name is a breathless whisper and unable to stop myself, I dip my head and kiss the very top of her right breast. "Why are you so patient with me?"

"Because you're worth it," I say, keeping my mouth on her skin. She shivers beneath my lips and when I envelop a perfect pink nipple with my mouth, the blissful sigh that passes her lips tells me how much she likes it.

I will break her of her fears. I know it.

Her hand is on the back of my head, holding me to her, and I let my hand drift down the gentle slope of her belly, resting between her legs. She's hot there, and wet. So incredibly wet. I touch her with just the tips of my fingers, delving deeper with every stroke, until she's moving against my hand, her legs spreading, her hips lifting subtly. I keep talking, telling her how beautiful she is, how I want to make her feel good, how much I need her to come.

Her eyes flash open as her body tenses and I wonder if she's close. Or if she's drifting away, letting her fears overcome her again. Her gaze meets mine, wild and confused, and I increase my pace, my thumb brushing over her clit again and again, and I know in an instant I haven't lost her.

I've finally fucking found her.

Leaning over her, I crush my mouth to hers, my hand busy between her legs, her body straining beneath mine. She breaks away from my kiss, a pained *oh* leaving her, my name soon following. My hand moves fiercely over her, circling her clit with my thumb, and she arches beneath me.

She's coming.

Her body is racked with shudders. Her skin is covered with sweat. My name falls from her lips like a chant, over and over, and then she's kissing me, right before she collapses as if her bones just melted. She's the one consuming me and I remove my hand from between her legs to clutch her close, roll her over so she's on top of me.

"I made you come," I whisper against her lips, the arrogant tone in my voice unmistakable.

Katie sighs, the sound of a deeply satisfied woman. "You did."

"I want to make you come again." I kiss her. "I want you to come on my cock."

"Ethan," she chastises, but I see the way her eyes flash.

She likes my saying that.

"Let me inside, baby." I tangle my fingers in her hair, pulling it out of the sloppy topknot. I remove the elastic band holding it in place and her golden hair spills over her shoulders, the ends tickling my face, and her familiar scent washes over me.

If my dick gets any harder, I might be in serious trouble.

"Like this?" She rotates her hips against me and I swear my eyes cross. "With me on top?"

"Whatever you're comfortable with." I brush her hair back and flip it over her shoulder. She's so beautiful like this. Her skin glows, her eyes sparkle. I put that glow on her face, that sparkle in her gaze. I'm the one responsible for making her feel sexual pleasure for the first time in her life.

I want to be her first and her last.

"I think I'd rather you . . ." Her voice drifts and her cheeks turn red with embarrassment. "I want you on top. I don't know what I'm doing."

Without warning, I roll her over so she's pinned beneath me and I kiss her, savoring her taste, the way she writhes underneath me. "I'll go slow," I vow. "And it'll be easier now that you've had an orgasm. You'll be more . . . open. More relaxed."

"I'm still tingling from it," she whispers, and I smile.

"Let's make it happen again."

KATHERINE

Now

He reaches for his bedside table and withdraws a condom from the drawer, tearing the wrapper and rolling away from me so he can kick off his sweatpants and put the condom on. I watch in fascination, fully taking in the length and width of his erection for the first time, and my throat goes dry. I know what he said, that it should be easier considering I just had an orgasm, but still.

Ethan seems big. Not that I've seen a lot of penises, but . . . yeah.

I don't get to stare and worry for long, though. He pulls me beneath him once more, his mouth fusing with mine, his tongue doing all of these delicious circles around mine. I love it when he kisses me. I love the feel of his hot body pressing me deeper into the mattress. The subtly insistent way he thrusts his hips against mine, the movement causing my thighs to spread and accommodate him. He's positioned perfectly to take me, his elbows braced on either side of my head, his mouth still on mine, his erection probing at my entry.

I refuse to let my fears take hold. Instead, I focus on the here and now. The way he smells, warm and masculine, clean and fresh. The tickle of his stubble against my cheeks, the taste of his lips, his assured touch.

Slowly, with infinite patience, he enters me. I tense up, my breath stalled in my lungs, my muscles seizing, but he keeps kissing me, coaxing me with his lips and tongue, easing the tension as he eases fully inside my body. He breathes my name against my lips and lifts up, his hands braced on the pillow as he pushes forward with his hips, embedding himself, going deeper.

I close my eyes and try to remember to breathe. His length stretches and pulls, causing a stinging sensation deep within, and I wince, a gush of breath leaving me when he withdraws almost all the way and then pushes back inside.

Oh. That wasn't so bad.

"If I move any more, any faster, I'll blow," he says, and I open my eyes to see the strain on his face, his lips pressed tightly together. "You feel so damn good," he mutters.

Shifting beneath him somehow sends him farther and we both moan at the sensation. I bend my legs, my thighs on either side of his hips, and he thrusts again. Withdraw and return. Withdraw and return. Slowly, so slowly, my body accommodating his, his mouth on mine once more, his hand on my breast, squeezing before he lets go.

"Lift your hands up," he demands, and I obey, raising my hands above my head, resting them on the pillow. He reaches for them, entwines our fingers and holds me there. Holds *us* there, bound together. Making the moment somehow even more intimate.

"Move with me, baby," he whispers and I do, my hips rising, my legs clamped at his sides. With his whispered encouragement I wrap my legs around his waist, anchoring my body to his and sending him as deep as he can possibly get.

It feels . . . amazing. So full. I'm completely connected to him, engaged and in the moment, lost to the sensation of his body moving above mine, within mine. Our hands tightly clasped, our fingers clenched around each other's, he bends down and kisses me, his voice cracking as he admits, "I'm going to come. Are you close?"

No, but that doesn't matter. I squeeze his hands, lift my head as much as I can to touch my mouth to his, and he increases his pace. His hips slap against mine, our damp-with-sweat skin loud in the otherwise quiet of the house, and then he stiffens above me, his fingers clamped so tight around mine it hurts a little. A hoarse cry sounds from deep within his chest and then he thrusts hard, just once, my name filling the air as his body is consumed with shudders.

I lie beneath him, reveling in his surrender, fascinated that we just did this. That we just had sex and I let him lie on top of me, let him inside my body. That he made me come with the touch of his fingers and I loved it. Only one hitch in the otherwise perfect evening and I somehow overcame it.

He collapses on top of me, his hands still wrapped in mine, his body heavy, his breathing labored. I disentangle one hand from his and stroke his damp hair, his back, feeling him shiver beneath my fingertips. I kiss his neck, his jaw, his chin, wherever I can reach, and he shifts away so he can look at me, his heavy-lidded gaze filled with satisfaction.

"Stay the night with me?" he asks and I nod, trying to bite back the smile that threatens to overtake me.

"Hungry?" When I nod again he rolls to his side, taking me with him and gathering me close. "Let me get rid of this condom and we'll take a nap. Then we'll fix something for dinner. Or order takeout. Whatever you want." He kisses my forehead and then exits the bed, padding into the connecting bathroom with a nonchalance I can only envy.

Maybe someday I'll feel confident enough to walk around

naked in front of him. Maybe someday I'll be rid of my hang-ups once and for all . . .

I'm already halfway asleep by the time he returns to the bed and pulls me into his arms. I end up sleeping like the dead, like I haven't slept in years, which I really haven't.

And for once, I don't dream.

KATHERINE

Now

I've learned a lot in my short life. Had a lot of terrible things happen to me. I've known tragedy, pain, loss, unspeakable violence.

Now I've known tenderness. Passion. Desire. Romance. I've known what it feels like to be held and kissed by someone you care about.

I also know what it feels like to be betrayed. I've experienced that particular feeling again and again.

Betrayed by my best friend Sarah, who didn't know how to continue our friendship after what happened to me. Betrayed by the media when a small fraction of them vilified me during the trial, made me out to be a slut who asked to be kidnapped.

My father betrayed me, and that hurt the most of all. How he couldn't deal with the guilt and the shame over what happened to me. His treatment of me filled me with so much of my own guilt and shame I didn't know how to cope. He hurt me beyond anyone else on this planet, maybe even more than Aaron William Monroe, and that will forever make me sad and filled with regret.

But this morning, when I wake up in Ethan's bed, my body naked and sore from his gentle abuse all last night, I feel on top of the world.

He's in the shower. I can hear the water running and I rub my hands over my face, trying to wake up. We stayed up late, talking and making love. Eating and laughing and touching and kissing each other until we couldn't keep our hands off of each other. I'm tender between my legs, my muscles ache, and my lips and cheeks are suffering from a serious case of stubble burn.

The shower shuts off and I hear the curtain being torn back. I imagine Ethan naked and wet, and my entire body aches with wanting him. He should've invited me to take a shower with him.

Oh well, there's always next time.

"Did you just get up?" I ask him, raising my voice.

He peeks his head around the cracked bathroom door. "Hey." His smile is wide, his handsome face and broad chest covered in drops of water, and I want to go to him but I keep myself rooted to the bed. I can see there's a towel wrapped loosely around his hips, fueling my newfound imagination. "You're awake."

"What time did you wake up?" I ask.

"About twenty minutes ago." He shrugs. "You were sleeping and I didn't want to disturb you."

"Maybe I wanted to take a shower with you," I say with a little pout, marveling at myself. Since when do I pout?

His smile grows. "Next time. I promise."

I like it when he promises.

He withdraws from the cracked-open door and I imagine he's toweling himself off. I hear a drawer open. The clank of something as it settles on the tile countertop, water running in the sink. I lie back and close my eyes, listening to Ethan's morning ritual and enjoying it. I feel so normal, so regular, so free.

I feel free. Like I've finally come over the other side of the mountain and survived. This is what life can be like with Ethan. The two of us together. Happy.

Complete.

His phone buzzes from where it sits on the bedside table, startling me, and I open my eyes, inhaling deeply to calm my racing heart.

"Hey, will you check that for me?" he calls from within the bathroom. "I'm waiting on a client to text me back and I think that might be him."

"Are you meeting with him today or something?" I ask as I sit up, smoothing my hair back from my face. I hold the sheet tight against my naked breasts, my modesty returning in full force with the morning light, and I hope like crazy my clothes sitting in his dryer are actually dry.

Though really I wouldn't mind if we didn't have to get dressed at all, just for a little while longer. I want him to come back to bed with me.

"We're supposed to meet next week, but he mentioned he's going out of town so we might move our appointment up. To this morning possibly." He pauses; the water turns on and then shuts off. "Can you check my phone please?"

Disappointment creeps in but I push it away. He has to work. I can't expect him to entertain me constantly. But maybe we can sneak in some time in bed before he has to get to work.

"You sure you want me to check your phone? No secrets to hide?" I tease.

He pauses. "Go for it."

I lean over to grab the phone from his nightstand, startled yet again when it buzzes once more. The message flashes across the screen, a phone number with an area code I faintly recognize, but no name attached to it.

Weird.

"Is it him?" he asks, but I don't answer him. I'm too busy reading the text that slowly makes my blood run cold.

I believe this phone number belongs to a former William Aaron Monroe? If so, please contact me right away. This is Lisa Swanson.

I frown, staring at the message, the letters blurring the longer I look at it. "This can't be right," I whisper, reading the message again, the name *William Aaron Monroe* flashing in my mind again and again.

William Aaron Monroe.

William Monroe.

Will.

No. It can't be.

The phone falls from my hands, landing on the floor with a dull thud. I can't breathe, I feel like I'm going to hyperventilate, and I swallow hard, close my eyes, fight off the dizziness. I need to get out of here.

I crawl out of bed, ignoring Ethan as he calls me from the bathroom, grabbing the phone because I don't want him to know about that message. Not yet. I dash toward his laundry room, the cold air that hits my naked skin making me shiver, but I push on. The moment I enter his tiny laundry room I crouch down and open the dryer, pulling out my clothes—thankful to find they're dry—and yanking them on, not bothering with the panties or bra.

My mind and body are numb. I have to go. What did that message mean? How could his phone belong to a *former* William Aaron Monroe? *The* William Monroe?

My William Monroe.

"Hey."

I turn on a gasp to find Ethan standing in the narrow doorway of his laundry room, his broad frame seeming to fill the entire space. I stare at him, really look at him, but I don't see it. Don't see my sullen, dark and emo teenage Will. Will's hair was so black, his face sharp and angular, though they have the same dark eyes now that I'm truly looking for it. Will's lip and eyebrow had been pierced, his tall frame lanky. The man standing before me doesn't resemble Will, not like this.

He just looks like . . . my Ethan.

"Already getting dressed?" His smile is easy and I hate thinking this, but he looks so incredibly good. So handsome, so comfortable in his own skin, so at ease with . . . everything. "I wanted to make you breakfast. Was that message from my client or what? I didn't see my phone."

"It wasn't from your client," I say, my voice a monotone. He frowns at me, his gaze so piercing, so intense, and I'm glad I already have my clothes on. They feel like a shield, like they can protect me.

But nothing and no one can protect me. Not anymore. The truth is dawning, thawing through my numb-as-ice brain, and I realize I've been lied to.

Tricked.

Betrayed.

Repeatedly.

"Are you okay?" he asks softly in that concerned, thoughtful tone of his and I want to punch him. Just smack his beautiful face, hurt him, make him bleed. Tear him apart, like he's doing to me at this very moment.

I say nothing, just hold out his phone toward him. He takes it from me, glancing at the screen, his face blanching as he sees the text I just read.

The text that has ruined my entire world.

He glances up at me, his gaze haunted, his expression a mixture of determination and alarm as he starts, "Katie . . ."

"Just tell me why," I cut him off, not wanting to hear any

excuses. I can't breathe. I'm hurt and humiliated and full of so much anger, so much rage over what he's done. How could he do this? And for what purpose? "Why did you lie to me?"

He shakes his head, confused. "What are you talking about?"

"Just—stop," I say, my voice low, my head starting to pound. "Are you trying to tell me that text wasn't meant for you?" Oh God, I can't believe this. I cannot even begin to wrap my head around what I just discovered.

"Katie, please. Calm down."

"Tell me the truth!" I shriek, surprising him. Surprising myself. My heart feels like it's been sliced in two. It hurts. What he's done, it hurts so bad. "Are you Will? *My* Will?"

Ethan doesn't say a word for seconds. Minutes. The longer he doesn't speak, the guiltier he sounds. "Look," he finally says. "I can explain . . ."

"Fuck you!" I've never said that to anyone in my life and it feels . . . good. Satisfying. Empowering. "Fuck you and your explanations. You *lied* to me. Got close to me, tricked me by pretending to be someone else, and then you get me in bed, have sex with me like it's some sort of sick joke and . . . now what? Were you going to tell Lisa Swanson all about me? How you fooled me into believing you're a good guy who's interested in me instead of someone from my past? Someone I'd rather forget?"

That last line is a lie. I'm just trying to hurt him and from the look on his face, I think it worked.

"Katie, stop. Listen." He grabs hold of my upper arms and I try to shake him off but it's no use. He's too strong. "I *am* a good guy who's interested in you. I swear. I care about you, Katie. I always have."

He always has. Those words touch me, despite my anger.

"Then why the lies?" I hate that I respond to his hands on me. My skin is tingling, my body warm at having him so near. I want to drop-kick him. Nail him in the balls with my foot and watch him slump to the floor, moaning in agony. Anything to see him feel even a fraction of the pain I'm currently experiencing. "Why, Ethan? Or should I say *Will?*"

He flinches, as if he doesn't like being called that. So many questions run through my mind, none that I can ask, because that would mean I care and he's the absolute last person I should care about.

Ethan is really *my* Will. My *Will*. I can't believe it. I seriously cannot believe this is happening. Why all the lies, the trickery? What did he hope to gain from this? I don't understand.

"If you could calm down for just a moment, I can explain," he starts, but his words only increase my anger.

"I don't want to hear your shitty explanations." I jerk out of his hold and push past him, but I hear him fall into step behind me, like he's chasing me through his house. I go to the living room in search of my purse and shoes and I find them both, slipping on my boots and grabbing my purse so I can sling it over my shoulder.

"Katie, goddamn it, wait," he demands as I make my way to the front door.

I pause there, my hand on the doorknob, my head bent. I'm not crying, which I find hard to believe, but I'm so pissed, so utterly baffled and in disbelief over what I've just discovered, I swear I'm in shock.

"I-I'm sorry," he says. "I can't even begin to explain what happened, how we both ended up here, but just know that I never . . . meant to hurt you."

Closing my eyes, I press my forehead against the cool wood of the front door. My mind races with endless questions. Did he do this on purpose? Did he really try to hurt me? Trick me? It feels like it. It feels like the worst trick in the world. And now that I've found out he's talking to Lisa Swanson, just like his father is, I feel utterly betrayed.

Completely destroyed.

Thank goodness I followed him back to his place. He'd suggested leaving my car and driving back here with him yesterday, but I'd wanted my car as an option in case I needed to escape.

And I've never needed to escape more than I do right at this very moment.

"I don't want to see you ever again," I say to the door, unable to look at him. I don't think I could bear it. "I don't know why you did this, why you wanted to trick me, but you did. You got one over on me. Congratulations."

I open the door and burst outside, running down the sidewalk toward my car. I can feel him behind me but he doesn't chase after me and despite everything within me yelling that I shouldn't look back, I shouldn't turn around . . .

I do.

He's standing in his doorway, his face full of so much pain, I feel my heart crack. "I fucked up," he says. "I'm sorry. I can't make you understand what I've done without a chance to explain. A chance to tell you everything."

"I don't want to hear it," I practically spit out at him, pushing down the curiosity that fills me. I unlock and open my car door, about to slide inside when I hear him say one more thing.

"I never, ever meant to hurt you, Katie. I hope you know

that. That's the last thing I ever want to do to you. I've thought about you every day for years. Wondered if you were okay, hoped that you were healing. When I saw you on TV . . ."

My heart sinks. It was the interview that caused him to find me. I should never have done it. "It doesn't matter anymore," I say wearily. "What's done is done. You had your fun. I hope this was all worth it."

I climb into the car and shut the door behind me, starting up the engine and backing out of his driveway. He watches me the entire time, his hands clutching the doorframe, his expression one of complete and utter pain.

He looks the way I feel.

The tears flow freely during the entire hour-long drive home. I don't know if I'll ever recover from this.

I do know that I'll never be the same.

ETHAN

Now

Rage fuels me. Makes me do stupid things.

I destroyed my bedroom, specifically the bed. I tore off the comforter and the sheets, threw the pillows so hard against the wall they knocked down the painting I had hanging there, some stupid abstract bullshit art I bought from a client as a goodwill gesture.

Always hated that stupid fucking painting.

Found my phone on the floor, discarded by Katie. Lisa Swanson's message still flashed and I went into the conversation, typed off a message, and hit send.

FUCK OFF BITCH!!!!!!!!!!!!!

Didn't make me feel any better, though, sending that message.

I run my hands over my face, through my hair. The one good thing in my life, the one girl who made me feel worthy of something, and I hurt her. Ruined our relationship as quickly as we formed it. Why the fuck did I do it? Why did I keep such a big secret from her? What did I really think I'd gain out of this, by lying to her?

Instead of being cautious and keeping my distance, I dived right in. Reached out to her, contacted her, spent time with her, grew to care for her all over again, fell a little in love with her . . .

And fucked it all up.

My heart hurts. It fucking aches. I rub a hand over my chest as I survey the damage, ready to do more damage when my phone rings. I grab it, see that the number has been blocked, and for some strange reason I think it might be Katie, so I answer it.

It's not Katie.

"Is this William Monroe?"

Lisa Swanson's voice is unmistakable.

"What do you want?" I ask through gritted teeth.

"Just to talk," she says hurriedly. Like she's afraid I might end the call. She's right. I'm ready to. "Your father . . . he said he was still in contact with you."

I close my eyes, letting the misery and dread course over me. *Great*. Given up by my father. Not a surprise. "I don't want to talk to you."

"Did you see the interview with Katherine Watts? I'll let you tell your side of the story, just like she did. The interview will be completely unbiased, just you talking. Nothing else," Lisa explains.

"You attacked Katie," I say. "You threw a few surprises at her—don't deny it."

Lisa sighs. "I had to. I won't do the same to you."

"I don't buy it. Not for a minute." I end the call before she can get another word in. I already said too much, revealed too much. She knows who I am. She knows how to get in contact with me.

My father didn't have this number; he doesn't even know my new name. I made sure of that. So how did he find out? Or did he? Was this all Lisa's doing? And if so, will she run off and tell him my new identity?

I press my hands against my face and scrub them over my cheeks before I run them up over my head, tugging on my hair.

Fuck. This is bad. Worse than bad. Not only have I ruined everything with Katie, I've put myself at risk for the media finding me. Hell, the media *has* found me. The chance my father could find me, too?

Pretty much guaranteed.

KATIE

Then

After everyone went to bed I sneaked into the family room and turned on the TV, keeping the volume low. It was almost eleven thirty. The show would start soon. I was anxious; my palms were sweaty and my heart was racing.

I would see him soon. Hear his testimony. Hear his voice. I hadn't heard him speak in so long and I missed it. Missed him.

Ridiculous, considering I really didn't know him, but true.

The commercial ended and the theme music started. A news show that had dedicated itself to the trial of Aaron William Monroe, it gave an update every night. Clips from the trial, analysis from lawyers who'd turned into TV personalities, recaps of testimony, of the crime, interviews with the victims' various family members.

I'd never been allowed to watch it. My parents were too worried I'd get . . . scared, I guess. They never allowed me to do anything. I wanted to watch it so bad. I wanted to see everything despite my fear, my hatred and fear of Aaron Monroe.

Tonight, though, I wanted to see Will.

I watched, anxious for them to get to the recap. They spoke of Will, flashed photos of him from when we were first discovered. He looked the same as I remembered, but that was a couple of years ago. I knew he'd changed. I'd changed, too. I'd grown a few inches, my hair was longer, my face not as full. I had breasts that I hid in baggy shirts and a narrow waist that the shirts covered up, too. I didn't want to grow up and be a woman. I was almost fifteen.

Couldn't I stay a kid forever?

The newscaster started talking about today's trial activities, spoke of Will's testimony. He was on the stand for the prosecution for over two hours and when it was time for the defense to ask questions, they didn't. That seemed to shock everyone.

It didn't shock me, because I knew Will had spoken the truth.

The TV shows went to footage of the trial, and there he was. Will sat on the stand, wearing a black button-down shirt, the sleeves rolled up, his expression earnest as he listened to what the prosecuting attorney had to say. I moved to sit on the floor and scooted closer, wanting to get a good look at him.

Just as I figured, he looked different. His hair wasn't as dark, not that unnatural black anymore, which confirmed my earlier suspicion that he dyed it. No more piercings, either, not on his lip or eyebrow. He looked older. His jaw was so strong, his expression almost unforgiving as he spoke of his father in this sort of flat, monotone voice. He squinted every once in a while and I wondered if he needed glasses.

I listened to his voice as he spoke. It was deeper and he sounded so much older. His shoulders were broad, his arms thick with muscle. He was a completely different boy than the one I first met.

Reaching for my wrist, I touched the angel charm that dangled from the bracelet Will gave me. I'd put it back on recently. My parents hadn't a clue who gave it to me. I'm pretty sure they didn't even notice I owned it, and I wasn't about to tell them about it.

They'd take it away from me. And the bracelet was the last link I had to Will.

The only link.

"Did you have anything to do with the abduction of Katherine Watts, Mr. Monroe?" the prosecuting attorney asked Will.

His expression turned stony. "No," he said vehemently. "I had nothing to do with it. I didn't even know he'd taken her."

"Only when you found her in the storage shed within twenty-four hours of the kidnapping did you know she was there, on the property."

"Yes." He sighed, a flash of vulnerability crossing his face. I recognized that look. It was one I'd seen many times when we'd been together. When he walked me to the police station. "When I first found her, I—panicked. I didn't know what to do, how she got there, and I ran away."

"Why did you run away?"

"I was scared. I couldn't believe there was a girl chained up in our storage shed." He visibly swallowed. "I was afraid if he knew that I knew, I'd be in trouble."

My heart cracked. He looked so sad, so . . . destroyed.

"But you finally went back to her. What happened next?"

"I told her I was going to help her escape."

"Why?"

"Because I couldn't let her stay in that shed. He was—he was hurting her. I couldn't risk it. Couldn't risk her life. He would've killed her if I left her there."

Tears streamed down my face. He was right. His father would have killed me. I knew it. Will knew it, too.

"So you saved her," the attorney said.

"It was the right thing to do." Will paused, clearing his throat. "It was the only thing to do."

KATHERINE

Now

I wake with a gasp, my heart thumping wildly, my breathing harsh in my throat. I sit up and push my hair out of my face, knowing the dream that I had wasn't really a dream, but a memory.

A memory of that night I watched Will's testimony on TV. He'd looked so different, so grown-up.

I realize now he'd looked a lot like Ethan.

Closing my eyes, I fight back the tears. I'm such an idiot. How could I not have seen it? Especially these last few days, when he'd reminded me of Will so strongly. Was I in some sort of strange state of denial? You'd think I'd want to find Will, to thank him for saving me, let him know how much he still means to me, even after all these years.

I flop back on the bed and close my eyes, sling my arm over my face. He hasn't tried to text or call me and it's been five days since I fled his house. He's either giving me time or letting me go.

That last part hurts. More than I'd like to admit.

Mom has been calling. So has Brenna. I've been short with them, blaming my mood on schoolwork. But I've neglected the papers I need to write, and the last test I took, I barely passed.

All I can think about is Ethan and what he did to me. How he lied. I don't understand why. What sort of sick thrill did he get out of tricking me? Is he really that messed up? I want to believe he sought me out with good intentions, but I don't know.

I guess I'll never know.

Despite it all, I miss him. I think of what we shared that night. How I bared myself to him, the intimate moments we shared. I want more. I wish I could have more, but I don't trust him. I can't trust anyone. I let one person into my life after so many years of never opening up to anyone and it ends in complete disaster.

I can't let anyone else in.

Ever.

Glancing at my phone, I see that it's almost six a.m. and I give up pretending I'll go back to sleep. I crawl out of bed and take a shower. Go about my morning tasks, getting dressed, drying my hair, eating breakfast, and checking my phone. I need to run a few errands and I'm about to leave when I receive a call from an unfamiliar number. I'm hesitant to answer it, should just let it go to voicemail, but something compels me to answer that call.

"Hello?"

"Katherine? This is Lisa Swanson. We need to talk."

Playlist

Music always tends to play a part in my writing process and this book was no exception. Here are some of the songs that I listened to while writing NTUA:

"Never Tear Us Apart" by INXS (Obviously. I adored INXS back in the day.)
"Lost Stars" by Adam Levine (This is for sure Will's song.)
"Atlas" by Coldplay
"OctaHate" by Ryn Weaver
"Daughters" by John Mayer (For Katie)
"If It Hurts" by Gallant
"Water Fear" by Katie Herzig
"Small Things" by Ben Howard
"Till Sunrise" by Goldroom featuring Mammals
"Pendulum" by FKA twigs (I loooove her music.)
"Medusa" by GEMS
"Ripped Apart" by Anthony Green
"Waiting Game" by Banks
"Every Breath You Take" by The Police
"Carousel" by Melanie Martinez
"Elastic Heart" by Sia with The Weeknd
"Round Here" by Counting Crows
"Teenage Dream" by Katy Perry (If you read the book—obviously.)

Ethan and Katherine's story continues in the conclusion to bestselling author Monica Murphy's darkly sexy, emotionally powerful two-part tale of forbidden love

Never Let You Go

Read on for a special sneak peek.

Coming soon from Headline Eternal.

ETHAN

The text came on a late Tuesday afternoon, the familiar ding indicating I received a message ringing loudly from across the room. My phone sits on the coffee table. I'm sitting in my recliner, tapping away on my laptop as I answer an email from a client.

When I finally send off the email, I get up and go to my phone, hitting the button to see who the text is from.

And proceed to drop the phone on the floor, I'm so startled by the name flashing on my screen.

Katie.

What do you want to talk about?

It's been a week since I sent that one text during a weak moment, when I was feeling particularly low and sad. I've taken care of myself my entire life. I don't remember my mom. Dad was never around and didn't care. I coped. I dealt with shit on my own and I preferred it that way.

Katie reenters my life and she's like a bright light I can't resist. Her warmth, her sweetness, the way she made me feel like a goddamn hero every time she fucking looked at me. I'd never experienced anything like it. I began to crave her. Need her. And once I lost her . . .

I'd never been so utterly alone, felt so incredibly lonely as I did after she left me.

You're willing to talk to me?

I hit send and wait anxiously for her reply. Within seconds I get it.

Yes.

Running my hand through my hair, I realize I'm sweating. Shit. How are we going to do this? Like two civil adults who can barely speak to each other? Will she want to meet me in public? If it's somewhere private, at her place or mine, forget it. I'm done for. I won't be able to keep my hands off her.

Do you want to meet me somewhere?

It's best to be in public, I tell myself. That way I won't do something stupid and risk her leaving.

How about the coffee shop you first took me to?

Her suggestion is perfect. Close to the amusement park, which is closed for the season. Near the ocean. In a public place, where I have to be on my best behavior. My fingers literally itch to touch her and I clench them into fists before I straighten them out and type out an answer.

That sounds good.

Tomorrow at three? Or is that too soon?

I smile at her response. Is that too soon? It's never too soon to see Katie again.

Tomorrow at three is perfect.

KATIE

I tell no one that I'm meeting with Ethan because it doesn't need to be said. Mom will freak out and Brenna will barricade herself in my house and forbid me to leave. I made the mistake in telling them immediately after I found out his truth, their shock and horror over who he really is reaffirming my decision to run.

But now I hate that they know and they'll hold this against him forever. There's telling your family things from your life in order to gain their comfort and sympathy, and then there's telling your family too much.

I went the too much route and I regret it.

Nerves eat at me as I make the drive, and my mind races. Am I wearing the right thing? Do I look pretty? Am I trying too hard? What do I say to him? What will I do when I first see him? Will I be able to face him, look into his eyes, find my voice and actually speak to him?

I'm scared.

Scared it won't be the same between us. Afraid that what happened is too large of an obstacle for us to overcome.

For *me* to overcome.

Somehow I end up at the coffee shop. I hardly remember parking the car, walking along the street, entering the warm, fragrant building, so many people inside buzzing with energy, chatting excitedly as they sip their coffee. I look around, my entire body quaking as my gaze searches for him but he's not there.

Disappointment makes my heart drop and I tell myself to shake it off. I'm early. Glancing at my phone, I see I'm here a whopping fifteen minutes before our planned meeting time and I go back outside, the cool, salty air like a balm to my overheated, over-stimulated body.

A park bench sits out in front of the building and I settle on it, my shoulders hunched against the cold, my head bowed so my chin dips into the soft infinity scarf around my neck. I wore black leggings and an oversized charcoal gray sweater, my hair up in a bun, my scarf a bright red color that probably draws too much attention. Pearl earrings that my grandma gave me for my twelfth birthday, minimal makeup, black flats. I didn't want to stand out so maybe the red scarf was a mistake? I look up and glance around, hoping to spot Ethan making his approach, but so far he's nowhere in sight.

What if he doesn't show?

Get a grip. You're worrying over nothing.

Pulling my phone out of my tiny crossbody purse, I open it up and check my email. Boring. Just endless sale messages. I'm not on Facebook, not on Twitter, not on anything. I check my text messages though I don't have any unread ones. I read the chain of messages between Ethan and me, my fingers hovering over the keyboard. I'm tempted to say something, but what?

I'm here!

Too eager.

Are you coming?

Way too anxious.

Where are you?

Too demanding.

Sighing, I shove my phone back into my purse and zip it

closed. I'm being ridiculous. He'll be here in minutes and we'll go from there. I'm wasting my time trying to figure out what I should text him.

"Katherine?"

The familiar female voice causes me to jerk my head up, my eyes widening when I see who's standing before me.

Lisa freaking Swanson.

"What are you doing here?" I breathe, glancing around, hoping like crazy Ethan doesn't choose this particular moment to appear. If he does, we're done for. Lisa will jump on this like a shark smelling blood in the water. She'll grab hold and never let go until we're both dead.

She sends me a look, one I can't decipher. "I could ask you the same question."

I gape at her. Is it really any of her business? "Having coffee."

Lisa's head dips, her gaze locked on my empty hands. "Hanging out first before you pick up a cup?"

I say nothing. There's no point in defending my actions. I'll just scramble and trip over my words and look like a liar—exactly what I am.

"Interesting location choice, too," Lisa continues, looking left, then right. As if she's trying to find someone. My throat goes tight and I press my lips together. "So close to the . . . scene of the crime. Are you trying to confront all of those inner demons, Katherine? This would make great TV by the way."

Irritation fills me. Fuels me. I rise to my feet, causing her to back up a step. I realize in that instant I'm taller than she is—and I'm of average height so this isn't saying much. I look down at her, dredging up any scrap of strength I can find within. "Do you consider every life moment TV-worthy?"

She tilts her head back, smiling up at me. "Yes. It's what makes me so good at my job."

Realization dawns and I step away from her, thrusting myself onto the sidewalk. A couple headed straight for me has to dodge around and I mumble an apology to their quickly retreating backs before I return my focus on Lisa. "Are you following me?"

Lisa blinks, the personification of innocence. "Why would you think that?"

She is. Oh God, she is. How *dare* she? "You are, aren't you?" I don't bother waiting for a response. She could defend herself till the cows come home and I won't believe a word she says. "You have no right to follow me."

"I have every right to follow you," she says crisply, her eyebrows rising up. I bet she figured I'd be my usual meek self. Well, forget that. "Agree to the interview and I'll leave you alone."

"Do you really think you'll gain my cooperation with bully tactics? I don't think so." I'm about to leave, turn on my heel, and get the hell out of there when I spot him. *Him*.

Ethan.

He's to my left, walking along the sidewalk, somehow a head taller than everyone else in the crowd. His brows furrow in that way he gets when he's concerned or agitated and I quickly shake my head, sending him a look that says *stay away*. My heart races as if it's desperate to leap out of my chest and chase after Ethan. As if it knows that's where it belongs.

I swallow hard, my gaze meeting Lisa's once more. Thank God she didn't notice Ethan making his way toward us. She's too busy talking to pay attention.

"You're making this difficult on me, Katherine. My boss

says he wants you included in this interview. Even if it's for ten minutes." At my eye roll she amends herself. "Five minutes. *Two* minutes, whatever it takes to get your opinion on Aaron Monroe and what he has to say."

I shake my head, trying my best to remain composed. "I refuse to allow you to manipulate me any further. You had your chance. Now please, leave me alone."

Without a backward glance I walk away. I can almost feel Lisa's angry gaze on me, her frustration coming at me in palpable waves. But I also feel something else, something full of . . . longing and confusion. Every hair on my body seems to stand on end and I rub my hands over my forearms to wipe away the chill bumps that have suddenly formed.

As subtly I can, I glance over my shoulder to catch Ethan watching me in the near distance. Unnoticed by Lisa, by everyone but me. Just another man in the growing crowd, his mouth tight, his eyes full of pain.

I meet his gaze for the briefest moment and I can feel him. Feel his presence, his strengths, his weaknesses, but most of all, I feel his unequivocal yearning reaching toward me. The yearning he feels for me. For this.

For us.

My body answers, everything within me growing warm and loose. I turn away, my breath short, my heart thumping, the blood roaring in my ears. One look at him, one single moment of our gazes meeting, and I'm lost. His hold on me is so incredibly baffling, so unbelievably dangerous, I'm not sure what to do.

Instead of going to my car, I dart into the narrow alleyway between the coffee shop and the building next to it. I lean against the brick wall to catch my breath, close my eyes for the briefest moment as I try to compose my chaotic thoughts.

Did I really think I'd be able to withstand Ethan by meeting him in public? We just saw each other with plenty of distance between us and I feel like I've been electrified by a live wire. What might've happened if he actually touched me?

I don't know if I would've survived it.

"Katie."

That deep, masculine voice slides down my spine, settling low. I open my eyes, my lips parting as I see him standing directly in front of me.

Ethan.

One stolen moment, a kiss, a touch . . . and she's hooked.

'*Owning Violet* owned me from the first page to the last. Ryder and Violet's chemistry is off the charts! Read it, own it, love it'
Katy Evans, *New York Times* bestselling author

Don't miss the first in the fabulous Fowler Sisters Series, *Owning Violet*, available now from

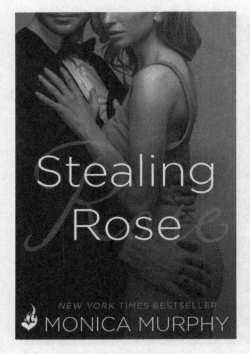

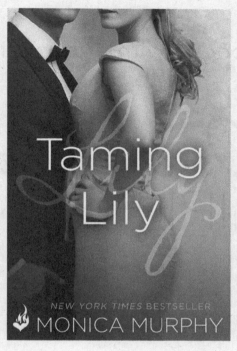

It all began with a proposition . . .
. . . to be his

One Week GIRLFRIEND

Have you read the steamy romantic love stories of Drew + Fable, Colin + Jen, and Owen + Chelsea?

Dive into Monica Murphy's spellbinding One Week Girlfriend series, available now from Headline Eternal.

We come from different worlds.

She's . . . perfect. And I'm . . . not. Somehow she wants me anyway.

So we'll grasp at what we can. She's my secret. And I'm hers.

The problem with secrets is they never last for long.

And when others discover we're together, they'll do whatever it takes to keep us apart.

All I know is: I won't let them. Because Reverie Hale? She's mine.

Don't miss Monica Murphy's

HIS REVERIE

and

HER DESTINY

One unforgettable love story.